Other books by Fred Patten

Best in Show: Fifteen Years of Outstanding Furry Fiction (2003)
Reprinted as:
Furry! The World's Best Anthropomorphic Fiction! (2006)

Watching Anime, Reading Manga:
25 Years of Essays and Reviews (2004)

Already Among Us; An Anthropomorphic Anthology (2012)

The Ursa Major Awards Anthology:
A Tenth Anniversary Celebration (2012)

What Happens Next: An Anthology of Sequels (2013)

Five Fortunes (2014)

Funny Animals and More: From Anime to Zoomorphics (2014)

Anthropomorphic Aliens: An Interstellar Anthology (2014)

The Furry Future : 19 Possible Prognostications (2015)

An Anthropomorphic Century: Stories from 1909 to 2008 (2015)

Cats and More Cats: Feline Fantasy Fiction (2016)

Gods with Fur: And Feathers, Scales, … (2016)

Furry Fandom Conventions, 1989-2015 (2017)

Dogs of War

Edited by Fred Patten

Dogs of War

Production copyright FurPlanet Productions © 2017
Cover artwork copyright © 2017 by Teagan Gavet

Published by FurPlanet Productions
Dallas, Texas
www.FurPlanet.com

ISBN 978-1-61450-346-0

Printed in the United States of America
First Edition Trade Paperback January 2017

To

William Shakespeare
(1564 – 1616)

"Cry 'Havoc!', and let slip the dogs of war".

The Tragedy of Julius Caesar, Act 3, Scene 1

Table of Contents

Introduction

by Fred Patten

This anthology is dedicated to William Shakespeare, the author of the famous line, "Cry 'Havoc,' and let slip the dogs of war", in his 1599 play *The Tragedie of Julius Caesar.* It is delivered by Marc Antony following Caesar's assassination, when Antony accurately predicts that Caesar's murder will not save Rome from tyranny, but will plunge it into bloody civil war:

"A curse shall light upon the limbs of men;
Domestic fury and fierce civil strife
Shall cumber all the parts of Italy;
Blood and destruction shall be so in use
And dreadful objects so familiar
That mothers shall but smile when they behold
Their infants quarter'd with the hands of war;
All pity choked with custom of fell deeds:
And Caesar's spirit, ranging for revenge,
With Ate by his side come hot from hell,
Shall in these confines with a monarch's voice
Cry 'Havoc,' and let slip the dogs of war;
That this foul deed shall smell above the earth
With carrion men, groaning for burial."

The "dogs of war" were well-known by Elizabethan England. Dogs have been used in warfare since antiquity. Their earliest recorded use was by the city-state of Magnesia in Ionia, in Asia Minor, in the mid-7th century B.C. Wikipedia says that in Magnesia's warfare against the rival city-state of Ephesus, "the Magnesian horsemen were each accompanied by a war dog and a spear-bearing attendant. The dogs were released first and broke the enemy ranks, followed by an assault of spears, then a cavalry charge." The earliest war-dog recorded by name belonged to the Magnesian horseman Hippaemon, who was buried with his dog Lethargos, his horse, and his spearman. King Alyattes of Lydia in Asia Minor (619 B.C.-560 B.C.), used war dogs in his battles against the invading Cimmerians from around the Black Sea.

Records of war dogs are steady from then on by the Greeks, Romans, and others. One of the most famous was owned by Lysimachus of Macedonia, one of Alexander the Great's generals who made himself a king after Alexander's death. When Lysimachus was killed at the Battle of Corupedium in 281 B.C., "After some days his body was found on the field, protected from birds of prey by his faithful dog." (Wikipedia) Most of the records of war dogs before World War I do not mention specific names, but there are many mentions of war packs. Xerxes I of Persia (ruled 486 B.C.-465 B.C.) used "vast packs of Indian hounds" when he invaded Greece. Attila the Hun (ruled 434 A.D.-453 A.D.) used large, heavy molosser dogs. During the Middle Ages, European royalty often made diplomatic gifts of war-dog breeding stock. The first official use of military dogs in the U.S. was in the first Seminole War of 1816 to 1819. Both sides in the Civil War of 1861-1865 used dogs, mostly to send messages and to guard prisoners.

War dogs came into prominence during World War I. Estimates of over a million dogs were killed in action. The most famous individual was Stubby, a Boston bull terrier stray who attached himself to the 102nd Infantry Regiment while it was in training at Yale University. Corporal Robert Conroy smuggled him on their troop ship to France. He participated in four offensives and seventeen battles over eighteen months. He was gassed and wounded. He was given a specially designed gas mask. He became adept at warning his unit of poison gas attacks. He captured a German spy during the Battle of the Argonne, which led the commander of the 102nd Infantry Unit to promote him to sergeant (probably a mock promotion for the 102's morale). After the war, Stubby was brought home as a hero. He was included in military parades with his medals, and was introduced to Presidents Wilson, Harding, and Coolidge. He was presented with a gold medal by General John J. Pershing. He later became the mascot of Georgetown University's Hoyas athletic team.

Another famous World War I war dog was Rags, a French mixed-breed terrier who was adopted by Private James Donovan. Rags mostly delivered messages between the 1st Infantry Division at the front and rear headquarters. He was also bombed, gassed, and partially blinded, but always returned for more. He also won many medals and awards. He was smuggled back to the U.S. by Donovan, who soon died at Fort Sheridan in Chicago. Rags became the Division's post dog until he became the pet of an Army major who was later posted to New York City. Rags became a noted NYC celebrity, often marching in parades and being photographed with politicians and Army generals. He lived to an advanced dog age of 20 years.

Still another famous dog came from World War I, but not as a war dog. In September 1918, American Corporal Lee Duncan found a starving Imperial German Army German Shepherd bitch who had just given birth to five puppies. Duncan found homes for the mother and three puppies, keeping two puppies which he named Rin Tin Tin and Nanette. Duncan brought the dogs with him to America after the war. Rin Tin Tin became a popular animal movie star throughout the 1920s. His films were credited with saving the new Warner Bros. studio from bankruptcy.

But not all war animals are dogs. When the prestigious British PSDA Dickin Medal was inaugurated in 1943 for animals that showed "conspicuous gallantry or devotion to duty while serving or associated with any branch of the Armed Forces or Civil Defence Units", the first three medals awarded went to homing pigeons that delivered messages resulting in the rescues of ditched aircrews. The Dickin Medal has also been awarded to horses and a ship's cat as well as to dogs. The most recent Dickin Award recipient is Lucca, a German Shepherd/Belgian Malinois bitch who worked with the U.S. Marine Corps and lost a leg in an IED explosion, presented on April 5, 2016.

Dogs of War presents 23 stories of anthropomorphic animals in military scenarios. Cats. Dogs. Hyenas. Lemurs. Mice. Rabbits. Wolverines. Wolves. Even mythological animals such as centaurs and pegasi. Animals have been fighting for humans—and for themselves—for millennia. They will go on for as long as warfare exists.

If anyone thinks that real rabbits can't be sons o' bitches, they haven't seen a warren of wild rabbits. Adams got it right in Watership Down.

Now anthropomorphize those rabbits, train them for warfare, and you have Nosy. And his carrot-spear, Wolf.

Nosy and Wolf

by Ken MacGregor

Luther stood shivering with eleven other young rabbits. It wasn't just the cold. The single, piercing eye of First Carrot was terrifying.

"We were afraid once," First Carrot said. His voice was lined with gravel. "All of us. The whole race. Scared little bunnies."

Luther felt sure he wasn't the only one in the line who was, in fact, still a scared little bunny, but he kept his eyes on First Carrot and tried his best to look brave.

The big rabbit had deep gouges crisscrossing his face, most of them over his left eye - the missing one. None of them knew his real name. It was like he never had one. He went on.

"But, that was a long time ago. Ancient history. Today's rabbit is a fighter. A warrior." He walked the line, stopping at each young rabbit and holding their gaze. "You, all of you, will be warriors, too. If you survive training." He shrugged. "Some don't."

A brown male two rabbits from Luther fainted. First Carrot spat on the ground.

"Get him out of my sight."

A nearby Carrot soldier dragged the unconscious male away. Luther never saw him again.

* * *

Luther and the remaining ten rabbits were assigned to an enormous instructor named Zinc. She was a Carrot Sergeant. Her fur was the same flat, silvery gray of the metal. She was easily the biggest rabbit Luther had ever seen: nearly the size of a bulldog, with a surly disposition to match.

Zinc glared at them that first day for so long they squirmed. Finally, she spoke.

"Today, you are tiny *mice*. Weak, useless, little nothings."

Luther cringed despite himself.

"However," the giant female went on, "when I am through with you, you will be *rabbits*. Strong, tough, all-grown-up rabbits. All you have to do is listen to me, work hard and try not to die."

She grinned at them. One of her big front teeth was missing a chunk on the inside corner. A white female raised her paw.

"Ma'am? How'd you break your tooth?"

Zinc leaned in so close, she and the female were touching noses. The little one twitched, but held her ground.

"I had a little soldier like you who asked too many questions. I bit him. Chipped my tooth on bone. Hurt, but it hurt him more, I bet."

The female wet herself. Zinc laughed.

"Congratulations, kid. You just earned your nickname. Little mice, this is 'Diaper'. You will call her that from now on. If I hear you calling her anything else, I will cut off one of your ears. Understood?"

The young rabbits nodded as one.

Zinc swung her attention back to Diaper. To her credit, the young rabbit was still standing at attention.

"Go get cleaned up."

The female scurried to the long, low wooden hut they were told would be their home for the next five months. Luther watched her go. He felt shame on her behalf.

"Hey," Zinc prodded him with a paw. "Nosy. Mind your business."

Luther blinked at her. He trembled slightly, but found his voice.

"Is that my name now? 'Nosy'?"

Zinc belly-laughed.

"You got spunk, mouse. I'll give you that. Sure. Why not? 'Nosy' it is. The rest of you got that?"

They did. No one needed to be reminded not to call him anything else. Several of them unconsciously touched their ears.

"Good. All right. First lesson of the day."

She pulled what looked like a large carrot from a sack next to her. It bulged with similar shapes.

"Who can tell me what this is?"

Luther, suspecting a trick, kept his mouth shut. An albino male lifted a paw.

"A carrot?"

Zinc shot him an unpleasant grin.

"Looks like one, doesn't it?"

The male nodded. But, there was sudden doubt in his pink eyes.

"Right. But, if this was the kind of carrot you eat, could I do this?"

Zinc pivoted her hips and hurled the carrot-shaped thing ten feet, straight through the chest of a hanging practice dummy. The dummy's ears flopped from the impact. It swung on its rope. The group of rabbits watched until it stopped.

The giant instructor handed them each one from the sack. Nosy found his heavy and awkward.

"Now. What are they?"

Slowly, tentatively, Nosy lifted his paw.

"Nosy?"

"They're weapons, ma'am?"

"Ding! Give yourself a gold clover, Nosy."

Nosy smiled. It fell off his face when Zinc pointed her carrot-weapon in his face. The point on hers was so sharp it was nearly invisible.

"We crafted these weapons to look like carrots. Why? Because carrots are sacred to our people. They are a symbol of rabbithood. This is also why our warriors are called 'Carrot'. First Carrot is the best of us. He or she has the highest kill count. You do *not* want to get on First Carrot's bad side.

"These things in your hands are called 'spears' and I will teach you how to use them. When I am done with you, a spear in your hand will be *lethal*. You will name your spear and keep it with you at all times. You will sleep with it next to your bunk. You will clean and sharpen it every day. Nosy!"

Nosy snapped to attention, attempting to emulate the way he'd seen grown up rabbits do it.

"Ma'am?"

"What is your weapon's name?"

Nosy looked at the thing in his paws. It was thicker at one end, tapering to a blunt, rounded tip. He hefted it, testing its weight and balance as if he knew something about combat. He met Zinc's eyes.

"Wolf."

Zinc's eyes widened slightly, then narrowed.

"Why?"

"It's a weapon, ma'am. It should be scary. And, a wolf is the scariest thing I can think of."

Zinc nodded. The ghost of a smile played at the corners of her mouth.

"We'll make a fighter out of you yet."

* * *

When he wasn't climbing walls, on his belly in the mud, sparring with his bunkmates, Nosy was sharpening Wolf. Zinc hadn't told him to do this, but when she saw him with the stone, methodically scraping toward the point, turning the spear and scraping again, she nodded. The other rabbits noted this and all started sharpening theirs, too.

On a drizzly, gray day, the recruits stood at attention, drenched to the skin. Nosy didn't like the musty smell of his own fur, but it was at least better than the rabbit next to him.

"Cripes, Guts," Nosy said. "Don't you ever bathe?"

The albino turned his pink eyes on him. They narrowed. His lip curled into a sneer.

"Why bother? We're just going to be in the mud again minutes later."

Nosy shook his head.

"You should bother for the rest of our sakes. Standing downwind from you is a special kind of torture."

"Quiet!"

Zinc sloshed through the sticking, squelching mud toward them.

"Today, we are going over the wall. You will be judged on speed, method and how many times you fall. Falling will cost you ten percent of your grade. So, try not to fall."

She called on them, one by one, to run the fifty feet to the high, wooden wall. It was slightly inclined away from them, but not enough to simply run up. It was ten feet high. The tallest among the recruits was just over eighteen inches.

Five rabbits (*no*, he thought. *We're mice.*) were already climbing when Nosy hit the wall. He leaped as high as he could, at least four feet, and scrambled for purchase on the rough wood. A splinter dug into the pad of his right paw and he winced.

Nosy managed to get another three feet, just behind Diaper, set to overtake her. She lunged forward, her back foot scrabbling on the wet wood. She lost her balance and flailed, claws digging furrows in the wall. She fell into Nosy. Her rear claws ripped a hole in his shoulder. They both fell.

Nosy spat.

"I had it."

"Sorry," she said.

He shook his head. Looking at the wall, he watched the others struggle on the wall. Guts made a mad dash, followed by a leap, trying to run up the near-vertical surface. He made it six of the ten feet before he fell.

"Well," Guts said, spitting out mud, "that's half my grade. So far."

The dirty white rabbit moved back several feet and did the exact same thing. Nosy shook his head. He slogged over to the edge of the wall, away from the others. He found a rough spot in the wood where he could fit the ends of his claws. He sought another one higher up.

Slowly, Nosy pulled himself along these rough spots. In an agonizing crawl, at a snail's pace, he dragged his tired, aching body up the wall.

At eight feet, almost there, his muscles started shaking. The wound in his shoulder burned hot. The stink of his wet fur filled his nostrils and threatened to make him sick. All he could hear was his own breathing, the beat of his heart. All he could see was the rough grain of the wood before him. His mind could only focus on the next handhold, the next few inches.

Finally, after what seemed like hours, Nosy reached the top. He pulled himself over the wall. Smiling, Nosy reached up a paw in a tired victory salute.

Then, his wet, muddy feet slipped, and he fell over the lip, straight down to the ground ten feet below.

He broke his arm. The crack shocked him awake and he screamed.

Medical splinted the arm and wrapped it in immobilizing plaster. Nosy had to cover it with a plastic bag during maneuvers in mud or rain to keep it dry.

In weapons training, he figured out how to fight with the spear using only his right arm. The first several matches, he lost. Under his fur, it felt like his body was one big bruise. He refused to give up, though, and he got better at one-handed fighting. By the time his left arm was healed, he could hold his own with just the right.

The left never healed quite straight. When they removed the cast, a permanent lump was revealed. Zinc poked at it.

"Your first battle scar. Won't be your last. You're healed enough. Go hit the climbing wall. Try not to fall this time."

"Yes, ma'am."

He didn't fall. He also noticed that the other recruits were going up slowly, using Nosy's method. He nodded at Guts when the albino reached the top ahead of him.

"You're pretty good at this. Faster than me."

"Yeah, well," Guts said. "I've got two good arms and I've been practicing a lot."

Training was brutal. It was either hot and dry or cold and wet. Muscles ached until they were numb. Then, somehow, somewhere along the way, they stopped hurting and felt strong. It was no longer agony to take a smack to the head with another rabbit's spear. Nosy, and the rest, shook it off and gave as good as they got.

The next few months went by faster than Nosy expected. It was almost testing time and Nosy and the other recruits had become friends, almost family. They were enjoying some rare down time after chow, sitting on the edges of their bunks, reading comic books or writing notes to family. Nosy was doing what he always did with free time.

A paw tapped his shoulder.

"Nosy."

Nosy lowered Wolf and set down the sharpening stone. He glanced up. Pillow, a brown and white male stood by him. Pillow had earned his name when he overslept roll call one morning early on.

"What's up?"

"You nervous about today?"

Nosy shrugged.

"No more than any other day, I guess."

"Are you kidding me?" Pillow asked. "We're *testing.*"

"Yeah, I know. We pass, or we don't. I don't see the point of getting worked up about it."

By now, all other eight rabbits who were still in the program were listening. Nosy looked at each in turn. They weren't mice anymore, that's for sure. These rabbits were lean and muscular. There was a hardness in their eyes.

They'll make it, he thought. *Most of them, anyway.* The ones who didn't, well, that's how it goes. He wasn't about to waste time or tears over it. Somewhere, deep down, a part of Nosy was appalled at this thought. Not making it through testing meant not making it at all. It meant not being a rabbit, and if you weren't a rabbit, you might as well be dead. The scared little bunny he used to be shuddered and despaired at what he had become. Nosy quashed the emotion, purposefully scraping the stone along Wolf once again.

"You're rabbits now. Either way. You're not mice anymore. Not to me anyway. No matter what happens today. Okay? Remember that."

Diaper smiled.

"None of us is more rabbit than you," she said.

Nosy shrugged. He sucked his teeth.

"Rabbit is rabbit," he said.

"Maybe," Pillow said, "but we all know who's gonna make Carrot here. You're the one we all look to, Nosy. I'm not afraid to admit it. I think it's good, too. Soldiers need leaders."

Nosy shook his head.

"I'm not trying to be anything special. I just want to protect my people."

Diaper put a paw on his shoulder.

"That, right there, is what makes you special."

Nosy flushed with a mix of embarrassment and pride. He was glad it was hidden under his black fur.

Diaper shuddered suddenly.

"When we go out there—when we fight—do you think the rumors are true? That we're going up against real badgers? And foxes?" She looked at Nosy's spear. "Wolves?"

Pillow shook his head.

"Nobody knows. The higher-ups won't confirm it. I asked. I did talk to a Carrot once. I met her in town, before I came here. She was at the bar, sloppy drunk. She said the predator gods were meaner than ours, but that the rabbit god was stronger. I guess on the front lines you find religion."

Nosy sighed.

"Whatever it takes, I suppose."

"Nosy? Do you believe in the Rabbit god?"

He looked at Diaper. The question seemed important to her.

"I don't know. I believe in my speed. I believe in my ferocity. I believe in Wolf. For me, that's enough."

Less than an hour later, they were lined up on the parade ground. They stood at attention, watching as the first group went through testing, waiting for their turn. That first group was solid. Every rabbit made it, and they named their Carrot. Their Sergeant shaved the stripe into the fur on his arm and hugged him hard.

Zinc stepped forward, snapping a sharp salute to First Carrot, who returned it. She turned toward her nine soldiers. She was bare-pawed, but radiated menace as she assumed a combat stance.

"Itchy," she called. The tan female moved up, swinging her spear to point at Zinc. They fought, and Itchy held her own long enough. She never managed to hurt Zinc, but she held onto her weapon and stayed afoot.

"Good," Zinc said. "You're a rabbit now."

Itchy rejoined the line. Pillow gently punched her on the shoulder. She grinned at him.

The next two in line made it as well. Nothing flashy, but they stayed up, stayed armed. They were rabbits, too.

Guts, the albino who had guessed wrong about the spears, narrowed his pink eyes and charged. Zinc used his momentum to throw him, disarming him in the same motion. Guts, who had always been more brave than smart, bunched his legs to leap. Zinc saw it and shook her head.

"Don't."

He did.

Zinc swung the boy's spear. To Nosy it looked slow, almost casual. She dropped low and whipped the butt of the spear in an arc. Flailing in mid-air, Guts tried to change course, but it was too late. Zinc slammed him in the head with the wooden handle. The sound made Nosy's stomach lurch. The male hit the ground in a heap of loose bones.

Guts worked his mouth, but couldn't form words. Zinc squatted beside him. Blood ran from his nose and pooled in the dirt.

"I said 'don't', idiot. Why didn't you listen?"

Guts shook his head, slightly as if to say "I don't know." He passed out.

Zinc cleared her throat and turned away from Guts as though he were no longer there.

"Guts was brave. No one will dispute this. But, it takes more than bravery to be a rabbit. It takes discipline, intelligence and the ability to think fast in combat. He wasn't ready. He was still a mouse. Guts is dead to us now, and we do not mourn mice. Next."

Nosy was next. He hefted Wolf in his paws, turning the orange spear so it caught the light. The edge was keen, deadly. He set Wolf down on the ground and stepped forward unarmed. Zinc's eyes narrowed.

"Why don't you bring your weapon, Nosy?"

He smiled at his teacher.

"I am a weapon."

Zinc shrugged.

"Your funeral."

He met her paw-to-paw. She was bigger, stronger and more experienced than he. Yet, Nosy held his own. He countered every blow; he sidestepped every throw; he gave her back what he was getting. After more than two minutes of this, both panting, neither giving ground, First Carrot spoke. His gravelly voice, though not loud, carried. Every ear there caught it.

"Enough."

Zinc and Nosy stopped, each paw full of the other's fur, but they were no longer moving.

"He's a rabbit, Zinc," First Carrot went on. "A damn fine one, too."

Zinc and Nosy separated. They exchanged nods of mutual respect. He retrieved his spear and looked to his right. Diaper was grinning at him. She would be next. Nosy smiled back. He winked.

"I softened her up for you."

Nobody else died that day, and the others in Nosy's group became rabbits. To no one's surprise, Nosy made Carrot. Zinc shaved his stripe, put her paws on his shoulders and looked him in the eye. She nodded and walked away. Zinc wasn't a hugger.

First Carrot gave a speech at the end of the day. It was about how proud he was of them all and how he knew they'd go on to do great things. He talked about their enemies: the predators and the monsters. How they would protect the young and the infirm, keep the rabbit race strong.

The whole time, Nosy was looking at the blood on the ground where Guts had lain. He knew he'd be seeing a lot more blood on the ground. Probably actual bodies, too, instead of just "mice" who had washed out.

He hadn't seen Guts leave the grounds. He wished he could have said goodbye.

He was a rabbit now. A Carrot even.

He pulled the stone from the pouch on his belt and sat down to sharpen Wolf. He could face the coming horrors to protect his people.

It didn't mean he had to like it.

When mankind is gone, how will the intelligent animals who replace him react to the apes still in their midst? Sami and the older Harun are from a company of the nomadic apes who have no settlements of their own, who get caught in the freezing north in a conflict between two other species.

The apes are looked down upon by the other species as the Darkened, too reminiscent of Man. But they have made a role for themselves, stretching far from their tropical homelands.

After Their Kind

by Taylor Harbin

Sani shivered as another hard gust of wind tore through his fur coat and the wool jacket underneath. The snow flew at him from every direction.

"If I make it back to the jungle, I'll never leave again."

Harun punched his shoulder. "Don't quit on me now," the grizzled ape said. "Pamela's out there with three hundred kin who won't survive once winter fully sets. I can't drag them back to Thraesh by myself."

"You're not dragging them anywhere in this blizzard. Can't see ten paces in front of me!" Sani, the younger ape, said. "We should make camp and wait for this to blow over."

"No," Harun said. "Coyel has the trail and we're not losing them again. Walk."

Sani gritted his teeth and took another step. His boot vanished beneath the snow. *Of all the jobs, why'd we take this one? 'Oh, it'll be simple,' he said. 'Just go find my cousin, who hates me, and her followers and convince them to come back.' We could have spent the days sunning by a river!* He walked with his head tucked into his shoulders, numb feet following the tracks of his colleague.

"No payment is worth this," Sani said. "And it's none of our business anyway. Pamela has the right to live wherever she wants."

"I don't care about her rights," Harun said. "We're here because we need to eat. Samantha needs to eat."

"You haven't been a father in twenty years," Sani said, grateful that the wind's howl muted his insult. He hated it when his own daughter was used to coerce him. It took more to raise young than providing the necessities. Yes, she ate, and she hardly knew him. One job led to the next, and then to another. He'd travelled most of Europa to provide for a daughter who seemed like a different creature each time he came home. But this time, they'd been promised a handsome bounty: one year's dwelling rights and a fifth of the local harvest. Maybe, just maybe, he would have a chance to reforge the bond.

"There he is," Harun said.

Sani looked. A red shape came towards them. The scout had returned. "What have you got for us, Coyel?" he asked.

The fox nodded east. "There's a clearing up ahead. The village lies beyond."

"Have they stopped?" Haurn asked. "Were you spotted?"

"They've gone into winter quarters," Coyel said, ignoring the second question. "They've cleared a patch of snow and dug burrows."

"Thank the gods," Sani said. "A day or two to rest, talk things over, and then we can head back."

Coyel grinned. "Only if they agree to come along."

"They will," Harun said. "Rayne's paying us to bring Pamela and the entire village back to Thraesh. I'm not in the habit of disappointing my clients."

"And, should Pamela refuse?" Coyel said. "Cougars are solitary animals; temperamental and independent. They do not like being challenged. You just might have to fight her and assert dominance over the lot of them."

"If I fight," Harun said, "she will lose."

Coyel dropped his grin. "What now?"

"We'll rest here for a time and wait till the wind stops," Harun said.

Finally, Sani thought as he flopped down against a tree. He pulled the water skin from underneath his jacket and took a long drink. The air stung his face. To his eyes, the winter forest was a crude mesh of white and brownish grey. How Coyel made any sense of it was beyond him.

"You're faring well," Coyel said, sitting next to him. "I thought you'd drop dead within three days." He wrapped his crooked tail around his legs, his namesake, a feature that had plagued him from birth. "Where will you go after this?" he asked.

"Some place where the sun is hot, the water is cold, and the fruit grows year round," Sani said. "And you? Thinking about which vixen you'll take next mating season?"

Coyel grimaced. "Have you seen them? Dull coats. Malnourished. Dim-witted. I'd be amazed if one in ten survived birthing a litter. If Rayne promised you a fifth of the harvest for retrieving Pamela, then one of us will starve. We can't survive by *farming*. A fox who doesn't hunt is no proper fox at all. Why do you think I spend so much time *away* from Thraesh?"

"Yet, you'll bed one nonetheless," Sani said with a grin.

Coyel turned away with a curt *hmph*. "Of course. I must keep appearances. What do you take me for?"

"I'm not quite sure," Sani said. "But I don't envy your position."

Coyel growled, but it gave way to a chuckle. "Cutting words. And I thought you didn't have a lick of wit." He motioned towards Harun. "That one, however, I am convinced."

Sani nodded. "All business, all the time."

"It must be quite painful, working with such a creature."

Sani watched Harun as he bit into a ration of salted pork. The old ape noticed him.

"How are you holding up?" he asked.

Sani wiggled his fingers and toes, trying to kindle something resembling warmth. He took another drink of water. "I'm fine," he said.

"Tell me if that changes. I need you here."

Sani nodded. *I need you here,* he thought to himself.

Everyone in the Jabril Company called Harun "father." He'd taken apes and chimps alike into the fold, and as far as Sani knew, none had left. A few young males had challenged him, and after they were defeated, Harun sent them back to work with a pat on the shoulder and those four words.

The wind died, at long last. Sani felt blood return to his face. Some rays of sunlight managed to break through the clouds overhead, and the places they touched exploded with color. It was a beautiful sight. But, was he needed here? *Samantha needs me too*, he thought. Yet, the company's reserves were running low, and none of the other males would make the journey. They all feared the Pack of Wolfenland, as did anyone who had sense.

Sani felt Coyel's eyes still upon him. He took another drink. "Painful? Yes, it is. But the strong will survive."

The fox nodded with approval, and then his eyes lit with a trace of fear. His ears perked, and he snapped his gaze towards the east.

"What?" Sani asked. "What is it?"

"Wolf call," Coyel said. "Towards the village."

Sani jumped to his feet and unslung the musket from his shoulder.

"What load are you going to use?" Harun asked while priming his rifle.

Sani grabbed his powder horn. "Buckshot. I never could hit a moving target with ball."

Coyel eyed the apes as they readied their weapons. "I've never seen it myself," he said. "*That's* the Secret Thunder and Fire?"

"The Last Men used different names for their tools," Harun said. "But Man is gone now, so call it whatever you like."

"My mother told me stories. She said that you made a pact with the gods for the lost knowledge of Man, but in exchange you were cursed with his likeness. That's why they call you Darkened."

Harun gave him a look. "Superstition."

"You're not Fire-Workers?"

"No," Sani said. "I got this musket from another ape who doesn't mind dealing under the table. Harun took his rifle off a corpse on a previous job. We don't vanish in clouds of smoke. We don't offer blood sacrifices to demons. Bury us in the ground and we won't come back."

"Pity," Coyel said. "I'd like some divine favor with wolves nearby."

You and me both, Sani thought. He closed the flash pan and cocked the hammer. The flint was worn and would have to be replaced soon. His jaw popped. He wanted Samantha. He wanted rest. Sani looked at Coyel, who looked to Harun, who smirked at them both.

"Let's see what's out there," he said.

Coyel took the lead. His ears folded back as they moved into the clearing. A knoll confronted them. The wolf cries were persistent as they drew near.

"Several of them," Coyel said.

"What are they saying?" Harun asked.

"Can't be sure. Sounds like they're leaving. If they used Man's Word, I would be certain."

"You think they know we're here?" Sani said.

"No," Harun said. "But if they're leaving, that's pretty smart of them."

They approached the crest at a low crouch. Sani glanced to his left and right every few moments. Somewhere in the dense forest were creatures who could think like him, but move like shadows and kill quick as lightning. If they were as good hunters as they said, then he wouldn't have time to scream.

Coyel signaled with a flick of his tail. They went to their bellies and peered over the crest. The village below was obscured by the roll of the landscape. The only evidence of a settlement were mounds of dirt that stood out against the snow. The rest blurred against the forest beyond.

"Can't tell anything from up here," Harun said. "Where's the glass?"

Sani went into his coat pocket and put the cylinder to his eye. "Something's moving down there."

"Hostile?"

"Can't tell. Sun's too bright."

Harun took the glass and scanned the area. "Might be some eager pups posturing, trying to act tough. Most rites of passage require them to defy the outside world and signal their place as the next generation. They love to put on a show." He pointed to a bush at the bottom of the hill on the left side. "I'll cover you from there until you get inside the village. Wave if it's clear."

"Who's going to tell Pamela the good news?" Sani said.

"I will," Coyel said. "We've met before, and she knows Rayne wouldn't send me unless he meant business."

"And if she doesn't believe you?"

Coyel smiled at Harun. "Your friend can persuade her."

They moved to the bush together. Before Sani went farther, Harun grabbed his shoulder.

"Step by step," he said.

Sani shook his hand. The old ape began arranging the foliage so he would be hard to spot at a distance, but still have a clear line of sight. Sani's pace was slow and careful. He couldn't walk fast on two legs, and his equipment made it difficult to stay balanced taking anything beyond casual steps. His eyes moved left and right.

"Is he any good with that rifle?" Coyel asked.

"I saw him knock a bull dead at two hundred paces," Sani said. "Not that it'll do us much good if there's a pack nearby."

"I'd say very *little* would do us any good if that happens. Are you sure there isn't some deity that owes you protection?" Coyel said.

"No, but if you can raise the alarm before any of those grey devils takes a bite out of my rump, I'll put in a good word."

They stepped around the first burrow. Sani shouldered his musket and inched a finger towards the trigger. A slight breeze took him by surprise. It brought a cold bite and a horrid odor to his nose.

"Urine," Coyel said. "They've claimed this land." The fox glanced back to the wilderness, to the invisible path that only his eyes could see. "But, why? We haven't crossed the border."

"Pamela couldn't have moved that fast," Sani said. He grimaced, looking ahead.

Coyel's ears twitched. His nose crinkled. He bolted and disappeared behind a leafless bush. Sani followed, waving and hoping Harun could see him through the glass. He wanted the old ape by his side. Sani checked the entrance of each burrow as he made his way to the fox. Coyel had found Pamela. Her body laid in a twisted heap. Blood pooled near her mouth. Parts of her hide were sliced open, other parts wet and matted from where jaws had latched and ripped.

"You fool," Coyel said, a hint of sadness in his voice. "All right, that's done. What now?"

Sani rested on his knuckles and sighed. *That's going to affect the bottom line.*

Two young wolves laid nearby. Their necks were broken. A third was barely ten paces away, but Sani couldn't identify the wound that had killed him. *Idiot*, he thought. *But at least she could fight.*

"Sani," Coyel said. "What do we do now?"

"Look for survivors," Sani said. "We didn't spend three weeks hiking in the freezing cold for nothing."

They climbed in and out of every burrow they found, but the village was deserted. The stench of urine clung to everything, erasing the victims from the Earth's memory.

"Something's wrong," Coyel said. "We found Pamela. Where are the others?"

Sani walked a short way, past the final row of burrows and into the woods. "If they scattered, it'll be impossible to account for them all. Maybe some of them were able to escape during the fight. Keep an eye out for tracks that—" His foot caught on a root. Sani reached out and braced himself against the next tree in front of him. He regained his balance and chuckled. "Too close," he said, patting the tree. "Might have split my head open if I'd bumped it on you."

Sani turned around to get his bearings. He shrieked.

Coyel appeared at his side. "What? What did you—" The fox stared, wide-eyed. He choked as a whine tried to come out.

The base of each tree before them was surrounded by corpses. Old and young. Male and female. Babes. Hundreds.

Coyel choked on his words. "Not a raiding party. This… couldn't have been a raid."

"No," Sani said in a flat voice. *It's not real. Can't be real.* "Wolves don't do this. Wolves never kill like *this.*»

"Unless they're at war."

Sani and Coyel started. Harun stood at the tree line.

"War?" Sani said.

"This was a coordinated attack. Planned to the last detail," Harun said. "The Pack is making ready." He brought them over to one of the trees. "It's called the Bloody Root. The victims are tied together by their tails, encircling the trunk. One or two are killed right off as a demonstration.

Most of the dirty work is done by young pups who've never tasted blood. They're forced to keep at it until they win or die."

He grabbed a canid by the ruff of its neck and held it up. Sani noticed that the marks were indeed too small to be an adult wolf.

"If we're still on the Thraeshen side of the border ..."

"Rayne will retaliate," Harun said. "Whole thing doesn't make sense. Little to no contact on the border for twenty-nine months, and now an incursion of this scale? What's their cause? Doesn't matter. They've never been the same since uniting under the Nation of the Three Darker Stars."

Coyel sniffed. "The urine's still fresh. We should go. Now. There might be a pack or two nearby."

"Count the bodies," Harun said. "Quick. I don't want to be here when the vultures come."

Sani and Coyel worked while Harun stood guard with the firearms. They circled around each tree, marking their progress by making notches in the bark. Each ring led them deeper and deeper into the woods. Sani kept looking towards the clearing. It became smaller and smaller in the distance, shrouded by branches. He wanted to run, drop everything and tell Rayne the dead couldn't be numbered. He wanted out, out of the forest where the shadows still watched him.

"How many?" Harun asked after several minutes.

"Two hundred and sixty-four," Coyel said.

"That should be enough," Sani said. "The village was supposed to be three hundred kin, exactly. With this many dead, no one will question the Pack's intentions."

"How many wolves would it take to do this?" Coyel asked.

"More than I've ever seen. More than I ever want to see," Harun said. He tossed the musket to Sani. "Let's move."

Coyel took the lead as they came out of the woods. As they passed the place where Pamela had made her last stand, Sani spat on one of the dead wolves. "May the crows eat you slowly," he said.

The wolf *stood up* and snarled. Sani gasped and fumbled with his weapon. It raised its head to howl. Sani whipped the musket to his shoulder and fired. He jerked the trigger and the spread went high. Few of the pellets hit their target. The wolf staggered, trying to stay on its feet. Blood dripped from its head and shoulder. It whined in long, chopped strains. With no time to reload, Sani dropped the musket and came at him with the knife. A thrust to the heart put the creature out of its misery.

"Trap," he said, wiping the blade on his coat sleeve. The rotten-eggs smell of burnt powder inflamed his nostrils. "They must have known somebody would come to investigate. Good thing I got him before he let off and told the others."

"No," Harun said. "You did the work for him."

Sani looked towards the knoll. The sun was at his back and he could see three grey shapes rushing towards them. He grabbed his powder horn and started to reload.

Harun dropped to one knee and took aim. "Get back into the woods. Climb a tree before we're surrounded." He pulled the trigger. The rifle cracked and felled the wolf leading the charge at one hundred fifty yards.

Sani turned away. He made it ten paces when two more wolves jumped from hiding and blocked his path. The first leapt and bit Sani's wrist before he could level his gun. They went down together. The wolf's teeth tore through his coat, the wool sleeve underneath, and drew generous blood. The young ape cried out and punched at its face, but the wolf shook its head and covered him with fresh pain. The second wolf pounced and snapped at his throat. Sani curled his right arm around his neck and turned his head as the wolf bit at his face. The drooling incisors ripped a piece of flesh from his cheek. The wound was shallow, but Sani cried out again.

Then, the wolf recoiled and began thrashing about. Coyel was riding its back, his tiny teeth latched to one of its ears. The other wolf released Sani's hand, distracted by his brother's peril. Sani grabbed the knife on his belt and lunged. The wolf noticed at the last second and dodged, but suffered a gash on its right shoulder. It snarled and assumed an offensive posture. Harun put him down with a bullet through the skull, and pulled Sani up by his good arm.

"Run!" he said. "Hurry!"

Sani reached for the musket. Harun snatched it up and pushed the young ape forward. Another wolf appeared and died in a blast of buckshot. The rest of them stood on the flanks, funneling their intended victims. Sani moved as fast as he could on two feet and one set of knuckles.

Run.

The pack closed in from all sides.

Run.

Sani heard their low panting, the kind all predators made when they had mind and body fixed on the kill.

Look, Daddy! Watch me go!

There was a corpse at the base of the tree in front of him. The first branch was still a way off the ground.

You'd better run, Samantha. I'm coming to get you!

Sani pushed with all his might and jumped. The body slid and gave way under his weight, but it fell against the tree and did not move any farther. He sucked in a quick breath and jumped again. His hand grabbed the branch. As Sani pulled himself up, he felt a draft beneath his feet. The wolf had also jumped, his stained teeth closed just beyond his prey's reach. Sani straddled the branch and leaned against the tree. His chest heaved. *Made it. Made it. Made it.* He repeated these words to himself a dozen times over until his body finally believed that he was safe, and calmed.

Below, the wolves tried to reach him with no success. The body broke apart into pieces each time they put their weight on it until it was a heap of branches. They could only look up at him with bright glaring eyes.

"Dogs," Sani said, and spat.

The wolves stopped growling. One of them smiled and said in Man's Word, "May the crows who eat your filthy flesh die, Darkened."

They started at the sound of a hammer being cocked.

"You first."

Harun had made it to a different tree, musket trained on the enemy. "Tell Aric that the Harun Jabril sends his regards and that your brothers' skins will fetch good trade."

The wolves gnashed their teeth and kicked at the air. Harun shot another one. The report echoed through the forest. The wolves barked and darted around the base of the tree, the old ape now the focus of their bloodlust.

"I've got plenty more," Harun said, waving his powder horn.

The wolves glanced at one another. They didn't want to leave. It was clear enough. But, one by one, they started to move back. With a final, hateful glance, they vanished into the shadows. Harun finished priming the musket and laid it across his lap.

"Where's Coyel?" Sani asked.

"Gone. Saw a wolf carry him off."

"He's dead?"

"He will be before dark."

Sani propped himself up and looked down. "Where's the rifle?"

"Dropped it. They might have taken it as a prize."

"I'm going," Sani said.

"Don't," Harun said. "You'll die too."

Sani searched for any trace of the little fox, but the sun was setting and the forest canopy blocked his view of the clearing. The rush of the fight left him in an instant. He gritted his teeth and moaned. The tears burned.

"He saved my life," he said.

"He was brave," Harun said.

Sani hung his head and let the sobs come. Three weeks in the wilderness. That wry smile and stinging wit were always there. Three weeks in the deep snow. That crooked tail was a welcome sight when the way was lost. Three weeks surrounded by the shadows that watched, and then the shadows had taken him.

"We failed," Sani said. "We couldn't save a single pup."

"Yes," Harun said. "But we know what happened. That'll help the others make peace."

"Rayne will retaliate," Sani said, crushing a pinecone in his hand. "He'll mobilize every last warrior to avenge this atrocity. Then, we'll have our war." He touched the wound on his face. It was beginning to swell.

"You have to tell his story," Harun said. "Our own young could learn much from Coyel the Quick. Course, he wouldn't have liked the name." Harun cleared his throat and attempted his best impression of the fox. "'Of course I'm quick. What do you take me for? A proper fox has to be quick. Why, I challenged my own shadow to a race. We couldn't decide who won, so we called it a draw.'"

Sani coughed as his throat convulsed between crying and laughter. "Yes, that does sound like something he'd say." He dried his eyes. "Coyel the Quick. I like that. If there was ever a fox nation, he'd be one of their great heroes."

"One fox for four wolves," Harun said. "Good trade, if you ask me. They got what they deserved." He spat.

Sani chuckled, but winced when he tried to flex his mangled hand. It took a great effort to unsling his pack and fetch the bandages. By the time it was wrapped, the night had come in full. The shadows were one great void. "What's the plan?"

"We'll sleep here tonight," Harun said. "Head out come morning."

"What about the wolves?"

"They've got other things to do."

"Coyel was our scout. You know the way?" Sani asked.

"Our tracks should still be there. The sun won't melt them," Harun said. "And if they're gone, we'll read the stars. Keep heading west. We'll run into somebody sooner or later."

Sani yawned. The battle had left him hurt and tired.

"Go on," Harun said. "I'll take first watch."

Sani nodded his thanks. "What a day. Found the remnants of a massacre. Killed a wolf and somewhere out there my friend is dying, wondering why I didn't save him. They'll honor the wolf who caught him with songs and mating rights. Oh, and there's a war coming."

"And you're not going to use that hand for a while," Harun said.

"Can't wait for tomorrow."

"Still want to go back to the jungle?"

Sani shook his head. "It's not so bad here. No tigers."

A whippoorwill called to a mate and received no answer. An owl hooted something wise in his native tongue.

"We wander the Earth, calling no land home. Everywhere, together and alone." The old ape looked at the young.

I need you here.

The young ape looked at the old one.

"Step by step," Sani said.

I'm here.

What a great idea! Transforming an army of human soldiers into fierce humanoid wolves to make invincible fighters!

Doesn't this sound like a great idea?

Think again.

Succession

by Devin Hallsworth

I was sure that the questions of whether I had murdered my father the king, and what this would mean for our kingdom, would quickly fade away as my subjects fully grasped the power they had been gifted through sorcery.

The spell I cast enveloped the entire kingdom and all of my subjects. From the most squalid tavern to the halls of this very castle, each and every former human paused to take in the spell's effects. They gazed at muzzles full of meat-ripping teeth protruding from their faces. They strode on paws instead of feet, and scratched at the fur that would now clothe them every day of their lives.

I had spared their hands and their ability to walk upright. They needed those to be able to pick up a sword and wage war upon our hated foes, of course.

"My subjects!" My voice boomed out across the hall where my closest advisors (and father's old sycophants) had been gathered. "For years we have lived in shame, under the conditions of a ruinous peace brokered by my weak-willed father due to his failure at the Battle of Devils' Ridge! Tonight I have taken the first step to rectifying our kingdom's woes! Each and every one of you has been given strength, endurance and speed you never dreamed of possessing before! The power of a wolf! With this and the fighting spirit of our kingdom's great warriors, we will crush the soft artists and philosophers who call themselves Guedans. We will rout their armies, break their lands apart, and feast on their kingdom's carcass until we have stripped it to the bone and grown fat upon its spoils!"

THAT finally got cheers/howls of assent out of my subjects. I had understood better than father ever did that the one thing that would always unite these self-serving knights and lords would be the promise of a successful war's wealth and glory.

"We will wash upon them like an unstoppable tide, prey upon them like a wolf feasts on sheep, shatter them like…"

* * *

I tried to console myself with memories of that heady time back in my castle, as everything went so terribly wrong. The boasting had lasted long into the night. My audience had been an eager one. We had all dreamed that night of a victory which would be sung about even centuries after the present age of sword and bow had finally passed.

"Get your damned hides over to the front! Drop those bows and shore up the left! You're obviously no good here!" My commanding general bellowed with all his might, exhorting what he could from the army at this desperate time.

The longbow men finally did as ordered. They dropped their bows and drew swords. They were poorly equipped for close quarters fighting, but no more so than it had turned out the rest of my army was.

They surged across the field of the dead and dying to join their brethren already engaged in battle. With their new muzzles the archers could smell prey a mile away. But their arm muscles had changed in subtle and unforeseen ways to alter the shape they had previously attained through decades' worth of archery practice. Archers who had learned to shoot perfectly soaring arrows through most of their human lives were struggling like amateurs as humanoid wolves. They ran across the battlefield as fast as they could; but our opponents did not have the same difficulties, and their arrows still flew true.

This was a fact that my advisors had warned me about over and over again as we had marched to battle. I had wished to maintain the element of surprise, while my generals had urged time to adapt the army to their new bodies.

I looked away from the battle and my thoughts turned back towards the direction of our kingdom where many, many miles away our cavalry horses still trembled in fear of the strange new predators who smelled exactly like hated wolves. The fact that when frustrated many riders had chosen to snarl at their steeds hadn't helped matters, either. In the end maybe one in twenty riders had succeeded in mounting their steeds, and even those had been thrown on the journey here while the panicked horses bolted away from the army.

I could take only small solace from the fact that the enemy hadn't seemed to have brought their cavalry to the battle either. A small mercy, but I greedily leaped at it like a starving man. Wolf.

Turning back to the scene of the battle, I felt my heart leap in joy as our ranks finally crashed upon theirs. The enemies' polearms had reaped a terrible toll on our army. There were almost as many dead as from the arrows. With their bodies so suddenly reshaped, few of the men could wear all the armor they had previously grown accustomed to. The kingdom's few smithies hadn't had any realistic chance of refitting so much armor in so short a time.

Modifying the straps to allow wearing a breastplate was the most that many men could do. Chain mail caught on fur in highly uncomfortable ways. Those in leather armor seemed to have made off the best, but many of those lay dead with heavy arrows through them.

But now that they had closed to arms' length with our hated foe, they were finally proving our kingdom's superiority. In close quarters, claw and teeth flashed just as readily as sword and spear. The enemy was unaccustomed to this level of ferocity. Their front ranks were ripped open as their powerful new foes surged in amongst them.

My lips were drawn back in a snarl as I began to dream that we would finally pay the enemy back for the blood they had spilled. The dour expression of my commanding general irritated me as he gazed along the edges of the battle, as though the clashing of sword and claw held little interest to him.

I was beginning to contemplate heading down to the front lines myself, leading with sword in hand as our forces gloriously devoured our soft foes, when a loud horn sounded across the entire battlefield. Every wolven ear, including mine, perked up towards that sound. It was the most ominous thing I had heard in my life.

The general's ears went back against his head as he stared off to the side. I followed his gaze and felt my heart stop as hundreds of armored and mounted knights surged forward from over a nearby hill and stormed towards our lines.

Cheers from human throats and whines from wolven ones were almost as loud as the thundering of hooves. My warriors did what they could with what polearms they possessed, but the hurricane of metal and beast that was a cavalry attack slammed into them mercilessly.

My general just shook his head in despair as I succumbed to the sinking realization that we had lost today.

* * *

It was now a week after that horrendous defeat. Our army was pushed almost all the way back to the border we had surged across when this war began.

I had taken this opportunity to seek out a nearby forest for a hunt, as hunting used to bring me such peace in my youth. Maybe it still would, if my hunting party didn't have to consist of nobles who were each more consumed with panic over the state of the kingdom than they were concern for the state of this hunt.

"There're rumors that the Guedans are in negotiations with the Pelans. We invaded them fifty years ago and they still hold a grudge over it. The Guedans are doubtlessly boasting of our heavy losses to them at this very moment," a foppishly dressed noble wailed for all the game in the forest to hear. I realized that this particular noble was well-known for never being seen in the same outfit for even an entire day, yet his clothes were still all exquisitely tailored to his new form. Did he have an entire army of tailors in his employ?

I growled loudly, then replied in a more human fashion. "The Pelans wouldn't dare! After we crushed them, we burned their fortresses and killed many of them. They wouldn't risk our wrath again after that." My sycophants didn't look particularly convinced.

I sighed and watched my youngest son instead. The eldest two had been crushed under the heavy hooves of armored war horses and he was my sole remaining heir. Worryingly, he had taken to his new form with unrestrained glee. Some days he almost seemed to forget he had ever been a young boy and not a young wolf.

He walked unclothed with ease on all fours, a bizarre feat considering his body had theoretically still been gifted with hands and bipedalism. I sometimes wondered if I had accidentally changed him more thoroughly than others.

He prowled through the underbrush and sometimes ran about, pausing to sniff at some patch of dirt and then carry on, tail wagging the entire time.

I tuned out the self-serving droning of my advisors and just watched. My son paused suddenly and then slowly began to creep forward towards a seemingly ordinary bush. I was just about to call him to me when he lunged forward and I heard the familiar squeal of something small dying.

Bouncing gaily upon his paws and looking very pleased with himself, my son came back to me with a dead rabbit clenched in his teeth. The blood dripped from his mouth as he set the kill before me and wagged his tail like a hunting dog. I heard one of my nobles retch, but ignored it as inspiration suddenly coursed through me like lightning.

I leaned down and gently scratched him behind his ears. "You may not realize it but you just saved our kingdom, son."

* * *

Our enemies banged their swords on their shields in ready anticipation of battle. My generals and army noted with growing terror that the enemies' ranks bristled with even more spears than usual. I was suddenly seized with a memory of watching a wolf unsuccessfully try to attack a porcupine.

But the fools in my ranks and the fools that were our foes had no faith in me. I alone wore a smile that was warranted that day.

"General, prepare to advance as I begin to cast. Do not hesitate and do not let the enemy retreat." I spoke confidently to the man commanding my army. Our armies' officers had not been filled in on the plan out of fear of spies amongst their ranks.

"Retreat. Right," he replied, not sounding remotely convinced. But like a good soldier he carried out his seemingly insane orders anyway. He bellowed out commands and got our mostly unwilling survivors of the previous battle moving forward again in the direction of the enemy.

They moved slowly, obviously certain that only death awaited them forward. I put their cowardice out of mind and focused my soul inward, to the place where I had stolen some tricks from the universe itself and learned to warp and shape the people who walked upon it.

This time though, I wouldn't be shaping my own subjects.

The enemy was gleefully taunting us and encouraging us forward. Their archers were just making ready to unleash a salvo when the changes began. Terror spread like wildfire among the ranks of the enemy. My own soldiers were confused at first. The enemies' ranks were heaving in bizarre ways, almost as if they were trying to free themselves from their heavy armor. But the confusion didn't last too long.

After all, every wolf knows the scent of a rabbit.

The chase began in earnest as the enemy dropped their weapons and armor. They fled as fast as their newly enlarged feet would take them back to their walled city. Now the tables were turned. It was our foes who struggled to survive in unfamiliar bodies, while my now experienced wolves chased them to the ground.

I had left our enemies their hands, minds, and human stance, knowing that they would make fine serfs as they worked the lands they used to own for their new masters. With such short bodies, they would never again wield a longbow or cavalry lance, nor would any of their countrymen.

The siege of their capital began that day. Our army camped around their walls and sang and howled and drank into the long hours of the night.

* * *

Construction of siege weaponry was a fascinating affair, one I was witnessing for the first time in my life from the safety of our camp.

I had tried negotiation with the king of the Guedans for two weeks, but was quite thoroughly vexed by his refusal to submit to my terms. In the end I had promised him that the second we breached his walls, our wolves would pour in and set upon his subjects like prey. But if anything, that had only seemed to make him angrier. Such an expression of pure hatred was surprising to see upon a lapine face.

I was watching the cutting of timbers to form a catapult when a messenger ran up to me with completely unexpected and frankly bizarre news. The gate to the enemy's city was open.

Certain that it was a trap, I dispatched a small force to investigate; only to be gifted with the unexpected.

The city was deserted! Empty. Barren of any living creatures. Despite our encirclement of them, it was as though every rabbit within had disappeared into thin air.

My generals urged caution while the soldiers muttered of curses. I waved both concerns off. It was time that our army entered the city and deprived it of all the spoils and wealth we had earned.

Only...

There wasn't any of that, either. The only things left for our armies to claim were the stone walls and bare floors.

* * *

I awoke in the morning in the former bedchamber of my enemy, which I had had refurnished from my royal pavilion in our war camp. His castle had a splendid view of what had been his city, and his bedchamber offered the best view of all.

Naked except for my fur and tail, I strode to the balcony and watched as the sun came up over the horizon. It cast its light upon all which I had laid claim to. We had not only succeeded in taking back the territories my father had so shamelessly traded away for peace, but we had laid claim to the entirety of the Guedan kingdom! Today's sunrise was beautiful to behold.

After a few minutes of basking in the serenity of that view, the screams started.

They began from a few quarters in the city below, then spread. I had no earthly idea what could be the cause of such commotion! Our armies controlled the walls, the gates, and the streets. My guardsmen burst through the door at that moment. I strode from the balcony with a raised eyebrow. One of them kneeled, panting heavily as he explained the news he had just received.

"Sire, the enemy is still among us! They erupted from hidden tunnels in the middle of the night, and slew many men in complete silence while they slept! All your generals are dead! The men are panicked and fleeing towards the gates! These rabbits built tunnels throughout this entire city while they were under siege! They could attack from anywhere at any time. We must flee the city, your Highness!"

Yes, rabbits have a natural talent for digging tunnels, I realized.

* * *

I would much rather have been out hunting instead of sitting in the throne room, listening to a bunch of good-for-nothings tally my failures.

"Besides the Guedans, the Pelans have laid claim to all of our provinces east of the river Tybelt. We have no forces that can stop them, short of the city of Lengsk," one such noble droned on.

I ignored him, remembering instead a hunting lodge I had rather liked in that region.

"That's a secondary concern," another noble broke in. "The Guedans have once again fielded an army, and are pushing at us from the south. They've created modified short bows and crossbows that they can use with their smaller frames. Arrows just appear seemingly out of nowhere and kill many of our supply convoys to the last man." Wolf. "The army has been running low on food for a week now."

It had been near a particularly stunning waterfall.

"Well, of course they are running low on food! They can't digest the starch in bread or potatoes anymore! They require more meat in their diet than any human ever did! Our cattle herds are rapidly dwindling to nothing! We'll have starvation among the general populace soon if we can't become human again!"

Now that I think about it, that was actually where father had first taught me to hunt.

"We can't! You heard our ruler yourself when he explained his sorcery. Once reshaped, it is far too difficult to reshape so many people again. He could possibly change a few hundred of us back to human with the strength he has, but not the entire kingdom."

He'd smiled a lot back then. I missed that smile.

"Damn him! You hear me!? DAMN you for damning all of us to starvation and defeat!"

My eyes finally unglazed at the sheer audacity of this... this... SYCOPHANT! Surging off the throne I waved imperiously at the advisors and lords gathered before me.

"I AM STILL YOUR KING, PEASANT! You would do well to not disappoint me any further! Or at least not any more than all of my subjects have disappointed me so far, with their cowardice in this war!" I roared at them.

They were all taken aback and I was just about to flop back into my throne, glad to have cowed them back into submission. But it was then that their hackles raised and teeth become bared.

"No. King is a human term. You are the Alpha." What I had seen as a throne room full of sycophants suddenly looked more like a large wolf pack. The nearest of the pack spoke as they closed on me and I shrank back, looking around desperately for the closest escape. "And weak Alphas get replaced."

Two castaways on an uninhabited island. A prey mouse and a predator wolverine. Which will be the survivor?

Of course, the author keeps you guessing…

Two If By Sea

by Field T. Mouse

Emerson had seen his share of storms. They were a familiar rite of spring and summer back home. Usually rolling in from the west, thick, tumbling clouds would carelessly blot out the sun. The air would build with electricity. Though a farmer, his father rarely complained about the weather. Count your blessings. That was his mantra. *He was always more spiritual than me.*

By contrast, the younger yellow-necked mouse viewed nature as a rogue force, accountable to no one. It both provided and took away with equal disdain. A nourishing rain could just as well become a devastating flood. *Does my cynicism prevent me from seeing beauty? Maybe father was half-right. We're beholden to nature. We need it more than it needs us. Doesn't that require a degree of respect?*

He tried to remember all this as the tempest raged around him. From his solitary cell below decks, he couldn't see much. He could hear, though. His keen, dishy ears swiveled atop his mousey head.

The wind roared. Waves crashed down like liquid cymbals, shattering upon impact, only to relentlessly reform for another go. Piling on, torrential, sub-tropical rains lashed the side of the modest battleship. The strain was evident, the sails drawn taut, every wooden beam creaking precariously.

The vessel bobbed and pitched without purpose. No angle was too steep. Emerson lost his footing and careened first into one wall and then another. He squeaked in pain, trying to fight the disorientation long enough to grab onto something. Eventually, he scrabbled his way toward the vertical bars in the circular window. They were metal. Like the lock on his door, they were designed to hold. *A death sentence should we begin to sink.*

It was no use begging to be let out. He'd already tried that. Predators didn't respect weakness. Besides, embroiled in crisis, the crew had completely forgotten about him. He wasn't a priority. He was their enemy. And they were his.

Why'd they bother taking me prisoner in the first place? Do they think I have information? Are they planning on torturing me? Am I going to be their plaything? He shuddered at the possibilities, but also from the chill in the air. All signs of warmth had long since vanished.

Grasping the bars that represented his imprisonment, the slender, golden rodent hoisted himself up to get a look outside. He was greeted with a spray of saltwater to the face. He turned and spat, squinting before taking another look. Visibility was low. Maybe a quarter-mile, if that.

Emerson had been the purser on his own ship, in charge of supplies. They'd been running dangerously low. The predators had all lines of commerce on lock down. He'd taken a smaller craft to meet with a potential black market provider when he'd been intercepted in port. It was a trap.

Was I careless? Should I have seen it coming? Outnumbered and outgunned, he'd surrendered immediately. *Having a strong survival instinct doesn't make me a coward. At least my crew mates got away.*

After securing the mouse, the predators had sailed away from the mainland. Emerson could only guess at their destination. One of the bigger islands, presumably. Upon the start of their voyage, the weather had been eerily calm. Maybe it was because he was prey, but he'd noticed. He'd felt a gnawing sense of dread. *If nature is divine, surely that was a warning.*

But they'd stubbornly sailed on, right into a developing storm. Now, their only chance of survival was to quickly lay anchor at one of the tiny, uninhabited islands along their path. The mouse pressed to the barred window, straining his big, fleshy ears to hear what was being said above deck. He could handle adrenaline. As prey, he was used to it. But he couldn't handle not knowing what was going on. That's when adrenaline bred fear. *It's the fear that paralyzes you.*

There must have been four or five voices shouting at each other up there.

"Did you see that?"

"There's a cove up ahead!" someone else claimed, most likely the navigator.

"Where? Are you sure? Hand me the telescope! And keep your paws on that wheel!" The captain's voice, deep and authoritative. Emerson recognized it from when he'd been brought aboard. The captain had looked him over, made a derisive comment, and ordered that he be hauled out of his sight. *Friendly fellow.*

"How close are we to land?"

"Did you *see* that?!" repeated the first voice.

"How can I see *anything* if if you have the—"

"There's another ship dead-ahead!"

"What?"

There were yips of surprise.

"It's an ambush!" growled a new voice.

"In this weather? Impossible." After a pause, the captain must have seen for himself, because he exclaimed, "A prey patrol boat? They're insane!"

"They must've been hiding in the cove. They're trying to prevent our entry."

"Have we stumbled upon a secret base?"

"They know they'll die at our paws eventually. Perhaps, seeing our approach, they've decided to go out on their own terms," a steely individual supplied.

"Shall I turn us around?" the navigator asked. "Captain?"

"We can't go back, idiot! The storm will destroy us."

"But if we head toward the enemy vessel—"

"Ready weapons?" the second-in-command asked with surprising calm.

The captain hissed lowly. "Ready weapons," he echoed, emphasizing both words.

His subordinates began shouting orders.

Before any of them could be enacted, there was a flash in the near-distance. On the briefest of delays, a cannon blast sounded. The predators, reeling from the suddenness of their situation, had spent too much time debating. The prey fired first, and the predatory ship took a brutal hole to the gut, pieces flying, voices crying. Every plank and beam of wood on the vessel vibrated from the force of it.

Emerson jerked away from the window, heart leaping in his chest. His brain and body were at a momentary disconnect. He could barely breathe. *Is this really happening?*

"Fire!" the captain roared, undaunted. He hadn't risen to such a high rank by losing his mettle under pressure.

A minute later, the wounded vessel turned and fired back. Boom, boom, boom! The starboard cannons, all of them. There were some cheers. At least one of the shots must've connected with the target.

"Don't let up! No mercy!' the captain bellowed.

Emerson, stuck in his dark, turbulent cell, tried to comprehend the irony of the situation he found himself in. He was prey. The attackers were prey. They had the same enemy. But they didn't know he was aboard. And even if they did, would they stop their attack? Unlikely. They couldn't. *I'm going to die at the paws of my compatriots. I'm going to be a victim of friendly fire.*

Frantic, he began throwing himself against the door. It was no use, though, and he knew it. He was too lightweight. The wood was thick and heavy, not to mention hard as a rock. The only thing he was going to do was bruise himself. The lock was solid metal. Without the key, there was no way to get out of here barring a hatchet. And he didn't happen to have one of those handy. *There's no way out. This is it.*

Boom, boom, boom!

The prey ship fired again.

Emerson, ears quivering from the concussive blasts, threw himself to the floor. It was purely instinct. There was no conscious decision involved. It saved him. The wall, including the window he'd been peering out of a few minutes ago, exploded behind him. By sheer fortune, the blast continued inward and took down the door to his cell, too. A cloud of dust and moisture swirled about in its wake, the rain and waves letting themselves inside.

Stunned and barely able to breathe, the trembling mouse got up. To his knees, first, and then fully upright. He gingerly massaged his ears. He couldn't hear the waves or the shouts of the crew. Just ringing, loud and steady.

He also felt sharp pains in his left arm. Little shards of wood had pierced him like splinters. His wrist, too, throbbed. *Must've injured it diving to the floor.* Closing his eyes, he quickly yanked the protrusions out and whimpered. He didn't know how long he'd been in here tending to himself, but he suspected it had been too long. He needed to get out of here. *Now! Move, move, move!*

Eying the space where the wall used to be, Emerson figured he had two options. Jump from here and swim unaided or go above deck and hope there was something he could use as a buoy or floatation device. Both plans involved making it ashore. As far as he knew, there were no lifeboats. Or, if there were, they were far too heavy for him to unleash on his own. He hadn't heard any voices since the last barrage of prey fire. *Is there anyone left up there?*

As much as his panic urged him to jump, he knew he wasn't going to be able to swim out of this alone, especially once the ship went under. It would drag him down with it. He needed help. Squinting, the mouse peered through the gaping, ragged hole in the wall and into the storm. They were faced away from shore. He couldn't tell how close they were to the cove. In this case, ignorance was not bliss. *It's not like it matters. You have no other choice.*

Long, thin tail whipping about like a counterbalance, he stumbled to the tattered doorway. He looked left. Then right. His eyes went wide. The broken body of a wolf laid at the bottom of a stairwell. Swallowing, he scurried toward him, clambering over the dormant figure and making his way above deck.

By now, his hearing had started to return. The storm was even louder up above. The rain careened into his face with disregard. He shielded his eyes with his good paw. When he glanced down, he noticed pools of red running across the deck. Blood, coming from mangled, dismembered predators. *Don't look. Don't look...*

But he couldn't help himself. Maybe it was morbid curiosity. Maybe he needed to know they'd ceased to be a threat. Emerson grabbed hold of a railing aboard the shuddering, sinking ship and scanned his surroundings. Mangled limbs and bodies abounded, covered in gory, wounded fur of multiple species.

The ship wasn't long for this world, either. Waves had cleared the bow. The sea was swallowing the vessel up, and it was using all its teeth. Gazing to the side, Emerson saw the prey ship sinking, too. Smoke was pouring out of all the windows. The sails were torn, and it unceremoniously toppled onto its side with a foamy splash. His heart sank.

Everything seemed hopeless. Pointless, even. *I can't be the only survivor, can I? How is that possible?* But there was no time to mourn. *Bury this moment before it buries you. You're prey. Prey don't give in.*

The ship groaned. As water flooded the interior, the angle of the top deck became steeper. Emerson began to slip. Jerking and jolting with manic energy, he clawed and scurried to the other side of the ship, bare foot-paws slapping on the wet, wooden surface. He lost his balance once or twice, cursing, crawling, bouncing back up each time.

Lightning struck high above, thunder rattling the world.

"Something that floats, something that floats," the mouse muttered desperately. *There has to be something. A chair, a barrel. Anything!* "Come on!" There were pieces of wood from the mast, but they were too heavy for him to move.

He put his paws on his head, ready to tear his fur honey-gold out. That's when he saw it. *The wheel. It came off! How? Who cares!* Breathless, he made his way toward it. It was mostly intact, too. It would float. And it was big enough to support his body across if necessary. While retrieving it, he had just enough clarity of mind to take the canteen of water off the navigator's broken neck. There was no time to forage for anything else. Slinging it over his own shoulder, he scooted the wheel to the edge of the ship, took several deep breaths and jumped overboard with it.

His wrist throbbed with pain at the plunge, the injured paw slipping off the wheel. The good one managed, if only barely, to hold on. Somehow he kept his head above the fray, gasping, chest heaving. His pink ears began to pale, his fur soaking through, and the earlier splinter-wounds stung from the saltwater. He could hear himself sobbing, but he wasn't consciously aware of making the noises. *Is this what an out-of-body experience is like?*

The fragile mouse clung to his makeshift life preserver with all his might. Hauling himself halfway upon it, he began kicking his legs in the water. Behind him, the predatory ship drew its last breath before disappearing forever.

The storm's waves, refusing to abate, lifted the mouse up and sent him hurtling forward down. *A good thing I don't get seasick.* He coughed as water tried to force itself into his airways. Up ahead, land. He was closer to shore than he'd realized. He was being pushed toward the island. After what felt like an eternity but what was, in reality, no more than ten minutes, he was in water shallow enough to stand.

He hauled the wheel ashore and fell to his knees, leaving imprints in the wet sand. The waves continued to claw at him. Everything was a churning mess of dull gray. More lightning strikes in the near distance yielded thunderous crackles. He wondered if the rain had slowed or if he was just so wet he'd stopped feeling it.

Collecting his senses, Emerson looked around him. It was, unfortunately, still raining. It was windy, too. Wreckage from the ship was beginning to surge toward the beach just as he had. Pieces of wood, clothing, books. Random artifacts of ruin. And there, clinging to what must've been the remnants of the crow's nest, was another survivor.

His eyes widened. It was a predator! *We must've come from the same ship. Just my luck. I wonder if he's one of the voices I heard shouting?* Short, stocky, with muscles that could rip an opponent to shreds, Emerson thought it was a bear. Upon closer inspection, he realized it was a wolverine. His short rounded ears and jet-black muzzle gave him a blunt, mean appearance. His bushy tail was waterlogged, drifting to the side of him.

Emerson briefly considered leaving him there. But only briefly. *If positions were reversed, wouldn't you want him to help you?*

Already feeling his adrenaline turning to fatigue, he fought against it and slogged back into the sea, pulling the dazed predator away from the wreckage and helping him ashore. With only one good paw, it was a painful process. He clenched his jaw, buckteeth biting into his lower lip. His ears tilted forward to act as umbrellas for his eyes. Eventually, he collapsed with the wolverine onto the white-pink sand. He stared at the surly heavens. He would've cursed them if he could think of the words.

The wolverine made a noise.

Sitting up, the mouse panted, "Are... who are you? Are you okay?"

Grunting, the wolverine twisted to all fours. His head snapped up. He bared his fangs.

Emerson's eyes widened. He scrabbled backward, tail and whiskers stiffening. "Look, I just saved your—"

The predator lunged.

The mouse chittered in alarm, the bigger male's claws tearing through his clothes and into his damp pelt.

"You attacked us!" the wolverine hissed, pinning Emerson into the sand.

"W-what?"

A flash of lightning above them briefly turned the wolverine into a menacing silhouette. "You'll pay for this!"

"I was on the same ship you were! Get... " Emerson tried to push him off. Rainwater dripped into his eyes. He closed them, heart hammered with fear. "Get off! Please!" He pushed, but there was no use. The predator was much stronger. "Stop it!"

The wolverine's thick, deadly paws surrounded his throat.

Realizing he still had a metal canteen slung over his shoulder, the mouse grabbed it and smashed it into the wolverine's muzzle.

He yowled!

Delivering another hit, this one a knockout blow to the skull, Emerson wriggled free. His paws shook, his whiskers numb. His whole body twitched with a mixture of a million things negative. He wanted to throw up. In fact, he tried to, but couldn't. So, he did the only other thing he could think of: he screamed.

Overnight, the storm dissipated, and bit by bit Emerson managed to drag the unconscious wolverine clear of the seawater's reach. Thankfully, the cove they'd found themselves in was framed by a gently sloping treeline rather than tall, jutting rocks. This meant they had a source of shade. It also meant they weren't trapped in place. They could venture out to search for food and water.

You make it seem like you're in this together. They were at war, weren't they? When push came to shove, it was everyone for themselves. *He tried to strangle you! Maybe it was a mistake to save him.*

Emerson rubbed his cool blue eyes. He didn't know anymore. He didn't want to think about these things. Or anything. He'd barely slept. *On the plus side, no time for nightmares.* The sky was currently a brilliant shade of azure, brightly dotted with impossibly white and fluffy clouds. *Like an inverted ocean. Except islands up there get to float away. Wish it was that easy for us.*

Sighing, he looked at the wolverine. He actually wasn't all that much taller than the mouse, but he was wider, denser. And not wearing a shirt, the muscles beneath his thick, oily pelt were impossible to miss. *He could snap me in two.* The darkness of his fur was offset by pale, off-white streaks on his head and backside.

Beneath the picturesque sky remained a messier sight. Random pieces of wreckage had wedged into the sand. Nature wasn't about to let its dominion be forgotten. Thankfully, no bodies were part of this. Emerson stared blankly past it all, toward the horizon. He felt hungover. *Someone will rescue us. Maybe even today. It's only a matter of time.*

Beside him, the wolverine stirred with a cough. This was followed up by a low groan.

"Welcome to the land of the living," the mouse said, reclining against a tree trunk with his knees bent. He loosely hugged his legs. "You're not missing much."

"Who are you?" was the groggy reply.

"I'm—"

The wolverine hissed. His body tensed.

Emerson recoiled. His whiskers twitched. "Don't think about attacking me again!"

"My head! Guh." The wolverine rubbed at it. "It's throbbing."

"Oh." The mouse cleared his throat. "Sorry. But you were sorta asking for it."

The wolverine remained quiet for a moment, finally recalling the struggle and being struck. "Mm." He sat up, arms reaching back and acting as stilts for his upper body. "Did you also break my ankle?" He winced as he tried to stretch his legs.

"Don't know anything about that. Welcome to the club." He held up his injured wrist.

"That is not your ankle," the predator observed dryly.

The mouse made a face.

The wolverine's fur, unlike the mouse's, was built for northern climes. The color seemed to absorb sunlight instead of reflecting it. His chest was already heaving from the heat. Thankfully, the direction the sun was moving, they'd be in the shade for most of the day. "How'd I get here? To the treeline, I mean." He rubbed at his head again.

"I pulled you," Emerson said. "Do you know how heavy you are? I should get a medal. Frankly, I don't know how you didn't fall out of that crow's nest between the ship and the shore." He fastidiously groomed at his whiskers. "It was a miracle you didn't drown."

"I don't believe in miracles."

"Neither do I, really. But our survival was highly improbable." *How can that be explained? Or, as blessings go, should it not be questioned?* "Fig?" He held out one. "I collected a few while you were out. The ones the storm didn't knock off. They're pretty ripe. They're good, if you like that sort of thing. I'd prefer a good apple, but the island is fresh out."

"Hmm." The predator narrowed his eyes. He inspected the fig. His usual diet consisted of meats and grains. He sliced the dark, sweet fruit it in half with his claws, licking at it. His eyes lit up. Whether this was good or bad was hard to say, but he gobbled up the insides immediately. He was hungry. "You *were* on my vessel," he said between mouthfuls. "You're the prisoner, aren't you?"

"Former prisoner," Emerson admitted, unable to look away. Watching predators eat was oddly entertaining.

"I was part of the detail that captured you," he remembered. He gulped, licking his lips. "I also gave you your food and water yesterday morning before the storm."

"Guess that makes us pals," Emerson replied dryly.

The wolverine puffed his chest up, tossing the remnants of the fig behind them. "When my compatriots come in search of my vessel, you will be a prisoner once more," he declared in his best warrior voice.

"Maybe." Tail roping around the tree trunk he was leaning against, Emerson folded his golden paws behind his head. He attempted to appear nonchalant, even if he didn't feel it. "Unless my side gets here first."

There was a brief pause. The wolverine hadn't considered that. "Doubtful."

"They were already here when your ship passed by, right? Stands to reason they'll be back."

"Back for what? To resume scouting this location for nefarious purposes?"

"If 'staying alive' qualifies as nefarious, I guess so."

"But your 'scouts' are not alive," the wolverine reminded bluntly. "They are dead."

Emerson's whiskers twitched. He lowered his arms and gripped his knees.

"How did you escape your cell? I doubt anyone let you out."

"It's a long story," was the slow, evasive reply.

The predator looked left, then right. "We seem to have plenty of time."

The mouse gave him a withering side-glance. "I'd rather not relive it."

"Typical prey. You cannot handle reality, so you pretend it does not exist. You live in denial, the whole lot of you. If your kind would only acknowledge that predators are superior in—"

The mouse sprung to his bare foot-paws without warning. His tail snaked through the air with agitation.

"Where are you going?" the wolverine demanded with a blink.

"To get some fresh air. Strangely, there's none in your vicinity." And that wasn't entirely an exaggeration. The wolverine had a pungent scent. Natural or not, the mouse wasn't used to it. It unnerved him. *Besides, I don't need to sit here and listen to him insult me. I'm not that lonely, am I?*

"This is your—" The predator yelped in pain as he tried to stand, too, forgetting about his ankle. He flopped back down and huffed. His tail hiked. "This is your fault, *rodent*. Do you deny it? Your people attacked *us*. If they would've granted us amnesty during the storm and let us come ashore—"

Emerson spun around in a fit of twitchy rage, fingers curling into fists. "This isn't even your territory!" he yelled. "Not this," he said, kicking at the faintly rosy sand. A cloud of it disappeared into the breeze. "Not that," he added, pointing at the glistening sea. "Every island in this region is *ours*. We came here to get away from *you*. But you couldn't accept that."

"We have a legitimate claim to these territories."

"How? We were here first," the mouse insisted.

"Nature doesn't reward first," the wolverine replied. "It rewards best."

"Don't lecture me about nature," Emerson spat darkly. He thought about his father's words, again. His parents' spiritual bent had led to them being pacifists. They weren't pleased when Emerson joined the service. But he'd been convinced it was better than doing nothing.

"Don't scurry from me, mouse!"

Without looking back, he corrected, "I'm walking, not scurrying."

The wolverine growled, incensed at his body's frailty and the mouse's lip. "There's nowhere to go! This island is too small!"

Emerson ignored him and kept going.

* * *

Seabirds veered and dove at sharp, random angles before rising up again, shrieking constantly. It was as if they craved attention. Emerson tried not to give them any, looking straight ahead. With all the rain they'd gotten during that storm, there had to be freshwater somewhere. The interior of the island was quite hilly and smothered with plant life. He kept an eye out for any natural pools.

As he searched, Emerson wondered why he didn't feel more remorse for those who had perished. He'd barely thought about them. There was obligatory sorrow, of course, but it remained on the surface. All of this had been traumatic because it had happened to *him*. What about those who hadn't made it?

You didn't know them. They were too abstract to have faces. He felt awful for thinking such a thing. But wasn't that how it had to be? *If you felt emotional pain for every individual death, you'd become paralyzed. You'd never be able to function. The only way to move on and stay sane is to let yourself become numb to it. It's a coping mechanism.* "I guess the wolverine's right. Maybe I can't handle what life has become," he admitted aloud. *Was there a time when things had been different?*

He wondered what his status was with the prey military. Killed in combat? Missing in action? Prisoner of war? *If I survive all this, I'll probably be promoted. Maybe I'll become a hero and, to boost morale, will be sent to fight on the front lines with the beleaguered troops.*

The idea rattled him. He'd been trained in the use of weaponry. He'd fired a gun or two. But he wasn't a fighter. He hadn't killed anyone. *Yet. If you had to, could you? You couldn't even let that wolverine die.* Sometimes, he wished he had the faith of his father, the grace of his mother. *Would that make me feel better about all this? Or is purity a matter of perspective?*

Of course, if a predatory ship came to their rescue, he was likely in for a very bad end. They'd no doubt place the blame for the loss of their ship on his big-eared head. *As the scapegoat, I'll probably be given an elaborate public execution.*

Emerson, realizing he was getting carried away, tried to squash these scenarios. *One thing at a time.* He'd finally found a freshwater pool. It was clear and still enough to reflect its surroundings. He tested it with his tail-tip. Shrugging, he bent down and dipped the canteen into it, filling it and greedily quenching his thirst.

"Ah," he panted. And then he filled it and drank again. Panting with relief, he topped it off a third time for the wolverine.

Momentarily quenched, he looked around self-consciously and began removing his frayed clothes: beige pants, loose, white shirt with several buttons missing, and his underwear, too. Even after his time in the sea and rain, he didn't feel clean. *Maybe it's all the salt. Or maybe it's your conscience.*

Stripped to his bare pelt, he carefully waded into the rocky pool and sank into the water. After adjusting to it, he splashed his face. Compared to his antagonistic beach buddy, he was a less striking sight. His trim, twitchy body was covered by brown, honeyed fur on his limbs and backside. His loins, belly, and chest were an off-white. To top it off, he had a golden 'collar' around his neck, which was the source of his species' name.

Emerson looked at his reflection in the rippling water. *I used to be cute. That's what everyone said. But, then, I used to smile more.* He couldn't seem to muster a happy face at the moment.

He splashed himself some more. Droplets clung to his whiskers and twitched off, his pink nose sniffing at the air. The breeze was fresh and fragrant. *Maybe I should explore more of the island, leave the predator to fend for himself. That's what predators do best, right? Why does he need my help?*

But, if he did that, he might miss the rescue party. And there *would* be a rescue party. Two ships gone? Someone would notice. Of course, there was a fifty-fifty chance of being rescued by the wrong people, but what was the alternative? Staying here and starving to death? He was hedging his bets on being found by allies. The fact that a prey ship had already been hiding here when the predators arrived gave him hope.

"I'll sail away from here," he breathed to himself, rubbing at his whiskery cheeks. "Far away."

Like all things, it was only a matter of time.

* * *

"I couldn't find any more food," Emerson said when he got back. "The figs that are left are rotten."

The wolverine blinked and looked up. "Surely, where there's *one* fruit tree, there's—"

"Probably," he interrupted.

"And?"

"I'm hungry, too, okay?" he griped. "But my main priority was water. And waiting for rescue. Here." The mouse tossed him the canteen.

The predator caught it, opened the top, and hesitated. He gave a few sniffs. "You first." He closed it and tossed it back.

Not having time to think, Emerson caught it with his bad wrist. He winced and dropped it. "Ouch! Dammit!" Huffing and retrieving it with his good paw, he scowled at the wolverine. "What's your problem?"

"I've seen the looks prey have given me. The same look is in your eyes right now. You'd rather I were dead."

"You don't know me."

"Drink it."

"If I wanted you dead, why did I save your life?"

"So I would be at your mercy."

Emerson laughed darkly, shaking his head.

"Drink first!"

"Or what?"

The wolverine gave him a death stare.

Rolling his eyes, the mouse took a healthy swig of water. He swallowed. "Happy?" Closing the canteen again, he threw it into a clump of nearby wild grass.

Stretching and reeling it in, the wolverine began to gulp the water down. He finished every drop.

"You're welcome." After a moment, the mouse sat in the shade of the twisty tree trunk he'd been leaning against earlier and observed, "Now that you mention it, it's funny how the tables are turned. Yesterday, you were giving me provisions. Now, I'm giving them to you." *Isn't that what they call poetic justice?*

"I am not laughing."

Emerson shrugged. "Not everyone has a good sense of humor."

"You don't strike me as military material," the wolverine said. He tossed the empty canteen away, wiping the back of his paw across his lips. "You weren't even wearing a proper uniform when we captured you."

"You're half-naked," was the retort.

"My posting dictates casual attire. It gets hot hoisted above the ship, left in the sun all day. Especially with fur like mine."

Emerson thought about it for a moment and replied, truthfully, "I'm pretty low in the ranks, myself." He paused and added, "I mostly handle ship logistics." Someone had to.

The wolverine eyed him curiously. He shook his head in confusion. "You don't fight?"

"If I'm called to, I will."

"But you don't prefer it?"

"We're not like you." His whiskers twitched. "You, your kind," he elaborated, gesturing at the predator, "relish conflict."

The wolverine shook his head. "That's not true."

Emerson scoffed. "I think it's pretty obvious that—"

"We're out for blood?"

"Aren't you?"

"Having a capacity for blood lust isn't the same as being bloodthirsty." Before Emerson could press him on that, he asked, "What is your side 'out for,' mouse?"

"Independence," he replied obviously.

The wolverine laughed. The sound was hearty and deep. "That almost sounds noble." His amusement faded. "Almost," he repeated. "If only you weren't thieves. We had a *mutual* government built on—"

"Mutual?" the mouse mocked. "Built on what? Respect? Hardly."

"Tradition."

"That's not enough. Before the split, predators held *every* notable position of power. No matter the government, they always have. Somehow, even with 'equal representation,' you gravitate toward the top. You dominate the hierarchy. The system is broken. There was only one option. It had to be imploded, given a complete—"

"Prey propaganda," the wolverine dismissed.

"The hard truth. You just can't accept you need us more than we need you."

"So, out of the blue, the whole lot of you decides to secede? Lands and territories previously belonging to all of us are solely yours? You could have talked to us."

"Talk is cheap when it comes to predators," the prey said. "You only care about action."

"Then, when we try to reach out to you, to restore order," the wolverine continued, "you resorted to terrorism. Arson, bombings. The first shots of this conflict were fired by your side, rodent. You killed first. Never forget that."

"You've been killing us since time began! We weren't getting fair representation. We never—"

"You've no fire in your eyes. All you have is your words."

"There's fire in me," the mouse assured. He put a paw over his chest. "It's in my heart."

"How saccharine! Adorable, even. I wonder if you really believe it?" He nodded mockingly, baring his teeth with amusement. "I'd expect nothing less from a mouse." He said the words as if it were an insult. "Of all the prey, you're the weakest, the most fragile. The most prey-like."

"I'm proud of my species."

"Then you are a fool, rodent."

"I have a name." Emerson felt his muscles tensing. Being in the company of a predator was bad enough. Having an argument with one? It was stressing him out.

"Well?" The wolverine opened his paws. "What is it?"

"Emerson." He waited for a caustic comment. None came. "What's yours?" he wondered, not expecting an answer.

"Reginald. My friends call me Reggie. You," he reminded, "are not among them."

"Alright, Reginald," he emphasized. "So, we don't see eye to eye. That doesn't mean we can't find a way to be civil."

The wolverine rubbed at his eyes. He still had a slight headache. "There is nothing civil about war."

"There are still rules."

"That is the first mistake prey make." Reginald grabbed at the wild grass, picking a few blades and releasing them into the breeze. "We are merely a few steps removed from the beasts, you and I. Our instincts are still strong. The only rule is to win. Survival of the fittest."

"I don't believe that."

"You're welcome to your delusions."

"Fine, you want to hear that you're stronger? That you're better?" Emerson got to his shins and knees and spread his arms in frustration. "You have us on the run. We're low on supplies, have fewer ships. You're just… " He shook his head. "Relentless."

"Most predators would take that as a compliment."

"Do you?" Emerson pressed.

Reginald tilted his head. "The tone in your voice is not complimentary."

"No," the mouse quietly confirmed.

"I joined the military with no hesitation," Reginald countered proudly. "My father and grandfather were both members. Even my mother is a nurse at one of our home bases."

"Sounds like a fine family tradition."

The wolverine couldn't tell if that was sarcasm or not. "It is. It's not about hunting or killing, as you suspect. Though sometimes that becomes necessary. It's more about structure, order. About staying in touch with our heritage, our instincts, maintaining our way of life. I've already been decorated twice for valor."

Emerson looked at the predator. His sharp claws. His bulky, muscular demeanor. Valor. *Does that include combat? I wonder how many notches he has on his belt?*

"What?" the wolverine demanded. He didn't like the look the mouse was giving him.

"Nothing."

"You've never killed before, have you?"

Emerson wasn't sure how to reply to that, only managing, "I'm betting you have."

"Only in defense."

"Really." It wasn't a question. The mouse looked away. *I wonder what it feels like? How does one live with it? Do I want to know?*

"Do you honestly believe all predators are out for blood? That we enjoy spending all our time fighting? How would a society function if that were the case? Do we have superior physical strength? Yes. In the ancient past, did we make it a point to antagonize you? Perhaps. Do we still?" He skipped a beat. "Superiority is woven into our fabric."

Emerson huffed. Each time it seemed like Reginald was coming around, he'd make a comment like that.

"Didn't you just admit we were stronger?"

"It doesn't matter," Emerson said pointedly. "The fact remains, after so many years, you *still* haven't won this war. We're a ragtag force at this point, barely keeping things together, and you can't get rid of us. You want to know why?"

"No."

"Half of war is strategy, maneuvering. Intellect. Maybe we don't have the brute force, but we're just as smart as you. Maybe smarter. You're the hunters? We're the hunted. And the hunted know how to evade capture. They're wired for it. You won't prevail until you stop underestimating our capabilities." The mouse shook his head dismissively. "And since your egos won't allow you to do that, I guess you never will."

Reginald's brown eyes wordlessly bored into Emerson's.

His ears, flushing with blood, burned red. He didn't back down. "Where were we going before we sank?" he asked. "I sensed the captain was in a hurry. Were you going to join an armada?"

"As you intimated, I wasn't exactly a high-ranking officer. I was a lookout," Reginald replied. There was a sheepishness in his voice. He'd been talking big, and it wasn't all bluster. But he wasn't exactly the predatory navy's top warrior. "We were set to meet our allies. Was it for an attack? If we *were* joining an armada, our absence wouldn't faze them. Our loss wouldn't be mourned." He took a slow, ponderous breath. "The mission always takes priority over the participants."

"Seems rather harsh."

"It is," he allowed.

Emerson closed his eyes and sat back down on his rump, leaning against the tree again. "And what about me? What was to be my fate?" Blinking, he gazed out at the skyline. "Was I going to be tortured? Forced into servitude?" *Or worse?*

"Prey have a low pain tolerance. Torture isn't very useful on them. Threats? Those work fairly well." Reginald let that hang. "We've found your kind have very active imaginations. The mere suggestion of something awful we could do to you can trigger a cooperative streak."

"And I was just beginning to like you, too," Emerson replied sarcastically.

Reginald frowned. "Do you want me to be honest or to lie?"

"What's the difference?"

"If you didn't want my company, you shouldn't have pulled me ashore."

"I couldn't just let you perish."

"I wouldn't have rescued you." It was spoken with no malice. It was simply the truth.

"Good to know," Emerson whispered.

There was an uncomfortable silence. For a moment, it almost seemed as if Reginald wanted to apologize. Instead, he asked, "What kind of mouse are you, anyway? Golden? Harvest?"

"Yellow-necked."

"Never heard of it."

"Well." Emerson tugged down the collar of his loose, white shirt, revealing the yellow-gold, almost caramel coloring on his neck and upper chest. It was brighter than the rest of his fur.

Reginald quirked a brow. "I see."

"What about you? What kind of wolverine are you?"

"There is only one kind that I know of."

"Really?" Why he was surprised by that, he didn't know. "In the whole world? Does that get lonely?"

The predator frowned. "What are you implying?"

"I just didn't realize there were so few of you."

"We're not terribly common, and especially not in this part of the continent. But we've always spread ourselves out," he explained. "As a species, we don't congregate like prey do. We don't require safety in numbers." Seeing he'd inadvertently offended the mouse again, the wolverine decided to revert back to one of their earlier topics. "In regards to our military strategy… "

"I'm all ears." Emerson's lobes swiveled.

"We expected this war to be over in a year, two at most. It's endured twice as long. You're correct in claiming you've put up a much fiercer resistance than our leaders anticipated. Timetables are dragging, costs are rising. The public is getting very restless. They want results. Soon."

Sounding exasperated, Emerson asked, "Does it really matter, though, whether you get them? Look at history. It's littered with bouts of predator/prey unrest. Maybe your side wins… *this* time. Maybe you regain control over this whole region." He waved an arm at their environment. "But as soon as the next generation comes along, it'll all happen again. It's a vicious cycle, stuck on repeat." He sighed. "Maybe it's hopeless. As long as we have our instincts, we're prisoner to them."

"Did I say that?"

"It was implied."

"And you blame that on us?" Reginald asked.

"By nature, predators are aggressive. The aggressive instigate. So, yes, you have more to answer for."

"I remind you that we're stranded here because a *prey* ship initiated a violent, suicidal onslaught. They wouldn't even consider a truce long enough to let us seek shelter in the cove."

Chastened, Emerson rubbed at his injured wrist. *That would require prey to trust predators. Trust has to be earned.* "They probably felt—"

"Always an excuse," Reginald interrupted angrily. "You refuse to give us the benefit of the doubt. In your own eyes, you are saints. The sanctimoniousness is off-putting." He struggled upright, gingerly testing out his left foot. He grit his teeth. It still hurt fairly badly, but he could hop around on one leg. He could handle pain.

"Where are you going?"

"I don't answer to you."

"You really shouldn't—"

"I drank a whole canteen of water. I need some privacy. I'm going to seek it."

"Oh."

"Unless you are afraid and require my protection?" If Reginald didn't know any better, he'd think Emerson was worried about him.

Emerson scowled halfheartedly. "I can handle myself."

* * *

Hours passed. It was mid-afternoon. The two survivors remained in the treeline on the cove, awaiting signs of rescue.

"What are you thinking about?" Emerson mumbled, standing and staring at his foot-paws. He'd been pacing back and forth with nervous energy until Reginald had demanded he stop.

Reginald fiddled with a twig. He broke it into several pieces. "What does it matter to you?"

"I've run out of topics. We may have nothing in common, but our conversation is healthier than my thoughts. It keeps my mind off things. And, besides… " He shook his head. It felt disingenuous to claim he was getting bored, especially after spending several days locked in a cell by himself, and then escaping a sinking ship in a freak storm.

"I was thinking about my mate," Reginald eventually said.

Emerson blinked, sitting down in the sandy, scattered grass. "You're married?"

The wolverine nodded, a sensitivity overtaking his visage.

"Children?" the mouse pried before he could stop himself.

"One." After a slow breath, Reginald sighed. "I want more. We both do. But I don't get home often enough… or, more accurately, at the right times," he added lightly, "to ensure that."

"Right."

"You seem surprised."

"When you said wolverines were independent and spread-out, I just assumed you were the sort… well, you know. To take lovers instead of actually be in love. You're so buff and gruff, I didn't think you could—"

"Feel that deeply? You thought I had no soul?"

The mouse twitched guiltily.

"Predators are susceptible to the same emotions prey are, even if it's in different proportions," Reginald insisted.

Again, Emerson said nothing.

The wolverine continued, "I don't get to see them often, of course. My family. My duties prevent it. But my salary provides for them, which gives me solace. I get letters now and then. I keep every one." He ran a large paw through his unruly two-colored head-fur. "Or I did. I lost them when the ship went down." He closed his eyes. He wouldn't say that made him sad, exactly. That would be too maudlin. But he felt regret. "They were the only thing physical I had of them."

"How far away are they?"

Reginald shook his head. "A week? The far end of our territory."

"What about a ring?"

"I didn't want to risk it getting stolen or lost should my body... " He trailed off and nodded. "In case something like *this*," he specified, gesturing around them, "should happen. I wanted it to stay with her."

"What's her name? Your mate?"

"Miriam. And my daughter... " The wolverine smiled. A big, toothy grin, the first sign of genuine happiness that had graced his face since they'd been stranded. "She's named after her. Miri. Isn't that precious?"

Emerson nodded. Hearing this wrecking ball of a beast use the word 'precious,' and mean it sincerely, was rather jarring.

"I wonder, sometimes, if Miri remembers my face. She's only three. Or if I'm just a vague, ghostly presence in her life? I feel guilty for not being there for her. I try to remind myself I'm keeping her safe, preserving her way of life. And that, were we not at war, I could be stationed closer to home. Maybe they could even live with me in some military port?" He seemed to be talking mostly to himself, now. "My mate, though... "

Emerson blinked, waiting for him to continue.

"She's glorious."

"I imagine so." *The only thing more intimidating than one wolverine is two wolverines.*

"Always a sunny smile. But, behind it, a sharp tongue and quicker wit. There's not an ounce of docility in her. She's just as aggressive as me. I had never met my match until the night we crossed paths. I thought I would resent being challenged, but it was strangely enjoyable."

"You mean you fight a lot?"

"Not in the way you're thinking. We butt heads, of course, but it's more like... foreplay," he decided. "We needle each other until one of us reacts. Energy spawns energy. Next thing you know, we're trying to pin each other down. And once we do, well... " He grinned slyly.

Emerson's ears became rosy-red.

"It's—"

"Glorious, yeah," the mouse mumbled, thwarting any details. He got the picture.

The wolverine continued, with rising reverence, "Coming together like that? With someone you care about? Two forces with one purpose? Is there anything more elemental, more pure? Although hate is far more prevalent in this world, I would not hesitate to say love is the stronger emotion. It takes such effort, though, to craft and maintain, that many turn to the easier avenue. The pleasure, though?" He licked his lips. "They don't know what they're missing."

Breaths shallow, the mouse cleared his throat. "I can't really disagree with that, I guess." In addition to being flustered, the mouse was increasingly confused. *Earlier, he was railing against me for no reason and now saying love is the better way?*

"What about your mate? What's she like?" Reginald pressed.

Emerson squirmed. He knew this question was coming. "I don't have one."

"Did something happen to her?"

"No," he explained simply.

"Are you not into—"

"There was never anyone for anything to happen to."

Reginald blinked. "Ever?"

Emerson shook his big-eared head.

"Why not?" the wolverine asked, showing what almost seemed like genuine concern.

Emerson gnawed on his lower lip. He wasn't sure how to talk about this. He didn't *want* to talk about this. *Besides, what does he care? I thought we were enemies? Predators can't really change, can they?* "It just never happened."

"Earlier, you asked if I got lonely. Did you ask because you are?"

"I'm not lonely." He twitched, adding lamely, "Not always."

Reginald waited for more.

"I'm not very personable, really. Grew up in the countryside, isolated." Emerson reeled in his ropy tail with his paws, fiddling with it. "I think it made me somewhat aloof. I've always had trouble making connections. Then the conflict began erupting between species. Death, destruction. I began losing uncles and cousins. The only way to protect myself was to seal myself off. And that meant love got cut out, too." He opened and closed his paws vulnerably. "It's not that I want to be alone. It's that I deserve to be. I'm a cynical coward."

"And what, aside suffering from a natural dose of fear, have you done to deserve such a label?" When Emerson didn't reply, Reginald prodded, "If I may give you some advice?"

"Not like I can stop you." The mouse, unblinking, stared across the sea again. It seemed infinite. It wasn't. Everything ended. This made him feel an intense amount of urgency.

Why is the gulf between who I am and who I want to be so much larger than any physical distance? I've spent so much time resenting people like Reginald. But am I any better? Aren't my biases just as blatant? Look at you. He's warming up to you, isn't he? You're still resisting. But, then, that's just like a predator: lure the prey into a trap and then pounce. My mind might be able to forget that, but experience won't.

"Your anxiety, as prey," Reginald recapped, "is such that the only way to safely process what you feel is to compartmentalize it, to wall yourself off. Otherwise, the intensity of the emotions would overwhelm you. There's nothing unnatural about that. But perhaps you are *too* talented at disconnecting. You seem like an introspective sort, a thinker instead of a doer."

Emerson nodded faintly.

"You've lived inside your head for so long that it's become second nature. It is a learned response. But, as such, can't it be unlearned? If you lowered your wall and ventured out a bit... " He held out his paws in an open gesture. "I've no doubt you'd attract more attention." He paused and added, "Friends and lovers alike."

"It's not that simple," he whispered.

"Isn't it?"

"If there's a wall inside me, I'm not the one who built it. Like you said, it's always been there. It has to be." He rubbed at his injured wrist, long, thin tail side-winding through the air. "Without it, I'd be having a mental breakdown right now." It was easy to forget he'd been present for dozens of deaths last evening. Too easy. *You're so good at forgetting when you want to.* "I can't survive if I expose myself to the world. It's not a safe place."

"Doesn't anything worth feeling or doing entail a degree of risk? A level of blind trust?"

Emerson didn't answer at first. His whiskers twitched. Then he said, "You're strong. I'm not. You can juggle love and hate in equal measure and not let one infect the other. I can't. You may have taken more lives than me, but I'm the worse of us." He hung his head. "What have I done to warrant feeling the opposite?"

"You live and breathe," was Reginald's reply.

"If only our governments shared that sentiment." Emerson, feeling an overwhelming sense of fatigue, struggled to his feet. *Maybe, in this short time, he has been changing. Maybe you can, too. Maybe you are and just don't know it. But is it worth the effort when the world isn't going to change around us?*

"Where are you going?" the wolverine asked. There was an uncertainty in his voice, as if the full effect of their heart-to-heart was finally sinking into his brain. Slowly, he was viewing the rodent as less a former prisoner and more a compatriot. They were both lost soldiers, waiting to find their way home. If they had one thing in common, maybe they had more?

The mouse grabbed the empty canteen, whiskers quivering, and muttered, "I think I'll go get more water."

* * *

On his way to and from the watering hole, the yellow-necked mouse paused intermittently to collect himself, and also to absorb the trappings of the island. No matter how hard he tried, he couldn't get over how different today was from yesterday. *How can nature change so quickly, so suddenly? And yet we, products of nature, cannot? Why do we get so stuck in our ways?*

The waters, once so wild and murky, were calm and clear, almost crystal. The colors were impossibly vibrant. Greens were greener and blues were deep enough to get lost in. The unique champagne-pink sand radiated an innate sense of romance. Peace permeated the warm, breezy air.

If only it was contagious. If only I could exist outside myself. Why am I always so lost inside my head, a prisoner of my thoughts? If I had died in that cove, would anyone have noticed? Would it have ended this war sooner?

His eyes began to sting. At first, he thought he was having an allergic reaction. But, no. The chaos of the past few years, culminating in the intense trauma of the last twenty-four hours and the ache of his buried loneliness? His dam finally broke. Emotion flooded him. It was suffocating.

I'd do anything to go home again. To be safe. To be loved. His breaths were ragged and desperate. *But you said it yourself: you view this war between predators and prey as part of an endless loop. That means, deep down, you see no hope for the future. Love only thrives in the presence of hope.* Ultimately, the outcome of the greater conflict didn't matter then. Inside, he'd already been beaten. *What if there's no coming back from that?*

Hugging himself, he shook, eventually collapsing to the ground and rolling onto his back. Staring at the zenith of the sky, tears glistened his whiskers, weighing down the tips. He sniffled and rubbed at them self-consciously, even though no one was around to see. *I shouldn't have survived that battle. Why did I? What am I supposed to do next?* He wiped his nose on his shirt and tried to stabilize his breathing. He'd been gone a long time. Reginald would be wondering about him.

Get yourself together, Emerson. You've escaped too much to give up now, pain or not. If life is a blessing, you're still in possession of it. You have to cling to every second. You're not a quitter. Prey isn't a curse word!

"No," he breathed weakly, raising up. "It's not."

He kept moving.

* * *

After collecting himself (and more water), the mouse had gone back to the wolverine. He felt emotionally spent. At some point, he fell asleep. He awoke, still tired, when sharp claws began poking at his side. He flailed in alarm. "What!"

"Look!"

"Hmm?" Sitting up dizzily, Emerson fought a yawn.

"It's a ship!"

"Where?" The mouse's head cleared immediately. The adrenaline started flowing again.

"There!" Reginald pointed to the north-west. "That little speck."

Emerson squinted. "Are you sure? Maybe it was a mirage. It's getting kinda hot." He kept looking, though. How good was wolverine eyesight, anyway? "Oh, wait." His heart stopped. "I think you're right." The sails caught the light just so. *There!* It *was* a ship. He held his breath. *Is it his people or mine? I can't tell.* He tensed up. *You'll find out soon enough.*

After a moment of silence, the wolverine observed, "I suppose we're going to be rescued, after all."

"I suppose so."

"I'm sorry, Emerson."

"For what?" the mouse wondered, blinking in surprised.

"This situation we find ourselves in. If I hadn't helped capture you—"

"It's not your fault, Reginald."

The wolverine tilted his head. "I thought you blamed me? I certainly blamed you."

"I guess I did. But maybe I was wrong," the mouse admitted. "Maybe we're all to blame." *That's probably why nothing ever changes. It's always someone else's fault, isn't it?* Emerson looked to the sandy, grassy ground and then toward the sunny, sparkling horizon. The ship was drawing ever closer. The flag was almost visible. The suspense was hurting his chest. His eyes welled up. He needed to look away. So, he did. "Hey, Reginald." His voice shook.

"You can call me Reggie," the wolverine offered, his tone gentle. If he was worried about his fate, it wasn't as obvious. There was an acceptance about him that the mouse hadn't noticed before.

"Reggie?" The mouse looked into the predator's eyes.

"Yes?"

"I'm sorry, too."

Combat in deep space—warfare between enemies in spacesuits in the hostile, airless void—that's always nasty. Each species will have its own version of professional space marines.

Including the hive-insects.

The Queens' Confederate Space Marines

by Elizabeth McCoy

"Listen up, larva," the squad leader told us, pacing in front of out tight-packed ranks.

We could hardly do otherwise, already in our armor, already loaded into the ship we didn't even get to see from the outside, already interlaced leg to leg with our neighbors. Her words were piped into our helmet-speakers, inescapable. She didn't need to have a queen's voice to enforce our attention.

"We're here because the pirates are getting bolder, taking ships even this deep in the Confederacy of Queens. We're in a converted freighter, if you dirt-sucking worms couldn't tell. We're bait. They board, we kill them. Got that?"

I raised a suit-gauntleted upper hand. "Squad leader, sir! Do we pursue when they retreat?" They would retreat. There was no doubt of that. We were the Confederation's Space Marines, after all. No pirates could stand up to us.

"Negative, drone. That's another squad's job. We keep them off this ship. If we get survivors when we're done, radio for instructions. Understood?"

Our affirmatives echoed in our speakers.

"Good. Now hunker down. It's going to be a long trip, and no telling when those motherless vermin will show up."

We did as instructed, setting our suits to a default stance that took the weight off our limbs. No one was foolish enough to unseal their armor, of course. Besides the squad leader's sure punishment, the hold

77

we rode in was excessively cold. It was going to be cramped for my lower hands, wrapped around my waist, but that was an egg-handling drone's problem; the warrior castes had wings instead, sleek enough to be ignored in suit-design. You learned to ignore the ache, if you wanted to succeed as a marine.

I wanted to succeed. I wasn't going back to the nurseries—not after making my case that I had a warrior's lungs in my egg-drone carapace, and not after making it through training. But no matter how far I'd come, I still needed to see combat to prove myself and secure my place.

The hold was too small to go wandering about, even if we'd been given leave to break ranks. That left conversation, in a quiet buzz across our squad channels. I tuned into all of them on one side, listening to the tenor of the whole, and scanned through each channel individually with the other side's speakers. It was a trick I'd realized the squad leaders used, and someday… Well, drones like me needed all the tricks they could get, to impress the brass.

Drones like me, who hadn't yet seen combat, didn't get invited into conversation much, either. That suited me, so far. I wanted to learn the internal hierarchy as well as the external one, and where their trigger-points were. Despite our discipline and training, the Confederate Space Marines are people under the armor, and there was no sense stepping on someone's foot by accident. Nobody would frag me, so long as I didn't screw up, but I might get transferred and have to start all over, still a drone and back to the lowest rank.

Most of the conversations were about food and sex, or sexy food, or foodie sex. The women were the raunchiest, of course. Female marines were almost always man-eaters, and that could be literal if they got carried away, but even the neuters of the warrior caste enjoyed the pleasures of life—and if I'd been an easily-shocked drone, I'd never have made it through basic training.

A more serious buzz caught my attention and I cycled back a channel.

"—privateers and not pirates?" one of the squad was saying. From the number attached to the comm channel, he was a drone like me, but with enough seniority—or patronage—to ask questions. (Just because we were the same caste didn't mean I'd get any help from him till I'd proven myself, though.)

"Act of war, if so," came the reply, from the warrior-caste he was talking to. I couldn't tell from the voice if the speaker was male, female, or a sterile soldier. "They're not so well-equipped, usually. Probably thrown out by their people. There's Confederates who do that."

What wasn't being said was that the dregs of the Confederation didn't take marines to mop up, and these pirates did.

"You think we'll ever find their home-worlds?"

"Bah. Who cares? They're vermin, and we squash 'em like vermin."

Another voice, definitely female, broke in. "Thought we were space marines, not pest control!"

"If we were pest control, 'Flower-belle,' we'd be after *you*," the gruff one retorted.

I listened to the banter till the conversation turned to food, then resumed scanning the channels again. Speculation about the pirate species was common, as were coarse jokes about them and their lack of sufficient legs, arms, or wings.

We eventually sat, carefully aligned, and tilted our armor into positions we could sleep in. I kept the public channels running quietly. That wasn't truly any plan to soak up the squad dynamics even in my sleep; I just drifted off better with a quiet buzz of conversation around me. It was never truly silent in the egg-chambers.

We woke, had our meals, joked that the pirates were considerately allowing us breakfast so maybe they weren't so bad—And the alerts sounded, strident, synthetic queen-screams alternating with deep, gut-shaking sounds guaranteed to wake any lazy maggot, and rouse us all to a fighting pitch.

The pirates' favorite tactic was to match speeds, interface their FTL bubble (a trick that shouldn't have been possible), and drop armored troops onto the hull of their victim. Explosives and high-potency acid ripped away the cargo-walls, and pirate warriors guarded the doors from the crew while others—it wasn't clear if all were soldiers—unloaded everything that hadn't freeze-dried from decompression. Then they left explosives to destroy the ship or cripple it enough to leave it dead in space, with no witnesses—which didn't work as well as the rest of their routine.

They hadn't changed their approach. A large section of the wall *crumpled*, creasing like fabric, and ripped away, exposing the iridescent sheen of the FTL bubble across the void. I was close enough to see the hull-chunk *twisted* out of its trajectory by some unseen force. Grav, light to start with in FTL pseudo-velocity, went entirely. My guts floated, but null never bothered a trained space marine, and our mag-boots cut in flawlessly. When the first helmets showed in the hole, our guns were ready.

The squad leader's *"Now!"* was matched by her first shot, centered in a pirate's faceplate. In brighter, steadier light, we might have seen the puff of gore freeze-drying as it left the suit—but we had FTL glow, ship lighting, and our own armor's spots. The enhancement cams didn't bother with niceties. And after that first shot, neither did we.

There was little element of surprise possible for us, and we'd just used it. More slugs took the other few helmets that'd been waiting to jump in, and we boiled out of the hold to follow up surprise with shock and terror. I sent my mag-grapple line up to the ragged edge of the hole and kicked off, boots releasing with my movements. To my sides, my fellows did the same, while the center-most of the squad, our leader included, used hand thrusters instead.

Obedient to training, we stuck with a buddy, organically pairing up—or re-choosing if an enemy's lucky shot crippled or killed someone. My partner and I lasted long enough to rack up two hits each and a shared kill, until return-fire sent an explosive into my one of my buddy's legs. The blast ripped the limb free, and I could only imagine the silence or scream; our comms gave privacy to the wounded.

I took down the explosive-launching pirate with a gut-shot that would at least keep it busy patching its suit, then turned to my partner to verify the armor had sealed the limb off, preventing full decompression. It had, though I had to slap one of my own emergency patches over the stub. The anti-shock drugs were good, but not perfect. I pressed our helmets together, snapping, "Fall back, soldier!"

She waved a hand in shaky acknowledgement and started the slow, three-legged crawl back inside the hold. I covered that retreat, double-wary as I had no partner for now and would need to find someone after my first was off the ship's surface.

There were more enemy than I'd thought. We were scattered in small groups, trying to engage them at close range. Their ship loomed over us like a malevolent gray moon. And as I watched, the FTL light dimmed and flickered over a trio of us as they closed with a single pirate—and one marine, marked as our squad's second-in-command in my helmet's IFF, was pulled free of the hull.

Tractor beam! I realized, though our own were too weak and dispersed for such fine work. But it hadn't crushed her, so I hoped it was weak enough… I raised a hand and shot my mag-grapple out again, aiming for her. Unorthodox, and I couldn't be sure it would hold, but I had to try.

Almost, it didn't work. The grapple hit her thorax, held a moment, was pulled free as the suit defenses pulsed a counter-mag field—and our squad-second lashed out a hand, grabbing hold.

I verbally commanded my suit to hold fast to the hull, then dropped down and grabbed that hull with my free hand, the suit-claws extended to dig into the metal. I looped the grapple's cord around my other hand as the line paid out, and commanded the armor to a death-grip. Instantly I felt the jerk and the strain, but didn't countermand my suit-instructions. Some of us were more expendable than others, and I wouldn't risk the pirates stealing someone and fleeing. Better a clean death than what the vermin might do.

I'd been talking to my suit, so someone else put in all-channel broadcast: "Squad-second in trouble!" That was followed by another: "Tethered! We've got her tethered!"

Space marines finished shooting their immediate targets, and space marine helmets turned to see what was going on. My squad began trying to converge on me—hampered by the pirates, who took that as a retreat and rallied themselves, forming up their own clusters and concentrating fire.

The grapple-cord was pulling at my arm, and all I could do was dig my free glove's claws into the hull and pray the mag-boots held. The tractor that had the squad-second was weak, but the only thing keeping us both from being dragged up was my suit, and I was glad I kept it in perfect condition, like an eager little drone trying to make a good impression. And even so, the grapple-cord was going to pull my arm off if no one could come help soon. The squad-second was trying to pull herself down the cord, but hampered by clinging to her gun as well; it looked like she wasn't in much better shape than I was, suit commanded to a death-grip on that end of the grapple.

The suit-comm crackled with the squad-second's terse, "They've seen our drone. Converging."

Some heroes would have let go, tried to get themselves killed mowing down the enemy; our squad-second knew too much tactical info to risk that if it wasn't a last resort. Capture and interrogation… We couldn't count on the alien pirates not having some way of getting past leadership grit and conditioning.

So she hung on, and I hung on, wishing the suit had enough power to reel in the cord. Feeling the hull slipping through my suit-claws, and hoping it was my imagination. Waiting for—

The alien pirate loomed in front of me when I looked up from checking my grasp on the hull. It was three body-lengths away, but with a gun that size, it might as well have had the bore to my helmet.

Cowards might've let go, tried to dodge. But my suit would hold fast even if my brains were outside my head, and I hadn't joined the space marines to break now. No way to get a gun to bear. No way to dodge. Nothing to do but hold the line.

The alien knew it, too. It seemed to take its time aiming. Maybe it was just combat-time, giving my mind enough of a pause to make my angry peace with death and consign my soul to the service of the Confederacy of Queens, here and in the afterlife. Die in battle, and move on instead of enduring another incarnation on the wheel, flesh served up to the youngling who'd take your place.

But combat-time, slowing everything around me, let me see the alien's helmet explode, not mine. Time snapped back to normal, as three other marines stomped up to me, double-time, one foot always on the ground so the boots could hold fast to the hull.

"Grab on!" the forward marine ordered the other two, and they locked their boots to the hull and added their grips to mine.

The forward one had bright red splashes painted on her suit, and I knew her nickname: "Flower-belle." She was experienced, not a marine who'd have looked at a drone like me twice unless she wanted a snack. But now she crawled on my back, pressed her helmet to mine, and snapped out, "Good job, maggot! You'll be a soldier yet!"

Then she stood up on my back, grabbed the line, and engaged her thrusters, shooting up the grappling cord while I stared. Something was strange about her red-splashed suit, but in the uncertain lighting, I couldn't tell what.

More marines were converging around us, and another one threw itself over my back and froze its suit, helping anchor me to the hull. Two more repeated Flower-belle's trick, bounding from our bent suits to the mag-line, and thruster-shooting up it. Others took defensive positions, shooting at the pirates who'd figured out anyone we wanted to rescue was *important.*

Even with the others holding the line, I was the one who'd been able to loop it. My upper arm was the one that was straining. My shoulder-muscles were tearing, a screaming pain that was in fact *worse* than anything in training, contrary to drill sergeant claims. I kept my mouth clamped shut on screams even though it made me nauseous. I wouldn't scream. I wouldn't puke in my helmet. And I *wouldn't let go.* No matter how many more marines were using me and my new back-buddy as launching pads to zip up that grapple-cord.

Head twisted awkwardly, I watched as Flower-belle got to the squad-second and then… yanked her down, which by equal-and-opposite reaction, pulled her up. The tractor beam made short work of that moment of slack—too fast for me or the other marines holding the line to react, and I could hear their curses where one's helmet touched mine, the second's radio-link relayed through the contact with the first.

But Flower-belle wasn't through. She got her feet on the squad-second's shoulders and back… and pushed off, bringing her giant gun to bear on the source of the tractor beam and starting to fire. It wasn't enough to push her down, and she was floating up.

The other marines had nearly reached the squad-second—and some of them extended their own arms, grapples flying out to hit the pirate ship's hull beyond the range of the tractor beam. They set themselves loose like petals in the wind, flying up to the pirate ship, and I had a brief moment of lucidity: another squad, taking a short-cut on their mission to get onto that pirate ship.

More of us had grabbed our squad-second and were using their thrusters to push sideways, out of the tractor beam's field.

Either the aliens increased power, or my suit gave out then. The pain went white-hot, and a scream broke out of me as the suit-arm pulled free of the rest of the suit—with my arm inside.

That triggered automatic suit protections: painkillers, to ease shock; suit-sealants to preserve air. The same things that'd happened for my first buddy's leg-shot. I was light-headed, with pain raging just beyond the drugs' wall. Squad-mates were shouting on the channel, or maybe against my helmet. The cord slipped through the grip of one of the others, but stopped when the arm… *my arm*… hit the other suit's fist.

It gave everyone else something to grab onto. One clutched my lost arm to her green-painted chest, while the other wrapped the cord around both fists and everyone who'd been holding me down shifted to them.

Marine way: when one of us goes down, two more will take up the cause.

With everyone around me, there was no way for me to crawl back to the interior of the ship, so drug-addled as I was, I saw when they got the squad-second out of the tractor beam's field. I saw her being pulled back to our ship's hull. And I saw Flower-belle send *her* grapple to a point right next to the tractor's emitter and reel herself closer to it, fast.

I still didn't realize why her suit looked odd. Thought it was the pain. Thought it was the drugs. Only understood when her open channel called, *"Tell the Queens I'm coming home!"* And then a joyous battle-shriek just before she triggered all those explosives and blew herself to the afterlife, along with blowing a hole in the pirate ship.

The remaining pirates must've realized they were in trouble, and began jetting from our ship to theirs on thrusters. Space marine guns shot at them, taking more down, but I couldn't see if it was a true rout. Maybe it was the pain. Maybe it was the drugs. Maybe it was relief that the squad-second'd been rescued.

Whatever the reason, I blacked out.

* * *

When I woke, medics were pulling my suit-helmet off and peeling me out of the rest of it while squad-mates stood around, stretching to look over the medics' heads.

"He's alive!" one said. "I saw his antennae lift!" And there was a great whooping cry, with the lights glittering on everyone's eyes.

The squad-leader's voice came from behind me. "Good job, larva! Brave as a Queen! And quick-witted as any female in flight!"

I unfolded my egg-handling arms as the suit came away—stiff and weak, but at least I'd be able to take care of my gear once the medics cleared me. My balance was terrible, even though I had all four legs; I wobbled as I lifted my antennae in a salute of everyone in the room. "My—my honor for the Confederacy of Queens, sir! My life for the space marines!"

The rest was a glorious party, in my and Flower-belle's honor, with medics fussing over me while my squad sang and toasted and told me how the pirate ship had been destroyed—and, finally, we'd taken some prisoners.

"Mammals, if you can believe it!" our squad-second said, resting beside me. "Not even reptiles. Who knew mammals could get so big and aggressive?"

I'd proven myself enough to ask questions and not get sneered at as a wet-winged cadet. "Think we'll have to take this fight to their homeworld, sir?"

"Might be these pirates are just pirates, and we can make peace with others of their kind," she said, generously. Then she spread her mandibles in a grin, flared out the remnants of her flight-wings, and cocked an antenna at me. "And if not? That's what the space marines are for, hero!"

If man breeds animals to be super-soldiers, or in this case super-helpers in dangerous climates, how can mankind keep its supremacy?

It can't.

But does it deserve to?

The Loving Children

by Bill McCormick

The sea of static flowing from his radio was filled with distant echoes of death. The screams ebbed and flowed with an eerie regularity. Gustav ignored them all. Whether they emanated from damned innocents or misguided heroes changed nothing. They were the bourgeoning dead. Gustav cared nothing for them.

Ever since his wife and children had been eaten by the brutes, he cared for little at all save the hunt. It was the only thing giving his life purpose. His little portion of revenge, delivered daily, efficiently, and with ice cold veins.

There were those who thought the creatures to be Aufhocker, shapeshifters, but he knew better. Neither slow-witted nor natural, these demons had been spawned from the depths of a laboratory, wrapped in the curse of good intentions.

One scientist had even insisted they would be the boon mankind needed in the mountains and other treacherous terrains, a true Lebensborn which would nurture hope and salvation where none existed before for those who needed help.

Every year, worldwide, over a thousand people get stranded, injured, or killed on mountains. The Matterhorn alone counted for almost a third of those statistics. Mostly due to idiotic tourists who thought it was as safe as the Disney ride of the same name. Oddly enough, Everest, the tallest mountain in the world, wasn't that dangerous. It kept its death toll to less than ten percent of its climbers by having regular guides who knew how to traverse its many nooks and crannies.

It might have also helped that the dead there were left where they dropped, used as markers for the next climbers. Corpses laid in climbers' paths tended to make great reminders that they should pay attention. Some, like Hannelore Schmatz, even became tourist attractions.

While there were, certainly, rescue animals and experts available, they were completely reactive. These new animals were to be placed in "high risk" areas so they could save people before they became statistics.

Not just mountains, either. Arctic and Antarctic wildernesses claimed their fair share as well. There were a myriad of locations the creatures could roam and be of service to man.

The scientist, Gustav forgot his name, made all these points and more in a colorful PowerPoint presentation on TV. He was the first one they ate.

That was forty years ago.

Gustav slid his modified MSR-338 sniper rifle back onto his shoulder and scanned the horizon. He could sense them near, but not near enough to be threatening.

He slid through the snow down the side of a hillock, barely four kilometers south of what used to be Freudenstadt, past the dark trees and into a gulley. He pulled out his binoculars again and scanned again. This time he saw one. They were hard to miss. Modified Komondors, the huge Hungarian long-furred sheep dogs, they could walk on their hind legs, manipulate machinery, and speak after a fashion. They had their own language, a collection of howls and grunts, that was surprisingly facile. Gustav knew about two hundred words of it. Enough to know when they were attacking and when they had other things to do.

He found that to be useful information.

He watched as the giant shaggy creature lumbered through the woods. Just under two meters tall, covered in white fur, weighing over ninety kilos, the beast moved with amazing agility. This one wasn't carrying any weapons. That confused Gustav. Normally they were never seen without their crossbows or swords.

Not that they needed them. If they got close to a human, they could kill and eat one without much effort.

Gustav unholstered his rifle and sighted the fiend. Unlike the "officially sanctioned" heroes who died with depressing regularity, Gustav knew how to kill them. He made his own bullets, each filled with a mix of napalm and fluoroantimonic acid. Even with that combination, only a head shot would kill. He'd tried to explain that to the government when the invasion began, but they'd dismissed him completely. They'd believed they could corral the beasts.

Three billion dead, and counting, proved them wrong.

Moscow, Vladivostok, Zurich, Lucerne, Amsterdam, Haarlem, Berlin, and Gustav's home city of Frankfurt, were among the many cities that now were gone, their citizens dead or scattered.

Aid from foreign lands wasn't coming. People tended to lose their minds when they saw pictures of their treasured sons and daughters dismembered and eaten. Gustav couldn't really blame them.

Gustav, in his own way, respected the devils. He even used their true name for themselves, Draugar, when he spoke, which was seldom anymore. The designation was fitting. They were, in many ways, a form of walking death.

They created villages, had culture of a type, mated for life, were clever beyond expectations when it came to engineering, and learned from their mistakes. The latter being far more than could be said for the European governments.

Gustav adjusted his sight and zoomed in on the Draugar. It was a male, holding a box of some sort. Gustav shivered when he realized what it was; a radio. One built by and for them. The design may have been alien, but its purpose was not.

He watched, partly in horror, partly in enthrallment, as it spoke and then listened. He knew that there would be no more group patrols now. They would be harder to find than they had ever been. Judging by their success thus far, avoiding bombs and bullets was a skill they'd perfected.

Normally, as a courtesy, Gustav didn't kill an unarmed opponent. He decided this was worth an exception. He adjusted for windage and gently squeezed the trigger.

Single tap lethal.

He smiled as the head exploded and the acid caused the fur around its neck to smolder. His smile went rictus when he felt two vice-like paws grab his shoulders. He was tossed into the air, pinwheeling randomly, until he landed directly in front of the largest and oldest Draugur he'd ever seen.

Though his muzzle was nearly black, his fur was bleached white, his eyes were clear, and his strength was clearly unabated. Age was not a detriment to him in any way.

He was wearing a deerskin jerkin and black trousers. Like all of them he was barefoot.

He moved, faster than any monster Gustav had ever seen. He grabbed the MSR-338, examined it, cleared the chamber, pulled the clip, and then, to Gustav's astonishment, handed it back to him. That astonishment was replaced by sheer terror when it leaned over and spoke.

"You. Come. Now. Follow."

The voice was guttural and the syllables slurred, but Gustav understood. That was something that should not happen. With snouts and recessed tongues, human speech should have eluded them.

Gustav shouldered the rifle and fell in next to the shaggy behemoth.

Dusk fell to evening and the stars shone brightly in the winter sky. The giant stopped, opened a pack under its jerkin, and offered it to Gustav. His first thought was to reject it, but he didn't know what he was being offered. He reached in carefully and pulled out a piece of jerky. Upon tasting, he realized it was venison jerky. Spiced differently than any he'd ever eaten but still quite good.

He looked at his captor in confusion.

"Way go yet," was all he got by way of an explanation.

They walked, silently, for another two hours until Gustav smelled the odors of civilization. Cooking fires, musk, and all those little scents that let the brain know that it was no longer alone.

They crossed a small rise, and Gustav gasped. He'd done threat assessments for the army when he was young, and grasping the size of a populace was something at which he was well skilled. There had to be over one hundred thousand of them.

Worse yet, judging by the range of devastation they'd caused, this was far from their only metropolis. They had to be breeding at a near geometric rate.

They passed a set of sentries and entered a main street. Gustav noted there were no walls around their city, just a mesh stretched overhead. He recognized the type. It prevented heat from escaping or being detected, and provided nearly perfect camouflage. Fear of invasion obviously wasn't on their list of things to worry about.

He wasn't sure what to make of that.

A few minutes later they were in a large building that seemed to have a military function. Gustav was aimed towards a table with several empty chairs. He sat in one and prepared for he knew not what. He was alive. That alone shouldn't be true.

His *de facto* jailer returned and set a steaming bowl of stew in front of him. A quick taste revealed it was also venison, also delicious, also different. While he appreciated the kindness, he was confused by it as well.

"Wolfrick," said the Draugur as he sat down across from Gustav. It took him a moment, but he realized he was being told a name.

He pointed to himself.

"Gustav."

Wolfrick shook his head.

"No. Tod Pirschjäger." The words were pronounced slowly, deliberately. "Death Stalker. You. Human name no interest."

So they knew him. He supposed he should be flattered, but he was still too confused to be anything other than baffled.

He began to assess his surroundings. The building wasn't abandoned. There were hundreds of bulky crates on the other side of the floor. Closer to a far door, he saw large rifles being carefully placed in similar crates. He was a weapons expert, and wished he could get a closer look at one. They were not like anything he'd ever seen.

Wolfrick noted his curiosity and called one of the workers over with a rifle. The worker handed it to Gustav without comment and walked away.

It had similarities to his MSR-338, but only superficially. The trigger guard was wider, the muzzle longer, the clip could hold thirty rounds instead of seven, and it looked as though it could handle fifty caliber ammo. He guessed it had a range of about fourteen hundred meters.

He set the rifle down and finished the stew. He was unsure what else to do.

"Guns help," said Wolfrick, "but slow. Need speed."

Gustav parsed through the meaning, and became aware of real fear for the first time in his life. They were looking for a way to kill humans faster and more efficiently.

"I hope you're not looking for my help," replied Gustav.

"No."

Another worker arrived and took the rifle away as they sat in silence.

"What do you want from me?" asked Gustav.

"Nothing. You honored. You will see. Watch. Witness."

"What?"

Wolfrick stood and motioned for him to follow.

They walked through the warehouse, past the rifles, out into the night, and straight into a nightmare.

There were banks of missiles on portable launching pads, with each pad attached to a small truck. Every missile had a white tip designating they were live rounds. An odd vestige of humanity. There was also a symbol on the side he didn't recognize. He turned to Wolfrick and motioned at it.

"Mist. Make humans go."

Gustav's spine felt shades of cold that he never knew existed. Biological weapons and poison gas had been outlawed long ago. Then again, as he thought about it, the Draugur had never been invited to those negotiations.

Gustav took it all in and looked Wolfrick directly in the eye.

"Why are you doing this?"

Wolfrick sighed.

"When young, loved humans. Humans taught. Humans fed. But humans hurt too. Humans killed. Humans made us feel bad. We…" he searched for the right words, "we tried be good. Humans made us do things. Bad things. We children were. Human children. So we thought. Humans bad parents."

Gustav had heard rumors of the Draugur being used as weapons in secret missions, but had dismissed them along with the usual prattle about UFOs, chemtrails, and lizard people. Maybe he shouldn't have been so hasty.

He looked at Wolfrick anew. He must be one of the first ones made. He had seen it all come to pass. Gustav wished language wasn't such a barrier. He truly wanted to know what happened and how.

He could never forgive the murder of his family but, as a soldier, he could understand the vagaries and horrors of war. He knew he'd done things he'd rather not visit in his dreams.

He watched as the missiles left in varying directions. He'd never felt so helpless in his life.

"You don't need to do this. There's always a way to work things out," Gustav pled. "Let people know why you're doing what you do. Teach them, put an end to this."

Wolfrick looked at Gustav hard and frowned.

"End is what we do. You ate our food, you know truth now."

Gustav had no idea what he meant at first. Then realization dawned. They no longer needed to eat humans to survive. That thought led to one he'd never considered. Why did they need to eat humans in the first place? That question he asked aloud.

"Food cost money. Prisoners free."

Gustav finally understood. Everything. True clarity of vision was accompanied by the sight of missiles launching in the distance. As they arced into the twinkling sky he laughed. The folly of fools was not to be underestimated. As each missile exploded high in the night sky, he could see a reddish mist growing across the horizon.

His laugh grew louder and louder.

"Fuck it Wolfrick, you're right. We all need to go."

Wolfrick smiled and began walking back to the warehouse.

"Yes, time for your children to own the world."

Rattlesnake soldiers? Well, why not?

It's said that those who succeed by treason are never villains, because it's the victors who write the histories.

Rattlesnakes, being cold-blooded, are perfectly suited for this.

Strike, But Hear Me

by Jefferson P. Swycaffer

The tale told by Plutarch is this: Themistocles strongly
opposed the proposal of Eurybiades to quit the bay of
Salamis. The hot-headed Spartan insultingly remarked that
"those who in the public games rise up before the proper
signal are scourged." "True," said Themistocles, "but those
who lag behind win no laurels." On this, Eurybiades lifted
up his staff to strike him, when Themistocles earnestly but
proudly exclaimed, "Strike, but hear me!"

My name is Yrella. Yrella Yma Lucile Marie Felderbaum, *Crotalus
viridis*. I am a Rattlesnake. I am also Sergeant Major for the Upshot
Regiment, currently on detached duty to oversee the emplacement of
anti-satellite screen projectors in this sector of the overall theater of
operations.

A Rattlesnake. Five metres in length, and as big around as an oil-
drum. Dark jade-green with yellow markings. Forty centimetres of fangs.
Powered-armor sheath with micro-manipulators.

It may not be something you see every day… but I do.

I was, at the time this all started, under something of a bombardment.
The enemy had been reaching for us with free-flight missiles. Our screen
projector jammed the navigation systems of guided weapons, save for a
few that used hardened optical-fiber links, unreeled from spools inside
the rocket, and those are of little use for indirect fire.

Our position was behind a ridge, among an outcropping of rocks. As
Rattlesnakes—and most of our unit are—we're quite comfortable with
this kind of terrain.

This can be deceptive; in fact, rocks are a poor form of protection, for, while they block some kinds of incoming fire, they have the effect of reflecting shrapnel and fragmentation, bouncing it around, increasing the number of casualties from explosives.

Still, it was nice to know that enemy rifle and laser fire are screened off. You take the trade-offs you get in the infantry.

I missed my old unit. The Upshot Regiment had been reinforced to a Brigade, and then the Rattlesnake Battalion was peeled away, and sent on this Engineering mission, to deploy signal jammers. I wondered if they'd downgraded the unit to a Regiment again, and whether the Old Lady— Persis Upshot—that's her name, and the name of her unit—ever got her promotion, even as a brevet. She'd been a Lieutenant Colonel for a long time, and was long overdue for a kick up the ladder to Full Colonel.

I was still permitted to call myself a Regimental Sergeant Major, even if I were only the senior NCO for a Battalion. It was a very mobile war… in that respect. On the ground, the front lines had stagnated, and some units had even begun digging trenches.

Rockets flew overhead, bursting somewhere behind. I wanted to turn off my brain. I could do that. Like all my kind, I wear an auxiliary cognitive prosthesis, but we just call them our brain-boxes. With them, we're of a high order of sapience, and even enjoy—if that is the correct word—sophisticated suites of emotional sensations. One of those was fear, although another one was courage.

We turn our brain-boxes off when we can. Life is a lot simpler that way.

Explosions up and down the line. Snakes died. I took my life in my coils and slithered, heading to the left, where the strike had been the heaviest. The medics had their work waiting for them. I made myself useful, showing discipline and strengthening morale. A few of the lads had turned their brains off; I made them put them right on again.

"No slacking! No hiding! Yeah, it's awful. What did you want? A resort hotel? A luxury cruise? You! Pick up your weapon. Strip it and clean it: I'm watching!"

You know what a Regimental NCO is? A flag, that's what. I'm a banner, and I wave, and people follow me. Like a banner, when I fall, someone else stands up in my place, and people follow him. Or her.

We Rattlesnakes are wonderfully egalitarian in that way. Not like the mammals. They *care,* and a whole hell of a lot, about what sex they are. It's all tied up in their love life.

Call me cold-blooded.

More explosions. I arranged the troops in better shelter, getting them to as much safety as might be available in the highly unsafe environment of a war.

The Engineers were tending the Big Black Box—that's what we called it. It was a self-mobile wheeled apparatus, too small for anyone to ride on, and carried the anti-satellite jammer. It had to be here. *Here.* Nowhere else would do. It all had to do with parallax, and geodesics, and a ton of other words I didn't know the meaning of. But as long as it was situated properly, and running, and not blown to scrap by an incoming round, the enemy was deprived, not only of satellite coverage, but air power, low-orbit space weaponry, and smart bombs. It protected this whole sector of the front.

Command told us where to site it. We obeyed. Our Battalion Commander is Major Stretch. Peggy Stretch. Human, like the Colonel. Stretch told me, once, that Rattlesnakes give her the willies. That's the army for you: if someone had a fear of heights, you know they'd be put in an airmobile unit, and if someone had claustrophobia, they'd become tunnel-diggers, faster than you can say—

Another close one. Bad. There were deaths. I did my song and dance.

"Get under cover and out of the way. You! Pick up your damned weapon. What is that, anyway? Not one of ours! Took it from an enemy? Shoots farther and straighter?" Wouldn't surprise me in the least. "Right, then, keep it. I'll turn a blind eye. None of my business, *so long as you use it!*"

Half the time they're like children, and half the time they're like devils.

Major Stretch came writhing through the stones, doing a right good job of it. A Snake could hardly have kept lower.

"Sergeant!"

"Sir!"

"We're taking casualties."

"Sir!" I had eyes. I had a tongue, and could smell the blood. I had pit organs, and could tell the difference between a soldier and a corpse. Corpses went cold.

"Find Captain Wright. Work with him to get them spread out. We're too concentrated. See if you can extend the line, rightwards. I'll take the left."

"Yes, Sir!" It was the only thing to say.

The rocks were good and sharp under our tummies. I gave a loud, sustained tail-buzz, as good as a whistle or bugle for getting attention.

Captain Wright, yet another human, gave his orders. I'm pretty sure he was male. He smelled that way.

Mammals.

We slid out. Wright had a tendency to walk, where he would have been better crawling. He had the wit to bend low. Maybe it didn't make any difference.

"C Company needs to spread out another hundred metres. Go with them to the flank. Give me a recce." Go and see what's to be seen, and report. My helmet was a command model, with binoculars built in. It compensated for a Rattlesnake's habitual myopia.

"Yes, sir." I tapped fifteen Snakes and gestured for them to follow me. Wright picked up twenty others. We moved out.

We were wearing body-sheaths, big belt-on vests made for our kind. Early models had arms, and that was absurd. They also tried making them with legs, and that was just about the stupidest thing anyone ever thought of. Rattlesnakes with legs. Fish with bicycles. Insane. Instead of arms, or hands, our vests have a surface with about five hundred fingers. They can work together to grip and hold and carry. They can wield and trigger a rifle, or launch a grenade.

There are some limitations.

I was lugging a pair of rifles, one on my right side and one along my back. Most Snakes carried only one. A heavy weapons team divided up the load of a repeating rocket launcher, not the kind our enemies were firing at us—big loads from an emplacement—but light anti-personnel and anti-vehicle rounds.

We spread out and wriggled up the slope, moving forward and to the right. We kept low, always moving in the crevices between the rocks. Before long, we came to the ridge-line, and got our first glimpse down into the next valley.

That was when I spotted the squirrel.

The squirrels weren't our enemies, any more than other Rattlesnakes would have been our allies. They were just on the other side, and that made them targets. This squirrel was an advance skirmisher, out in front of an assault Battalion, working its way up the ridge from the opposite side.

I threw four quick expert loops about him and squeezed, hard.

Someone always raises his hand at this point and says, wait, Rattlesnakes aren't constrictors.

No, not by nature. It's something they have to teach us in Basic Training.

Also, I didn't constrict him; I crushed him. Caved in his ribs and broke his spine in three places. Constriction means steady, smooth squeezing, so they can exhale but not inhale. It doesn't take much of that and the victim loses consciousness from asphyxia. But it takes a mammal a good long time to die that way, around five minutes. Another Snake takes twice that time.

Breaking their spines is quick.

Gunfire.

The skirmish line was long and spread out, coming diagonally up the reverse slope from the valley below. How had our surveillance missed them? We were still supposed to have satellites and aircraft and other fly-over imaging. But the squirrels were wearing camouflage netting, and, for all of that, their fur was a dirty brown by nature. It was hard, even staring down the hill, to make them out. They blended in to the rocks, dirt, and low clinging scrub-brush.

Ground squirrels, not tree squirrels. Hole-diggers.

Like us, they'd been changed, morphed by the science of the age. They'd grown in the process, a metre and a half in height, with clever manipulating paws, capable of working just about any weapon a human might wield.

We were on the high ground, and they were exposed on the hillside. The firefight was short and hot and very fierce, but the advantage was ours.

Captain Wright was still in sight. I waved some tick-tack at him, and maybe he saw it. That was when I made one of those decisions that sway the course of history. I rallied my baker's dozen rattlers, and went on the attack, back to the left again, along the crest of the ridge.

Was it a stroke of tactical genius? Or was it blind stinking luck? You tell me. We came to the top of a knob, what hikers call a false summit, and caught the rest of the squirrels in a murderous enfilade. We shot right down along the length of their line.

Starship gunners absolutely live for the once-in-a-lifetime opportunity to maneuver against an enemy's stern and put missiles up their engine vents. Aircraft pilots dream of riding in a foeman's six and shooting the length of his fuselage. For infantry, it's an enfilade, sitting at the end of their aligned ranks and shooting them down the long way. You can't miss. It's murder, pure and simple. I burned out the barrel of my first rifle, and that's why I carry two. It was ten minutes of the nastiest work I've ever done, and I enjoyed every microsecond of it. It was a combat infantry - Snake's best fantasy. I wouldn't have traded it for thirty days of leave.

And... that was the end of the war.

Not the end of the skirmish, not the end of the attack, not the end of the bombardment. The end of the war. The jammer was too vital, too strategically important. If they'd knocked it out, they'd have still been in with a chance. But when the attack stalled, the overall situation ceased to be tenable.

Captain Wright came up to me and slapped me up and down with his hands, a celebratory caress the way my kind likes it. More gently, I tickled his palms with my tongue, and gently butted him in the shoulder, the way he, at least, likes it.

"That was a firefight!" he crowed.

"That was better than anything in a textbook," I agreed.

"They were almost on us! If you hadn't rushed the hillcrest, there was nothing to stop 'em!"

"C'mon, they're squirrels. We eat their kind for breakfast."

He laughed, and, since my brain-box was on, I knew how to laugh also. It's artificial, but still feels good.

Then we came back to ourselves, and faced the ugly business of looking for survivors. The casualties were spread out in the typical statistical bell-curve, from dead-on-the-spot to mere scratches, with every possible variation of harm in between.

The squirrel Battalion surrendered first, then their parent Regiment. We let them disarm and come forward to help with the wounded. There'd been hits among our side, too, and we were just selfish enough to want to tend those first. So, by and large, we let them sort out their people, while we saw to ours.

Somewhere in the middle of this informal fraternization, their Headquarters ran up the white flag. Before sunset, official terms of surrender were being drawn up.

My side was a coalition of Guerramancy units, about thirteen Divisions in size. The enemy was a working force, also of Guerramancy formations, roughly twelve Divisions strong.

We were both from the same polity.

It wasn't a civil war, not in the usual sense. Just an ordinary working war. That's how the Guerramancy does its statecraft. Other Republics hold elections. We trade bullets instead of ballots.

Your neighboring province cuts off your water? War. They slap a trade embargo on you? War. Magisterial corruption? High unemployment? Offended cultural values? War.

Since wars are expensive, their respective *casus belli* tend to be serious issues. In the early days of this form of government, there were wars over insulting movie reviews and disappointing roundball games. But the system of governance by warfare is self-correcting—very much like the Free Market, there is an "invisible hand" that establishes a working balance.

There is a tireless band of abstract philosophers who argue for representative democracy instead, where decisions get made by a Council or a Parliament, with votes taken on everything, and the members of the Parliament elected by the people.

Of course, the immediate question is: who's going to enforce the decision of the Parliament? Does anyone honestly believe a province is going to *consent* to the loss of water rights or the imposition of a tariff? My brain-box is running; I know how to laugh. Go on, tell me another one.

Now, okay, I'm willing to be fair. Not all wars get fought out on the battlefield. I'll get to this in a bit.

That day, the war was over, and we were happy. Our Battalion had done critically strategic duty, and Wright's Company had saved the day. Wright was the hero of the hour, mentioned glowingly in dispatches, celebrated by military and civilian publicists alike, and he ended up with a medal for Valourous Heroism out of the affair. There were even rumors of a Knighthood. He named me for a medal, and that didn't happen, but at least *he* knew what my role had been in our victory.

Or maybe Major Stretch should get credit. She's the one who told us to extend our line.

One of the other Battalions got demobilized in the sudden new peace, but it wasn't made up of Rattlesnakes, so I didn't much care. The Brigade was knocked down to a Regiment again, and Colonel Upshot didn't get her promotion.

Most of the Regiment went back into barracks quarters. If another war didn't break out fairly soon, there would be more demobs. Our Battalion, having some Engineering expertise, was sent back to the battlefield, to help clean up. There were unexploded bombs to be dug up, and other dangers.

It was strange to be over the same old ground again, the same rocks and little worn grooves in the dirt where we'd slipped and slithered. The hillside was quiet, with a soft wind purring through the low, prickly underbrush. The ridge-line was still somehow ominous, and I couldn't help myself from stationing a look-out at the top, even though I knew that no attack was forthcoming.

Here was the rock I hid behind when the barrage struck. Fresh chips and scars showed in the native stone. Here was where one of my Snakes died, and not well, half-torn open by an airburst. Here was where

Major Stretch had her command tent, not much more than a lean-to of waterproofed canvas.

Now we had similar tents laid out for our use, as opposed to how we'd slept during the war, coiled in the cold night air. Luxury beyond luxury: our tents, now, had radiant heaters. We basked. Food was issued in big wads, the sort we needed to unhinge our jaws to engulf, the kind that took half a day to digest. During combat, we were fed in little nuggets, which were made available to us throughout the day. Little snacks, but nothing like a proper, heavy, stomach-distending meal.

I was stretched out on the ground, behind a nice warm shelf of rock, happily digesting, with my brain-box off, when I sensed something was wrong. I wasn't asleep, but not really awake, either, just drifting in a comfortable reptilian half-doze. My eyes may always be open, but I wasn't paying much attention to what I could see.

Still, it seemed that a lot of the guys were moving away, across the slope, into a little up-and-down gully or gulch. After about the fifteenth Snake had wandered that direction, moving with the kind of careful innocence that is a sure sign of stealth, I let myself come awake. I turned on my brain-box.

Fifteen? Fifteen Snakes of the unit, going off somewhere hidden?

I hardly needed an augmented brain to know what was going on: liquor.

To be honest, I was half-tempted to overlook it. Let them get wrecked. To essay a bad pun, let them get a nice buzz on. Boys will be boys, and Snakes will be Snakes. We get drunk easily, and it takes a long time to wear off, but this was a battleground clean-up mission, and the higher levels of discipline weren't necessary.

On the other hand, they'd been careless, and I'd seen them. Also, it was a little insulting, at a professional level. Right under my nose? So I snuck up after them, going around a bit so I could come close without being seen, or, I hoped, heard.

Oh, boy: right again. They were working on a good messy souse. Someone had smuggled in a small barrel of the strong stuff, and they were belting it back, quite pouring it down their gullets.

I almost jumped on them then, but that was when I overheard some of their loose talk.

"Oh, Captain and *Sir* Wright," one of my Snakes hissed. "*Sir* bloody up his digestive sphincter, holier-than-thou Donald Shaw Wright. Stab his soul!"

Insubordination from drunk soldiers. What a surprise.

"We don't have to take it," someone said, his voice slurred.

"You're damned right we don't! We don't serve under him by choice. He's a hot-head. He's a fool! He spends our lives like surfeit-water. He washes his clean little hands in our blood!"

One of the wiser heads writhed a bit, and looked away, not willing to meet the gaze of the leader, the instigator. "So what do you figure to do about it? It's the army." He said it the way another might say, "It's fate."

"We take action," the leader said. I recognized him, then: Bien-Soir Othniel Tait Rattlesnake, Riflesnake ordinary, the sort who'd been made Corporal and then busted down again to Private, repeating the cycle at least twice. One of those who was good, and good-for-nothing, all at the same time.

There was still time. I could have acted then and saved him from the consequences. But before I could even lift my head, it was too late.

"Tonight, I'm going to kill him. You just see if I don't."

Ah, Bien-Soir, that's execution-style talk. And, bless me for a fool, I *still* was trying to think of ways to spare him.

"Ah, that's just wild talk," one of the others murmured.

"Is it? Listen. You all know the Lericom Regiment, run like a tidy little dictatorship by Miss wouldn't-get-her-feet-dirty Piper. Piper Lericom. I know a guy in one of her Companies. Had a Captain just like our own." Here he spooled off another long list of insolences, too dreary for me to bother repeating. As well, some of the words he used are those a Gentlesnake would not set down on the record. "Well," he went on, "there was a guy in that Company who didn't figure to put up with a Captain like that, not for another minute. Next firefight the unit was in? Ah, the poor Captain took an enemy round. Not in the front, but not in the back, either. You got to figure these things. Any fool of an asp can shoot someone in the back, but if you get 'em in the side, when they're turning half about to gesture back to their troops... Oh, so heroic. 'Follow me! Death or glory!' Boys, you listen to me, when those are the only two choices, I make it death, but not *my* death. No, no, no. His!"

"Won't be any firefights out here, you know," someone said, and you'd almost imagine it was a complaint.

"Ah, you haven't got the brains you were born with. Is your brainbox on, or off? Wake up, you worms. *Unexploded ordnance!* This ground is peppered with warheads that didn't detonate properly. What do you think we're here for? Easiest thing in the world to find one, rig it to blow, and then, all kind of innocent, ease him into the right place."

"Just talk."

Just talk. Just foolish, drunken talk.

No such luck.

He slid a detonator around his vest, passing it from one mechanical finger to the next. "Radio controlled. All nice and safe. And there's a big rocket, buried under the gravel, just up the hill a way. Lucky for us it didn't explode. It would have done some hurt. I found it on today's sweep, and sort of covered it up some, keeping it from sight. Tomorrow, first thing, I fix the detonator. Then…"

"What if he doesn't walk over to it, just for your convenience?"

"Then I'll get him another day. Bust me to Private? Risk my cloaca in an uphill charge? He ain't no officer of mine."

I could almost have wept. The brain-box gives me that option. The higher emotions are complex, and sometimes very confusing. I've never been completely sure they were a good thing to give to our kind.

But duty and idealism were also built in, as well as respect for the law. I didn't have any real choice.

I reared my head up high, striking position, and gave out a nice, long, shrill burst of the rattles. The nest of Snakes spilled their liquor in a massive spasm, startled into sudden reflexive coils.

"Attention! Eyes front! Hold tight! Don't move, not a twitch! Liquor and mutiny! Illegal assembly! Conspiracy to murder!"

"No!"

"Not us!"

"Only him! Only him!"

"Silence!" Another long, hard, strong rattle, sounding much like steam escaping from a valve. "Straighten that line! What are you? Soldiers? I've seen ballet dancers in better formation! You, and you: take that thing away from him." The detonator was quickly sequestered.

"It wasn't us…"

"You *listened!*"

"We was gonna report it."

That was such an obvious and transparent lie, I didn't even bother to respond to it. "Seize him. Latch on to his vest. Bind him. Get some fastenings. Strap him up, good and tight. You can squeeze the breath out of him, for all I care. Save the firing squad from having to do their duty!"

That was over the top, and, in truth, I had no intention whatever of allowing any harm to come to him, including self-harm. He was going to be held under tight security, monitored every minute. The firing squad was going to have its due.

All Hades on a shoestring, this was just going to stink.

I detailed a guard-of-dishonor, and made sure the incriminating keg of liquor was brought along also. One of the more enterprising Snakes tried to spill it out, but I was ready for that, and kept it from happening.

The liquor, the detonator, the buried enemy missile, my testimony, and the rather compulsory testimony of the others in the little drinking party… It was enough.

Conspiracy to Mutiny, Conspiracy to Murder. A list of lesser crimes half as long as my tail. The trial was a formality.

Captain Wright—Donald Shaw Wright—I had actually never known until that scene in the gulch what his full name was—watched the court-martial hearing with a sad look on his face, almost of incomprehension. He was a good officer, so good that he didn't even realize that anyone could think ill of him. It didn't do his reputation any good.

There were no more rumors of a knighthood.

Bien-Soir Rattlesnake was made to lay out in a line, sideways, and the firing squad aimed at the sweet-spot, three head-lengths behind the poison-glands. Following some damned-fool tradition, handed down from beyond anciently, one of the Riflesnakes was given a blank cartridge. There are as many theories of why this should be as there are Snakes to pass the time in idle speculation. I've heard it said that it was so no-one could be sure whether or not he'd fired an actual shot. That, at least, is certainly a load of scat. Anyone who's fired a rifle will instantly know the difference between a live round and a blank.

My theory is it's so any member of the firing squad can *claim* he fired the blank, as a defense if anyone is grieved at him participating in the execution of a popular comrade. There have been cases where every single member of the squad claimed to have fired the blank.

Finis and exit, Bien-Soir, and may you rest in peace…you black-livered, cowardly, drunken, foolish renegade.

I was afraid this incident might have moved our Battalion up to the top of the list for demobilization. Instead, the axe fell on the next unit over, and now the Upshot Regiment was at one-third strength. But instead of breaking us up completely, they reinforced the Headquarters Platoon, and attached a Strategic Signals Company to us, making us a communications and intelligence link. Before long, a Brigadier General made us his Command Regiment, and, bless me if I'm lying, we were breveted a Brigade again, understrength and all.

We serve that kind of an army.

I was saying something about wars not needing to be fought.

The headquarters commando was summoned to the fortress and base, where Colonel Upshot made her decisions. It wasn't much in the way of a fortress, having few emplacements and only a perimeter of woven-wire and coiled razor-concertina fence. It was sited in the center of a broad, grassy field, with good defensive lanes of fire. A patchy forest surrounded the area. The equivalent of a Division was usually stationed here, although, with downsizing, it was less at the time. As it was nominally peace-time, no General was in command, only Colonel Upshot.

Persis Upshot, human, was rather the Grand Old Lady of the region, reputed for strategic elegance and consideration for officers and enlisted personnel alike. Her campaigns had led to victories in something like a five to one ratio, which put her well ahead of most of her colleagues.

A gaggle of officers sat about a conference room, in the heart of the base. It was a proper command center, concrete walls, electricity, water, even air-conditioning, which, at the time was set at far too cool a temperature for my comfort.

I shouldn't even have been there, but, as no one knew more about the ready-status of our troops than I, my presence was, in the quaint old terms, requested and required.

You can't expect me to tell you much about a human by her appearance; they all look the same to me. But even across species boundaries, there was something inspiring in the way Colonel Upshot bore herself. She spoke softly enough, but with serious power lurking under her voice.

"Our next action," she said, and then paused, looking around herself. "If 'action' is the correct word…" She smiled thinly. "We're going on a terrain drill, out on maneuvers. We're going to display ourselves. We're showing off, just a bit."

She stopped then, while the coffee ritual took place. Unpalatable, vile coffee! No Rattlesnake would go near that poison. Mammals!

"There's a war in the offing," Upshot took up, while the others leaned back in their conference-room chairs and sipped at their mugs. Even the aroma… Pffft! I had to hold my rattles tight to keep them from shrilling an alarm.

"As usual, it doesn't much matter to us who's threatening whom. War is our business, but, as businessmen say, the customer is always right. Our customer doesn't want to pay for an actual fight, and has made a kind of bet with his enemy. If we, as a military unit, can demonstrate our prowess in combat maneuvers, the actual fighting can be dispensed with. It is time for us to show the world what we're made of."

Colonel Lericom, her junior in seniority, had some questions. "Do we have security and assurance? How do we know this isn't some kind of ambush, or a trap of a subtler nature? While we're one place, the real attack comes somewhere else?"

"It's true that your absence leaves this base weaker than I'd like, but I think we can still defend against anything this enemy is about to put together. You, of course, will be constituted as a full fighting force, with supplies, weapons, ammunition, communications… Everything. I wouldn't send you out with simulated weapons to an unknown route-of-march, although there may be some play-acting along the way. No real skirmishes, but make-pretend, to show that you can react to unexpected events."

"There will be observers?"

"Yes. They're the whole point of the affair. You have to make them aware of what this Brigade is capable of accomplishing in the field."

Upshot stood. "I have all confidence in you. I know you can make this work. If you succeed—and I truly believe you shall—then the enemy will make terms without shots being fired." She paused, and her expression grew stern, although I thought that, just perhaps, it was a mock sternness, one of those nuanced mixtures of emotional tones humans are fond of. "If you screw it up, be prepared for some serious handling, not by the enemy… but by me. Go out and do your best."

My Snakes were in the command cadre, linked to three other Brigades. The whole strike force was put into giant transport ships and landed by assault-barges on the shores of a lonely piece of coastline. What land it was… what *planet* it was… we never learned. We had several strategic goals, all for demonstration purposes. The principal goal was a forced-march from the beach to an inland mountaintop, thirty kilometers.

Sunrise to sunset.

Full pack, and unit heavy weapons.

It was summertime, temperate latitudes, so we had sixteen hours of daylight. But it was hot, and too much heat makes a Snake go woozy. Too cold, and we get slow and sleepy; too hot, and we get brain-baked. Not our clamped-on brain-boxes, but the organic thinking matter we're born with.

Beautiful start. We were dumped in the surf where the salt water, brisk and astringent, was about a metre deep. My people aren't much good at swimming, but we're able to hold our breath for long enough to shove through the breaking waves and find the shore. We hit the sand with clockwork precision. Every unit landed exactly upon its designated zone. Nobody drowned; nobody ditched their equipment. We formed up and shoved inland. As a headquarters formation, we kept to the middle of things. Skirmishers and scouts roamed well ahead. A rear-guard was established. The maneuver elements followed the right roads and trails. It could have been a walk in the park.

Inland of the beach were bluffs and headlands, which we clambered up, keeping our proper spacing. A Squirrel couldn't have crept through the gap between Battalions. Then we spearheaded our formations and went, hell-for-leather.

Behind the bluffs was a belt of maquis, low, dusty scrub of some piney, spiny bush. It tended to grow together in networks, so shoving through it was a chore. We Snakes quickly got the knack of tunneling along at the roots, and made the best time.

There was a creek to cross, and a flag to capture, and, all per orders, a retreat from a presumed obstacle, so we had to circle around and find a new direction. Now we were in the shade of large, cork-barked trees, gray behemoths, hiding pleasant little glades of damp grass and fronded ferns. This was where we made our best time. The terrain felt wonderfully home-like to us. Perhaps our distant, native ancestors had lived in woods like those.

More challenges, more obstacles. There was a deep, steep river-gorge, which we had to find a way across. That set us back an hour. Then a simulated air-strike, with denominated casualties, and we had to role-play wounds and medics. Far better to do it as make-believe than in reality.

Up into the hills, and then the mountain-flanks. We slogged along, coordinating the other units, maintaining cohesion and control.

Sixteen hours? We did it in thirteen. There was enough daylight left for a battle, had it been a real march against a real enemy.

The real enemy was no more than a scattered group of observers, watching with worried expressions, seeing the maneuvering of an experienced army and the labors of disciplined soldiers.

For us, it was a good training exercise, a forced-march and a bivouac, ending with a campfire under the stars and big slabs of meat for every Snake and all. For the would-be enemy, it was a very clear object lesson: don't mess with an army that can accomplish a fully-armed point-to-point across unfamiliar terrain. We showed what we *could* do, and the enemy was wise enough to take it to heart.

Their coalition fell apart, and their diplomats came, hats in hand, to talk terms.

The Guerramancy isn't blood-thirsty. We don't make war for sport. It's a science, and an art, and a craft, but the most important thing is, it's a discipline.

War is how we make our decisions.

As Regimental Sergeant Major, I have the paradoxical position of having nothing to do, and everything to do. I'm not formally in charge of any specific aspect of operations, but I put my nose into everything, keep an eye on every phase of a campaign, and, at least in seeming, keep the whole affair running smoothly, with no more than a word or two in the right place. Well, all right, sometimes strong language is involved. I'm not precisely in the line of command, but functionally just outside of it.

I don't get invited to command conferences, at least not usually.

We'd taken the mountain, scared hell out of the observers, proven that a Heavy Infantry Division can march like lightning, and scotched a war before it could start. Fine bit of campaigning, and, other than the pretended casualties, very few of our soldiers had gotten hurt. A few scrapes, a few falls, the usual summer-soldier sickness, often as not petty malingering. I honestly think we could have defeated an enemy infantry force one-and-a-half times our own size, even at the end of that grueling cross-country scramble.

Now, the word got passed that I was wanted in the command hut.

Captain Wright was nearby me, and summoned also. It was all right for him; he was an officer. I'm not.

"What's this all about?" I wondered.

"Not a clue," he answered. I hadn't expected anything different.

"Your Battalion looks good," I told him, as we wandered, him walking, me gliding. You could go a long way before seeing two more disparate life-forms.

"I guess they're over their sulk."

Their resentment after the execution.

"I reckon. It wasn't much of a mutiny. No planning. No thinking."

He shook his head. "Such a damned waste, though. Such a miserable waste." I had enough experience with humans—and a brain-box that emulated a man's emotions—to know his mood. Weary, forlorn, and regretful. But he was the kind to cope. He wouldn't let his troubles haunt him for long.

The command hut was just a square-sided frame-tent, stood up in the shelter of one of those immense gray trees. The Headquarters Platoon kept a perimeter clear, but let Wright and me pass. He held the tent-flap wide for me, a bit of consideration I might not have expected from an officer.

Inside, a crush of ranks, nearly all human, stood about, clustered much too close together, all talking loudly. I knew most of them. I was most impressed to see Colonel Lericom, commander of one of the Regiments in the day's exercise. Major Stretch was there also.

Human psychology isn't one of my specialties, yet even I could sense a mood of deep concern. I also had the impression that their conversation had come to a very sudden halt the instant I'd put my nose among them. Among ordinary enlisted-rank humans, this might have been attributed to ophidiphobia. For some reason, a lot of humans become uneasy when face-to-face with five metres of Rattlesnake.

Colonel Lericom told off a Lieutenant to serve as Officer of the Guard: he went outside and monitored the periphery, guaranteeing our privacy.

I was beginning to have strong misgivings.

"All right, everyone," Lericom said, not loudly, but with the kind of force of personality that commands everyone's attention. She looked around herself, as if taking stock of the assembly, just one more time.

"You're probably wondering why I've called you here," she said, her lips twisted up just a bit. Everyone laughed, a bit more loudly than the pallid antique of a joke warranted.

"As most of you are aware, there are going to be further rounds of force reduction." Demobilizations. Everyone was now completely silent, and watching the Colonel with all their attention. "My Regiment is for the chop. You all know the Liftleg Brigade: the axe. The Beefjoint Regiment: cut to the bone. Everything pared back to Headquarters units. Placeholders. If a large-scale operation comes up, reinforcements and replacements will fill in. Nothing we haven't all seen before. But some of us are wondering if there might be an alternative."

If I had hackles, they would have raised.

"We're in an unusually advantageous position," she went on. "We're assembled in full strength, with access to transport. I've had the landing craft retained. They put us down on the beach; they can pick us up again. A short jaunt, a quick drop, and we can be… anywhere we want. In force. Fully armed."

Colonel Lericom was discussing an unauthorized maneuver.

No… I could no longer fool myself.

Colonel Lericom was discussing mutiny.

"The officer cadre, those of you who are here now, have all given me your private approval and support. Staff have drawn up plans. We can do this, if we all pull together. Is there any one of you who wants to nix the operation? Say the word. Each single one of you has the power of the veto, but only if you speak now."

Did that include me? I sensed it did not.

There was only silence.

Lericom turned to face me.

"Will the troops follow?"

That was what she asked me, but it was a foolish question. The troops would never know the difference. A legal attack, or an illegal one: they would look exactly the same to Jack Rattlesnake with a rifle at his side.

Would *I* follow?

I couldn't have been fooled, the way the troops could be. I know too much.

I said that my role, in the heat of battle, was much like a war-banner, a rallying standard, an insignia on a pole, which the troops would follow. If I lead them to the right, they follow to the right. If I press forward, they press. If I cry a halt, they halt. I'm only echoing the true commands of the officers. I don't make the decisions. I just make sure they're carried out.

This rebellious cadre, this mutinous assembly, this council of treason, *needed me*. There were too many ways I could break up the operation. I was a key working part of the strength and success of the Brigade. With my help, victory was vastly more likely than without it, and with my determined opposition, defeat was absolutely certain.

They could, of course, simply kill me. That would release me from the onus of the ethical decision. But they'd lose my expertise, my skills, and the long years of my experience. With me dead, the Brigade would lose a good part of its cohesion, just as a unit does when its banner falls in battle.

The other Sergeants would pick up the slack. I wasn't indispensable. Just a damned strong asset.

And I'd just a short time ago watched a good Snake get shot in the heart for very much the same thing.

The officers here could command me, but they couldn't suborn my loyalty. If I kept faith with the Guerramancy, I could not join this revolt. If I kept faith with Colonel Lericom…

I said, "Yes," and my voice did not waver.

Lericom gave me a look I couldn't decipher. I moved forward, and let go a half-second buzz of my rattles.

"Yes, I said. But you will hear me. I may be a willing participant in this crime—" I said that with much force. This *crime*. "But my soldiers are innocent. They don't know. They *won't* know. That's my price. You guarantee their lives, when the courts-martial convene and the charges fall."

Colonel Lericom nodded. "I agree. The executions start… and stop… with those in this tent. Now get out of here. We have a campaign to plan."

I let myself out of the tent.

Colonel Piper Lericom is an officer and a gentlewoman, and she recognized the value of my word. No one was assigned to watch me, to follow and report on whom I spoke with. I could have gone directly to the communications tent and made a report, but I'd sided with the mutineers and they knew that.

Things happened very quickly.

We didn't have to travel overland back to the beach. The transport craft turned out to be gravity barges, able to fly overland. We queued up by unit and got ourselves loaded aboard. From that point, until debarkation, we were nothing more than cargo.

We were put into starships and conveyed right back to our headquarters world, the planet we'd set out from. Our target was our own home base, where Colonel Upshot had given us our briefing.

The intelligence phase of the operation was carried out perfectly. No one knew we were coming. The big transports fed us back onto landing craft, and the barges set us down, as gently as anyone might have wished, into a large grassy meadow, in the late afternoon, on a planet we knew well, under a familiar sun. The grassland was ringed with a tree-line, and little stands of woods spotted the field. We'd held maneuvers through this terrain scores of times. Most of us could have navigated it blindfolded.

Colonel Lericom had chosen a wise course and a sensible plan of action. She could have had us assault-landed, right onto the base, square in the heart of the opposing forces. Then it would have been a face-to-face death struggle, a general melee, no retreat possible, and victory to the most ruthless.

Instead, we were going to make a strategic approach, perhaps an encirclement.

At the moment, we were very tightly concentrated, and thus highly vulnerable. The first order of business was to disperse ourselves into travel formation.

The next was... travel.

Now we performed, for real, what we had, so very recently, done only to show off.

My Battalion set off, came to the edge of the meadow, and burst into the trees of the forest.

The opposition—I could not bring myself to call them "The Enemy"—was in our own well-known military base, a proper formal station, with barracks buildings, a security perimeter, a fence, and weapons emplacements. But they, too, were horribly concentrated.

We were unseen in the circle of woods, but the base was in the middle of a broad clearing, another sun-dappled meadow. I remembered the wide killing ground in front of the razor-wire fence. Our units could skirt the clearing, so we could strike from any angle. It was one of the rare cases where exterior lines of communication gave a solid strategic advantage.

Now, Lericom earned my respect again. Instead of ordering a full-speed charge across ground to try to take the base by surprise, she made a demonstration attack. The largest part of our force was held to one side, while a light Battalion went forward, on the far left flank, to make a raid on the base's front gates. They shot high, over the heads of the soldiers at the guard-post. It was a declaration, serving proper notice.

The defenders were deer. Or antelope. I'm not totally sure of the difference. Morphed animals, with high, domed foreheads containing advanced brains. They didn't need brain-boxes the way we reptiles did. They'd been pseudo-evolved to sophisticated intelligence. They also had hands instead of fore-hooves, walked upright in a two-legged stance, and had a herd-instinct that made them natural soldiers. They followed orders well, and if a detachment was sent on a dangerous mission, a "forlorn hope," they went to it with fully willing self-sacrifice. All for the good of the flock.

They were also dead-eye shots with scoped rifles.

The sentries at the gate returned fire. That made it legal for our diversion force to take deadly aim.

Inside the base, alarms blared and sirens screamed. Doors slammed, hooves pounded, and there was the sound of shouting.

It's a lovely thing to put an army base into full alert.

In a strange way, we became aware, then, of Colonel Persis Upshot's own awareness of us. Instead of thrashing about in a panic, the defenders snapped to their stations. It was as if a single mind and will were controlling them all, and that mind was Persis Upshot.

That was the first time in the operation that I seriously considered the possibility that we would lose.

Lericom let another formation be seen, at a different angle of the base fence. They got good and close, and began tearing up the chain-link fence, bundling up the razor-sharp concertina wire with sensible caution.

The defenders shifted their resources to meet the new challenge. Lericom released another unit, a full Regiment this time, and opened a new attack front. Meanwhile, the first two attacks seemed to falter and the troops drew back.

Feint and probe. Lericom knew her business. She was keeping the axis of the main attack hidden, not yet ready to commit to an assault that *had to win*. She could dart back and forth like a fencer with an epée, keeping the opposition off-balance, scoring points, making them wonder. But when the time came for it, it would be an all-out shock-assault, like the edge of a logger's axe, not a delicate fencing blade.

The trouble was that Colonel Upshot knew this game perfectly, and had been playing it longer. Little probes and sallies emerged from the base, exploratory attacks, feints, and then, when we least expected it, a reconnaissance in force.

It was led by a Major, but Colonel Upshot was controlling it. The attack unbalanced us, and compelled Lericom to commit units she would have preferred to hold in reserve.

The base's heavy-weapons bunkers opened up. We'd already sited on them, and knocked them down with our own rockets. We weren't here for a siege. We were here to pry the oyster open, not to crack through the hard shell.

Or maybe that's a mixed metaphor. I'm not sure. My expertise is not in poetics.

Lericom withdrew the forces that had been revealed, and for the space of half an hour, there was near-silence. Weapons popped, and rockets fizzed, but it was at a slow cadence, not the full rambunctious pandemonium of a true fire-fight. The opposition obliged our fondest wishes, by forming up into maneuver units and sallying forth into the surrounding fields.

What was Upshot up to? Everyone wondered, and many feared.

I think Lericom had taken instincts into account. The deer, or antelope, *wanted* to be out in those green, grassy fields. They felt trapped inside the cage of their fortress-base. They didn't want a siege any more than we did.

Thus were planted the seeds of their defeat. If they'd stayed in place, nicely bottled-up, we'd have been days and days levering them loose. But when they came out to meet us, they forced the issue into a short, sharp time-frame. It would be all over in just hours.

Whether we were to win or to lose—that still hung in the balance.

Our force had just come from a training mission. We were fit and disciplined and in condition. We were ready. And no one has ever accused Colonel Piper Lericom of being a poor tactician.

The trouble was that no one had ever doubted that Colonel Persis Upshot was a *better* one.

We attacked their formation in the middle of their deployment, putting them into disorder. Then we hit the other side of the camp, and tore open a new section of the fence.

They maneuvered. We counter-maneuvered. Lericom kept hitting them where they were the thinnest. More of their force came out into the meadow. They lay themselves flat, hugging the ground and some of them digging with camp-shovels to make rude trenches or firing pits. We let them extend their lines... and then attacked from other directions.

All of this was in aid of a specific strategic goal that might not have been obvious: minimization of casualties. Lericom wanted to win a battle of maneuver, not a slug-fest. She didn't want the ground littered with countless dead.

Colonel Upshot must have known this, and, strangely, seemed willing to cooperate. The opposition was playing the same game. Who was showing the greater weakness? And yet it was a war of friend against friend: we were all in the Guerramancy military, and no one wanted to win at the expense of large-scale destruction.

Only a fool zeroes in artillery on the strongpoint he wishes to capture intact.

My Snakes were given the go-ahead. We shot out from our hiding place in the woods, now fully exposed to daylight and incoming fire from the opposition.

The *enemy.* They were shooting at us.

We returned fire, but only in a suppressive role. We took casualties, but we were moving fast, and we came up to the base perimeter essentially intact. This was one of the places where the wire had been peeled away. We were through, and began spreading out into the buildings, storehouses, barracks, and workshops of the base. There was a quick firefight at the power shed, which we won handily. We turned off their electricity. For good measure, we cut their water.

Had they shouted for help? Had they signalled for reinforcements and backup, for air and satellite coverage, for heavy armor, for all the big bruisers that an infantry assault could not withstand?

Of course they had! We were on a tight time-table.

My Snakes spread out, jumping forward with bounding overwatch tactics, always moving, bypassing defenses. We moved the way water flows.

Lericom helped us out: she showed a large formation, rampaging out of the woods and hauling hard for the fence, over on the other side of the base entirely. That drew away enough of the defenses to make our job possible.

Hit them where they aren't. Get there first with the most. Concentrate and puncture.

Kick them in the ass, don't just spit at them.

If it had been a game of chess, where every pawn was the equivalent of every other pawn, Colonel Upshot would have won. But she was burdened with the lesser troops. It is immodest of me to say this, but we Rattlesnakes were worth more than our equal numbers of Deer. The Colonel should have invested in a hardier species. A *nastier* species.

Nobody loves a Rattlesnake... but no one fears a Deer.

Too, once the battle reached this level of detail, fighting one-on-one, from building to building, an officer as elevated as a Colonel loses touch. Upshot had no way to bring her skills to bear.

We took casualties crossing each roadway and lane and alley. We took casualties from snipers on rooftops. Whenever two or more of us were, temporarily, close together, we took casualties from grenades. When we split up and moved independently, we took casualties from defensive crossfire.

But we kept advancing, always one body-length closer to our objective.

The Snake ahead of me was first through the door into the command bunker. An officer inside shot him dead with a pistol.

I was the second through the door. I shouldn't have been. It was a risk I shouldn't have taken. But I was there, in the right place and at the right time, and didn't wait to send another in my place. My rifle barked, and the officer with the pistol fell.

The others put their hands up.

A handful of Lieutenants, some Captains, two Majors, and Colonel Upshot.

"Stand your troops down," I said.

"No," she answered.

"Your successor can surrender as easily as you can." I pointed my rifle.

"My successor can die as easily as I can. We aren't going to surrender."

"You've lost."

Colonel Upshot shook her head, a small gesture, which I had trouble interpreting fully. A refusal, or a denial, or just a personal rejection of bitter fate?

"You've *lost!*" I repeated. "I've captured you, and the rest of the battle is pointless."

"Actually," she said, in a quiet voice, the voice I knew to be capable of great vigor and immense force, "my troops are doing pretty well. We're pushing back your assaults on all fronts. You've succeeded in a brilliant lightning raid to get this far, and you've captured me. But I'm not indispensable. My subordinate officers—the ones outside, in direct control of my troops—can coordinate affairs. We have dispersed communications. We aren't dependent on a central comms room. All they have to do is hold off defeat *long enough for reinforcements to arrive.*"

That was undeniably true. There was a time limit, and it was approaching rapidly. I could almost hear the roar of aircraft, the thump of rocketry, the clank-and-grind of armored fighting vehicles.

I thought about shooting one of the Lieutenants, but gave that up immediately as a bad job. Several more of my own troops came storming into the command room, but when they saw I had things under control, they went back out again. Wright was leading them further through the base compound, seeking to knock out their heavy weapons emplacements.

Colonel Upshot was right.

"I don't want to die," she said, "and so I'm willing to bargain with you. I suppose you don't want to die either. So we can trade. Life for life. When this siege and hostage-holding are relieved, you'll be taken, tried, and shot. Shot, just as one of your Snakes was shot, a little while ago. You'll be stretched out in a line and shot in the heart. But that doesn't have to happen, if you surrender. Now."

I'm not fearless. I listened.

"I'll sweeten the deal. Surrender your detachment—a Battalion-sized raid, wasn't it?—and I'll spare them, too. And that Captain Wright. Captains Jaynie, Vost, Bückel, Ariella… The lot."

I said nothing. I listened.

"More? You need more? Major Stretch. I can save her. She doesn't need to be shot."

The words came from my throat without my volition.

"Colonel Lericom?"

Persis Upshot looked at me with eyes nearly as cold as my own.

"No."

I turned off my brain-box.

The Colonel was suddenly in the room with a primeval serpent, lacking the gift of higher cognitive functions, and wholly without any of the refined emotions. I knew hunger, anger, fear… and nothing else.

Loyalty was gone. I could betray my unit, my command, my people. I was capable of any act, simply to stay alive.

I opened my jaws and let my fangs show. I'm afraid I dropped my rifle, and most of the accessories gripped by the fingers of my combat suit. Nothing seemed important.

"Outside," I said. I didn't know if she could understand me. My speech was slurred. But, "Outside," I said again, and butted her in the right direction. The Snakes with me didn't understand what was going on, but they helped me out, herding the group of captives through the door and out into the sunlight.

We marched them toward the sound of fighting. They resisted. I pushed.

Before long, we came within sight of one of their fighting positions. "Hold your fire," someone shouted. "It's the Colonel."

Upshot, to her rather great credit, prepared to snap out a series of orders, which would almost certainly have opened with, "You will not surrender!" I gave her a hearty bump with a curve of my flank.

When I knew that her soldiers were watching, I opened wide again and menaced her with bare fangs. Longer than your arm, cold and bony and white, with milky venom dripping from the vents near the tip.

One of my Snakes, quicker on the uptake than most, shouted, "Surrender! We have your Colonel!"

Some of the opposition heeded. Some didn't. There was confusion. Orders were given, and countered, and counter-countered. All attention was focused on the immediate stand-off, drawing effective control away from the several battle-fronts. Officers called back for instructions, then for clarification.

Colonel Upshot claimed she wasn't indispensable… but she was an extremely important personage, the Brigade's commander, founder, and eponym. The Upshot Brigade.

The Upshot Brigade didn't surrender, but it lost enough cohesion that our forces were able to cement unassailable tactical positions and force theirs into immobility. Their maneuver elements gave up, one after the other.

Before long, we, the rebels, were in control of the base, and the opposition forces were prisoners under guard.

Captain Wright came up to me and, quite courageously, turned my brain-box back on.

I withdrew my personal threat from the Colonel's person. If I could have blushed, I would have.

"Do you surrender, Colonel?" Wright asked politely.

Colonel Persis Upshot gave him the military honor of accepting her surrender. I wasn't an officer; it wouldn't have been appropriate. Also, I'd acted in a low fashion, making personal threats against captured personnel.

The reinforcements arrived, about eight minutes too late. There was nothing for their aircraft to strafe, for their rockets to target, for their tanks to overrun. They took over the situation anyway. More units showed up, including infantry—even a Battalion of Rattlesnakes—and put the whole area under martial guard.

There were trials. I was acquitted, given that the Colonel had refused to surrender. It was a fine legal point, but Colonel Upshot herself spoke in my defense.

The mutiny, of course, was completely legitimized. Colonel Lericom was promoted, from Lieutenant-Colonel to full Colonel, and Major Stretch became a Lieutenant-Colonel. Our units were advanced to "Guards" status: we become the Lericom Brigade of Guards. It gave us better access to reinforcements and replacements, and moved us farther down the list of units to be demobilized in peacetime.

We got away with it.

We did the right thing.

We won.

We're the Guerramancy, and war is how we make our decisions.

Who would want to live in a democracy?

Warfare against the Gods! Against their mythologicals, too.
Centaurs, pegasi, minotaurs, harpies, and the like.
How well do they fight together?

End of Ages

by BanWynn Oakshadow

CHAPTER I ~ In Vino Veritas

"General Bacchus! The humans are changing their formations into smaller units with a wider array of combat strategies. It suggests another attack on the Strait."

"No surprise there. We all know that whoever controls that strip of land between two bodies of water wins this damned war." Bacchus noticed the downfallen expression of the young pegasus. Still a yearling. *This is insanity! Men forcing us to put our children in the middle of a war.* "What is your name, Child of Pegasus?"

He was a tiny thing, his legs still a tumble of sticks, wings still shedding bits of the fledgling fluff. *A child willing to fight to the death before he ever has a chance to experience life. This one, and ones like him made men so easy to hate.*

"I am called Ferallus, General, out of Synanee and Horanden." The names were so hard to say past the lump in his throat.

"It is fine and proper to mourn your sire, little one. When you speak his name, remember that you speak the name of not just your sire, but that of a hero as well.

"What did you see of their organization?"

"The camp is spread out so far that it makes us attacking a form of suicide. It also makes it difficult to catch many with a single kind of attack. Each formation has its own cook fires, water barrel, latrines... likely is 360 Men in six..."

Bacchus sat up and looked intently at the yearling.

"… will stop any arrow or javelin, but I think that they will not block… with no shield or spear, just short swords and what… the new horror from their factories of death. Leonidus de Vinci and Plato are said to have invented a shoulder mounted cannon… goes through the bodies of any but the giant-class, and are making over… probably has no more than ten to twenty. I would say closer to ten than the twenty.

"Behind them was a long triumph…the back of the triumph probably means slings…or kneeling archers."

General Bacchus listened with more and more amazement at this tiny child's professional observations, suspicions, calculations, evaluations, counters, and meanings. What he had not been able to get a look at, he extrapolated, and it just went on and on. Horanden had been a natural-born strategist, and Ferallus had obviously inherited that and more.

Bacchus took several deep swallows of his wine and listened to his scout continue his report.

"There was something large, very large and very long so far to the rear, I could not see anything but a shape under a tarp. A witch and her cauldron was directly between it and the soldiers. Her rising fog blocked my view, although one soldier breathed a whiff of it and fell to the ground retching and helpless.

"General Bacchus, what happens if the wrong ingredients are put into a witch's potion?"

"Various things could happen, all of them bad. I see where you are going, but how?"

"No bags. Flat container folded into a bag so it opens by itself. Load in a bit of anything alchemical… hold breath, close eyes and drop at the right time. That means whoever… precision delivery… she isn't worth even one of us!

"Back to what else I saw, or didn't. No one that I saw wore the red crest of a commander. This seemed odd to me. Senior commanders… rarely seen outside of the command… move the actual command center between them so often that I can't tell where they are. But, I should see junior commanders.

"The huge trenchers of food being carried that disappear… I found one! Two soldiers were carrying one… Several minutes later… camouflaged. We may not know how to get to it, or what is in there, but we know… A satyr with poisons crossing the water with General Hydra's support… capability of any in the Mythos forces."

The little pegasus was croaking by the end.

"Oh, little one! I am so sorry. I had my eyes closed and was envisioning all as you described it. Amazing. But I did not wet your throat, though mine I kept well lubricated. Here, have a couple swallows of this. I spent the tiniest bit of the divine into it to sanctify it so that it would restore me more completely. It will probably have you buzzing around like a bumblebee."

Bacchus was not far off the mark. Ferallus's eyes opened wide, his hooves danced in the dirt, and his restless wings stirred up little dust devils.

"I-should-I-go-and-see-if-Ican-find-out-where-the-junior-commanders-are,-General-Bacchussir?"

"Go! Go! Burn some of that off before you pop! If you locate them, don't let them know that they are discovered." After the pegasus scout had left, General Bacchus mused, "Hmmm, should have gone with one swallow instead of three."

Ferallus saw two male griffins and called them up for a high conference. They snickered and agreed.

Ferallus flew back to camp and got a female griffin to go along with the plan.

When he was back in position, he signaled the three to begin their romantic waltz in the sky.

The enemy humans cheered and seemed to be betting on the outcome. Others were shaking hands with themselves in the bushes.

Watching thinking animals, or some mix of man and beast having sex seemed to drive humans nearly insane with lust… even mosaics of them. Watching griffins going at it hot and heavy right overhead was a chance not to be missed.

While they were watching griffin porn, Ferallus did a sweep of the tree line. He was flying faster than he ever had, wind actually screaming through the feathers of his head, eyes closed to bare slits. It was wonderful! He gave the signal to move the action to where he was. As soon as they reached that spot, Ferallus delivered a present. One griffin appeared to lose, while the winner flew off with the female to consummate in private. In other words, fly back to camp and laugh their tails off.

"GeneralBacchus-I-found-out-why-I-saw-no-commanders. Eight-squads-of-fifty-archers-four-on-each-side-and-in-the-trees-anywhere-that-put-the-Strait-in-range-on-both-sides-of-the-approach. They-are-under-camouflage.

"Commanders-called-orders-through-messengers-carrying-the-bucket-of-water-boys.

"I-saw-a-satyr-running-from-General-Hydra's-center-of-operations. He-was-carrying-wine-for-you.I-took-it-and-message-then-sent-him-home-turned-towards-General-Chiron's-camp-I-picked-up-some-supplies-there-as-well."

"What if I had sent him myself rather than use aerial?"

"Then-you-would-be-being-an-ass-sir.Satyrs-are-in-camp-messengers-and-not-my-responsibility.You-made-me-Senior-Scout-Messenger-Strategist.It-is-not-your-place-to-put-in-camp-messengers-on-my-field.You-have-no-excuse-for-endangering-the-satyrs. My-fliers-or-the-rest-of-the-camp-through-arrogance.If-you-don't-like-it-I-will-happily-resign-and-hand-the-tangled-mess-over-to-you. In-the-future-work-the-chain-of-command-bottom-up-or-take-over. There-isn't-any-in-between."

"Bacchus-sir-you-know-it-is-time-to-grow-up-and-be-a-leader. Drink-yousef-blind.Bugger-anything-that-moves.Do-things-just-to-piss-off-General-Chiron-and-Colonel-Right-Head.But-we-are-almost-gone,and-as-much-as-you-want-to-get-numb... We-want-to-live-to-see-tomorrow-a-week-a-month-years.If-you-don't-get-off-your-divine-ass-and-help-none-of-us-will-ever-see-any-of-them!"

Ferallus was still buzzing, and his hooves were tapping. Though slower than before, his speech was still near a blur.

Ferallus was gritting his teeth and his wings were drooping.

"Ferallus, are you hurt?"

"No-General-Just-some-muscle-strain."

"Lift your wings straight out."

Bacchus called to a passing satyr: "Onasmus, find Doctor Hippocrates and send him to me to treat damaged wing muscles on an injured pegasus yearling."

"General-why-does-Geedubius-insist-on-these-very-risky-attacks. He-loses-far-far-more-troops-than-he-kills-or-captures-any-of-us."

Bacchus sighed and took several swallows of wine. He started to give the young scout a swallow.

"Don't you dare, you old fart!" Hippocrates shouted. "If this young one is truly the get of Horanden, the only way he would fly hard enough to injure himself would be to score a major hit on the enemy, rescue one of ours or an innocent of theirs... Or if an irresponsible, senile, old fart caused him to do it. How many swallows, Bacchus?"

"You don't understand. We were plan..."

"Bacchus, the whole time you are talking, this one is in agony but, taught by his sire, he refuses to show it. How many swallows?"

"Three."

"Three would make a giant giggle. How could you do that to a child?"

"I am sorry, Ferallus. I wasn't thinking."

"I-forgive-you-Lord-Bacchus-but-'I-wasn't-thinking'-doesn't-cut-it.
You-are-General-Bacchus-of-the-remains-of-the-only-Air-Corps-of-
all-the-Mythos.You-are-not-allowed-to-not-think.Be-a-falling-down-
drunk-goat-buggering-foul-mouthed-rotten-father-boy-buggering-
irresponsible-disrespectful-sheep-buggering-sack-of-harpy-bungholes-
puss-oozing-tool-of-a-decrepit-old-fart-that-we-love-well-before-all-else.
But-don't-you-ever-not-think.That's-how-people-get-killed.People-like-
me-and-everyone-else-who-counts-on-you.Until-you-get-decently-
drunk-and-your-puckered-brown-winker-gives-birth-to-your-head-you-
are-more-of-a-liability-as-you-are-a-leader."

"That is the kindest thing anyone other than my sons and their gets
has said to me in... 187 years. You understand. Thank you, Ferallus.

"Get this ointment rubbed into his shoulders and all the way across
his back."

Hippocrates smiled and nodded at the yearling, "Bacchus has needed
that chewing-out for a long time. Good job. Now, if you leave the binding
alone for three days, you will heal.

"Apprentices and Bacchus, watch what happens when your little
divine fortification is neutralized.

"Two big swallows, Ferallus. Good lad!

"By Apollo's silk ladies' panty collection! He was not going on your
energy, Bacchus! Your damn potion caused him to take energy wherever
it could find it from his own body, muscle tissue, body fat... all of it. He
should not be able to readjust a divine potion! You almost killed him. Ten
more minutes in the air and he would already be dead. I'll give him this
potion to neutralize the imbalance. You drink this one down."

After Ferallus had swallowed, he asked, "What's it do?"

"It is going to give you a twelve-hour migraine, so you don't forget
to never 'not pay attention'. Bacchus, you do not use children to impress
them about the god they serve. I am going to go, so shut it. I do not wish
to speak with you any longer today.

"When you two are finished, one of you locate Ferallus's kit and pack
these skins in it. Loss of them shall be Bacchus's punishment for being a
stupid ass."

When Ferallus had mostly recovered, though he showed many
more ribs than before, Bacchus returned to the discussion at hand. "Did
your sire teach you of the war between General 'Goldilocks' Custer and
Alexander the Great?"

"Yes. General Custer lost his entire company, his scouts, his reserves
and the camp prostitutes, including his mother, sister and three brothers,
along with his own life because of an overblown ego...

"Oh, that is why you asked. Geedubius is now working to keep General Montgomerius, whom he hates with all his heart and black and twisted soul, from claiming victory. He dreams of standing on that deck with the banner unfolding over his head proclaiming his victory. He is not fighting against us as much as he is fighting for his own glorification and Montgomerius's humiliation.

"By Cerberus's hemorrhoids! That means Montgomerius is in a position to make it a race. He cannot be close enough behind… Bacchus, sir, we are in a pincer with Montgomerius's troops coming at us by both sides!"

"Actually, it is more like Montgomerius is pulling our cheeks apart and Geedubius wants to… well, he won't kiss first or cuddle after, so no date for him.

"Forget about Montgomerius for now, Ferallus. He is well taken care of.

"What is your opinion about what tactics they will use?"

"They are obviously drawing us in for our cavalry to be decimated by their hidden archers. It's a trap to lure us in too deep."

"That is an excellent job of reconnaissance and of making a very precise report. I will adjust our strategy here and with our other generals. You've given us enough to give us time to set our defenses and save many lives. Your father would be very proud of you.

"Ferallus, I am reassigning you. You are far too good to be wasted staying in one area while another is under attack. I will have you travel to whichever area has most need of you. Now I must ask one very important question of you…"

Before he could finish, Ferallus grinned, "Nope. You screwed up. I'm the one in pain, so you lose two skins. No take-backs or do-overs. But, if you reach very gently… I'm sorry, your hands are way too big. It will hurt… more."

Bacchus called over a satyr. "Which wing?"

"Right wing up top. So close to the front it feels like it will fall out on its own."

The satyr got the skin and ran off before Bacchus could reach it.

"I'll get you, you thieving little bastard! I'll tea bag you for a week, you good-for-nothing grandson!"

Ferallus stepped up and wriggled until a skin fell out from under his left wing. Bacchus got it and gave the colt a slap on the haunch. It stung like a horsefly big as his head, and made Ferallus proud. The General was treating him as he would any other of his adult soldiers. Bacchus did not look at him and see just a yearling, but one who had earned his way to adulthood. Now it was just a matter of letting his body catch up. His father *would* have been proud!

Bacchus hated watching the young one leave with his head high, chest out and strutting in parade form. But at least now, if the little one was killed, he would die a soldier, the equal of any and better than some. Bacchus cried that he had to think and do such things. He drained the first skin and reached around for another.

A centaur galloped across the rolling field and came to a halt in front of Bacchus. "General Bacchus, sir, General Chiron is planning a new tactic today. We have no men to ride us, and you know why. The dryads and others nimble with the bow will still ride, while the rest of us will carry straw dummies to keep up appearances and soak up some arrows. Centaurs and riders will use bow and arrow."

"Thank you. My scout saw something he wasn't supposed to see. It may be best to hold off the new tactics until we see if the haystacks work. Has there been any word from the Mariners?"

"Sir, from what I was able to discern, two sisters will come at the Strait, one from each side. They say that the haystacks should be able to stand the two smallish tidal waves, but you might want to position them ten arm-lengths further back. Are there any messages for General Chiron, General?"

"Tell him that I am bringing a Hekatonkheire into battle."

"Hades! A giant with near to a hundred arms and a nearly limitless supply of stones… that would slow anyone down."

"Ask General Chiron to have his giant-class soldiers lay in regular piles of stones along the lead-in to the Strait, and between the haystacks. I want a very large pile of stones just inside cannon range for when we signal the Hekatonkheire to join the party."

The centaur said, "I would estimate no more than a week before another Mace of reinforcements arrive."

Bacchus said, "Twenty sphinxes, part of a flight clearing islands, flew in last night and are added to our roster."

"Is there anything else for General Chiron, General Bacchus? Supplies to help the upcoming ceremony, perhaps?"

More centaurs crested the hill. Twenty in all, and each with four large amphorae of wine, but for the colt in front carrying two.

"I am most grateful, but there shall be no Bacchanal until this war is over. It would be too disrespectful to those who are still falling. Please take them back with you. I know my limits of self-control, and that of my sons and theirs."

Bacchus yelled for the young pegasus, "Ferallus! By Sister Sarah, quit lazing around, you feathered mule's ass. You have been resting for almost five minutes. Time to put your butt back to work! Give these donkeys with delusions of grandeur whatever we have that is to their taste. Then kip on back and find out how the hot tar and bladders are coming along. They need to be hot when they are picked up."

A satyr running past stopped when he heard the General. "Hush, Pops! With all disrespect to the General, people are talking. Ferallus, that stunt has really boosted morale. I have been to the hot tar project. They are keeping them hot and easily broken in a hot sulphur spring." He saluted the god and ran off.

"What did he mean by 'stunt'? Your report to me did not mention any stunt."

"Uhm… well, like when I saw their commanders I realized that my bowels and bladder were full and I kind of…"

The centaurs laughed themselves hoarse.

Bacchus laughed so hard that he fell off of the stone he had been sitting on.

"Aide! Where in Hades is Bodacious?"

"I'm right behind you, as always, General." A minotaur stepped around to the General's side to keep him from seeing the hidden stash of wineskins under the bushes behind his back.

"Bodacious, give Ferallus a medal!"

"Which medal and action, General!"

"I don't care… give him 'the Grape and the Vine' for shitting and pissing on the enemy commanders!"

Bacchus roared to Ferallus, "By Posidon's middle fin! Screw the last position I assigned you to. You are now my personal messenger, cleared to take whatever action that you think will piss off the enemy. By all the other gods, though none so as fine as me, I think I like you, son. Now go find me a couple more skins, dammit! No, get the skins from the navy; they have the good stuff. Go to them bearing this scroll. Come back with their strategy… and wine. Move it! Fly on over to Chiron on the way, and mark out the exact positions and numbers of archers and commanders you blessed. But get a bite first. You're showing more ribs than feathers."

"Lord Bacchus, I can't fly for a few days."

"That's right. Once again, I am sorry. You felt more like one of my sons than a soldier, and I gave you their measure to drink. How did you crap on them without being seen?"

"Monster porn, General."

"What is monster porn?"

"It is when men get all hot and horny watching us mate. I arranged a fake aerial mating battle, and when they were close enough to take the blame, I dropped my payload. They don't have a clue that they were scouted."

Bacchus turned to the centaurs. "Who is commander of this squad?"

"I am, General, Senior Light Troop Leader Damascus Sword Dancer."

"Senior Troop Leader, you've seen my aerial messenger/scout. Do you have anyone who is fast, steady enough to take instructions, and a lot smarter than most of you so he remembers them?"

"I believe that Hoofer Second Class Whirlaway Blenheim would best suit your needs. He is being wasted standing in formation, and will hurt the enemy many times more carrying information than he will with a bow. Serving you now will give him a better understanding of how to maximize combinations of different kinds of soldiers so that he becomes a respected strategist."

"I'll take him! I think that he and Ferallus here will get along fine. I will take the amphorae that Whirlawa Bloodman is carrying. They will be used by our soldiers for pain-control in surgery, blessings of new marriages, deaths and births, not for revelry."

"As Lord General Bacchus commands! Hoofer Second Class Whirlaway Blenheim, you are now reassigned to General Bacchus."

"Troop Leader, you and the Girl Scouts are welcome to sell cookies back in the encampment if you wish."

The troop trotted out of camp and Bacchus had another laughing bout. They had laid a trail of fresh horse apples leading all the way to the border.

"Ferallus, let's get Whirlaway settled in, fed, and introduced around.

* * *

"I want everyone to meet our newest scout and messenger, Whirlaway."

"He is going to be working a lot with Ferallus until he gets settled. Ferallus dropped road apples and drained himself all over the enemy junior commanders!"

Bacchus had to wait for the laughter and cheers to subside before continuing.

"If you haven't been told, listen to this one and pay attention to his ideas. He looks the babe, but this babe is Horanden's get, and his sire's blood runs hot in him. He knows the numbers and placement and of what approach may be the most effective. But, while he may have his father's mind in strategy, he has not a satyr's gift in theft! Turn around and bring back my wineskin, Ferallus, you thieving bastard!"

All of the pegasi cheered Ferallus loudly. This one may be Hornaden's get, but he had the soul of a satyr.

Ferallus mouthed the skin to General's Aide minotaur Bodacious, who drank and passed it to another pegasus, who mouthed it to Whirlaway, who drank and gave it back to Ferallus.

He had Whirlaway hoist the skin. "General Bacchus! Thanks for giving us the good stuff!"

"Get back here so I can pluck your wings like a fly, you backstabbing, deceitful, moldy pair of donkey balls!

"By a siren's salty slit! I've absolutely terrified Whirlaway. Be kind to him; he still believes that being a god means something."

Ferallus said, "Whirlaway, come with us. We'll get you a place to settle where you won't get buggered by a minotaur in your sleep."

The centaur gave a small snort but looked afraid to do more.

"Whirlaway, you can relax and smile. This is Bacchus's camp. and is as odd and twisted as he is. By the sagging buttocks of all the gods! If we may die tomorrow, then let's laugh as much as we can until that final second."

"By Hera's nipples!" the others cheered. "He is Horanden's get, with Bacchus's voice!"

"Ferallus, your sire would be so proud of you."

Bodacious strode up and fastened a ribbon around the tiny pegasus's neck.

"By the order of the Divine General, Lord of the Bacchanal, Divine Commanding General of the Mythos Air Corps, and Decrepit Old Fart, Bacchus, Ferallus is hereby awarded the Order of The Grape and The Vine, for his split-second decision to humiliate and demoralize the humans by voiding bladder and bowel upon their commanders. All salute!"

Everyone faced away from Ferallus and dropped their trousers, lifted kilts or robes, or raised tails and shook their asses at him. Outside camp, salutes were formal. In the living areas of the camp, troops were free to be children, whatever their age, and had made the bare-ass salute the standard symbol of respect.

Even Whirlaway had to snort at the "Divine General Bacchus" and "Drunken Old Fart" when both were equally honest.

They all wanted to see the medal and gathered around him and headed to Ferallus's flop while discussing strategy and fallback plans. Ferallus settled Whirlaway on a spot to bed down right next to his own.

They shared a couple bites of hot grain mash and some of Bacchus's wine, watered.

"Whirlaway, take the medal off me and stow it in my kit, please. Thanks. Help me up. Wings. Bacchus has your first assignment."

Bacchus saw the little pegasus and centaur galloping to Generals Chiron and Hydra.

The minotaur handed him a large skin when he saw Bacchus trapped by the guilt he felt for every death or unforeseen act of heroism or sacrifice. Each shoved a javelin of fire deeper and deeper into the god of orgies, excess, drunkenness, and joyful abandon.

CHAPTER II ~ A Horse of a Different Color

Ferallus and Whirlaway split off, each to a different General at about the midpoint.

Chiron was drawing out routes for attack, fall back zones for multiple wave attacks, and medical facility locations. He had a few humans who were still loyal to the old ways, eighty centaurs, and a couple dozen dryads and nymphs handy with a bow. What he didn't have was time for babes in the middle of a war.

"Sorry, little one but not now. I have battle plans to refine."

"With all due respect, General Chiron, I was sent by General Bacchus to give you the report of my scouting mission. The information is worthy of attention, sir. Senior Light Troop Leader Damascus Sword Dancer can vouch for me."

"Well, I have to admire any fledgling who can talk back to me, even politely. What do you have to tell me?"

Ferallus looked at the geography on the map. "Six widely spread-out turtles of near sixty men with… will be dropping hot tar and Prometheus's Fire on them." He continued to give the numbers, types and position. "…because four junior commanders and 200 archers on each… them are sufficiently trained as archers… Anywhere they can get a straight shot at the Strait. A couple commanders also have wet and stinking uniforms. I needed to go and they were right there…"

Chiron laughed and slapped him on the other flank.

"You are with the perfect commander. I am sorry for dismissing you earlier. Your observations are accurate, professional, and will save a lot of lives. What would you recommend?"

"They lost about 250 and a cannon before dawn this morning. General Hydra has her girls retrieving it. They have 400 archers, 360 men in turtle shield groups, 250 men… delivered to one location we now know of, but

131

at least one more that remains hidden. What or how… mystery. 60 more men with minotaur slaves along with three war machines of unknown abilities arriving tomorrow. Almost forgot the witch.

"There is one light in the darkness."

"And what would that be, Child of Pegasus, get of Horanden?"

"If one of the hidden forces is Cerberus, he hasn't made this side of the Strait his 'walkies' spot."

General Chiron laughed and rubbed his eyes.

The troops were completely shocked; the brilliant General never laughed! Ever!

"I think that I like you, Ferallus. Now, let's turn to war. We have 80 Cavalry, near 60 Air Corps (mostly light), plus 20 satyrs (mostly drunk and horny), 70 Mariners (most of whom require open sea to be effective), 7 Giant Class, and no Infantry."

"General, we have an Air Corps, and they do not. The best they can do is shuffle and hide their aerial countermeasures. If we stay ahead of them there, we still have a slight chance of finishing General Geedubius's forces and being dug in while the wall is being built to keep reserve forces from coming in."

"Second is while cannons may be more powerful, they are not as versatile or mobile as giants are. They give us another great advantage. Your cavalry has inflicted heavy losses in every engagement. That is floating in their heads, and they will be halfway useless from fear in a major strike.

"The Mariners are set to send two tidal waves, one on either side of the Strait.

"We know the location of one underground bunker and which tent the food for it is coming from. I am going to see if General Hydra will get two satyrs loaded with poisons across and into place once it gets dark. Tonight we will also try dives to drop alchemical ingredients into the cauldron.

"They will probably use one cannon loaded with grapeshot for the spread. The other probably with ball shot for power, although if he is willing to sacrifice his men, and we both know he is, he may fire both with grapeshot… if they even suspect where you are, General, whatever is back there is just for you.

"His primary objective was originally to capture slaves, secondary to stop us from reaching Crete and digging in… now he wants to make us pay for his mistakes and deny Montgomerius anything left to claim. He won't be shooting to wound and disable anymore.

"If you appear to be falling for the Strait, have titans throw… now and come in along the water from both sides and take out the archers instead… one turtle will come out to at least… waves can take them out. The satyrs will scream from the haystacks, and you can turn and strafe again to devastating effect over and over. Any panicking men… in the water letting Pan's crew disable them.

"That is my assessment, General."

"Your assessment? You were not given these plans? You planned it out on your own?"

"I'm sorry, General. I misinterpreted what you meant and gave you my own evaluation. It wasn't my place."

"Relax, little one. I am trying to discover if you are a natural-born strategist."

"I am Horanden's get, General."

"That explains it. Now I wish you were one of my troops.

"Well done! Off with you."

CHAPTER III—Some Like It Wet

Instead of heading back to camp, Ferallus made a detour to General Hydra who stated that she had received the scroll and verbal message.

"General Hydra, I know that Whirlaway has delivered the scroll and other message to you. I have been going over tactics with General Chiron and tomorrow will be very unexpected. I am to give you a reconnaissance report from my flyover and planning with General Chiron."

"You, a child, were planning with General Chiron? I find that to be more than a stretch."

"General Hydra, I am Horanden's get, and it seems that I have some of my sire's skills as well as what he taught me while he lived. If Generals ask my opinion, I answer to the best of my abilities. If they find me lacking, I can be dismissed like an insect. So far, both General Bacchus and General Chiron have found something of value in my words.

"I don't mean to be disrespectful, but I know that this will be insubordinate. We have few enough left who are able to fight and cannot afford to throw away any asset, not even the words of a child."

Colonel Left Head laughed, "Bang! You just got hammered!"

Colonel Right Head advised, "Laws in time of war are there for a reason. When we start making exceptions, all we gain is chaos. You know what you must do."

"You are such a stuck-up prick!"

"We need to find a way to cut you off and let you live with Bacchus."

"I am going to cut both of you off if you can't remember that we are at war… and losing. This is exactly why I am General and you two are Colonels. By the other gods, I'm getting another migraine."

"Then you will be glad to know that Hippocrates just gave General Bacchus a twelve-out migraine for injuring me while trying to impress."

Colonel Left Head said, "You should see how impossible she gets during PMS."

"Colonel Left Head," they all snickered at the name, "I think you and I have much the same sense of humor. But right now, I want to save as many lives as I can by dealing with the General in which she can direct and assist me with the distractions of insults. I mean no disrespect."

"None taken. When you are right, you are right."

"I shall not pursue the insubordination charge. Let's turn our attention to the war."

"This is what I saw on my flyovers: 360 turtle formations; 250 witches, two cannons, what might be a cannon of godlike proportions, and I discovered that something or -things are in underground bunkers waiting to be used. I would love to find a way to follow the feeders, wait for them to open the trapdoor, and then drop Prometheus's Fire in them. I have asked both Generals about getting two satyrs armed with poison to their camp near the tent that the trenchers of food for underground bunkers come out. Could you get them across in the dark?"

"That should pose no problem."

"It could make a huge difference if your girls could watch for those carrying trenchers and identify where the camouflaged bunkers are. With luck we can roast them before they are even used.

"The trees for thirty rods on either side of the Strait are full of hidden archers. The satyrs are going to scream from the safety of the haystacks, which will be repositioned like this. The screams should keep the centaurs and riders, also with bows, safer while they strafe. Many of the panicked are going to fall or jump into the water. Do you think anything bad might happen to them?"

Left and Right heads chuckled.

"The archers go from here on this side of the Strait and from here to here on your current side. 400 archers with commanders. A lot of your girls are going to have short-term boyfriends. Can any leap out of the water to grab an archer too close to shore or on a branch?"

"Not many, but a few. It is well-thought. My girls are in a position that makes it very difficult to exercise their abilities. If you think of other ways to engage them, it will be appreciated, Son of Horanden."

"When they recover from a Scream enough to return to position, they will still be confused and their minds susceptible. Sing them a pretty song and they will come to the dance."

"I like that one very much. Our thanks."

"The centaurs are going to be hitting here and here at the same time, and then working their way up and down, again and again until they run out of targets. When the centaurs split off in both directions, the satyrs will scream from the haystacks.

Before, we thought the tidal waves would be best timed to take out the token force of humans in turtle formation. The air corps is taking care of everyone behind the forces mentioned.

"Now, the third cannon changes things. They must be willing to sacrifice their troops by shooting through them to get to you and your marines, or General Chiron and the Cavalry… lure to blow up as part of a trap.

"These may allow us to take out all their archers and make a full third of their infantry into our troops without us shooting even a full quiver."

"You look as if there is more you need?"

"General Bacchus is sorely tortured. He is the god of revelry and joyous excess. When he sees the young ones like myself fighting in a war, instead of overhead playing air ball… you know him."

"Of course, and very honorable for you to think of it and brave to ask."

"Yennyll, two large skins of our best wine for the scout strategist here."

"Hey, Ferallus! It ain't a medal, but take this. You stood up to the Bitch and the Prick. You earned it." Colonel Left Head spun his neck around and released a silver wreath with copper leaves that spun in a straight line to him.

He caught it in his mouth and flipped it so that it settled around his neck.

"I would appreciate it if we discussed these things first, but I agree that he is more than a step above the average soldier, as was his sire."

"It is highly irregular! We must maintain discipline and regulations!"

Colonel Left Head warned, "You should probably run now, things are about to get nasty."

He settled the skins. "Thank you, General Hydra, Colonels. Soak 'em 'til they don't float anymore!"

All three heads chuckled before looking at each other with fire in their eyes.

Ferallus turned tail and galloped, even though it hurt. Still he heard the argument and "ow"s and squeals. Apparently the 'argument' had deteriorated to biting.

CHAPTER IV ~ "Back to work. I love war!"

"Alright! That's enough! Let's get back to the battle plans if you commanders can fit it into your tea party schedules."

Commander One said, "Yes sir, General Geedubius, sir! Sorry sir!"

"Apologies are for women and have no place in war! I won't have them in the command tent. Just thinking about it makes me want to puke!

"We lost 235 heavy armor infantry with that little stunt of building rafts and tying them together to cross to the other side. No one could defend because a breeze blew the witch's smoke in their direction! They got one of my cannons! How many did they lose? I'll tell you. They lost zero and we never even saw any of them. Soggy bitches.

"So, who was it who fouled up my orders? Which of you lost my cannon? Which of you cannot follow simple instructions?"

Commander Two said, "General, I suggested a tarp... we explained that our scouts found..."

"It's too late for your excuses. My job is to come up with Strategy. Yours is to carry it out. It... Was... Not... Carried... Out!

"What's your name, Commander?"

"Dementius sir!"

"Well, Commander Dementius, you have failed me for the last time. Anyone who knows the name Geedubius knows that failing me once is too many times.

"Give him to the fish bitches!

"Someone promote me a new Commander."

General Geedubius lit a fresh cigar and puffed on it for a bit. "Damn, this is good. Where do you find these, Colonel Cannabis?"

"I grow it myself, General, and have satyr slaves roll them. I add just a tiny bit of an herb to the tobacco that makes the cigar relaxing to smoke."

"Congratulations, Commander. You are my new personal Aide."

"Thank you, General Geedubius. I won't disappoint you!" *Which is why I have a box of cigars with twice as much herb in the cigars, to keep you mellow and happy, you narcissistic psychopathic asshole.*

"Back to work. I love war!"

Commander One said, "They know about the witch, but only what we want them to know. The other cauldron is under camouflage on the bank, ready to be tipped into the water."

Commander Two said, "They have counted all six turtle formations, but don't have a clue that the first two are sacrificial lambs manned by peasants and slaves. They've seen the Triumph, reserves, wounded tent. They think they have accounted for our number. Those archers are going to be a hell of a surprise."

Commander Three said, "We have three of the eight-cannon turtle war machines from Leonidas de Vinci and Plato's factory in Sparta on the way. They know we have something big with the two cannons, but no clue what it is."

Commander Four said, "…"

"By Athena's case of the clap! There is a Commander Four?"

"We are waiting for the newly promoted Commander Four to arrive."

General Geedubis said, "Just wait until they try to advance for close combat, and we open the hatches."

Commander One said, "General, isn't placing a third of our forces as archers right by the water a bit risky?"

"Nonsense! We are dealing with animals here, not people! They can barely count their own hooves, let alone deduce my strategy."

Commander One said. "But, General…"

"There is no "But General", dammit! Nobody overrides a Geedubius decision. When I give an order, the questions are over!"

Commander Two said, "General Geedubius, sir. I had an idea that may work well with your order. If we were to include twenty archers in with the lambs, they can create chaos, maybe even kill something, and allow some lambs to survive and create more distraction."

"By Zeus's third testicle! You are a spineless girl instead of a soldier! Since you want to save lambs so much, you get to go out in rank and tend your flock. Sing campfire songs. That's an order! It may lift your spirits enough to kill something before you all die."

"Aide, promote me a new senior commander and send him in here."

"Yes, General, right away, sir!"

A soldier with new rank insignias sewn on crookedly entered. "Senior Commander Achilles reporting as ordered, General Geedubius."

"Now you are Commander Two. Their air superiority rules out the human gliding wings."

The General's Aide said, "They still think it is a trap rather than an assault, so all their focus are going to be on the perceived greatest threats."

"General, what is the assault order on the Strait?"

Another new Senior Commander reported for duty.

"You are now Commander Four. Start strategizing and stuff."

Commander Four said, "Two sacrificial lambs. Let the archers take out what they can, don't worry about the lambs, but when it comes to the centaurs and minotaurs aim to kill the animals. This is a war, not a zoo."

Commander Two said, "When the damn horses charge, we fire the cannons with grapeshot. That is what the lambs are being sacrificed for. We may even take out their General if he is overseeing from the right spot. We are free to wipe them out... at any cost. Is that correct, General?"

"Pretty much. Unless it backfires, in which case your ass is going to be hanging in the breeze."

Commander One said, "We still keep 'Big Bessie' covered. She is for when they have no choice but to send in the giants, cyclopes, and other huge mental midgets. In practice, she heats up too much to fire more than four times a day. But when she does speak, she makes a titan's fart sound like a bird's chirp."

Commander Two said, "Let them drop anything they want on the witch. We have what we really need already. She's expendable."

General Geedubius said, "Then the assault. Triumph first, then the first pair of turtle formations, followed by two turtle cannon machines. They are arriving tonight when they cannot be seen. One formation and one machine will split to each side. The last two formations and then the last cannon machine goes right up their ass and keeps going. Archers will merge with formations from areas where they can effectively shoot with relative freedom. We are ending this hemorrhoid of a war."

The General's Aide said, "General, we have a full Mace of a thousand supposedly already here on the beast's side of the Strait. Shouldn't we coordinate with them?"

General Geedubius puffed on his cigar until it was smoking like a chimney, "What? And let that mincing Sicilian boy-lover claim the victory? Never!

"When General Montgomerius gets here, we will all be humpin' centaurs, or all of you will be dead trying! Is that understood?

"What can 200 animals do against a fully armed, fully trained Mace of 1300, plus our specials, plus our new war machines, plus Big Bessie? Are you seriously worried? Can you possibly be that yellow?"

"No, General, Sir!"

He handed a cigar to the General.

* * *

CHAPTER V ~ Rising To The Challenge

On his way back to Bacchus's camp, Ferallus saw Whirlaway being attacked by harpies. Two on the ground weren't moving. Before he could get there, he saw the centaur knock another down and stomp its head.

He caught up. "Cut my bandages!"

Whirlaway had more scrapes, cuts, rips and bruises than skin. All of him was covered in harpy shit. He did as he was told. Soon Ferallus was batting them to the ground with his wings, Whirlaway was using his blade, and both were kicking their rear hooves.

The remainder fled and it was over. Nine harpies lay dead at their hooves. They ran to the nearest stream and helped each other get clean. Whirlaway did most of the cleaning.

"Ferallus, how about if tonight General Chiron has one of his giants, with wine vinegar cloth up his nostrils, pile them on a flat leather piece, not a bag, tuck it closed. Then he could carry it close to the human encampment, whirl and throw over the trees. That waking you up in the middle of the night will ruin your day."

"By a dryad's knothole! Whirlaway, that's brilliant! That's what my sire would call using unexpected resources to maximum effect. We need to get your cuts healed first."

One of Ferallus's wings was sagging and the other trailed in the dirt. Whirlaway moved to that side and helped his friend rest the worst wing across his back while they made their slow way back to camp.

"Ferallus! Get your feather farting ass over here. Whirlaway, I am going to tear two of your limbs off if you do this to me again. I have been worried sick. Both of you missing. No messages. I was about to go looking myself."

Bodacious, the minotaur Aide, said, "Pan, two manticores, two sphinxes, two hippogriffs and two pegasi are currently searching for you at this old drunk's command. About 5% of our Air Corps and a son if that tells you anything."

"Shut up!"

Whirlaway spoke up, "We got lost. We thought we smelled you, but it was just a dead harpy."

"By hermaphroditic Hydra's hymen! I knew that you were one of us!

"You are both seriously injured. By what?"

"Harpies."

"Bodacious, one of the tiny skins of the special stuff."

Bacchus squeezed the entire skin into his mouth, appeared to be concentrating very hard and then carefully spat the wine back into the skin.

He handed it to them. "Don't worry about the backwash. One swallow each. No more."

They did as directed and felt like they were tingling all over, on the outside and the inside too.

"By Medusa's extensions and weave! Ferallus, I'm totally healed! Thank you, Bacchus! I take back two of the nasty things I was going to say about you."

Bacchus just nodded.

Whirlaway explained his plan.

Bacchus just nodded.

Bodacious gave the orders. "You have good minds and work well together. I leave your activities to yourselves for now. Bacchus will be mostly stone-cold sober for the next five hours or so."

"Bodacious, how many times in this war has he done that?"

"Counting you two... twice."

Ferallus took Whirlaway back to their kit and had the centaur add the laurel to the medal. They took one of the two skins of General Hydra's best, and replaced it with a good but not great vintage, then returned to Bacchus and surrendered the skins to Bodacious who did no more than raise an eyebrow.

* * *

Ferallus sent Whirlaway to Chiron first with his idea so that they would see him as more than a satchel with legs for delivering the mail. He was also told to give an honest and complete review of Bacchus's troops and capabilities and then about General Hydra's girls, and then return General Chiron's message about needs he had that the Air Corps may be able to loan out.

Ferallus wingwaved when he saw Whirlaway heading back to camp, and the centaur waved back.

Ferallus hit the ground at a gallop. "General Chiron! Sir! I have this message for you from General Bacchus. It, much like Bacchus, is useless. At least for now."

He handed the 'message' to the General.

It was written in crayon and showed two horsies, one with wings and one with arms, using a giant hammer to crush the enemy camp.

"If you will permit, General. On the way here, those requests gave me an idea that may actually be worth something."

"Ferallus! Disrespecting your commanding officer is a court martial offense!"

"I beg the General's pardon, but I would never speak to or of you in such a manner. I would never knowingly hurt the General Bacchus we love so well, but it is exactly that kind of disrespectful and stupidly childish behavior that keeps him going even while he is dying on the inside. We cannot do this without him, so we do what we must to help him survive. Another reason is he used some divinity to heal Mythos Air Corps Scout Messenger First Class Whirlaway Blenheim and me. He is going to be sober for six hours."

"It seems my decision was better than I knew."

"A keen observation. I have not had much respect for how Bacchus runs his camp, but you are correct; he is the god of wine and revelry. He would waste away in mine."

"We are grateful for the respect you have shown towards centaur culture and consider you to be one of us now. First names are fine, rank if it is official."

"Hold, soldier. You are trembling and your eyes are somewhat glazed. When is the last time you ate?"

"Right before flying here, General. I was settling in Whirlaway and had a couple bites of his mash and some watered wine."

"That is not a meal. When is the last time you had a meal?"

"Uhm... I think it was three days ago."

"Canter First Class **Princessnesian Princequillo**, take this little thing to the mess. Do not bring him back or hear a word he says until he has finished off a large warm mash, two apples, and a large stein of small beer. Am I understood?"

"Sir, yes Sir!"

"Follow me."

"This is too important! I can't waste any time!" Ferallus begged, threatened and tried to turn around.

When he returned to General Chiron and the map, he looked and felt much better. He had not realized how close to the edge he had been running.

"There we go! Now you don't look like a corpse out for a stroll. Now tell me about your idea."

"You mentioned dryads as being among the archers astride a centaur archer. They can be put to good use right now. Have them sing the hornets to allow their hives to be gathered into bags. A few of those dropped on the archer line right before the attack ought to keep them occupied."

"Senior Aide Forego Forli, a Bronze Hoof, please."

"Right away, General Chiron."

The aide returned just a few minutes later.

General Chiron turned to the winged messenger. "Ferallus, in a single day you have, on your own, developed four plans that I know of that will increase our chances of victory, and will definitely avoid many casualties. Lower your head."

He did as ordered and Ferallus felt something placed around his neck.

"Mythos Air Corps Scout, Messenger, Strategist Commander Ferallus av Synanee ga Horanden, it is my privilege to award you The Bronze Hoof of the Centaur Cavalry. Congratulations!"

He looked around and was shocked. Every centaur had dropped to one knee, fist on chest.

Ferallus dropped to one knee, spread two white wings to their fullest and bowed his head to the centaurs.

* * *

"My head feels like my skull is on Vulcan's anvil. Are the regular forces ready to go?"

The Newest New General's Aide said, "Regular troops are ready."

"How about the heroes? They don't have a clue about the pits. Are Odysseus, Perseus, Jason, Bellerophon, and Orpheus ready for action?"

The Newest New General's Aide said, "No, General!"

"By Cerberus's wormy steamers! Why aren't they ready?"

The Newest New General's Aide said, "They are piles of bones, General!"

"How the Hades did that happen?"

The Newest New General's Aide said, "Vorpal Bunny, General!"

"By a harpy's tasseled titties! Who put the Vorpal Bunny in there? That is one of our most valuable special forces!"

The Newest New General's Aide said, "With all due respect, you gave the order, General!

"I don't judge, General. I merely observe. You had several skins of the reinforced wines from the new distilleries in Athens, and may have been slightly inebriated when you decided to improve their morale by giving them a pet. Your new Aide tried to dissuade you, and you had him tossed out in the water… like the others."

The General said, "Oh, well. Everyone except me is expendable, anyways."

"Are the empty wine barrels in place?"

"Yes, General. The tarp is hammered down tight in case of wind."

* * *

A high flyer scout saw the column of purple smoke at General Chiron's camp and relayed the 'request strategist' request to Ferallus.

Ferallus grabbed Whirlaway and chose to gallop.

"What is your feedback on this?" General Chiron asked. "Once the archers have been dealt with, I plan to use naphtha-fueled arrowheads that produce a ground-hugging poison fog. What say you?"

"Too much for too little gain, General. But if fired at night, sleeping soldiers will take more damage and lives than in day time. They will also ruin enemy night vision. That allows daytime flyers a chance to work at night with a clear destination with a known altitude. Two passes from each flyer all from different directions dropping tar, oil, and flame. The giants can toss their harpy sacks. Let them try to sleep in that, and then have fun with rocks! Centaurs and their riders to arch arrows into the camp. One of their wells is close enough to the water for selkies to make that short a distance over land and befoul it. Satyrs on our bank scattered and screaming at will should keep us fairly safe. We'll laugh our asses off at their kicked ant hill. We should always look for chances to bolster our morale, even if it results in relatively minor damage.

"We should take care to not target their archers. We need them right where they are…

"General? What is that light? I can barely look in that direction."

"Don't look. Burning star metal burns bright enough to blind, even from a distance. We use small amounts of it with special eye protection to melt the stone and make channels for fresh water in to each troop area, and another for waste out."

"Does it melt metal, too?"

"Yes it does… oh, you brilliant gem of a soldier! We have six. I will get you four of them, and a satchel to carry them in. Don't worry if they seem small. One should be enough to permanently disable a large mystery machine."

"Please note for Whirlaway Blenheim's service record that his rank is "Mythos Air Corps Messenger, Scout, Stategist First Class."

"His idea about tossing the harpies gave me another."

"Tonight is for chaos, morale, and to identify hidden threats. The humans are clustered the closest in formation. After the archers are plucked, if huge sealed bags filled with oil are given to the giant class forces, we can come close to ending this while they are still busy recovering from the massacre of their archers. They would need all the oil from Air Corps as well. We can fill them so they are ready to pick up."

"I would say to use them tonight, but there is not enough time to get them made and filled at both camps in time. Tomorrow, the smoke from the burning oil will keep them from targeting flyers.

"After the first two turtle formations are clear, I will explain to them in a moment, two titans toss two blocks each to close the Strait and give the humans no way to move toward us in formation. The giants swing and hurl oil bags over the trees and into their camp. They move to a new position and repeat until they are empty, move to the nearest rock pile, and do what makes them happy. The oil also goes into their underground bunkers. Light the oil, roast most of the troops, General Hydra moves the flames where they are needed with waves. They have to retreat back, and we take the camp."

"Why did you say to let the first two formations cross freely?"

"General, this is from no one piece of information or observation. It is just this rolling feeling in my gut that something is wrong."

"Your sire's gut was rarely wrong. Let me know what you will of me."

"Leave the first two formations unharmed. Guide them out of the firing zone on the Strait. Those are sacrifices. General Geedubius is going to shoot the cannons through them to get you. He does not even pretend that any of his other forces will engage. They are the trap within the trap.

"I say that we are better than him! We do not kill except when we must! Most especially, we do not kill civilians, innocents, or the helpless! Even war does not justify their deaths at our hands except by accident. We actively seek to kill the Commander, but that is to put an end to his poison today, and make the skies full of Air Ball and grassy fields for Polo tomorrow! I believe we will gain a hundred more for our side without showing all we have, such as the tidal waves. Even if they do not join us, we avoid a hundred weeping scars on our souls! If we do kill them and they turn out to be slaves, is anyone still going to have the stomach for the hard things we must do? Will we care if we win the war or not once we reduce ourselves to the level of the men we despise?"

He was working hard to get the words out while standing at attention and sobbing.

Only when his eyes cleared did he see that every centaur had lowered themselves to both front knees and held fists over their hearts. Each head was bowed to him.

"Your tears show your noble heart. I will notify the other Generals."

"General Chiron sir, we can use the third Hekatonkheire from the back of the crescent. Would you please manage him with your other giant-class?"

"Certainly!"

"Their cannons with grapeshot can do a lot of damage, so let the big boys get the injured and dead out of the way quickly in addition to happy rock throwing. We leave no dead behind, be they centaur or sacrifice."

"And yes, General, we know medals are for parades and showing to grandchildren. But we have to have enough time to reach our flops before we can stow them."

"Ahhh… go home, both of you! You are bad influences on my troops."

"Thank you for the honors, General. We will do our best to be worthy of them."

After they headed to their General, Chiron's eyes followed them. "You already have, young ones."

"Tandornus and Vamitia, take tarps and load half the harpies onto each. Throw from opposite sides to maximize spread when the night attack commences. Use Air Corps Messenger Strategist Whirlaway Blenheim's suggestion about vinegar rags in your noses.

"The rest of you, if you do not have other specific orders, start making the sealed bags and filling them with oil."

* * *

"Damn, I'm going to miss this war. I think I'll get something going with Troy after this. Give me something pretty with tits for a trigger. I can give us a war in a month, and make it look like it's their own damn fault!"

Commander Three bemoaned, "But it won't be as much fun as crushing monsters, mutants, and abominations."

"Commanders, send out your stealth assault squads two hours after sunset."

The Newest New General's Aide said, "Sir, they have night fliers, and some of them are flamers."

"Are you questioning a Geedubius order?"

"No, General."

"They're expendable. Even after the battle this morning, the beasts are not going to believe that we were hurt so badly that we have to wait until tomorrow to attack again. They are going to expect another attack."

"These troops are merely going in to create some chaos, give them easily defeated forces to keep them underestimating us. Can animals even anticipate? If they are really lucky, they may even kill something as well."

A member of one of the stealth assault squads, in violation of orders, had been using the officers' latrine. He heard every word. He collected the other members of the stealth assault squads very quietly, and discreetly shared that bit of strategy amongst them. They developed a plan of their own.

* * *

Ferallus sent Whirlaway to General Hydra to explain the night's plans.

"Many will go to the nearest water to clean. This is something your singing lures can do, isn't it?"

"It is, thank you."

"We will avoid this area so that some of your girls can befoul the well there."

"You have my gratitude. This will do much for morale."

"Wait for falling signals in this color and pattern. They mark spots we need your waves to drift the burning oil to, too."

CHAPTER VI—You Are The Wind Beneath My Wings

Bacchus saw the white shape flying towards the camp. The pegasus circled twice and then forced the General to dodge falling meadow muffins.

"You little bastard! You have to land sometime, and I know where you sleep!

"By Herpes' Kiss! I wish that he were my son."

When Ferallus landed, Bacchus merely asked, "What took you so long?"

"General Chiron saw that I was on the brink of starvation and forced me to eat. Then he was impressed with my scouting and asked what I thought would be the best strategy. He liked what I suggested. Here, here and here… ignore sword and shield and use all archers. Move the haystacks in this line to maximize confusion and panic, and at the same time provide better safety for the centaurs and their riders.

"Then the big one!" He explained the oil bags. The camp was set to work making and filling them.

"Whirlaway is planning with General Hydra to see if it was possible for sylphs and nymphs to sing as many as possible out before the battle starts. The tidal waves will come when the centaurs attack, and the turtle is on the Strait there.

"I also asked if her people could put one or two of your stealthiest satyrs with some poison. Now that we know where the food for the bunkers comes from, it doesn't matter where they are, if the food is poisoned on the way.

"I also made an unordered side mission to recover some valuable resources.

"General Chiron asked my advice about his planned aerial bombardment and lethal gas weapon attack.

"Yes, General. I suggested night bombardment. And this… there… this… and just for sheer nastiness, this and this. Oh, best not to forget these!"

Bacchus looked fairly recovered. Not enough to plan anything more than a trip to his throne in the outhouse, but there was somebody home. He smiled when Ferallus opened his wings to let two more wineskins swing free.

"Hah! Good lad! I like you. I really do. Respected your sire a great bit. Admired him, but he was more of Chiron's temperament.

"He didn't laugh enough."

"My sire loved me, but he was as disciplined at home as though our house was in a war zone. He was raising me to be the same. I'm glad I found you, Bacchus."

"You know that before your first flight feathers finish growing in, you have a good chance of being killed in battle. Even if you are terrified, and you are far too smart not to be terrified, you know to laugh now more than any other time. Squeeze each second as if it were a grape and drink in joy like a good wine."

A nearby satyr stopped and said, "While Whirlaway was here less than an hour and terrified of you and afraid to laugh, Ferellus got him settled on a bedroll right next to him and said, "Whirlaway, you can relax and smile. This is Bacchus's camp and is as odd and twisted as he is.

"By the sagging buttocks of all the gods! If we may die tomorrow, then, let's laugh as much as we can until that final second." I think he gets it, Pops."

"Little one, was it a horse rolling a swan, or a swan doing a horse?"

"I can go get one of each. You try both and see which one gives birth to something with wings, and which gives birth to an alcoholic blowhard."

"You should have been born a satyr. They are your brothers in their hearts."

Once again, Whirlaway ended up reporting as Ferallus finished. He hung around and the two said in unison, "Is that a Bronze Hoof?"

It looked like the General would be good and drunk by game time.

"Now go get the commanders of the hippogriffs, manticores, every damn thing that flies and is on our side."

The General was starting to look maudlin again, so Ferallus grabbed Whirlaway.

"No more, Bacchus! You know that we love you, but I will not stand silent while we are insulted by you anymore. We young ones do this horrible thing so that you can have Bacchanals where everyone celebrates for a thousand more years. We get to be part of making that happen! Do you have any idea how honored and privileged we youngsters are to be part of this, the greatest defining moment of Mythos history? We don't want tears. We want the same respect you would give any adult soldier. Drink for us, but drink a toast for luck and laughter. We deserve better than your tears. I just wanted you to know how we see it."

"Thank you, Ferallus. I shall stop my tears and celebrate my young heroes as they deserve to be honored.

"Bodacious, put one skin under the bush with the others you hide from me. This one will be plenty. A child just told me to remember the power of joy."

The god of wine turned back around, gasped for breath several times, and then did the impossible… He dropped his wine skin. On the other side of where Ferallus had been standing was a large wineskin inflated with air, covered with tar, feathers and topped with a chicken head. Around its neck was a sign that read "For Pappa Bockbockbockus".

He looked around and caught Ferallus and that young centaur, Whirlaway head to head and stomping hooves in laughter.

When you can't find joy, count on those who care about you to make some. His tears were happy ones and sweeter than wine.

The two scouts went to their bedrolls so that Whirlaway could take off the medals, stow them, and they could exchange information.

They got hold of Pan and explained the poisoned food plan. They left it to him to find the satyrs and poisons.

CHAPTER VI ~ Assume The Position

"Pan! Pan! Get your fuzzy ass over here. Obey your father just once so I know what it feels like!

"What took you so long?"

"I was drinking wine from your hidden stash, Pops."

"Are those haystacks ready?"

"Yeah. Heavy as a Cyclops' balls, though."

"I want you and your brothers to move in the haystacks, ten here and the other ten here, all close to the bank for maximum reach into their camp. There is a hornet's nest of archers in the trees on either side of the Strait, so turn the haystacks to face that way.

"We are going to make every single one of them night-blind. Don't scream tonight. The archers cannot discover that they have been spotted.

"When you hear the horns, or see the dropped message cloths, you and the boys scream your throats raw. You are going to keep doing that for the centaur archers. They will make pass after pass with some of Hydra's girls doing cleanup on each sweep.

After the archers are dead, keep screaming into their camp while the centaurs continue back and forth, arching arrows into the heart of it."

In short time the orders were given.

"… Once they reveal anti-aerial emplacements, they become primary targets for all troops!

"Priapus! Priapus, you wanker, get over here!"

"Back off boy, a step back or you are gonna put someone's eye out with that thing. It's my own fault. She was there, long, thick and had a reservoir tip. How was I supposed to know that your mother wasn't a condom?"

"Pops, didn't the four hours of screaming tell you anything?"

"I though it meant I was doing one hell of a job.

"This young one has been awarded the Grape and Vine and a Bronze Hoof in a single day of his first week as a soldier. Pay attention and learn something."

"I suggested that Dryads sing hornet nests into bags. If delivered to us in time, we can drop them on the archers just before the centaur's first strafe. Those stingers should distract them."

"By the Kraken's ass crack! I should make you a General! Grab some food and rest. Priapus, you bring back the hornet sacks. Try actual work just one time."

Priapus turned and headed off. "Screw you, Pops! I'm on it."

"Sir!" Ferallus came to attention before General Bacchus.

"I may have to strangle you in your sleep."

"General! I did have one tweak I wanted to make to the hornet plan. We don't know what they have in the tents or what they really have in the back four formations. It may be a good idea to hold half of the hornets back for emergency response."

Soon, the troops were listening to their orders. "The centaurs use powdered starmetal to melt stone for their camp water distribution. It melts metal, even metal under canvas, quite happily, and once dropped requires only a ball of Prometheus' Fire to get it going… and blinds any troops who look directly at it… forever."

"The camp is making and filling giant bags of oil for the giant class to lob over the trees. After enough, their camp becomes a funeral pyre.

"Lord Bacchus, just tell me what you want slagged and consider it a pool of very hot metal."

"What's with the 'Lord Bacchus' crap? Oh… I understand, little hero. You've lost your heart and want me to know that you feel honored to have served under me. Is that it?"

"Not lost heart, General. Just facing reality that this might be the last time I get to tell you that, because I am going to fight proud and take a couple hundred with me as my honor guard."

"Then you are not your sire's get, after all. He never gave up. Never! If he was one against a hundred, he would fight until he fell, and then he would crawl to where he could fight bleeding on the ground and when a spear pinned him to the ground, he would throw rocks until they crushed his head."

"That was Horanden, and you are not his offspring. Get out! Not out of my presence, not out of here, I mean get your smart, heartless ass out of my Air Corps, because we don't need you! We need Horanden's true get. On my command as military commander and as a god, you are no longer welcome here. If you find Horanden's true get, send him to me for we desperately need him. Hundreds of lives are his to save or waste."

It took three large skins to get the god of revelry to stop weeping.

It took a lot longer for the young pegasus, both wings dragging in the dirt and bleeding.

Colonel Bodacious caught up with the yearling. "Ferallus, wait… please. I need to speak with you."

"Didn't you hear? I'm not Ferallus, I am just an imitator of him."

He looked at Bodacious. "It's too much, Bodacious. It's too much. How can I keep him and me and Whirlaway and you and Pan and the rest from going to pieces… and help direct the war… and plan and develop strategies out of our nonexistent resources… and be responsible for anyone killed if I make a mistake? How, Bodacious? I get three awards of honor in a single day and it isn't enough! Tell me how! Please, Bodacious, please tell me what to do. I'm five years old, so tell me how to do all that!

"Mamma's last gift was to get me here where I could find a home and make a family of my comrades. I did. With Bacchus and the satyrs and comrades in camp. Most of them do a whole lot more to win the war, but they still made me family. Now, even that is gone."

Bodacious leaned against him, gently stroking. "Don't stop. Keep talking."

"Mamma died from the wasting sickness. Our housekeeper stole anything she could carry. She wouldn't even help with Mamma's grave. I had to do it with my nose or hoof one stone at a time. When I was done, I talked to her a long time about how much I loved her and how she showed her love for me. Then I grabbed a butcher knife with my teeth, pushed it into the stones.

"Dead is better than being cold, empty, and alone and feeling dead inside. I threw my head down and felt the knife go through my throat. I remember all of it again. Away from Bacchus, it all comes back. I'm cold, empty, alone and feeling dead inside… again. Mamma can't help me again. Please show mercy and let me go find my knife."

"Oh, Ferallus, you magnificent child. You weren't giving up, you just reached a place far, far past anywhere a child of five years should be.

"Please let me help you to decide if you want to live. If Bacchus doesn't pull his head out, I will resign my service and go to find a home for me and my pegasus and centaur sons."

Ferallus found himself wrapped in the warm, very strong and comforting embrace of the minotaur who sees and hears it all.

"Ferallus, I need for you to do something for me. Close your eyes and breathe deep three times. Now with each breath in and out, look deeper. What do you see?"

"Do you mean the sparkles? I see them all the time."

"When did you first notice them?"

"When Bacchus took the wine from me laughing, he swatted my haunch hard enough to bruise. It made me happy because he was treating me like any other soldier.

"It's strange. I feel like I've been here for a long time but can't remember anything here before that scouting mission. Everyone in camp thinks I have been here a long time.

"After the smack, I felt like I had a home. That night two tiny sparks kept buzzing around while I was trying to sleep. There just gets more and more of them, but I am used to them now."

Bodacious used the ever-present wine skin to rinse the scrapes on the pegasus's wings and got him turned around.

Bacchus roared at the first sight of the minotaur and pegasus, "What in Hades is he doing here? He is banned and you are disobeying direct orders. What game are you playing, Bodacious?"

"No game Bacchus, this is emergency first aid. You seem to have slipped your head so far up your own ass that it is choking you, you heartless, ungrateful, arrogant, short tempered, childish piece of shit! That's what it's about.

"Put a hand on him, Bacchus. We both know you can feel any lie made when skin to skin.

"Now ask how old he is."

"Why? He's at least ten or he would not be in combat."

"Ask him!"

"How old are you, Ferallus?"

"I am five, Bacchus."

"By Hermes inflatable foreskin! I have falsely wronged you so horribly. Come here, child." He rocked the yearling, letting now be enough for a while.

Bodacious pointed out, "Bacchus, all of you are so used to seeing the glow. You've forgotten your own histories."

"Oh. Oh! The yearling is of one of history's greatest strategists, is an empathic demigod, and is a five-year-old child that I yelled at and treated that way."

"Ferallus, when your sire was twenty he had not, and could not have, accomplished all that you have done at five years," Bodacious put in.

"Find your heart, Ferallus. You may very well be the fulcrum that determines the balance of what remains of this war. I free you to make your own decisions and even to change Air Corps movements and tactics based on your second-by-second observations. The other two Generals you may advise."

"I wish that Bodacious had never asked those questions. Now I just feel cold and empty and alone again. I don't want to remember. I can't not remember. Please, just let me go so I can make all the hurt go away forever. Just let me go."

"You mean that. The only thing you want from us is enough mercy to let you go so that you can kill yourself."

Nod.

Bodacious said, "Bacchus. Other than this camp, he truly is a five-year-old child all alone in the world, and has already committed suicide on his mother's grave. If you cannot do right by him, I shall."

"Ferallus, would you feel less alone and empty if I was your pappa and all the other satyrs were your brothers and uncles?" Ferallus nodded against his chest.

"Not to make you feel better, but for real and forever?"

Ferallus looked up and nodded, his smile back where it belonged.

"Oh, my newest son, you are going to surprise Pan into accidental obedience."

"I doubt that, Pops. I spend a lot of time behind these bushes spying and drinking your wine. If you didn't do right by him, dawn would have seen you short a pegasus, a centaur and a son."

The minotaur said, "I would be with you."

"When he gets mad at you, he pees on your wineskins, and telling that is my pay-backs for you stealing my apple."

"I gave General Chiron my gut feeling about something. Based on things my sire taught me, now grown into instincts. He has agreed to allow the first two shield turtle formations to cross the Strait unmolested and be taken out of the firing zone. They are sacrifices and know it. If they cannot do anything about it, they are not soldiers. They are just made up enough to be mistaken for soldiers."

"General Chiron will allow them to cross unmolested if you and General Hydra agree."

"Ferallus, you take over. I am going to sit here, get drunk and scratch my balls."

"Pops, with all due respect, I will take your orders, take your wine, but I'll be buggered by a cyclops before I'll scratch your balls!"

"Get out of here before you are awarded the My Foot Up Your Ass."

"Yes, Pappa Bacchus!"

He got to the pegasi camp and was about to chow down again. Whirlaway stowed both their Hoofs.

"First General Bacchus. The same day General Chiron. When is General Hydra going to award you, little brother?"

"C'mon, I'm already blushing to my pinions. Oh, Whirlaway, don't let General Chiron see you going around wearing medals."

Everyone laughed and no one was jealous of the awards. No matter how many he got, it never changed how he treated his comrades one bit. He still felt junior to, or intimidated by many of them.

"Whirlaway, I'm glad you are camped with us. You're already a good friend. Keep your ears open too. The veterans here know a lot more than we do. We can learn a lot from them."

"The General needs two heavy flyers for a single sweep and night drop over the center of the human encampment. Big boys who can handle one or two arrows and get back safely. One light flyer able to carry burning Prometheus' Fire and drop accurately from high altitude and return. Sphinxes, please select two of your flight to assess merging abilities. Report to General Bacchus!"

"Now will you give me a chance to eat and drink? If General Chiron sees me so much as hungry again, he's going to skin me and use my hide as the awning of his command tent."

He curled around himself on his bedroll. He was feeling crushed by all that was happening, even the good things. A satyr skipped over and sat down, using the pegasus as a backrest. "Thanks. You're fluffier than any of our other brothers. I know you're scared and tired. But you're not alone, Ferallus. I didn't call you 'brother' lightly. Everyone here needs you, brother.

"Everyone here is also helping you stay up and on your hooves until the job is done. You can rest tomorrow after we've won."

"Brother, how are you called?"

"I am Fellatio."

"Thank you. I received the Grape and Vine because you commented on the stunt.

"Fellatio, I took one of General Hydra's best and replaced it with average stuff. Are you up to a drinking party tonight? Well… that answers that. I can see that you are very up for it. Get our other brothers and some friends to join us. Pegasi need someone to squeeze the bag for us."

The satyr grinned—actually, they always seemed to be grinning, "You got it!"

"I don't think you have a clue about how many friends you've made, and the respect you've earned."

"I'm just a fledgling and still too young to understand the rules."

"Brother, I swear that you are a satyr with wings. No wonder Pops adopted you."

"Thanks! I need to go over plans again."

He fell asleep instead.

* * *

CHAPTER VII—Sky Rockets In Flight...

In the night the assault squads left for their missions... revised... by them.

Shortly after, both giants tossed their payloads.

The sound of vomiting filled the night.

Two creature with huge bat wings flew low over camp. The cannons were a good distance apart, angled for the Strait, so the manticores spilled the pouch on the large cannon instead. Waking up covered in harpy crap and pieces of dead harpy created chaos in an army of orderly formations. Everyone searched for a place to get clean. General Hydra's girls were taking a short holiday on land inside the camp perimeter. Many found new boyfriends to wedge under tree roots a long way down, while the sisters sung more and more of them close enough for a hug.

Fire was dropped on the star metal, and night became day.

* * *

The next warning was called when two bright torches dropped from the sky. It had to be a high flyer trying to light the ground for some reconnaissance.

By the time anyone around the wine casks and tarp imitating the super cannon had wrapped several layers of cloth over their eyes and took stock, 15% of the troops were at least temporarily blind.

* * *

The drop was the signal for the centaurs' archers to launch the naphtha arrows.

These started wreaking havoc on the nearly blinded troops.

* * *

Full flights of day and night fliers dropped rocks. They picked up more and repeated.

Loud bangs began to come from every direction, and flyers began to fall.

The signal for 'last drop and return to base' was given.

Five pre-assigned flyers dropped bags in the cauldron before the smoke became caustic. The cauldron bubbled over and flowed downhill until it reached an area of ground that melted away. Screams echoed from it for several minutes.

Ferallus flew a single, low-level circuit, carefully spreading a light dusting of star metal. When fire hits, bunkers become easy to see.

The two satyr assassins heard vomiting, moaning, gurgling, and then a whole lot of silence from three different bunkers. They smiled, and General Hydra had Colonels Left and Right Head take them back across.

When they finished, the Air Corps headed back to General Bacchus's camp where a landing strip had been marked out with torches. All the injured were able to fly back. A hippogriff with part of her head gone was the only fatality.

* * *

While the three branches of the Mythos Army had some fun before the end, the humans' secret assault squads removed their armor and weapons and laid them across their arms. They marched to the centaur camp. When they were far enough from General Geedubius's encampment, they lit torches and announced their surrender every few paces.

They were no longer expendable. They were well-fed and well treated. They were prisoners of war, and were restrained in a humane manner. All-in-all, it was far better than they had expected.

Two announced that they had basic field medic training.

General Chiron said, "By prancin' Apollo's animal wives! I have the start of an infantry!"

One of the prisoners begged to speak to an officer. Finally they took him to General Chiron.

"What is it? We appreciate the peaceful surrender, but still have a war to wage."

"General, I am Private Darmiar. I was one of the shoulder cannon light artillery. There are twelve of them. They are easiest to load with the muzzle up. They get sprinkled within formations rather than being clumped together. The vulnerable shields mean they can aim only overhead most of the time. Anything other than a smooth, clean muzzle and the fire powder inside will make the whole thing blow up. Small packets of sand not tied closed can save a lot of your flyers. Ten more need repairs and are stowed away. I know where."

"They had a dummy cannon in the back. We know the real one is behind that. They were waiting for our giants before they revealed it. What was your father's name?"

"Nabius, sir!"

"Troop Leader! Grab rider straps and take Mythos Infantry Senior Sergeant Artillery Specialist Darmiar Nabius to General Bacchus. Thank you, Sergeant. You and your men have nothing to fear."

As they started bouncing their way across the field, the soldier was sick until they reached a gallop and the ride became smooth. He laughed with delight.

The two field medics moved to the hospital tents. They took care of broken bones and stitches, leaving the more skilled doctors to focus on the seriously wounded.

* * *

Sleep is a luxury in the military, but instead, the wine came out. It seemed that almost everyone had stashed a skin in reserve for the last night. Very few thought Mythos would survive tomorrow, so screw a couple hours of sleep in exchange for a few last hours with good comrades.

Ferallus made the first toast. "To our boss, the Lord of Flatulence!"

* * *

General Geedubius laughed to himself. "Finally, it comes with the dawn! All that everything else has been leading up to. The final battle, teaching beasts the true power of Man. I can hear it in the night, smell it, and taste it like the thick copper taste of blood."

"On the morrow I am finally free to teach the animals that they cannot defeat human ingenuity and numbers with falling turds. My skin tingles and my nipples explode with delight!"

CHAPTER VIII ~ You did it, you damn dirty...not apes!

It would probably be the last day he had the chance to do it, so Ferallus wore his medals and the laurel around his neck.

He dropped the signal for the centaurs to charge up the sides. Two hornet sacks on each side of the Strait were for the archers. Satyrs stood ready. The turtle formation was not moving yet. The Mariner signaler asked if he should go.

Ferallus dropped "no".

As soon as the centaurs started towards each other up the sides, the signal for the satyrs to scream was dropped. Humans scattered, some jumping into the water. They returned to position just in time for another strafe.

The centaurs turned and began another strafe. They signaled the satyrs to scream again when they spun to head back. The girls jumped in after each strafe and got a surprising number of enemy archers.

That was it. Repeated three more times, and there were not enough archers left to make a difference.

Six centaurs were dead, would not survive, or needed to be aided on their way.

The last five had been killed by Geedubius when he ordered the cannons loaded with grapeshot and fired at the centaurs through the trees… and his own archers.

Ferallus signaled the order for the Giants to throw oil. Bags began flying over the trees. They landed on humans who suddenly felt very flammable.

The Mythos centaurs continued firing over the trees, one in five a fire arrow. Soon pools of burning oil spewed orange flames and black smoke, turning the camp into Hades. Screams that no human could make marked two more bunkers. The sprinkled starmetal melted away the hidden covers of nearly every hatch. Burning oil was sent to each of them. When each giant was out of oil bags, they happily switched to rocks. The Mythos Air Corps moved in with hot oil, sand and fire, dropping these on areas where soldiers were trying to regroup.

* * *

"Perfect! The beasts are as stupid as milk cows." Geedubius happily ignored the loss of what was probably 700 of his 1300 soldiers. It was going to get much worse as the burning oil spread.

"Dump the river cauldron. Send the lambs, and uncover the light ballistae. As soon as those slimy mudfish try to escape the poisoned water, mow them down with the ballistae. The lambs will soak up whatever the goldfish have left."

* * *

Ferallus was supposed to stay out of direct combat, but he decided to take a chance. He dove and dropped star metal and fire target flags at the cannons, a packet in the cauldron and two hornets on the witch. One must have crawled out and been angry enough to sting him on the neck.

General Hydra kept the burning oil moving with waves in search of underground bunkers. One pass caught the star metal and it blazed. It was short of the cannons, but quickly burned their wooden ramps and platform. All four cannons rolled away or were tilted at odd angles that made all but one of the smaller ones unusable.

That one was remounted and usable in time to watch the lambs crossing freely and getting away without dying.

The humans advanced. When they were three fourths of the way through the water, Ferallus dropped the hold tidal wave signal. Aerial units with oil, tar and fire circled, but waited. The scattered sound of shoulder cannons exploding boosted morale. The sand would save many lives.

Banks of ballistae began taking a devastating toll on the flyers until their fire finally hit the oil. It lit it, and the ballistae, and the men using them.

Once visible under the turtles' shields, the 'soldiers' proved to be peasants and slaves; all but one who was in the uniform of a high ranking officer. Geedubius managed to kill 17 Mythos troops, and wound 11 others with grapeshot through the trees.

Geedubius' Triumph began marching down the Strait. Ferallus dropped the Titans' throw-block order. Four blocks of stone the size of two horses and a chariot crashed on top of the Triumph, eliminating two thirds of the formation and sending the others back or into the water.

* * *

Ferallus saw the steam around the bend. He flew to look, dropping a second throw-rock signal for the giants. He saw the huge cauldron being dumped. He added two signals to forces a long distance away on both sides. Cyclops and two giants to assist to the east, and the Horanden to the west.

He flew down to General Hydra. "General, there is poison in the water behind you! You are in a trap! If you and your troops do not cross the Strait to the water on the other side, you are dead."

"Thank you... child! But I will order my own troops, if you please."

"General! If you do not get yourself and your people moving right now, I will tie all three of your necks together, piss on you for lube and slide you across myself. Now do it!"

There was something in his voice. The General did not even realize she was doing it. The child was not out of sight and she was issuing his orders.

* * *

When Ferallus was up again, he was able to see another set of uncovered ballistae aimed at the flyers. He climbed to the six Chimeras, pointed out the machines, and told them to flame them and the soldiers manning them; but to come in at an angle that would keep them safe from the shoulder cannons. It was only partially successful. Some were taken out, but the weapons hit a manticore, a griffin, and a pegasus. They were forced to drop tar, pass after pass, until one of General Hydra's waves drove the oil where it was needed. They had not known about the two ranks of heavy duty ballistae behind the other until they and their operators went up in flames. Only the griffin was able to fly out of the fire zone. At least ten shoulder cannons had exploded. A second sweep took out the odd weapons and those who fired them. Back to sweep light and heavy ballista, while Geedubius rolled out Big Bessie.

The oil still burned and another 300 more of Geedubius's men were dead.

Two giants, one cyclops and a Hekatonkheire all closed their eyes and began throwing stones as fast as they could pick them up. Screams allowed them to narrow their aim.

An angry and deafening shout got them to stop. The giant cannon had finally been pushed out of cover and had shouted her vengeance. The corner of one of the blocks disappeared, and its cyclops came to a bloody end.

No one could approach the huge cannon until it cooled. The greenery near it was curling and turning brown. It was hot. It needed a long cool-down period. Ferallus signaled the giants to have fun with rocks.

He was heading back to the Generals for reviewing tactics when he heard a scream. He looked up to see a nymph falling from her pegasus; an arrow in her side. A lucky shot from below. He maneuvered himself to let her fall on him. He had expected it, but screamed as his wing broke. He had to land on water, but the spin was towards the wrong side of the Strait. He made it as close to the bank as he could, and felt her pulled off of him. He managed to drop the satchel of star metal onto the bank before he went under. Even part of his head was under by the time he felt himself being pulled free.

"Get him to the medics, quick."

Ferallus managed, "Stop, you fuzzy, misshapen, six-legged bugs. Must tell Generals, help me save them—"

"By Athena's buggered owl! He's Horanden's love child with Bacchus! Tell us what they need to know. One of us will gallop to each camp. One of General Hydra's commanders is listening here, too."

"Cauldron is trap to send high flyers falling. I dropped two hives near her. Other four formations real. Large objects coming from behind. Don't know what they are. Two new cannons in place in less… than… hour… Four cannons ours. They must - hidden ways - handle flyers - real battle… mu… tell…"

By the time he finished his report, he was too near death to go to healers, but they were on their way to him. Several wept when they saw him.

"Stop crying and do something to stop the bleeding. Start pouring clean water over him. Do you still want to court martial and hang him, General Hydra? All three of your heads together aren't worth a tenth of him. Get a bucket brigade and stop that poison from burning deeper. Help me roll him over."

"Oh, gods! He's been shot in the neck!"

Hippocrates put a wad of cloth there and leaned heavily on it, but did not look hopeful. He had stayed up a long time after the 'sting'.

Hippocrates could do little until the ongoing damage was stopped, but had no way to do that. One of the other great healers of the Mythos army was Asclepius. The once towering and mighty Olympian god of healing was now a fragile old man led by a boy. He could not see well, but laid his hand upon the yearling and started to gently fade, even as Ferallus started healing. The boy tried to pull the god back. He was already mortally wounded by his lack of worshippers.

His smile was glorious. "You make me so happy to be able to give this to you, child. I have earned my rest. This one is the first newborn god of the new age. He is already a demigod in power. I choose to give what is left of me to this hero, both healing and the last of me that is divine. A large heart and larger future lay ahead of him than can be said of me."

As he faded, every creature that ran, walked or flew paid homage to him and saluted.

A laugh was all that was left of him, and that too faded.

"Look! A thin layer of fur on his body and fluff and tiny feathers on his healed wings!"

"Look at his feathers! Each one has gold around the edges. He is Divine!"

* * *

Whirlaway galloped by and grabbed the pouch. "Anyone who isn't a healer, get your asses back to the fight. There's a war being fought, if you hadn't noticed."

"Call in infantry!"

Several hundred of Geedubius's infantry came up from behind the centaurs and wreaked awful havoc on them as they slaughtered their way to General Geedubius.

Now, that was war as he ordered it to be. He didn't question where the men came from.

Once the Infantry was inside and halfway through the camp, the centaurs regained their feet and began to decimate the frontline troops who had to keep lifting shields to block falling rocks. Those riding the centaurs jumped off as their comrade mounts switched to sword and shield and leapt the stone blocks and engaged.

It was time for the slaves and their handlers to arrive with the new war machines.

* * *

When he woke, Ferallus, looked up and saw Bacchus smiling. Hippocrates bowed.

"There's the hero!"

"By Hephaestus's mithril dildo! You're uglier than Cerberus giving himself a muzzle to lipstick menage-a-toi!"

"That coming from a drunken version of the three hags' shared ballsac!"

"It is you, Pegasus! I know I promised not to cry for my young heroes, but let me have a couple happy ones, okay? I thought I was going to lose you. Did you really tell General Hydra that if she didn't do as you said right then that you were going to tie her necks together and drag her across?"

"I just wanted my Pops to be proud of me. Never respect for anyone, but always respect for everyone."

Bacchus picked him up very gently. "I am very proud of you, Pegasus. Very proud. You saw, evaluated, made decisions, and ignored all three Generals as you started throwing orders left and right."

In spite of the care, being lifted hurt and Ferallus could not stop his wail.

"Son, listen to me. Close your eyes and find your sparkles. It is hard to do when you are hurting really bad, but you need to find them. Now one by one send them to where it hurts. When they are easier to move, move more at a time. Keep going until about a quarter are left. The others will return soon, and you don't want to go empty. That is horribly dangerous."

Ferallus relaxed, moved and smiled, "I'm just sore now."

"No, child. You do not have advanced experience for healing. You did pain management on yourself."

"You saved ninety-six humans in those dummy formations. Countless of our side's lives. Allowed us to re-evaluate our plans and you are about to see them go into effect.

"Over half of their formations were killed by your oil, and you roasted Special Forces in two or more underground bunkers. Another three were poisoned; a third seems to have been empty… or at least nothing came out."

"Why do people call me Pegasus and bow?"

"How did you become one of us, lad? You glow with a small amount of the essence of what makes us gods"

"It doesn't matter, Pops. I'm just one of the troops… for a little longer at least."

"Pegasus, lad. It does matter. You are the first new divine since we gods began to weaken. I must make that clear… we need to know how you became divine so that we know where to look for others."

Divine or not, the yearling was still a child, one who was weeping, "I don't want to feel it again. Please ask Bodacious. Please."

"Of course I will. You don't need to think or remember the other part for now. What was the first thing you remember here?"

"Uhm… nothing, until that scouting flight, and then I was walking up the hill towards you and the Air Corps."

"There will be a military tribunal after. You knew that there was going to be a price to be paid when you did it."

"Yes I did, Pappa Bacchus. But I actually thought of you and decided, "Screw the rules. I'm gonna save some lives and win a war!"

"Oh! My medals burned off."

"They were collected and are being kept from idiots who would clean and polish them. They represent so much more as they are.

"So, are you ready to watch the end of the war… not battle, the war?"

"Can't answer with my mouth so dry, *hint, hint*."

Bacchus chuckled while drizzling a couple swallows down the young one's throat. He carried the child to watch what he made possible.

"Geedubius had no more cannons. Placing all four of them together must have been somebody else's mistake. The remounted belcher had not been locked down and shot backwards though several tents, killing the one aiming the cannon and several in said tents.

"Remember all the dummies tied to the backs of the centaurs? Remember the reports of humans taking minotaur slaves to the camp? Remember the three contraptions you couldn't identify?

"Sixty live human 'slave handlers' replaced sixty of Geedubius' troops with cut throats and were dragged away in the night. The three machines are from the Munitions Manufacturing Factory in Sparta. The 'slave' minotaurs Red Rock, Tornado, Oscar, Little Yellow Jacket, Bushwhacker, and Blueberry Wine are inside, excited to see what they can do. This should be fun.

"Oh look! 400 of Geedubius' light infantry are attacking the centaurs from behind. Oh, dear us. Look how so many are past the stones already—there go the rest.

"We made it look as if we were falling for the witch, who turns out to be none other than Sadamyuh herself; very powerful but very stupid. Still smart enough for the water poison trap. That would have worked and killed almost every mariner, if it was anyone other than you reporting it. We came in at her loaded with oil and Prometheus' Fire. Then we banked and doused every tent and covered structure still remaining after your oil bath."

"By the Furies' Fishy Fuzzy Snatches! Another hatch! That's a basilisk, a badly burned and pissed off basilisk!"

"I had more pouches left."

"Whirlaway has it. Wait."

The little centaur waved three flags.

A giant got the pouch and threw it at the basilisk. The other giant threw the fire, and the basilisk's threat was eliminated. A stone giant was no longer a threat to the humans, either. He would become a statue and symbol of the sacrifices it took to fight the way to somewhere to call home.

"Whirlaway has been directing operations and orders from Generals Chiron and Hydra and me. Who would have guessed that you both had it in you? A yearling terrified and shaking at our banter, now one of the primary directors for entire forces of our generals.

"You should have seen it when Geedubius' Special Forces died before they could even climb to daylight. It seems they were open territory forces. Thought there were gorgons in one. One of them almost made it out before becoming BBQ.

"General Geedubius personally ordered the first two shield formations to advance on the Strait. But the infantry were in the way and had to weave and press their way through. When in place, one set off the purple smoke that signaled the attack. 400 from the front.

"He ordered the first two war machines to advance behind them. He repeated the order several more times, getting more furious every second, until he ordered the last two shield formations to attack the war machines for ignoring his orders. He was so busy screaming and cursing that he missed the tidal wave that took out about 520 of his soldiers on the Strait. Satyrs' screams caused 21 to jump into the poisoned water; 13 were lured to the depths; and everyone else fought to be the ones to finish off the rest.

"Back in the camp, one formation broke off and surrounded Geedubius, who was grateful for the safety until he realized that they weren't his soldiers. They crossed the Strait with flags to identify them as the Mythos soldiers.

"The 'slave' Minotaurs had fun seeing what the war machines could do… using their last human troops still in their formations as our target practice, while the new Mythos Infantry, formerly Geedubius' Infantry, was mopping up everyone not in formation.

"The Mythos soldiers turned over Geedubius and returned to the battlefield. The enemy still had around 250 soldiers while the Mythos had only around 68 centaurs, 55 aerial, and 60 marine troops; a couple cannons and the three cannon machines and 380 light infantry. Most tried to run, to meet up with the forces of General Montgomerius, but there was no way out. Three turtle cannon machines blocked the way back. Shoulder cannons, bow and arrow, Air Corps circling overhead, and stone-happy giants convinced all of them to surrender."

CHAPTER IX ~ Sparkles & Bronies

The dead could finally be seen to. The Mythos bodies went on pyres, and the humans were buried. They dug a long trench and wrapped each body in waxed cloth and laid them reverently. Healers worked non-stop on the wounded. Their only breaks were a quick sip of gin from the still in their tent. They tended to cycle between clowns one minute and self-pitying maudlin whiners the next, but they did good work. Only two more died.

The humans were buried by their traditions, with markers made for those who could be recognized. The Mythos were sent free on the pyres or to the sea bottom with stones.

The lambs looked horribly confused. Their dead had been laid to rest with honor. They were being fed good, warm food and small beer or watered wine. Many went up to the 'monsters' and hugged and cried their gratitude. Women pushed centaurs away from the stoves and ovens and shooed them out of the kitchens. Soon, good food was coming out fast.

An infantry soldier ran up to Pegasus. "I was assigned to check all the bunkers. Got you these from one. Rabbit feet are lucky, right?"

"How much luckier do you think Vorpal Bunny paws are?"

Pegasus laughed and looked in the bag, "No, this is not right. You keep one. Me, Whirlaway and one of our satyr brothers will get the third. How does that sound?"

"Like I've been told to expect from you."

* * *

The titans were finally free to start hauling huge, blocks of basalt from where they had been cutting them, in a quarry three coves further down from the encampments. One human ship tried to stop them. A single cut stone was thrown at them, and the ship ceased to be a ship.

They began to build a giant curved wall in an arc going from bank to bank of the Strait on their end. They built in sections of fifteen times the height of a man and twenty long strides thick, each one another defense. They had weapon emplacements with a giant and a Hekatonkheire, armed with huge piles of stones. They had the 24 cannons from the three turtle cannon machines, Geedubius's large canons, a belcher—the other had been too close to the star metal and was ruined—and 12 repaired shoulder cannons. There were odd v-shaped indentations periodically along the base at the wall.

The giant and the Hekatonkheire were extremely happy when one advanced unit arrived to scout the situation and report back. Bloodstains don't report much.

In twenty hours the first two sections of the mainland wall were completed. The titans built stairs and weapons placements at the top. The first were the 2 larger of Geedubius's cannons.

The Mythos people who had chosen not to fight or had decided to stay with the humans started appearing in a steady flow, with wagons of supplies, families and housewares.

The word was spreading for the Mythos creatures to come home. Singly and in groups, they came out of hiding and made their way to what had been Crete.

Citizenship in the new hard-fought home was no longer free for those who had not fought. They were told that all would be explained at an Assembly soon.

Part of the wall was done. The rest of the defense spread in a long line.

The reinforcements arrived the next morning. The Commanders spoke quietly for several minutes before agreeing that even a two-thirds completed wall was a bad sign. They ordered the war machines rolled into place.

On the signal, every defensive emplacement, including the v-shape for aiming Big Bessie and giants opened fire. They focused on the humans' officers. A single volley eliminated them.

Seeing nearly a quarter of their forces dead or wounded in less than fifteen minutes after entering the zone claimed by the Mythos, the humans turned around and headed back. Their soldiers refused to pull their war machines, and they were abandoned. Their slaves left formation, grabbed the machines, and followed the Mythos signalers on top of the wall who waved them in. Centaurs went out and collected all of the wounded. When it was safe to do so, they assigned the healthy humans to burial detail. They gave the humans a bag of small silver coins to put on the eyes of their dead.

Soldiers saw their dead and wounded being tended by the enemy, where their own Generals had left them laying in the dust. By ones and twos, then small groups, and finally two whole squads with leaders, the humans took off all armor and laid it along with their weapons across their arms. Their dead were laid out in the burial trench. They were called over to identify whom they could for grave markers, and to honor their dead brothers in arms.

The dead were covered. The soldiers and their equipment were brought inside, had their wounds treated, were fed, given a place to bed down, and several skins of wine to ease their fear. The next day the prisoners all joyfully joined the Mythos Army of Free Crete.

* * *

The other two Hekatonkheires remained on duty at the walls at the either end of the six coves. Montgomerius had troops at both walls, but the constant barrage of stones was deadlier than his war machines. He decided that the cost was too high and retreated. In the night, another 230 surrendered quietly and were lifted over the wall. When the Mythos whispered the offer of land and freedom over the wall, 190 more. Montgomerius had both divisions meet up far from any walls. He discovered that nearly half of his command had been lost without his knowledge.

The Army of Free Mythos went out with their cannons and giants. They collected both of Montgomerius's was machines. The hundred civilians that followed the warriors explained their offer for any who chose it, and left. As they left, they were directed to go past the rawhide circle that Geedubius was bound on. Mongomerius hated Geedubius as much as Geedubius hated him. He ordered his men to ignore the wailing general.

Montgomerius had to report that Geedubius had lost all his troops and been taken and was killed by harpies. Then he had to report that he was returning with only 170 men. He was left alive so that he could report that attacking again would never be worth the cost.

* * *

"How about Sicily? No one gives a crap about it. We don't even need an excuse to declare war."

"And those lithe, black-haired boys, glowing after rubdowns of olive oil. Their taut, young buttocks… I mean every officer needs an aide de camp, don't they?"

"Seeing them shedding their robes and swimming in the clear water, teasing and playing together until they lay out to rest and dry…"

"Enough already, General Sodomitieus, General Pedophelius! Who cares why we go? Let's kill people already!"

* * *

There were two formal assemblies after everything had been accounted for.

All except those on defense duty attended.

Geedubius was stripped to his skin. Priapus brought forth a jar. He rubbed some of the ointment, that no one wanted to know the origin of, on Geedubius's member. This caused it to rise to stiff erection, to the point of pain. It was destined to stay that way for life. He was outspread on a large rawhide frame. This was rolled well outside the wall being constructed. The frame was braced, and he was left out for the harpies to use as stud service for as long as they chose to let him live. As he was being rolled away he screamed, "You can't do this to me, you filthy animals! I am Geedubius! Do you hear me? I am Geedubius!"

Laughter followed him all the way to his last home.

Before Pegasus was brought before the Generals, General Hydra awarded him the Waterspout for saving so many of her forces. Regardless of its propriety, those lives merited the award. And the two Colonels' heads were having a field day teasing the General for jumping to a child's orders.

"Pegasus, do you understand why you are here?"

"Yes, General's I do."

"Why do you believe you are here?"

Pegasus began listing violations of regulation.

"You are your father's get.

"That is not why you are here, little one. What is the difference between a hero and a traitor?"

"Success and good PR?"

"Save us all. You are already your new father's son."

Even all three of the General's heads laughed loud and long.

It took a long time for the cheering to stop.

"Relax, Pegasus Reborn, you are here to be cherished, not punished. I do have a couple questions of my own that you need not answer if you do not wish to.

"Pegasus, how old are you?"

"I am slightly over the five-years-old limit for non-combatants."

"How long have you been able to fly?"

He looked sadly at the nearly naked pink limbs that were supposed to be wings, "Over a year... almost fourteen months, General."

Shocked whispers swirled. Pegasus was the equivalent of a 10-year-old human child.

"What is the minimum age to serve in military capacity in a zone of combat?"

"It is ten years."

"So you lied your way in?"

"I believe so, Generals. I don't remember coming here. I think Mamma sent me."

"Why did your mare let you join?"

"It hurts too much! Can I tell later?"

"Of course, hero."

Bodacious wrapped a comforting arm over his back. "Now I have Pops and my brothers and uncles like Bodacious, Colonel Left Head. And General Chiron. They can help me say I love you and good-bye to Mamma."

Chiron stumbled a bit. He had not known that Ferallus felt that way about him. Chiron spoke the verdict: "On this, the first day of the Mythos Army of Free Crete, we modify the code to allow orphans to join service that they feel less helpless, surrounded by their fellows to guard and guide them. We have many vacancies in the command structure of the new army, and we are happy to accept thrice awarded... What was that? Four times awarded Pegasus Reborn as a First Lieutenant."

Someone must have spread the word. Nearly everyone in the crowd turned away and bent down to wiggle bare butts to Pegasus. They also decided to get seriously falling-down-drunk to honor the hero.

"There are unpleasant tasks, laborious, some even foul. But all need to be done to free up personnel who can keep our new home safe and growing.

"First, all of you who were not smart enough to avoid fighting at our side, you and all the Mythos coming home to us are full citizens effective immediately. You are free to pick a plot of land suitable to your needs, build your own home, plant and harvest, breed and slaughter, and raise happy children. We ask that only, when you sacrifice, you think of those Mythos who made your bounty possible."

The crowd was totally silent. Land? Their own? Crops and livestock their own? Share with those who made it possible and give thanks in the old way? They were still trying to remember how their mouths worked when the God of Excess continued.

"We started with nearly 10,000. We finally reached our home with under 200 Mythos and 210 humans who survived. Those who fought at our side helped us make it home. They have paid their dues. Do not expect to get what they have without some cost.

"To all of you who chose to remain neutral, give us three years' service and you shall be made a full citizen."

"To all who fought against us, give us five years' service and be made a full citizen.

"Those who are paying in years will receive a small amount of gold each year to save or spend as they wish, along with a new set of clothing and sandals. We don't want slaves indentured for a number of years.

"Our offer is extended to those who we forced to surrender in the final battle. Join with us doing your 5 years in the military, or leave your armor and weapons behind.

"Any skilled tradesman or artists paying time can do so by practicing their craft.

"In all instances, settling or building homes or farms on any of the islands that are now ours is by permission only."

"Finally, I declare that in two months hence there shall be the first Bacchanal in seven years!"

He started to leave them to their cheering and toasting. Two titans passed him, each carrying two perfectly cut blocks of white marble. They set them in place and four sculptors set to work.

From the first stone chip to fall, the humans dashed to claim them. They put them on leather thongs, and tied them around their necks.

"I want every statue of Pegasus Reborn to be of him as he is, how you knew him. No powerful thing with wings outspread and forelegs kicking."

Hydra said, "General Bacchus, Pegasus Reborn seems to have more of the divine in him that can be accounted for by our beloved healer..."

He explained to Colonel Bodacious that he first noticed his "sparkles" inside "on the day I swatted his haunch as I would any soldier. That was the day that he felt at home again. It started with two 'sparkles that were buzzing around when he closed his eyes and kept getting more and more all the time.'

"Losing home and family... his mother... you will laugh at me but... he committed suicide on her grave. He still remembers the pain. He believes his Mamma sent him here where his first memory was that scouting flight."

"Pegasus, think of your feelings about your sire and dame and me."

"I loved and respected my sire, but he would never cuddle. Mamma made everything warm and safe and happy. I could play without Sire giving me stern looks. She was a lot like you, Bacchus."

"That is what I thought, hero.

"It wasn't anything we did to him except to trigger what was already there. His mother had to have had a speck of the divine to send him to where he could find what he needed when he sacrificed himself."

Bodacious said, "Bacchus provided the warm love that he missed and gave him a giant, silly family to play with, and it started. He really is a true divine."

"How strong is he?"

"Demigod around Pan... No it's growing. It must be the stone chips. He's not a demigod. New gods for a new age are being born! Pegasus is the first of them!"

Both Generals shook their heads. "Another Bacchus? At least as powerful. Where can we sign up to immigrate out of this madhouse?"

"Why don't you two join the others and drink to the hero?"

"I have a hero to care for. It was an honor to serve with both of you. I will never admit that in public, of course."

When they reached camp and Bacchus took Pegasus to his bedroll, there was a very sad young centaur already there weeping quietly.

"Whirlaway! Did no one tell you that he was going to live?"

Sad child turned to fierce combat warrior in a blink. "Yes, General. I have been waiting to find out where the court-martial is to exile him.

"By your pustule ridden ballsac! I'm going too, and there is not one little thing you can do to stop me, even if you are a god!"

"You have known him less than two days."

"I don't care, he's my brother!"

Bacchus laid Pegasus down on his bedroll.

The little thing was asleep almost immediately. He had done his job and could finally rest.

"Whirlaway, hold onto these medals for your brother. Do not allow them to be cleaned or repaired, only left as they are after the poison water, and one given after. They speak even more highly of his heroism. I never saw or heard anything about the silver and copper laurel. How many of these things did he get in just two days?

"Whirlaway! On your hooves for your commander!"

"For your outstanding duty and addition to the Mythos Air Corps, imaginative and laughingly disgusting use at every opportunity to turn anything you could think of into a weapon, your calm head on the battlefield and your outstanding bravery and loyalty. For carrying on for him when Ferallus fell, I bestow upon you the Order of The Grape and The Vine."

Bacchus left the two young friends to comfort each other.

* * *

In the morning there was no sign of them. He called for Pan and Bodacious. Only the minotaur answered the summons.

"Where are Pegasus and Whirlaway?"

"I don't know, Bacchus, but there is a scroll on your rock."

Dear Pops,

By now, I suspect you know that you are missing your satyr, centaur, and pegasus sons, as well as a big and varied handful of Air Corp Mythos, a half-dozen centaurs, and a good handful of Hydra's girls. We took a good many humans with us. All of them got married last night. Eat life in big bites! My brothers are very young and need someone older to help guide them, to keep them happy and rotten to the core. We stole half of your wineskins until the vines we stole take and start producing grapes along with everything else we need… or want. We also stole your private, fancy galley for off-coast, night, torch-lit, adults-only, nude swim parties. Oh, I buggered your houseboy. I can't tell you where we are going, but I have heard that there are some killer waves to surf at the isle of Kimolos.

With absolutely, positively no respect at all,

Pan

"You sneaking, thieving, deceitful, horny, maggot filled scrotum! Get back here! Give me my wine! I will hunt you down, I will squeeze you back into a sperm, you sack of rotting meat and harpy farts!

"Aaah… now that's what I needed! I feel much better."

Bacchus sat on his rock and grabbed a half full wineskin. No wine or any other liquid came out, just the foul smell of sulphur, harpy feathers and rotten meat making him gag and his eyes burn. There was a bit of paper rolled up in the mouth of the skin. He pulled it out and read, "Gotcha! Lots of love and no respect, Pegasus and Whirlaway."

He laughed himself off his rock.

"Yup! They're my sons!"

What if uplifting animals had happened early enough that World War II had had rat soldiers? Would this have made warfare any easier for human soldiers? Or harder?

Or would it have made much difference at all?

Humans or rats; soldiers will be soldiers.

Shells On the Beach

by Tom Mullins

1917

The lab wasn't so much hot as it was humid, a stark contrast to the cold British winter outside. Built inside of a bunker meant poor ventilation and a stark decor, with bare pipes and wires lining the walls in dark stripes. Brigadier Powell removed his hat to wipe the sweat from his balding head and followed the Private down a concrete hallway. They stopped outside of a metal door and the Private asked the superior officer politely to wait outside. Powell grunted in the affirmative, waited for the Private to disappear through the door, then stuck his calloused fingers down his collar in an effort to relieve himself of the uncomfortable heat that was building underneath his crisp uniform. A moment later the Private returned followed closely by a short man in a greasy lab coat and thick glasses.

"Brigadier Powell, so good to see you," said the scientist, offering his hand.

"Indeed," Powell said with a frown, grasping the hand but taking great care to not let the sleeve of the lab coat touch his uniform. The scientist was a good foot shorter than the military man. "I've come to speak to you about your research, Avery. An informal inspection, if you will."

"Of course, of course." Avery normally came across as a man with a rather nervous disposition, but today he instead wore a gleeful smile. "Private, you may leave us."

"Yes, Professor." The soldier gave a smart salute and then marched off back towards the entrance.

"Please, Brigadier, if you'll follow me," said Avery, opening the metal door and leading him into another barren hallway, this one with doorways that led to various offices, sleeping quarters and storage rooms. Powell followed, his frown still dominating his jowls.

"You've had six months, Avery. Command feels you have gone too long with little results to show for it," said Powell.

"Too long? With respect, Sir, translating advanced chemical formulas from German is no easy task. Not to mention that Steinkopf has awful handwriting."

"That doesn't change the fact that we have not received a proper report from you in three months. Only vague notes and promises of... something. Now Avery, we demand to know what the Germans were working on."

Avery spun to face the Brigadier with an excited grin. Powell couldn't help but take an anxious step back at the sight of the smaller man's enthusiasm.

"The bulk of the research was about a new type of mustard gas. What they were hoping to achieve was a formula that killed much faster and lingered longer, making indoor areas completely uninhabitable for months at a time."

"Did they succeed?" asked Powell. His cheeks threatened to turn a shade of grey.

"No, thank God, it was a complete failure. But it was in these failed experiments that the real discovery lay. They were testing the gas on rats, you see, and there were some unexpected side effects. The rats didn't die. Instead they thrived in the most bizarre fashion." Avery locked eyes with Powell. "They grew." The scientist paused, waiting for the officer's reaction. But Powell furrowed his thick brow together, less than impressed, then gave a small cough.

"Avery. Our best agents nearly died to get that research. You better have more to show me than just some overgrown rodents."

"Oh, so much more," said Avery quickly. "You see, it didn't just stimulate the rats' growth hormones, it completely mutated them and their synaptic nerves." He held his hands out in front of him, his gesturing becoming wilder as he went on.

"If I wanted to hear gibberish, Avery, I'd take a boat to visit the Huns. What are you trying to tell me?"

Avery looked around the empty corridor, and his beady eyes, amplified three sizes by his glasses, shone brightly. "I'll show you," he said, then led the way through another steel door. Brigadier Powell found himself in a busy lab, surrounded by other men in similar white coats working with various chemicals and equipment, while others stood back observing or taking notes. All were wearing heavy rubber gas masks with wide lenses. Powell's hand instinctively covered his face as a sharp and acrid stink violated his nostrils. Noise hit him like a wall. Cages upon cages filled every available space: on shelves, on desks, even on the floor. Each cage was occupied by a single rat, squeaking in a combined cacophony that made the Brigadier wince.

"Should we be wearing masks?" he asked as he glanced at the other scientists, quickly pulling a red handkerchief out of a pocket to cover his mouth and nose and trying not to gag. But Avery just waved his concerns away.

"Oh, don't worry about the smell. Short term exposure doesn't have any harmful effects on humans, unless you have a weak stomach," he chuckled. They approached a heavy metal door that was set into the concrete wall at the back of the lab that reminded the Brigadier of a bank strongroom. Pulling a key from his coat pocket, Avery unlocked the door and slid back the iron bolt. The professor, with an enormous grin, motioned for Powell to enter the room beyond. It was very dim inside and the strange smell, although not as sharp, permeated everything. But it was the heavy scuffling noises that drew the officer's attention. Avery hit a switch and a single orange bulb slowly revealed the room.

"This is the first subject to survive more than a month. We exposed it to our own modification of Steinkopf's gas."

"Good God," Powell muttered, eyes wide.

"The results are very encouraging." Avery grinned and fidgeted, barely able to contain his exuberance.

Powell stared at the rat. It was the size of a Labrador, with front limbs that were much too long for it, and a tail as thick as a snake that slowly swept across the floor with a gentle swish. The rat stared back through the bars of its large cage, looking at Powell with calm and inquisitive eyes.

"It's a monster."

"We like to call him George," Avery said with a smile. George's ears twitched slightly at the mention of his name and he turned his gaze to the scientist. Realising his mouth was hanging open, Powell composed himself.

"It's still just a very large rat, Avery," he grunted rather loudly in an attempt to hide his shock and disgust. "This is not what we were hoping for. We need a weapon."

From a cluttered desk, Avery picked up a large piece of card with various shapes drawn in different bright colours. "George, how many triangles can you see?"

George moved himself to the very front of the cage in an awkward display of overly long limbs and peered closely at the flash card. After a few seconds the mutated rat tapped his front paw four times against the metal bars.

"Correct."

Powell gawked at Avery then studied the board himself. There were indeed four triangles.

"And how many blue shapes are there?" Five taps. Correct again. "Good boy, George." Avery handed George a piece of bread who delicately plucked it from his hand with his long nails and ate it.

"George was exposed to the gas just over a month ago. We estimate he currently has the intelligence of a four year old human child."

Powell thought of his own young son, and how he had just learned to count beyond ten. Noting the Brigadier's silence, Avery picked up a sandwich and held it up so George could see it. George sniffed at the air and looked around, nose twitching from side to side.

"He loves ham and French mustard," Avery muttered to the Brigadier. He looked back to the rat. "Now George, this is yours if you can say my name."

"You can't possibly be serious?" Powell did his best to scoff at the idea, but his deep voice wavered just slightly.

"Hav! Hav-ry!"

The rat's voice was coarse and raspy, like the words were a struggle to spit out.

"It spoke…"

"His vocal chords are still not very suited to human forms of language. But we think we can improve them by tweaking the chemical formula and maybe some minor surgery. Brigadier, this is your weapon! Imagine, once we perfect the process we could have soldiers, warriors, just as smart as humans but twice as fast and able to sense danger a mile away. And of course they would be loyal only to the British Empire, programed to follow orders without a moment's hesitation."

Brigadier Powell stood in silence, chewing his lip, while he shared his gaze with the thing in the cage. He tried not to see just the hideous mutant before him, but the potential the experiment could contain.

"What do you need?" he asked. Professor Avery's smile grew.

"A larger laboratory and research space. And the finest chemists and geneticists in the Allied Nations. Brigadier, we are going to change history."

1943

Rodney Brown sat at the bar top with his short legs dangling from the stool. He removed the cigarette from his mouth to take a sip of the small brandy. The trumpet player finished a marvellous solo, and Rodney set the glass down and clutched the cigarette between his teeth so he could give a proper clap. The old pub was plenty cosy but had just enough room to fit the little four-piece band in the corner and fill the rest of the space with a couple of wooden tables and chairs that were in desperate need of a varnish. Rodney had once heard a lady describe the pub's wallpaper and general decor as "ghastly", but he honestly couldn't tell or care for that matter so long as the thick curtains did their proper job and kept any light from escaping the windows into the dark night beyond.

The band played *It Don't Mean A Thing* well, but Rodney's attention was focused on the woman who had just started to sing again. He couldn't quite see her through the haze of cigarette smoke, but he could hear and smell her, despite the tobacco. And she both sounded and smelled beautiful, like the sea at dusk. Even if her face was a little hazy.

The song ended with a jazzy flourish, and the pub's occupants applauded with a whistle or two thrown in for good measure. Rodney joined in the hurrah, putting his hands together, but the rest of his senses were still focused on the singer who was now waving and laughing at the entire pub. Her gaze settled on him for a moment and she glanced away, her smile faltering. He realised he had been staring. A second later she was smiling and chatting with some of the musicians, but a nervous look back in Rodney's direction told him all he needed to know. Rodney sighed and slurped down the last of his brandy. Of course a woman like her would never give him the time of day. Or any other human woman for that matter.

Rodney was a rat. A little over four feet tall with a longer torso and shorter legs compared to that of a human, covered in brown fur, complete with a long tail, ears on the side of his head, and a lengthy and very sensitive nose. More importantly, to him anyway, he was a Sergeant in His Royal Majesty's British Army. The highest rank so far achieved by a rat.

Rodney looked away from the band, but focused his nose and ears on the woman, content with letting her soft laughter wash over him. He signalled the aging bartender, Milligan, for another brandy. The

Sergeant's eyes must have followed his nose however, as he soon found himself gazing at her misty face. Milligan noticed.

"As fine a gentleman as you are, Rod, I don't think you'll garner much luck with young Phoebe there," Milligan said, passing him a new glass. "She has a rather particular taste in men."

"Let me guess, those tastes include tall, handsome and tail-less?" He took a quick sip of the booze.

"Without putting too fine a point on it."

Rodney sighed and shook his head. "Do you ever think… With men like me?" he trailed off.

"Rodney, mate, you fellows have only been walking about for twenty years. Most of us still need time to get used to it." Milligan saw the despondent look spread across Rodney's face and added, "I'm not saying it won't happen, just give it time. The world isn't ready for it yet."

"You're right, Milligan. I may not like it, but you're right." He took a long drag of his cigarette and wondered what it might have been like to be born twenty years from now. Probably very dull, he thought, stamping the spent smoke in a nearby ashtray.

The band started up again with a Glenn Miller tune, and Milligan took the opportunity to change the subject.

"Your lad's doing right well tonight," he smiled and pointed at another rat, hunched over in front of an old drum kit, smoothly keeping time with a stick in each hand and third wrapped up in his tail. He wore a near identical uniform to Rodney's except with only a single stripe stitched to the shoulder. Instead of brown fur, like Rodney, his body was cloaked in a dusty grey. Rodney simply sat and listened to the music. The song was an instrumental, and he found it much easier to enjoy without the singer to distract his thoughts.

The music ended and the pub applauded again, a little louder this time as the band made it clear they had finished their set for the night. The rat drummer shook hands with the rest of the human players, all of whom wore similar uniforms.

"That was some good playing tonight, Eric," Rodney complimented his fellow rat as he approached, shaking his hand when he reached the bar. Rodney's hand brushed against a long scar that ran down Eric's palm and wrist. An identical mark was visible on his other hand. To most people this was just an ugly scar, possibly the result of some unfortunate accident. But to other rats, and some perceptive human soldiers, it was a tell-tale sign that Eric O'Hare had not been bred from other mutated rats but was in fact a force-grown mutant himself, and had, at one point in his life, been a mere ten-inch laboratory rodent. A force-grown rat would have one of their front phalanges, or "fingers" as it were, surgically repositioned to act as an opposable thumb, whereas bred rats, like Rodney, could be chemically engineered to be born with natural thumbs.

"Thanks, Rod," O'Hare replied, nodding. "I just wish we could get a replacement snare. The darn thing's starting to ring if you hit it in the wrong place."

"I'd put in an order, but you know the response we'd get," Rodney chuckled and then lifted his glass. "Drink?"

"No thank you, Sergeant." O'Hare raised a scarred hand. "I have an errand I need to run. Plus I need to get some rest for the big day tomorrow."

"Very fair. Well, goodnight then, Eric."

"Goodnight, Sergeant. I'll see you back at the bunker."

Lance Corporal Eric O'Hare waved Milligan goodnight then walked out of the pub, a wash of cold air creeping in through the door as he left. Rodney turned to his near empty glass.

"One more, Rod?" asked Milligan. The rat shook his head, and instead nursed the remains of his current brandy. Rodney made a point of staring at the shelves of bottles behind the bar, being very careful not to look at the beautiful smelling woman who was now talking and laughing with three other young men from the village. After only a few minutes of half listening to their rather benign conversation on the shortage of tinned peaches, Rodney finished the brandy, dropped a few shillings on the counter, and wished Milligan goodnight.

"Good luck tomorrow, Rod. I'm sure it'll go smooth as custard." Rodney simply smiled in response before leaving.

The air was cold outside and made his nose and whiskers sting a little. He lit another cigarette. The tiny glowing ember warmed his muzzle only a modicum as he strolled up the street, but it was enough.

"Oi! Put that out." Rodney turned to search for the harsh voice in the dark. He saw the outline of a policeman's domed hat on top of what was presumably a policeman's body. It was too dark to see the bobby's face very well, but Rodney guessed from the way he strode towards the rat, arms swinging roughly up and down, that he wore an expression of anger.

"I beg your pardon, sir?" Rodney asked.

"Are you deaf? I said put that out," the policeman barked, pointing at the cigarette. Rodney recognised the voice as belonging to one Constable Baines. A tall man by human standards, he towered over Rodney, making it ever more evident by standing barely a foot directly in front of the Sergeant. Rodney resisted the urge to take several steps back. Instead, he looked rather bemused at his cigarette then back to the Constable.

"Why?"

Constable Baines sucked a lungful of air through his nose, puffing out his chest slightly. Rodney could see his face quite clearly now and saw his eyes narrow at the question.

"Blackout laws."

Rodney stopped himself from laughing by turning it into a convincing cough. "Sorry, Constable, but I don't think the Germans can see a lit smoke from across the channel."

"Laws are laws, soldier," he spat the last word like it was poison.

Rodney kept his face level, but felt anger sting the back of his throat. He technically outranked the bobby, and yet he was quite literally being talked down to. And he bet he knew why.

"And frankly… Brown, was it?" Constable Baines went on. "Frankly I don't care what you think. I will not have your kind putting good, innocent people in potential danger."

There it was. *Your kind.* Rodney blinked once very slowly. He took a step back, dropped the cigarette onto the paved street, and stamped it out with his boot. He looked up at the policeman with the widest smile he could manage and said, in a very cheerful voice, "There we are Constable, no harm done."

Baines glared at him for a few uncomfortable seconds. "Good. Bloody keep it that way," he snarled before turning and marching off down the street. Rodney watched and listened to the vile man leave, hearing the bobby mutter something about 'bloody vermin' under his breath.

War is good for very little, Rodney thought as he returned to making his way up the gentle hill, but it is good for bringing people together. Rodney had been born fifteen years ago, which made him the mental and physical equivalent of a thirty-year-old human man, due to the rats' accelerated growth process. He had experienced much prejudice in the first ten years of his life; not allowed to vote, drive, or even eat at most pubs. He'd put up with politicians arguing with each other about whether he and his brothers were "real" people. He'd found himself the butt of cruel jokes and even crueller beatings by the less than accepting general populace. Often by blinkered men much like Constable Baines who were too narrow-minded to accept the unusual. But a lot of that changed in 1939. Suddenly the lab rats had a use and a purpose. Forced to work and serve beside these strange anthropomorphic rodents meant that human soldiers actually got to know the creatures, saw their worth and skill, and even, on occasion, became friends. And a serving man's opinion meant a lot to the folks back home.

Rodney still remembered the first rat to be promoted to Sergeant, back in '41. The lucky sod had his photo taken shaking hands with Winston Churchill. The Prime Minister had made a speech about the solidarity of man and rodent, how they were all children of Mother England, no matter what the circumstances of their birth. It had been published in every paper in the country.

But, he thought as he listened to the annoyed bobby stamp away, a few humans still saw him as just an animal, an experiment, or even an abomination depending on your religious inclinations. The uniform he wore, no matter how proudly, didn't matter too much to some people, no matter how many stripes were pinned to his shoulder. After all, as far as he knew, there were no rats that weren't employed by the military as they had been bred specifically for service. They were, for all intents and purposes, tools of the army.

In saying that, the giant-rat super-soldier idea had not worked out quite as the army had planned. The mutant rats were indeed smart and fast, but an aversion to running headlong into danger had been the idea's ultimate downfall. No matter how hard the scientists tried, they just could not breed out the rats' exceptionally strong survival instinct. However, the rats did make excellent engineers with their small, flexible bodies, dexterous fingers, and penchant for problem solving. A good rat mechanic could fix a broken jeep nearly three times faster than any human could.

Rodney pulled himself from his thoughts when he realised he'd passed the last of the houses. He continued by some old sheds and through a grassy field that led to a cliff, a gentle breeze making his ears flap. Beyond that was the English Channel. Set near the edge of the cliff, however, was a small, grey concrete bunker. It had been built sometime near the end of the first Great War as a watch point, was ultimately abandoned in 1920, and had then been commandeered by lost sheep and the occasional drunkard as a safe resting place from the constant wind and frequent rain that blew in from the ocean. At present, it was home to a very small group of military rats, the sheep and tramps having been evicted over a year ago when the army reclaimed it.

The rusty door squeaked but opened easily. Rodney stepped inside and closed it with his tail. The bunker was not particularly large, but with only five rats to accommodate, it served its purpose comfortably. He walked through the makeshift mess hall which overlooked the ocean, if you peeked through the long and thin pill box style window in the concrete, and into a short corridor where the soldiers' bunk rooms were located. Three Privates shared a single room while Rodney and O'Hare were allowed a room each to themselves. The Privates' door was closed but light was creeping through the crack, which meant that they were probably playing cards before bed. Rodney was not particularly strict about lights out, so long as his men worked hard throughout the day.

A loud clatter from one of the equipment rooms turned Rodney from his own door. A tin of whale meat in brine rolled through the semi-open door and stopped against his boot. He knew who was responsible before he even looked, and not because he could smell their scent.

"Charlie," he sighed, "What have you done now?" The equipment room door slowly opened all the way, and a small, pointy face poked out, looking rather sheepish despite its inherent rat-ness.

"I'm - I'm - I'm sorry, Sergeant. I was just cleaning down the shelves and—"

"Charlie, it's gone eleven. You should be getting some rest." Rodney kept most of the bite out of his voice. Charlie was one of those poor rats where the chemical therapy had gone a bit… wonky, for a lack of more scientific term. While most mutant rodents were intelligent and often more quick-witted than was good for them, Charlie was about as bright as a busted bulb.

"Besides," Rodney continued, moving into the room to inspect the damage, careful not to tread on the carpet of cans, "didn't you clean these a few days ago?"

"Yes, Sergeant, but I thought they could use an extra bit of polish."

Rodney blinked and twitched his whiskers. "Charlie. They're shelves." Although he couldn't deny that the slabs of thin metal did shine quite nicely under the bare light. "There comes a point when you're just dirtying a perfectly good rag. Now sort this mess out, and go to bed."

"Yes, Sergeant!"

Rodney headed back into his own room and closed the door, leaving Charlie to scamper about the store room.

"Twit," the sergeant muttered. He sat and leant back in a squeaky wooden chair, letting his mind drift. A feeling of melancholy washed over him, the booze not helping, as his thoughts wandered back to the singer in the pub.

"What do I do, Auntie Imogen?" he asked a small cage on his desk. In the cage was a small brown rat. The rat wasn't really his aunt. However they were actually related, although he did not know enough about genealogy to know exactly how, so he just called her Auntie. They had both come from the original group of rats from that mysterious lab during the first Great War. While he was descended from the mutants, she was descended from a control group. A perfectly normal rat.

Rodney watched as the tiny animal just squeaked and scratched at some old newspaper. He thought about the woman with her gorgeous voice. He wondered if she looked as beautiful to humans as she smelled to him. He knew humans often judged things based on sight, which was a concept he had trouble grasping. Some fathead had once told Rodney that all rats looked the same. He knew the man had meant it as an insult, but Rodney actually agreed. Rats did all look the same, just like all humans looked the same, bar the color of skin, hair or fur. But everyone smelled and sounded so distinct that it was impossible not to remember who was who. He hadn't said that to the man in question, instead Rodney had suggested that he go soak his head, which had not been received well at the time.

He chuckled and shook his head at the memory, then yawned, a good signal that he should get to sleep. In bed, in his night clothes, he tried to put the woman out of his mind. He needed to focus on sleep. After all, tomorrow was the big day.

* * *

The wireless warbled out the pleasant crooning of a Noel Coward song, accompanying two rats as they vigorously rubbed their oddly shaped black boots. Rodney knocked on the door frame, with his uniform smartly buttoned over a belly full of porridge. Privates Coney and Cavy looked up from where they sat on their bunks.

"Morning, lads."

"Morning, Sergeant," they replied in unison.

"All ready for today?"

"Just giving 'em a final shine," Coney said, motioning to his boots.

"Very good. Have either of you seen Charlie?"

"Yeah, I saw him outside sweeping up the leaves," Cavy said, and pointed his nose in the general direction of outside.

"How's his uniform looking?"

"Good enough, Sergeant," said Coney.

"Smarter than he is, in any case," said Cavy, getting a chuckle out of the other Private.

"Keep it to yourselves, lads," Rodney said, forcing a frown to stop himself from laughing. He smelled O'Hare, and turned to see him approach.

"Sergeant."

"Morning, Lance Corporal."

"The captain's here. He's waiting outside."

"Very good. I need you to finish preparations, Lance Corporal," Rodney ordered. "As for you two, get dressed and help O'Hare."

"Yes, Sergeant!" the three called out. Rodney gave them a brief smile then headed for the exit.

Rodney found the Captain standing at the edge of the cliff, the wind threatening to claim the cigarette that he pinched between two slender fingers. Captain Bonham, a thin man in his thirties with thinner framed glasses, stared out across the Channel and watched the waves crash around each other in messy sprays of foam. When he saw the rat approach, he took one last suck on the cigarette then flicked it over the edge of the cliff where, presumably, it joined the waves smashing the rocks below.

"Good morning, Brown," Captain Bonham greeted Rodney.

"Good morning, Sir," Rodney said with a smart salute. Bonham quickly returned the salute and took the opportunity to make sure his peaked cap was jammed tightly down around his head.

"How are you this morning, Sergeant?"

"Bloody cold, Sir." Rodney tilted his head against the wind in an attempt to stop his ears from flapping violently against his own skull. It was a miracle he hadn't lost his side cap already.

"Yes, it is a bit nippy up here," Bonham chuckled, tightening his coat around him. "I assume your boys are all ready for today?"

"Of course, Sir. We're just tidying ourselves up a little bit."

"And, Brown, the uh," Bonham paused and cleared his throat. "The rest of the town seems to be getting ready as well." The Captain peered over his glasses at Rodney in a look that was somehow disapproving yet wonderfully amused at the same time. Rodney, now suddenly rather concerned, looked around and saw several of the villagers milling about some hundred yards from the concrete bunker, halfway down the hill. A larger woman in a floral head scarf was handing out sandwiches, while a group of men were talking amongst themselves.

"Oh bollocks," Rodney muttered.

"I don't suppose you know what this is all about?" asked the Captain. He hid a grin in that smug way only a British officer could achieve, usually reserved for moments when someone has achieved something ultimately harmless yet potentially embarrassing.

Rodney quietly swore. "We posted some notices that warned about today. We just didn't want to cause any panic. It was not supposed to be a bloody open invitation."

"Ah yes, I did see that as I passed the green grocer. 'There will be a loud bang at noon on the twelfth of July.'" Bonham quoted. "'Do not panic. The Peevey Bay Artillery Section will be testing their new Channel defence Howitzer.' Really, Brown, you might as well have included an RSVP. Well, no harm done in any case. I just hope your lads can still perform with a bit of an audience."

"Of course, Sir, we won't let you down."

"I know you won't, Rodney, but it's not me you should be concerned about." His voice took a more serious tone. "It took a lot of convincing to get HQ to agree that an all rat artillery section could operate successfully without human supervision. Even more to get you the new gun. Do yourselves a favor and be brilliant. Because I'm not sure what will happen if the higher-ups hear of anything less." He pulled another cigarette and a book of matches from his jacket pocket and tried to light it unsuccessfully against the wind. "Damn it."

"I understand, Sir. Thank you." Rodney looked over to the small group of nosey villagers and frowned. "With any luck, they'll lose interest and go home."

* * *

The villagers did not lose interest. In fact, interest seemed to spread through Peevey Bay with a swiftness of force that could have rivalled a hurricane. An enormous group of people had gathered upon the hill and by the cliff. In fact, Rodney had ordered Charlie to put out a length of rope and told people not to cross it, just to keep them from getting too close to the new Howitzer. Some enterprising villagers were selling pies and drinks for a conveniently inflated price. One man had brought along his guitar and was strumming a simple tune. It looked almost like a fair.

"Don't they have anything better to do?" Rodney asked O'Hare. The two gawked at the expanding crowd from the safety of the bunker wall, the unspoken authority of the rope keeping the villagers a thankfully decent distance from the rats' home.

"Well, there's no cricket today." O'Hare's reply made Rodney snort.

Just before noon, the five-rat Section fell in just outside the bunker. Rodney, wanting to put on a just a little bit of show for the humans, marched his soldiers to the Howitzer less than a hundred yards away. They dragged with them a small wooden crate on a trolley. A few of the villagers clapped and whistled. It was not a rousing ovation, but it caused Rodney to smile and hold his head just that little bit higher. The small crate was opened once they had formed up around the gun. Inside were several gleaming brass shells. One however, had a bright blue stripe painted around the case and the word BLANK stencilled in large black letters among other smaller identifying numbers. The special blank had been made for the test, and contained no explosive, just a firing charge and a simple metal projectile that would splosh harmlessly into the ocean. It was this shell that was loaded into the breech.

As Rodney ordered his Section through the procedures, the crowd descended into silence, growing ever quieter as the moment approached. Nearly twenty children stood with their hands clamped tight over their ears, and faces scrunched up in preparation for what, to them, would be the loudest sound in the world. At the sight and sound, Rodney felt a small tingle of excitement. In that moment, he was the protector of Peevey Bay. The defender of England. He imagined the cheer going up when the gun fired. Through the cacophony of odors, he could make out the distinct natural perfume of Phoebe, the singing woman from the pub. And while he couldn't see her, he certainly hoped that she had a clear view of him.

"Number one gun, ready!" a crouched O'Hare shouted out.

"Number one gun, fire!" Rodney ordered.

"Fire!" yelled O'Hare. Cavy pulled hard on the firing lever. Nothing happened. The rats stayed frozen. Rodney sucked in a sharp breath through his nose to stop himself from groaning. Charlie opened his mouth to voice his confusion, but quickly shut it when Cony glared at him.

A murmur started in the crowd. It began quiet but grew louder, sounding like a distant swarm of bees. Children looked to their parents, confused. Cavy wrinkled his snout and pulled on the lever again, but Brown shook his head at him.

"We follow procedure," he said quietly. Then, louder, "Unload!"

O'Hare checked the firing pin was released, then opened the breech and removed the shell, then placed it very carefully back into the box. His face soured ever so slightly.

The crowd grew restless, wondering where the promised big bang was. Most of the adults began to gossip with one another as they watched with raised eyebrows. Some of the children were much more vocal, loudly asking their parents why the gun didn't go off, some even complaining, crying, or demanding that they wanted to hear the boom.

"Squad!" Rodney shouted at the rats in formation. "Forward... March!" He caught Captain Bonham's eye as they moved back across the field and the human gave him an encouraging look. Rodney tried to smile back but his frustration was written clear on his face, even despite his rodent features. It was the crowd that was really getting to him. Rodney could have handled boos. Or shouts, or names. Or even the simple dismissal that 'them bloomin' rats can't do anythin' right'. He'd been handling those his entire life. What he couldn't quite handle was the dejected disappointment that rolled over him from the crowd like a thick fog, and seeped in through his round ears. At least it was very easy to focus one's attention while marching. Eyes front, arms up to breast pocket height, tail curved and tucked against the small of your back, left, right, left, right. He paid no further attention to what the crowd behind him did, it was none of his business, he didn't care. Except that he did care. But he did his best not to.

"That could have gone a lot better," Rodney sighed when they had fallen out and retreated to the inside of the bunker. "What happened?"

The rats looked around at each other in search for an answer, but mostly found shrugs.

"Not really sure yet, Sergeant," O'Hare offered. "Could've been any number of things. Dud shell, faulty firing pin, dirty chamber, too much grease…" He let his answer hang in the air. "Honestly, probably a case of plain bad luck."

Rodney let out a single laugh and shook his head. "It was definitely not our day today," he muttered, stroking along the top of his muzzle. A creak signalled the bunker door opening, and Captain Bonham stepped through.

"Atten-SHUN!" Cavy yelled, and all the rats stood rigidly to attention. Rodney gave a salute that Bonham returned before removing his cap.

"Sergeant Brown, do we know what happened out there?" The man seemed just as disappointed as Rodney. The replacement of the old gun was, after all, Bonham's doing, and he was just as invested in its success as Rodney was.

"We don't know yet, Sir. The damn thing just didn't want to go off," said Rodney, shaking his head. Bonham's shoulders sunk somewhat.

"Well then. A man can hardly be blamed for faulty equipment. And I thought you all looked rather dashing today, so well done there. For now, just find out what went wrong, and I'll send a man to fix it."

Most likely a human man, Rodney thought. "With respect, Sir, when we do find the problem we should be able to fix it ourselves," he said, a little more forcefully than he had intended. Bonham's eyes flitted around the room, and he fidgeted with his cap.

"Yes, of course," the Captain said. Although his eyes did not meet with Rodney's. "Well I do need to be off now. I have a meeting back in Bexhill this evening, and I promised Freda I'd take her out to afternoon tea. Finding a spare spot of free time is rather challenging these days." Bonham realised that he was rambling, coughed, and put his cap firmly back on his head. "I'll leave you gentlemen to it. Goodbye." He smiled, turned, and exited, the bunker door clanging shut behind him.

"He doesn't think we can fix it, does he?" Cavy said, smirking.

"He means well," Rodney said. "I just wish he'd place a little more faith in us."

* * *

Rodney jolted up in bed, heart pounding, the haze taking a few seconds to completely lift from his panicked brain before he realised it had been a loud noise that had woke him. A very loud bang indeed. Auntie Imogen squealed and rattled about her cage in a panic. He almost fell out of bed and got dressed with a speed that impressed even himself, shoving his untied bootlaces into his socks before stumbling out of his room and into Private Cavy.

"Private, what in blazes was that?" Rodney demanded, whiskers twitching in confusion.

"I—I - I don't know, Sergeant!" Cavy stammered, the poor sod still trying to button up his shirt.

"It's the bloody Germans' is what it is!" Coney appeared dressed in just boots and trousers, clutching an old Lee-Enfield rifle to his scrawny chest. "They're trying to bomb us!"

"You idiot, that was no bomb blast," muttered O'Hare. The Lance Corporal looked as if he had woken up fully dressed in his working rig. The only clues that he had been awake for less than a few minutes were the dark rings under his eyes, and the heavy droop to his tail. O'Hare turned and looked pointedly at his Sergeant. "It was artillery fire."

It took Rodney a few seconds to put two and two together, but credit must be given that he had just been violently roused from a deep slumber.

"Where's Charlie?" he asked quietly. The two Privates glanced around as if expecting Charlie to fade into the foreground.

"He's not in his bunk," Cavy had started to say, but Rodney was already marching out the exit with speed. The other three rats scrambled after the Sergeant into the cold black of midnight, smelling their way across the grass to the new Howitzer which they could all hear sat uncovered. The sharp smell of gunpowder was strong and fresh. Charlie stood a few feet away from the gun, looking dazed and lost, like he couldn't remember where he had placed his wallet. But the thrashing of his tail gave away his panic. The contents of a toolbox lay sprawled by his feet. Rodney stomped up to the Private, their noses barely a few inches apart. Charlie leant back and swallowed. His feet stayed rooted to the ground.

"What did you do?" The Sergeant's voice was barely more than a whisper.

"I tried to fix it." While Charlie's answer was somewhat louder than Rodney's question, his voice came out much smaller. "I didn't mean for it…" he trailed off meekly. Rodney stared. He stood and stared for nearly a full minute, not knowing what to say, his muzzle tensed up in rage.

"You complete and utter tit."

"Yes, Sergeant," Charlie squeaked as he stared at his boots.

"Get back to the bunker," Rodney muttered.

"Yes, Sergeant."

"Privates. With me." Coney and Cavy nodded and headed off. "Lance Corporal. Check the Howitzer."

"Yes, Sergeant."

As Rodney marched back to the bunker, his narrowed eyes focused directly ahead and his ears standing rigid despite the wind, the three Privates exchanged nervous glances as they followed. Or more accurately, Coney and Cavy exchanged glances with each other, and threw worried looks in Charlie's direction. Charlie, thin shoulders slumped, kept his eyes fixed two feet in front of him.

The cold chill was just as prevalent back inside the bunker as it was outside. It did nothing to improve Rodney's mood, who seized the opportunity to turn on Charlie.

"What in God's name were you thinking?" he spat.

"I just wanted to try to fix it," Charlie murmured, and winced away from his Sergeant. "To show you I'm useful. I know you don't think I'm very smart."

"So far, you have failed to change my opinion." Frustrated and confused by his own anger, Rodney huffed and stepped around in a tight circle, needing to see something that wasn't Charlie's sorry looking face, before he returned to the guilty rat and jabbed him the chest with a thin finger. Coney and Cavy looked on motionless, not daring to interrupt the Sergeant's rant.

"You do not, I repeat, DO NOT!" Rodney screamed, "Touch the Howitzer without my permission!" He opened his mouth to continue, but Lance Corporal O'Hare hurried through the door. He wore an expression that did not bode good tidings. Rodney silently prayed in vain for this ordeal to just end.

"Sergeant, I've secured the gun. But…" Normally very calm and composed, the Lance Corporal shifted around as he searched for right words to deliver the impending bad news. "It seems… The Howitzer was not pointed directly at the ocean when it was fired." He stumbled over the word 'fired'. "Judging by the direction, and angle of elevation, it looks like we might have fired on Norman's Beach."

Everyone stared.

"Good God," Rodney breathed. Norman's Beach was a beach town, a little to the east of Peevey Bay, known to the locals as a lovely little holiday spot with its charming stretch of sand that stuck out from the mainland like a geological finger.

A macabre cloud of dread fell over the rats. Rodney slumped into a nearby chair and held his head in his hands. The Section stood in silence, too scared to move.

"Blimey…" whispered Cavy, disturbing the silence. Then the Private wrinkled his nose and looked up. "Hang on, if we shot at Norman's Beach, where was the second bang?"

The others frowned and the tension eased. Cavy was right, there had been no explosion.

"Not to mention no sirens or screams," O'Hare added.

"Maybe it did land in the sea?" Coney offered.

O'Hare shook his head. "It was definitely pointed at Norman's Beach. Not to mention we still should have heard it go off."

Rodney sat up a little straighter, a thread of hope unravelling before him. "Cavy, check."

Cavy didn't even nod, he just dashed into the Privates' bunk and returned a few seconds later with a pair of binoculars. He went to the thin, horizontal window of the bunker and leant out with the binoculars pressed awkwardly against his eyes, the human built tool not quite fitting around his muzzle.

"Well, Norman's Beach is still there," he called back. A collective sigh of relief ran through the rats.

"Then what happened to the shell? Charlie definitely fired something," said Coney. Charlie flinched.

"Um, I think it might be on the beach," Cavy responded, still looking through the binoculars. "It's too dark to say for certain, but there might be a small… hole in the beach."

"Well, that's okay, isn't it?" asked Charlie, trying not to stutter. "If it's a dud, then we've got nothing to worry about." He smiled and looked around for encouragement. "It's just a shell on the beach."

"A dud shell," Coney muttered to himself and nodded.

"Thank God it didn't explode," said Cavy gratefully.

The relief that had set in did not surrender easily. Compounded by tiredness and prior panic, it had coated the rats' minds like thick marmalade, sweet and satisfying. But as the soldiers' minds started to churn their relief began to evaporate, replaced instead by fresh terror.

"Oh, Christ." Rodney couldn't help but tense back up, his whiskers quivering. "It's an unexploded shell." His brain tingled in fear as he imagined a group of small children playing on the sand in the mid-morning sun, before one of them trips, his foot catching on something metallic and heavy, and then… Smithereens.

"What do we do, Sergeant?" asked O'Hare.

"I don't know," Rodney said

"I don't understand," said Charlie, "We're safe, it didn't go off."

"It didn't go off," said Rodney, turning on the Private, "which means it's a live bomb just waiting to blow the legs off the next poor sod who comes along and gives it more than a gentle wiggle!" He opened his mouth to swear but a piercing ring caught the words in his throat. The telephone. Everyone stared at the green mound of plastic that hung on the wall. It rang again. Rodney took a few deep breaths to calm himself and clear his head. He walked over, carefully lifted the receiver and placed it against his large ear.

"Peevey Bay Artillery Section, this is Sergeant Brown speaking." His whiskers shivered in panic. "How may I help you?" His voice seemed to go up an octave and he winced.

"Brown? Bonham here," said the crackly voice on the telephone. Rodney's tail stuck out nearly as rigid as steel. "I've had some worrisome calls in. People say they heard a blast up on the hill. Is everything okay out there?"

"Erm…" Rodney searched for something to say. He knew he had to inform the Captain, but he couldn't think how to break the news of accidental friendly fire. "Captain. Something has… happened."

"What has, Brown? Is everyone alright?"

"Yes, Sir, we're all fine," Rodney struggled to get the words out. "You see…" He glanced at Charlie. He had never seen the stupid little bugger so miserable in all his life.

"Brown, I need to know what's happened. I can have a platoon sent out to you in ten minutes."

"No! No, Sir, that won't be necessary. That sound, it was a lightning strike, Sir."

Charlie looked up suddenly in surprise, his eyes as wide as saucers. The other troops looked around confused as well. There was a pause on the other end of the phone. Rodney imagined Bonham questioning what he'd just heard.

"A lightning strike? You're quite sure? The forecast didn't mention any storms."

"You're quite right, Sir. No storm, just a freak flash of lightning. Struck right on the edge of the cliff. Gave us all quite a fright." He went on, invested in the lie. "For a few moments we thought it was the Germans."

"Oh, don't be silly Brown. But I'm glad to hear everything is peachy. Now if there's nothing else, I'm afraid I'm going to head back to bed."

"No, Sir. Goodnight, Sir."

"Goodnight, Brown."

The clack of the plastic handset being placed back on the receiver echoed around the concrete walls. Coney and Cavy couldn't help but give Rodney an eyeful of shock.

"Thank you, Sergeant," Charlie said, quietly. Rodney couldn't help but wince.

"Oh shut up, you bloody trumpet," Coney said to Charlie.

"Sergeant, that shell is still out there," O'Hare pointed out to Rodney. "We can't just—"

"Leave me alone, you berk!" Charlie shouted back at Coney.

"Flippin' bellend!"

"You take that back!"

Rodney shut his eyes against the eruption of immature name calling and angry advice. The Privates were spurred into arguing what should or could have. O'Hare tried to sort them out, but was immediately drawn into the verbal fray at the scowled questioning of his mother's promiscuity. A doubly bizarre lure as O'Hare technically did not have a mother. Rodney's small fists clenched as the din boiled in his mind to a near breaking point.

"Everyone bloody pipe down!" He barked the order like it was a magic spell, his deepened voice hitting the rest of his Section like a wave, knocking away their own voices and silencing them.

"We are Britain's only all rat gunnery platoon. But right now that is nothing to be proud about. They've basically relegated us to the home service, to defend a town the Germans couldn't give my Auntie's arse about, with a gun that can't do boo to a naval assault. They don't like us, they don't trust us, and even though they created us, they don't think we are capable of defending our homeland!" He paused and glared at them, daring them to say otherwise. But no one spoke up, so Rodney continued, starting to pace back and forth. "Well, I'm not prepared to prove them right. Not tonight, not ever! So I'll tell you what we're going to do. We're going to find that shell and bring it back." He smiled and was glad to see everyone smile and nod with him.

"And then lads, we shall never speak of it again. To anyone."

The rats let out a cheer. Not quite an hour later they were swiftly making their way along the stretch of road that led to Norman's Beach. The two small towns were not very far apart, separated by a grassy meadow often frequented by farmers from either town wanting to feed their cows. On the opposite side of the road the crashing waves of ocean could be heard. Coney had stowed the rifle and located his shirt, while Cavy had covertly requisitioned a wheelbarrow from the front yard of an unsuspecting villager.

The five rats trudged down the road, being careful not to draw any attention to themselves. They had the distinct advantage of being able to hear and smell their surroundings quite clearly, although occasionally one of them would trip and stumble on a crack in the road.

Getting down to the beach was easier than expected. They avoided passing through the village of Norman's Beach itself by scooting behind the vicarage, and aside from an easily dodged troupe of drunken farmers belting out a chorus of *Yes, We Have No Bananas*, the soldiers were met with no other human activity.

"Ugh, I hate the beach," muttered Coney as they sneaked through the sand.

"How can you hate the beach? It's so lovely out here on a clear day," Cavy said just as quietly.

"Shut it, you two, and keep your eyes peeled," Rodney hissed. The beach was not so large, but the Sergeant realised that finding a seven-inch bomb half buried in the sand was probably going to be a rather difficult task.

"How are we s'posed to find it in the dark anyway?" said Charlie.

"With any luck you'll give it a great heaving kick. That'll solve us two problems," Coney snorted. A beam of light paved a path of white sand directly in front of them. O'Hare had switched on a torch. He passed another to Rodney.

"I could only find two," O'Hare said. Rodney switched on his own torch, being very careful to point it directly down the beach, and not towards either the village or the ocean.

"Good job, Lance Corporal. Everyone, try to smell out metal or gunpowder. And for God's sake, be careful."

The shuffled slowly and carefully along the beach, keeping their eyes and noses alert. After twenty minutes of silence and no luck, Cavy let out a grunt.

"Can someone help me with this damn wheelbarrow? The wheel keeps getting bogged down in the sand."

"Why did you bother with a wheelbarrow?" Charlie asked. "It's not like the shell's that big."

"Because, you muppet, I don't fancy carrying a two hundred pound chunk of metal all the way back to Peevey Bay."

"Lads, quiet!" Rodney held up his hand in a signal to stop. "I think we found it."

Ten feet away there was a large divot in the sand, almost like a crater. At the bottom of the crater something glinted in the torchlight. The smell of grease and gunpowder lingered in the air, overpowered by the strong salty scent of the ocean. Coney and O'Hare carefully approached the metallic shine, while Charlie took a nervous step backwards. Coney scraped away the sand.

"This is it, Sergeant!" he whispered. Rodney breathed a sigh of relief. But they weren't out of the woods yet. With a gentleness that one would treat a fragile infant, the rats excavated the heavy shell from the beach and placed it in the wheelbarrow, packing in big handfuls of sand to stop the bomb from jostling around. They switched off the torches and pointed the wheelbarrow back from where they came. As much as they wanted to race back to the bunker in Peevey Bay, they were also terrified of hitting a bump or crack in the road in just the wrong way and having who-knows-what happening to the unexploded shell. So by the time they trudged past Milligan's bar, up the main street towards their bunker, it was well into four o'clock in the morning, and the first vestiges of pale yellow light were starting to trickle through the clouds on the eastern horizon.

Exhausted, Rodney just kept moving, holding the side of the potentially explosive wheelbarrow to keep both it and himself steady. When he saw the sign over Milligan's bar he smiled.

"Nearly there, lads," he panted. "Just fifteen more minutes." He looked around at the tired faces of his section. He was fully prepared to let them all sleep for the entire day, if they wished. That was his plan anyway. As for Charlie... He'd deal with Charlie tomorrow. Rest first, then punishment. He turned his face back up the street. They were so close to home now.

"Oi! Stop right there!" The harsh voice cut through the early morning and made Rodney wince. No, not now. Any other time but now.

"And what," barked the tall figure of Constable Baines as he marched towards them, "do you 'orrible lot think you're doing?"

Rodney fought through his fatigue and straightened himself to face the bobby. "We're just out for some early morning exercise." He smiled. "Nothing wrong with that, is there?"

"Exercise!" Baines scoffed. "Not bloody likely. That wheelbarrow looks mighty suspicious. What's in it?"

"Sand," Rodney replied. He was suddenly very thankful they had completely covered the shell. The other four rats remained silent, and gathered behind Rodney.

"Sand? Why would you want a wheelbarrow full of sand for?"

"To make it heavy. Like I said, Constable, we are exercising."

Baines narrowed his eyes, and huffed. "Well, it just so happens that I don't believe you. You're up to something, and I'm going to find out." With that he reached into the sand. The privates all gasped. Rodney, quick even for a rat, grabbed Baines's wrist before he could get any further, and pushed it roughly away. Baines looked shocked and insulted, and held his wrist as if he had been burned.

"How dare you! I am a Policeman!"

Rodney had had enough. "You are a Constable, Sir. And I am a Sergeant in His Majesty's Royal Artillery, meaning that I outrank you. Now do me and my men a favour, and leave us alone."

"You call these men?" The tall man pointed behind Rodney. "Your rank means nothing to me, freak."

Cavy and Coney were quick enough to grab Rodney's shoulders and arms to hold him back. The Sergeant fought to free himself. He had never wanted to belt someone in the face so hard in all his life. But he stopped struggling when O'Hare stepped forward to face Baines.

"Baines is it?" O'Hare asked, craning his neck to look the policeman in the eye. "Right, now listen. You're going to bugger off now, otherwise I tell my mates here your little secret."

"Secret; what are you blabbering about?"

"The reason why, after fifteen years, you're still just a police Constable."

At this, Baines's entire face and body seemed to tighten up. "You shut your gob, boy," he hissed.

"And when you tried to enlist in the army, they wouldn't take you because—"

"Shut up!" The Constable's mouth clamped shut, and his pointed finger hovered angrily in the air, unsure who exactly to point at. Eventually, he lowered his arm, turned and strode away. Over his shoulder he shouted angrily, "Your Captain's going to hear 'bout this!" The bobby disappeared from view and the whole section let out a sigh.

"What were you on about back there? What secret?" Rodney asked. He got behind the wheelbarrow and started to push.

"Yeah, tell us!" The Privates looked to O'Hare with a mixture of confusion and curiosity.

O'Hare snickered, "Asthma. The sod's got asthma. Army won't have him 'cause of it."

"That's it?" remarked Coney looking disappointed. "That's not very scandalous."

"I know. But apparently it's his secret shame, or some bollocks." O'Hare shook his head.

"What about him not getting promoted? They don't stop you from being a Police Sergeant just because of asthma, do they?" Coney questioned the Lance Corporal. But O'Hare shook his head.

"I am a rat of my word, lads. Mostly." He grinned. "Even if he is a bull-headed bastard."

"I won't disagree there," Rodney murmured. "Eric, how can you possibly know this?"

"His wife told me," came the answer.

"What were you doing with his wife?" asked Cavy. O'Hare grinned slyly.

"A lot of things Constable Baines can't. Gets too out of breath, you see."

It took a few moments for the rest of the rats to get his meaning, but then all at once they whooped and let out loud whispers of "Cor!"

"I didn't bloody hear that," was Rodney's only response. He couldn't help but smile just the same.

No more interruptions assailed them on their final trek to the bunker. However, the last leg of their journey, despite being a short walk on any other day, felt endless. Between the lack of sleep, the several hours already of steady walking, and the ever present notion that they were carrying a volatile explosive, the night had left all five of the rats exhausted and tense. But they did finally arrive at the dirty white stone building, and none could have been more relieved, staring at the entrance with a sleep driven hunger. The door was just wide enough to accommodate the wheelbarrow, and soon they all sat around it in a rough circle within the makeshift mess hall.

"What do we do with it?" Cavy said.

"I reckon we throw it off the cliff. If it goes off, blame it on the Krauts," said Coney.

"Maybe we can bury it?" Charlie said. Cavy glared at the younger rat and scoffed.

"I got a better idea. We push you off the cliff holding the damn thing," Cavy sneered.

"You shut it, you—"

"Lads!" Rodney barked. The last thing he wanted was another argument. Dealing with the shell was stressful enough.

"But Sergeant," Charlie said, "He keeps -"

"I know, Private," Rodney said. "Cavy, close your gob. Charlie, do us a favor and make some tea."

Charlie shot a filthy look at Cavy, and then nodded at Brown. He got up from his chair, took a step forward, and somehow managed to stand on his own sloppily tied bootlaces. Rodney and the others watched in horror as Charlie pitched forward, propelled by his own inertia at the sand-filled wheelbarrow. The falling rat threw his lanky arms out in an instinctive attempt to grab hold of something. Rodney tried to leap out of his chair to catch or tackle Charlie out of the way, but his trousers had barely left the seat as Charlie crashed into the side of the wheelbarrow. It tipped, sand spilling everywhere, and hit the concrete floor with a clang. O'Hare, Coney, and Cavy all dived away, eyes bulging, desperate to get as far away as possible. Rodney landed on top of Charlie with a crunch. He shifted his panicked gaze to the side and watched as the heavy shell bounced out of the wheelbarrow and onto the bunker floor. The most intense sensation of fear that he had ever, or would ever experience gripped his heart and squeezed with icy fingers. The shell bounced a second time on the concrete, then rolled across the floor with a sound like a drill, before finally smacking loudly against a wall and sat there. Rodney couldn't breathe. He just stared at the stationary tube. Nobody moved. The shell continued to do nothing.

Rodney forced himself to breathe. He slowly stood up. Too afraid to speak, he gestured for his soldiers to stay still. He crept up to the shell as if it were a small, vicious dog. He stared at it some more. The shell had a blue stripe painted around it. He picked it up. The word BLANK stared at him in large black letters. They hadn't seen the markings in the dark of the night, amidst their initial panic.

"You bastard," he whispered at the shell. Rodney set the shell on a chair for all of his Section to see. Then he wandered into his room and collapsed into the bunk. He gave the slumbering form of Auntie Imogen a tired glance, for a moment almost envious of her simple life. Rodney laid his head back on the pillow, sighed out the stresses of the night's ordeal, and fell asleep.

This is an anthropomorphic-animal fantasy, but this is what modern warfare really feels like.

Yeah, with the personal touches, too.

Cross of Valor Reception for the Raccoon, Tanner Williams, Declassified Transcript

by John Kulp

Hello everyone. My name is Tanner Williams.

I'm so glad you all could make it. I'm not used to this kind of talking, but I've been through five of these already, so you're getting treated to the good version. Every one of you here at the Shawichuka Raccoon Veterans Center deserves every bit of effort that's gone into fluffing me up like a poodle ready to win an academy award. Though, to be honest, I don't think any self-respecting raccoon actor would be caught dead in a hand me down tux stitched for a ferret.

Okay, there's some laughs! When I gave this talk up in the big city, I got nothing but crickets. I think they just couldn't imagine a ferret tux fitting me! Hate to break it to you, but it wasn't a lie. Ask my mom. I think she's back there in the third row—the woman with the wonderful scent of pecan pie and lilies. I won't spoil the whole story, she tells it best of course, but it was an act of charity when my grandfather got mugged and left within an inch of his life out on business in a bobcat city. Thanks to her for being here, by the way; along with my sister Leah, my uncle Jim, and my best friend Jonas. They've all given me so much support growing up here in Shawichuka.

I'd also like to take a special moment to acknowledge my Uncle Brady, the reason I joined the army in the first place. I know you're out there: Wave your paw, please! There he is, right in the back left. Could you all please give him a round of applause? That good raccoon used to feed me cookies and tell me war stories whenever he could pull me away—used to drive Mom mad.

Now, these introductions and reminiscences are all good and sure are wonderful—it's been ages since I've seen so many raccoons in one place—but a small town raccoon can get carried away, and I don't want to bore anyone. You're all here to hear about me and my good otter friend, Matt 'Fishbreath' Tallow, surviving Aurochabad.

You know, when you see pictures of the War of Protection, you usually only see the dusty, stuffy cities; rows on rows of tan houses with the thin dirt roads in between all packed shoulder to shoulder with carts and people from the surviving native species. I like to say this is because journalists love getting pictures of explosions, and there's not much point for the bad guys to be setting explosions out in the suburbs. Even when they show the rural areas, it's all desert, sand, and those ramshackle white stone buildings like you'd expect an archaeologist to uncover.

Aurochabad is green. It's a town right along the Alumm River. There are big palms that look like overgrown pineapples, grass all over the place, and even a few forests if you'd believe it. The houses are pretty spread apart too, except for in the center of town. Most of the roads we traveled along were surrounded with big overgrown farms of wheat or wild tall grasses.

All the quiet in between towns is really unsettling. Every time you pass a farmhouse or a cluster of buildings with no one around, you can't help but wonder whether they just shied away from the war or whether they were porcupines, otters, polecats, or another of the species that the caliph ordered executed.

Going into the town of Aurochabad stood my fur on end like a storm was rolling in. The sudden narrowness of the road didn't help, especially after so long driving in the open. Out there, we could cover miles through the scopes of our rifles. The sudden tan walls of tightly nestled buildings was claustrophobic. He's no canine, but I'm sure Matt could smell how uneasy I was. His whisker twitches said he felt the same.

I don't think any of us were even surprised when a tremor shook the humvee. The deep boom that followed a split second later confirmed what we all figured, an IED had just gone off. Our team lead Natalie flattened her ears, grabbed the radio, and barked at our squad leader for a status update. She was answered immediately.

"Greytail 3, Greytail 3, this is Greytail. Small arms fire from the rooftops at my 10 o'clock. We have contact from an RPG team up ahead—unknown location. Missed Saltlick 2 by the fur of their ears, but can't pin their position. Get the turrets surpassing, haul your bleeding tails into gear, and throttle up the engines—copy!" Natalie didn't get to respond, though. Our squad leader clicked off from the little radio handset still gripped tight in her limp paw as blood blossomed across bullet holes in her vest and throat. Honestly, she deserved to be the one up here telling this story. That woman was much better at all the organizing and leading than I could ever be, but she was in the driver's seat next to the fuc—freaking empty window. You know, if we got replacement glass after the last ones got all shot up and turned cracked spiderweb white, then she'd still be alive. Isn't that screwed up?

Billy the shrew, up at the turret, was gone as well. I heard him shoot off three bursts before it went quiet. Well, the small arms kept rat-a-tat-tat-ing all around us, but the sound of the mounted gun is so distinctive with big banging rattles that shook our tin can deathtrap and jittered my paws like you wouldn't believe. I knew he was done for.

I think what saved us is that Natalie's foot never left the pedal. She was a dog, you know? German shepherd. God, it's hard to say that. It lets me see her again; how she'd sternly inform Matt and I that we did well on a training exercise, but couldn't keep the twitch of a wag out of her tail. That's who she was right up until the end. She believed in us. She wanted everything for us. And as soon as she got shot, she put everything she had left into stomping her foot down on the pedal to make sure we didn't stop moving.

The humvee went careening with nothing on the wheel and we rammed into a wall to the left of the road. Another stroke of luck was that my squad lead's 10 o'clock was my left, so the gunmen couldn't get a good shot on us. I bet there were some on the other side, but either way I think it was fate pulling the wheel with Matt and me ducking and shaking like fall leaves in the back.

There was no time to think right after the crash. It knocked the wind out of me like an oxen linebacker. I checked Matt over immediately since he was on the side that hit the wall. He survived, of course, but I could tell right away that the crash got him. It was his tail and left leg. When we hit, he decided he needed his arms, so he shoved his hip at the door and pulled back his shoulder. All the force of the crash rammed through his knee and thigh first. He cracked his kneecap, jolted his leg near out of the socket, and his tail yanked up against the seat's tail access hard enough to snap the bone right near the base. Even so, he could fire a gun. I bet he fancied himself a martyr, though he'd never admit it. Probably wanted to shoot overwatch while I made a dash for it. What a romantic idiot.

I tugged for a few solid seconds before managing to undo the button. That's what the buzz of combat does to you. The most complicated processes become perfect clockwork that you slide through like nothing, while the simplest stupid things are pure hell and trip you up. Fumbling with the button that I just had to push down to let out his seatbelt was like solving a Rubik's Cube under gunfire. They like raccoons in the army because of our steady fingers and good sense of touch, but I couldn't keep my paws from shaking.

I'm sorry. I need to take a moment for myself. Trust me though, this is the good version. Last few times I was stress panting like a malamute in a desert by this point, even with all this gratuitous AC. What is it, twenty degrees in here?

Well anyway, that moment coming out of the humvee wasn't my first time in combat, but all the fights before had been long range skirmishes where we could drop a threat before they posed any real danger. We had better guns, better equipment, and better training.

This was a situation like I'd heard of listening to my Uncle Brady as a kid, one that you see in war movies. On the TV, there's always this moment where everything hits; the mortars erupt, all the bad guys start shooting, and the world goes quiet except for the ringing in your ears. I thought that was from the intensity of it all, not that some grenade bursting next to you was simply too loud for your ears to take. I figured your body just shut down everything that wasn't important and you became something more, like a masked hero from the comics—every sense heightened and acting on flawless instinct like a feral beast on the prowl. There was some part of me that really wanted this, too. Back in high school before I enlisted, I dreamed about having that moment of perfect clarity where things exploded to my left and right and bullets lit up lines around me as I dashed through the storm of enemy fire to be a hero.

I guess that it was like that, at least a little. There wasn't any sort of numbing silence or sensory overload, but the gunfire was damn loud, terrifying, and all around me. There were more than a few furs on my hide that wanted to give up; but I couldn't, not with Matt hurt.

I slung his arm over my shoulder and hoisted him up to my side. He tried to help with his good leg, but his crooked tail made it too painful for him to move much on his own. When I got him out, though, limping and wincing each time his tail shifted beneath him, he didn't act the infirm. I couldn't think of anything but getting him, excuse me, us over to one of the thin alleys in between two of the tall tan buildings that would afford us cover. Matt, on the other paw, had his rifle up, emptying a clip at the rooftops and darn well anything else in sight that moved.

He's a damn good shot too. He says he hit a half dozen while I was preoccupied with getting us the hell out of there. You can never believe him on the number, of course, but they don't let a stubby legged otter into combined species recon for his hundred meter records.

Matt shouted at me right after we ducked around the corner, but I couldn't hear what he was saying. I motioned to my ears, then gestured down the narrow alley. He shook his head and peeked around the corner out to the road. He looked back at me with his ears flattened, as much as those clamshell ears could flatten at least, and then allowed me to help carry him farther into the alley.

The sounds of gunfire had already ebbed down to an occasional patter. I tried to listen for the telltale growl of a humvee from my platoon in hopes they'd seen us and were going to loop around after having killed most of the enemy soldiers on the rooftops. Of course, even thinking that the enemy soldiers had suffered as many casualties as us was wishful. Besides, with Matt firing off his semi-auto right next to me, my ears weren't in any real shape to listen. I don't know how canines do it with ears twice the size of these little round stubs of mine.

He shifted on my shoulder and then turned his head to me with a big toothy smile. "Good thing I was there to get you out of that mess, huh Tanner?" Matt had an odd sense of humor like that, but hell if in that moment of adrenaline and anxiety it didn't sound to me like the most hilarious thing I'd ever heard. I never got used to hearing jokes from an otter with a demeanor like Matt's. You take the roughest pirates you can think of from the storybooks—Halftail Bill, Bloodear, the Diamondback Brothers—Matt was lean and mean like they wished they could be. A long haphazard scar down his left cheek topped off his look. He loved to scare recruits with the thing.

The joke was adrenaline stabbed in my thigh. He grounded me back to reality and in turn I did my duty of hauling his crooked tail off of the street. Aurochabad isn't a big town, but it has more than a single road to it. I lugged Matt around a leftward bend in the alley, between two clustered irregular rows of buildings, and then took a right as soon as I could.

The street we came out at wasn't half as wide as the one where we crashed. Matt was in full-on soldier mode again. Even with his bad leg and how excruciating it must have been to drag his broken tail along the ground, he continued to scan the street with his rifle braced at his shoulder. The main road had been empty—everyone was likely cloistered away at the sounds of gunfire—but this one had some activity. A huddle of tan furred squirrel kits stared petrified from behind a toppled fruit stand four houses down. A thumbs up and a grin from Matt sent them scurrying into the nearest building.

An adult goat off the right froze in front of us. Matt indicated for him to run off with two flicks of his gun; a gesture that was immediately obeyed. As soon as the street was clear, I dashed across as fast as I could with a half lame otter on my shoulder. I was right to move quickly, because I heard the crack of a gun firing and the telltale zip that meant a bullet had passed near me.

I tried to return the favor Matt had done with his joke, telling him to keep his disgustingly fish-smelling fur off mine so I didn't have to shower every day for a week after, but it fell flat. He did make a crack about my mask though, saying they ain't never seen a raccoon and think I must've just painted my fur to steal their livestock. Again, not a funny joke. Darn near speciest, if I say so myself, but Matt always knew when the right time to make those bad jokes came and it made me smile real wide.

There wasn't another road past that second stretch of buildings, just a ditch for drainage and a haphazard mix of grain fields and towering brush. I froze for a brief moment to consider my options. The Al-Abgeer soldiers likely couldn't make it down from their roofs and over to the edges of town for a minute at least. That meant time for me to find somewhere to hide, or at least bunker down to make good use of Matt's semi-auto.

What I didn't expect was an oryx woman in a snow white hijab frantically gesturing me towards the back door to a building on my right. I glanced at Matt, down at his injuries, and then helped him over to the door. She said something in her language, but I couldn't speak it. Only one guy in our entire platoon could.

She let us in, sat us at their table, and fed us. I still can't believe they were so kind to us as complete strangers. It's humbling that they thought so much of us and what we were doing in their country to protect us like they did.

Matt and I were resting in their guest room where there was a crash and a bang. Then there were gunshots. The Al-Abgeer army had seen us come into the building and came back to kill us. Matt and I fought them off, but it was too late for the oryx couple. It was horrible, dreadful and…

After they were dead, I—

I

I can't fucking lie anymore.

206

I see you over there on the stairs, Terrence! Go back to your seat. If you try to take this mic away, I'm done. I won't let you parade me around like a kit who won a fucking spelling bee anymore. This is my home. If I want to tell my kin what happened, I God-damn deserve the chance! I'll go back to all that bullshit after this speech, I promise, but only if you let me keep talking.

That's what I thought.

Look, I don't need these notes. That last bit, they wrote it for me because they didn't want the truth. It doesn't play into their little story about what the army is like. Wouldn't it be so romantic if I avenged the deaths of the kindly Al-Abgeer family instead of what—what really happened? Yeah, that's why they wanted that version. It's prettier, how they want all the impressionable kits to think of war.

The home smelled like spices and dirt, with a slight coppery tang. It was an unfamiliar smell, but oddly welcoming. I hadn't been in a place that smelled that safe and homely since I got to Al-Abgeer.

The two oryx sat us at their table and fed us. I got nervous when her husband put his hand on Matt's, but it wasn't anything threatening. The look in his face was like when someone on the street tries to get a soldier to take their kid home with them to live a better life. He said something neither of us understood and then his wife rushed out a side door.

She came back in holding a dirty black and white picture. Her husband took it from her and pushed it in between Matt and me. The picture was of the oryx couple standing in front of a wide fenced-in field of wheat. In between them, the woman's hooved hand scuffled the fur on the head of a young Mediterranean otter girl.

Real fucking good shit, right? They wanted me to put that bit in. I mean, that's the whole reason for the war. It's the War of Protection. We're there to help all the victims of the genocide and take out the fuckers who did it in the first place. And here I am with a sweet family who lost an adopted child to that horror show. That is the shit they put on posters. Well, I refuse to say any of it unless they let me say what happened after. There was no way in hell they were going to allow that.

But those two, the oryx, they were so sweet. I just—Matt and I were humbled by them. We'd been fighting for so long out in the open country with no one but the other guys in our platoon to talk to; and our friends, they're like a pack of sharks dropped in an aquarium. You forget about the people who actually lived here, what they're going through.

After dinner, Matt and I crammed all our shit into the small, barely furnished guest room. They set out some mats for us, said evening prayers, and then left for their own bedroom. Matt and I—well, we took advantage of the opportunity.

I can only imagine what the father thought when he walked in on me muzzle locked with the otter. The two little cups of tea he'd been holding clattered to the floor in little bits and the faintest of bleats escaped him. I bet he figured right then and there that the Caliph had a point. We outsider species were bringing decadence to his country.

He slammed the door shut and Matt and I jolted upright. I'd been playing with his short fuzzy ears while we were kissing and, well, I guess that's information you all don't need to know, but I couldn't have been caught more ill-prepared for the moment than I was right then. Matt looked at me, dumbstruck. I was shaking. My fucking raccoon paws supposed to be all steady and shit shaking again. God.

I got up, moved to the door, and gestured Matt over. Somehow I'd forgotten his broken tail and leg in the heat of the moment. He didn't move of course, and I didn't go over to get him. There wasn't time. I waited next to the door with my own rifle braced against my shoulder, dreading what was going to happen. Was the father running to tell all the Caliph's men? Were we about to be cornered and brutally executed like I'd heard a group in the rabbit division had been the week before? I looked back to Matt. He had to have been just as freaked out and terrified as I was, but he just smirked and coyly licked the muzzle of his gun. God, when no one else is looking, that otter is such a fucking otter.

I—I do love him for it, though. Feeling his paw slip over mine when gunfire echoes near our humvee, or his rudder tail poking and prodding me while I'm trying to sleep in the squad tent. He makes me squirm and blush nose to ear and I have to work real hard not to let anyone else notice. I swear he knows all my buttons and exactly how hard he can push any of them without letting our secret slip. He never let anyone find out about us. I guess I fucked up with that one, didn't I?

Hah. You don't know whether to laugh, jeer, or keep sitting in awkward fucking silence like you're doing now. Maybe you could walk out like Mary Lingh just did. Yeah, Mary Lingh. She used to babysit for me almost eight years of my childhood. That right there shows just how much she actually cares.

Maybe this'll help you all choose. The father who let us in out of gratitude for what we were doing for species like his adopted child, who probably saw a something of his little girl in Matt, the man who fed us and offered us a place to sleep—he opened the door and had an AK with him. He raised it. I adjusted my aim just slightly and shot before he had the chance to. I put three holes in his skull before he dropped, then half a dozen more. My ears rang.

The mother must've heard. She came out, saw her husband, and shrieked. I shot her too. I don't know if I needed to. I shouldn't have, but my brain was already numb right there.

You know, I didn't even mention Liam. Liam was a cat; he rode shotgun in our Humvee and survived the crash. I didn't rescue him and I can still remember his screaming as I carried Matt away.

I'm a selfish fucking shitbag! I decided Matt's life was worth more than Liam's and more than either of the Oryx's. Well, he's a good guy. His might be, but mine sure as fuck isn't.

I—give me a moment. I think I got something itchy in my mask fur. Us coons—we always got a fucking excuse, don't we?

After that, well, it was night when we went back outside. I didn't even look around to see if anyone was coming. My mind was numb. If anything, that moment that I said how I used to wish war would get— where everything goes all quiet and your ears ring and everything is all surreal. I could still smell the blood. I couldn't forget it. I still can't forget it.

As much as he didn't act it, I think Matt was also really shaken up by how I shot the Oryx couple or how they attacked us. I can't stop remembering the happy swish of his rudder and twitch of his ears when they showed him the picture of their adopted otter.

Those people were his reason to fight. And I got them killed.

I mean, we'd both seen innocent civilians shot before. Its war, shit happens. Sometimes when you're patrolling they come too close. They didn't know enough about how our army operated back then. They didn't understand warning shots and they didn't get how we were afraid of IEDs and people attacking in civilian clothes and no uniform. But this was different. Those are mistakes.

What I did wasn't a mistake. No, it was a mistake, but not that kind of mistake. I meant to shoot the guy. That's why when I stood by the door with my gun ready and aimed, unlike all those other dumb times my raccoon instincts actually kicked in and my arms didn't even fucking shake.

It was a mistake, though, kissing Matt. I'd wanted him alone with me for so long. We were in training together; same batch, even. Going in, I was sure I'd be the only gay guy there, and I wasn't about to let anyone else know. It was tough enough in middle school when I got caught with this other raccoon, Trevor Jacobson. The kids were brutal. They beat me so hard, so many times, that my mom had to pull me out and tutor me herself for a few years. I would've given up training long before I let anyone else know.

Actually, it's pretty funny how I found out about Matt. This lynx named Fred bled me dry in a night of poker. He convinced me to snatch an issue of *Otter Abandon* from Matt's footlocker instead of giving up dessert for a week. I would've told him off for asking the only raccoon in the room to steal the magazine, but I figured it was better than losing dessert. We knew Matt had the thing. Whenever the otter was off to the bathroom, he'd flash us the cover with this coy grin born in owning something he knew we wanted.

I got up early the next day and waited until right when he hopped off the bunk to get up myself. That way I could unassumingly slide past and peer over his shoulder to catch the combination to the locker. I committed the numbers to memory and was off as soon as I heard the snap of the lock opening, him none the wiser. I returned the night after he'd gone to sleep and carefully clicked the footlocker open. *Otter Abandon* was on top, but I couldn't help my curiosity and thumbed underneath to see a pristine, scentless copy of *Musky Musties*. At this point I knew something was up. No one's porn mags were pristine anymore. Sure enough, past *Lovely Lutrines* was a wrinkled and worn issue of *Knot Sorry* with the same wonderful fishy smell as the otter.

I was in complete shock. I hadn't even considered that anyone else in training with me could be gay, let alone the muscular, wise-cracking otter. It should have ended there, but somehow knowing he was gay flipped a switch in me. Sure, there were a lot of hot guys around, but the fact that this was the military put a damper on my desires. Why bother crushing on boys when you know that none of them are ever going to want you back? I learned in high school how that was a recipe for self-loathing. But every time we changed after that, I wondered if Matt was checking me out. I certainly looked at him in a different way.

The whole thing built up to the point where I had to hide a blush and corny smile every time he was around me. My squadmates began to notice and heckled me about being a turd-pusher. None of them really believed it, though. They were just joking around. Matt, however, saw right through me.

Just last week, I asked him when exactly it was that he realized I had the hots for him. He told me that there was a morning when I was sitting up in bed thinking that no one else was awake. I was just looking across the bunks at him with dreamy eyes. He also says I was contouring his body through the air with my paw, but he's the type to make the story nicer at the truth's expense.

That evening, I sneaked off to the bathroom with a copy of *Vix* that had made its rounds after being snatched from a hapless fox. I left it on the floor of the stall. It was just there for cover. Matt came in a minute later. He called, "Tanner?" and I stopped what I was doing and shuffled my pants on. My ears were burning with heat as if somehow Matt knew that he was the target of my fantasies. I opened the stall door to look up at him, the insides of my ears bright red and my muzzle flush with heat.

He asked me if I was "fucking gay." But I understood from the tone of his voice that he was actually asking, just in a way that allowed him an out if I said no.

I didn't say no. I told him the truth.

He said he saw how I'd been looking at him.

I said I wanted to borrow *Knot Sorry*.

He cuffed me for stealing *Otter Abandon*, but we both knew he didn't actually care.

Our first kiss was a week later. We shipped off for deployment a month after that.

I'm sorry. I get carried away when I'm talking about Matt.

Anyway, we stumbled through the trench outside the Oryx couple's house. I wanted to get us out of the town. We could survive the wilderness for a while and make our way around to a road to get picked up, but I couldn't bear staying around the town any longer, not after what I did.

The problem was that I didn't have any splints in my pack. As much as Matt tried not to show it, I could tell that he was really hurting. Since otter tails are long enough to drag along the ground, with a break like that it's damn near impossible to keep it still enough not to hurt like hell.

I brought him out into the brush about half a mile before I stopped and told him that it seemed like a good spot to rest. I helped carefully set him on his side to rest on his good leg. My heart was still pounding and I was flush with anxiety and fear, but the otter's smile melted my worries away.

I looked him in the eyes and pressed my nose to his, but I didn't dare kiss him again. It felt wrong after what happened. I knew we'd be kissing again the next day, and maybe the day after if we got rescued and found ourselves a moment when no one was watching, but after what happened that night I couldn't bring myself to do it right there. He didn't press me either. Beneath all those muscles, the creamy brown and white fur, and the wit and sarcasm is the sweetest man I've ever met.

We made it back to the road the next day, hiking south to avoid the town. Delta platoon picked us up. They went into Aurochabad to clean up any remaining resistance so that the military could keep using the road and picked us up on their way out. Matt was splinted by their medic and airlifted to a hospital from which he was sent home. I served another three months before they let me come back to get my medal and give all these talks.

Matt's been traveling with me. He doesn't come to these speeches since we've been afraid of people figuring us out, but I guess that's behind us now.

That night in the field of tall grass is something I will never forget. As much as he's said he owes me his life, I owe him mine too. Laying on the ground nose to nose, the broken otter knew exactly how to fix me.

Thank you for your time.

This is another story about man losing out to his creations.
But are the creations really that different?
As Walt Kelly said on another occasion, "We have met the enemy and he is us."

Last Man Standing

by Frances Pauli

The eggheads always said we'd never do it, but they never once said it wasn't possible. Sitting on my knapsack in a mud-filled trench, this seems like a ridiculous thing to ponder, but the thought lodges in my brain as soon as our Captain gives word the monsters are restless. They'd never said we couldn't do it. They'd only trusted us not to be stupid.

And we'd failed in spades.

Next to me, Joe chews a wad of tobacco-free chaw and rubs his flamethrower with a cloth that looks about as clean as my boots. Nervous, that kid, but who could blame him? We didn't sign up for this. Not really. We put our names down, sure, but back then our heads had been overflowing with humanity's last stand, with glory and victory and all the abstractions that real warfare hid behind.

Ideals might spawn bravery in the recruitment meetings, in back alleys and empty schoolrooms, but they feel like a thin shield now. An abstract, tissue paper barrier between our trenches and the enemy. We're right, of course. We have to do this, but here in the mud, it's a lot harder to believe we'll succeed.

Harder to believe we'll survive, win the war, save the humans.

The night sky lies thick and black above us. No stars and nothing but a pale outline to show us where the Rockies stand. No moonlight. No idea what we're facing or when tonight's action will start.

At the beginning, we'd expected it to be easy.

"You need a dip yet, Mack?" Joe holds his chaw tin out, rattles it too loudly.

"No." I whisper it, only a breath of sound and still the hairs along my forearms lift. Proper sparse hairs. Nothing at all like the Augmented, and yet a shiver takes my spine, a memory flashes through my head.

Becky had started with the eyes. Maybe they all do. Maybe that's the first place it shows up when you muck about with a person's DNA. Who knows, really? Who cares? Point is she came home from work one day, skipping with joy to show me her new eyes. Cat's eyes. Creepy as fuck, and of course I screwed it all up.

I kick one boot against the other to dislodge the filth and try to remember she's a freak now. It doesn't matter if we fought about her eyes. The eyes had only been the beginning.

"You hear that?" Joe again, too loud for the frontline. Maybe the last frontline.

We've been at this for over a year now, and each week etches another layer of optimism from our hearts. We had them out-armed, outnumbered at first, but then half the folks back home, you know, the ones we're here risking our asses for, well, they all up and took the augmentation.

Like lambs to slaughter.

Now we don't even know who we're fighting for. Maybe ourselves. Maybe as the last dregs of ordinary humanity, we just can't bring ourselves to stop.

The first skirmish proved disastrous, of course. We'd expected to fight a war, expected the enemy to be civilized, to shoot back at us. I've changed units four times since then. They shuffle us around so we don't know how few of us are left. Makes sense, I guess.

But that first night, we'd been ready to win. We'd had piss and fury in our veins, huddled behind our fancy barricade with superior weapons and a heap of righteousness on our side. Until they came at us.

Until we heard the growling.

We had no idea how unlike us they'd become until we saw it in action. Teeth and claws and no fear at all in their first rush. Who wouldn't have run from that? Most of us ran. Hell, I ran.

Still heard them tearing us apart. Still heard the damn noises they make.

We didn't even start shooting until the shock wore off. Until it was too damn late.

They're calling this the last front. Nothing left past the Rockies, and the damn Augmented hold everything behind us. So we'll go out trapped, I suppose. Maybe. Unless we can hold them here. But I can already hear the guns firing in the dark, already hear them snarling.

* * *

The Pinkies had had a lot to say before the first battle. Afterwards, all we could hear was their whimpering. All we could smell was the piss they'd shed in fear.

I nudge Jerry in the rib and he shows me a fangy grin. We got 'em, that smile says, and the swish of his tail confirms it. His pelt's like smoke in the night, and only the gleam of his teeth and the shine off his rifle give him away.

Except I can smell the jackass. He's too damn excited for his own good.

I scratch behind one ear and tilt my head, catch the sound of whispering from their desperate little trenches. Tobacco scents waft sweet tendrils between the stench of terror. God, they always stink of that. Like we're some kind of demons, like they didn't start this whole thing.

We just wanted to be left alone, to live as we liked, do what we wanted with our own bodies. Nobody needed to die, not one person. Now, so many deaths trail behind us that I fear we'll lose our humanity before we win. I glance at Jerry, so excited to kill.

How can we get back to the ordinary world now? How can we go back to the office, go home again, and pretend this hasn't changed us? Damn Pinkies forced our hand, and maybe, they made us into what they'd always feared we were.

Animals.

Wrong again, Pinkies.

Captain Mayes stalks between our lines, hooves clipping against stone and rubble. He's going to order us out soon. I can feel it. But he's worried too. He tosses a suspicious glance at Jerry. Us preds make him nervous. Hell, after the first few frays, we make ourselves nervous. They keep us out of the brass now, keep us in the lines where we can let the instincts do the most good.

Sure hope we can rein it back when this hell is over. Won't be a win at all if we have to become what they hated to get it. Even if it is their fault. Still can't come home to the missus with a bloody muzzle.

I still don't get how we ended up here. Why the Pinkies had to go all superior. So much weaker than us, and yet so sure they should own everything. They're so convinced we're a mistake that they tried to lock us up, undo us. Their laws and bans and boxes pushed us to it, in the end.

Not our fault, Pinkie. This is on you. You're not so superior now, are you? You've heard the howls at midnight.

Now they know their reservations will never hold us. Their doctors will never cure us.

They cannot unmake our kind, cannot wish us away.

I don't even think we lost one soldier that first fight. Not our unit at least. Mayes marches past again, swishing his oxtail and flexing both arms behind his back. Prey or no, he's still a scary dude. He'll give them hell as much as Jerry will. Horns like razors and a damn tough hide under his IBA.

He stops and raises one arm high over his head. He'll signal the assault any second, but he spares one last look at Jerry. At me too, I suppose. The wolf in me wants to snarl at him, to curl my lip and show him what's to come. I rein it in, though. I've got a lot more control than Jerry.

His throat warbles a low purr. Ready to go.

We're ready for anything.

Except, maybe, going home when this is over. Maybe, we'll never be ready for that.

* * *

We got in a few that time. I know we did. I can still catch the stink of singed fur on the wind. The fire worked like a charm, but the screaming was horrendous. I huddle beside the first fire we've been able to build in days and tell myself the shivering is from the cold.

It just proves they're not human, the noises they make. No reason to have doubt about that. Once you hear the bastards howling, you have to know it. You chant it in your sleep afterwards. They're not people any longer, and it's not like we didn't warn them. The damn reservations were for their own good.

I've lost Joe. Damn kid got too cocky and ran ahead. A bear-man took him down, a huge hairy bastard with claws like… Poor kid. Captain wants me to write his wife. Shit. Dear Mrs. Jones, I'm sorry to inform you your husband was torn to pieces by a bear-man.

No. it was a bear. They don't deserve the *man* anymore. We tried to be reasonable, to provide a safe place for them to keep their freak-of-nature bodies out of our society. We don't care. Just don't want to have to see it. Be animals if you want to be animals.

Now, they can just be dead.

Captain says only one of us is going to make it out the other side of this war. I believe him, I do. I'm just not sure anymore that it's going to be us walking home after the dust settles. Rumors going 'round about augmentation rates in the cities, scary numbers. They swear it's just Augmented propaganda, lies to scare us out of fighting.

No way everyone can possibly want to be a freak.

Just my Becky.

* * *

The caveman has rediscovered fire. Son-of-a-bitch. They burned half of Omega Squad before we worked out what they were up to. Fire. And they call *us* animals. Scared the shit out of me when I saw the flamethrowers. Not just ordinary scared either, deep bone-level scared.

Made me want to run. Ha! No way am I saying that aloud. But still, you know, the wolf thing. Captain Mayes says it won't be a problem. Now that we know what they're up to, we can hang back. We can let them burn out their fear on the cold ground. We can wait.

When their napalm runs out, then they'll be ours again. Too many good men dead, though. Too much carnage already. They've drawn their blood, Mayes says. Now we'll show them how to really do it. It makes me uneasy when he says it, makes me twitch a little.

Earns me another suspicious look.

Well, he's the one that says it. Kill them all. His mouth makes the words. I just imagine doing it. Jerry too, if his tail is any indication. My housecat's used to twitch like that. Mr. Sprinkles. He'd make that noise too, right before he pounced.

We'll make sure none of them come out the next round in one piece.

It's us or them. All or nothing. I just want it to be over.

* * *

The new captain sends our unit in first, scouting sort of, but pushing the line forward a little as we go, testing the boundary. He wants us to work out where they're hunkering, I suppose. Doesn't take long.

The beasts come at us before we hit the suburbs, and it's a massacre. They've figured out the flames and they wait just out of reach for us to burn the fuel off. Stupid. Doesn't matter how much you shout, *hold your fire*, when they're snarling and scratching like that. Everyone shoots. Everyone goes dry.

Sometimes, the bastards don't wait. They run right through the flames. Maybe they're not human *or* animal.

I get separated from my unit and end up facing this big guy. He's part cow or some shit. Horrible horns coming right out of his hair. He snorts, and I know I'm going to buy it. This is it for me. Game over. We're standing a good ten paces apart when he sees me too. Nothing but dust and rubble between us. He's faster. He has hooves, for Christ's sake. I'm out of fire, and hand to hand is *not* an option.

I've got a standard issue pistol in my belt, but we both work that out at the same time. The bull bastard charges when I reach for it. His hooves rattle my bones, death music. I imagine the letter they'll send home. Gored by a bull-man. Except there's no one to send it to.

My Becky is one of *them*.

The pistol sticks and my vision narrows to a tunnel. At one end, I'm gearing up to die. At the other, a monster is bearing down on me. His head lowers. How does he brush his hair around those things? Does he have his hats specially tailored? Insane laughter bubbles from my lips. I stagger my legs and bring my left arm up.

My right is busy trying to free a pistol that may not even slow this asshole down.

His horn goes right through my arm. I think it scrapes a chunk out of my side also, but the pain is so thick and I'm screaming so loud that I can't be sure. His head jerks and tries to tear free, but the son-of-a-bitch is stuck and I'm too close to passing out to do anything but scream and strike at him with the pistol in my free hand.

I slam it against his temple twice before I register that it's there. In my hand. I just want his head to stop moving so bad, but... Things are going dark fast. Still, I get that thought out and there's nothing to do but press the gun into his fuzzy hide and pull the trigger.

His eyes roll, white at the edges and full of nothing but fury. Nobody's home, and not just because I've blown his brains out. Never going to forget those eyes.

Never.

* * *

The science jerks may be right about the aggressive thing. I hate to admit it. I saw Jerry bite through a guy's shoulder in the Denver fray. He just sank his teeth right into the jackass and tore him up. Even after the guy stopped kicking.

It burns into your head, something like that, watching your best mate gnaw on a body. Maybe the pred thing *is* getting out of hand. Maybe. It still gives us the edge. It still keeps them on the fly. Cause they're really running now. Maybe, they'll never stop running.

The new brass is predicting total domination in a month or less. They're talking about reservations for the remaining Pinkies. It would serve them right, locking them in their own cages. Find out how they like being rounded up. I can't see there being many of them left, though.

This never was a survivable fight.

Jerry's stalking through camp like a peacock, proud as hell and ready to eat them all if he has to. I wonder if he knows. Red stains on the fur around his muzzle. Creepy shit. I wish he'd stop crowing and take a wash. Show some trace of remorse. Wash off the blood, Jerry, and sit down. You look like an ass, like an animal.

Besides, I can smell it.

Hope I don't end up eating anyone.

I'm probably gonna be sick if I do.

* * *

I'm on my own. Got separated again. There's just too much panic when they start roaring and rushing at us. I'm in the trees now, but I can hear them. I can hear the crunching, the shots in the distance.

And I'm bleeding a lot.

I don't know who's left, either. Maybe it's just me. Maybe this is the spot where humanity bites it. It's not funny, but I laugh anyway. Maybe I've already lost my mind.

All our power, our weapons, the sum total of human intellect, and we're still decimated. We still lose. There's no denying that now. We're losing this shit hard.

Maybe I should have liked her new eyes, the tail even. Was that where I went wrong?

I hear branches cracking, too close. Voices that growl too much to be my unit. Doesn't really matter where I fucked up now. Doesn't even matter if we were right or not.

I just hope they shoot me.

God, please don't let them eat me.

* * *

We completely destroyed them, but I'm not sure it feels like it should. I mean, they tried to herd us up, lock us away. Still, this is massive, way worse than anyone expected, I think. Even the brass. Then again, nobody could have predicted these numbers.

I lost my shit in the last fray. Don't even want to talk about what I did, but that's war, right? We all do things we don't talk about after. I think that's how it works.

My left leg is hamburger. Stepped right into a last ditch grenade. The medics swear it can be rebuilt, but the transgenic docs in this place are more worried about rebuilding *me*. The pred heavy factor, they're calling it. We scared the shit out of them out there. Now they want us all to add a meeker animal just to be safe. Like I want to be a damn squirrel, for fuck's sake.

Maybe they'll let me pick something cool like a mongoose or one of those nasty Tasmanian rodents.

Anyway. We won. Still think it should feel better somehow. Mostly, I'm just really glad it's over. Over. Now we get to work out what to do with the shit we won. All the shit.

Nobody like them left in the cities even. A whole fucking Augmented Nation.

Maybe they'll let me be part badger.

* * *

They said we wouldn't stop, until they had the last man. Well, I think I might be him. They've got me in some transgenic hospital in Denver. New Denver, they're calling it. Everyone's talking about the future here as if there is one.

My nurse looks like a cat. She reminds me a lot of Becky, really, but her fur is orange and she's got little black tufts on her ears. I probably should have known Becks wouldn't stop at just farting around with contacts. I shouldn't have kicked her out when the tail grew in. When the fur showed up.

The guy on the next bunk's in worse shape than I am. His leg is ruined, but he doesn't even notice. Massive guy, and the fur. Shit. It's making me want to sneeze, but he'd probably strangle me if I did.

He keeps arguing with the staff, too. Wolfie doesn't want another augmentation, it seems. Huh. Maybe their new nation isn't the paradise they think it is.

The cat nurse wants him to pick a bunny or some shit. Not this guy. He's a fighter. He might even be the wolf who ate Travis in that last round. He doesn't want to be a rabbit, that's for sure. Hey, genius, a badger isn't a rodent.

The doctors come to council him. They pull a curtain across like it's going to help. I hear them arguing, but it's obvious Wolfie isn't going to win. Not like he can run away on that leg. When he shuts up, it's my turn.

My doctor's a dog… for real.

His nose twitches when he talks to me. Do I stink, Fido? You got any idea what damp fur smells like, asshole?

He informs me they are offering two options. I can die of my wounds or I can let them fuck with me. No choice at all, is it? My body's too sore to fight, too damn tired to battle infection or mend itself. I imagine shooting him in his furry face, and he smiles. He assumes I'll choose augmentation, of course. His furry fingers pull open the curtain and he leaves with a final promise the nurse will help me make my selection. The one who could easily be Becky.

How would I know anymore?

* * *

My Pinkie roommate is a piece of work. This guy. I'm stuck getting a ground squirrel minor augmentation and he's got the balls to whine about having a proper animal. Sad sack he is. Stinky. He smells like fear and judgment. I suppose I should feel bad for the asshole. I mean, his side lost. Last of his kind and all. Last man standing.

Did we go too far?

He's nervous, I guess. I remember when I got my wolf. I'd wanted to impress the boys down at the pub. All of them were fawning over Jerry's panther. I wonder where Jerry is now. Haven't seen him since the last fray. Since the medics found me and dragged my sad carcass to transgenics.

I sure hope Jerry made it out all right.

The whiny guy takes the catalog from the nurse, a hot kitten with orange fur and a cleavage worth writing home about. Anyway, he doesn't even open it, and I catch him glancing my way. Maybe he thinks he's being subtle. Maybe he's going to take a slow death after all.

I tell him not to sweat it. The pity I offer is probably half guilt, but he looks terrified of a damn paper catalog. "Whatever you pick, buddy, it can't be worse than a squirrel."

I can see he doesn't want to laugh, probably doesn't even want to talk to me. Too bad.

"Ground squirrels aren't the same as tree squirrels." He's a natural smartass.

"Whatever." I shrug and try to impress him. "I doubt I'll still be hung like a horse when they're done with me."

Pinkie actually laughs at that.

He glares at his catalog, and the nurse comes back to take me to prep.

"Sayonara, buddy." I let my nerves keep me talking. "Good luck."

He laughs and tells me to hang onto my junk.

No kidding.

I hope I don't end up with a cocktail frank. Stupid Pinkie reminds me of more than that. I forgot how nervous I was the first time. I forgot how it felt to touch bare skin until I'd grappled with that guy in the last battle. Weird. I'd forgotten that, too. Maybe the pred heavy factor *was* real. The animal had gotten in my head. Maybe.

I forgot a lot out there.

* * *

I peek at the catalog after they drag my new mate off to be neutered. Poor sack. He was shaking like a squirrel when they wheeled him out. Now that's funny. Somehow I can't picture that furry bastard enjoying a nut or two on the neighbor's lawn.

But I can't picture myself with a tail, either, with fur and eyes like Becky had showed up with.

Nothing in this catalog looks like Wolfie. I suspect they don't want me with anything that powerful. Just a token change for me, something to make me one of them. To wipe out the last of ordinary humanity.

Maybe I should take the death. I probably should. It would have been easier, somehow, out in the trees with the gunfire and the howling. The hospital bed is too normal. Even with Nurse Kitty attending. The time for noble sacrifice has passed. I think I might want to live now, even if it means a tail.

I imagine the wolf asshole with a huge squirrel tail and can't help but smile. It'd serve him right. But I'm just trying to distract myself and not doing a good job of it, either.

Nurse Kitty makes a few suggestions. I tell her skunk is right out, and she manages to make me laugh. When she giggles, the human shows. Her hands too. They're furry but long fingered. Human, even with the claws at their tips. If you focus on her normal bits, she's not bad looking.

Nice smile. Only slightly fangy.

"So what'll it be?" She grins.

There's a housecat in my catalog, but maybe that's too ordinary for her. Maybe they like to mix it up. How would I know? I didn't keep Becks around long enough to find out. God, I can't do this. How the hell am I going to fit into a society I know dick about. I consider asking the nurse what she thinks. Will that make me sound like a pussy?

Not even funny in my head.

"Why'd you do it?" I hear my voice, but I hadn't meant to say it. Maybe I'm not asking her. It's Becky I think of.

"Because I wanted to." Nurse Kitty sounds just as pissed as Becks had.

I can't stop myself. "Then why are you all so touchy about it?"

She leans forward and wrinkles a nose just like Becky would have. "Maybe because we can smell how much you don't like us."

"You can smell that?"

"It's like a superpower." Nurse Kitty stands up and gives me a look. Not angry, but not happy either. Do I really stink?

"That's kind of cool." I mutter it, but her eyes widen. "I mean, I didn't know you'd get extra senses and stuff."

God. I sound like an idiot.

I wonder if Wolfie is half squirrel yet, if his Johnson will shrink up right away or if it takes a while. The catalog claims there's a *genetic accommodation* period. It uses terms like *transition* and scares the shit out of me. Maybe they'd put a bullet in me if I asked. Nurse Kitty might.

Except now I see more sympathy in her gaze. She's softened a bit. Maybe I smell scared too. Or nervous. Either way, she brings me a valium and smiles when I swallow it without arguing. She takes the catalog from me and thumbs through it. Shows me a picture or two.

"How about a rodent?"

I shake my head. "You got any horses in there?"

It's funny that time. I could show the wolf guy my horse junk and get the last word in.

Nurse Kitty has a pretty laugh.

"I think I'd make a lousy vegetarian," I tell her.

"Maybe something, omnivorous?" She holds the catalog open facing me and taps a picture of a Raccoon with her finger. I almost manage not to notice the claw. "This one's cute."

Cute, she says. It looks like a bandit, but maybe the mask does it for her. Maybe she's into bad boys.

"Fine." I nod. Cute it is.

Just not a squirrel.

We lost the Transgenic War, even if they said we'd never have one. We lost ourselves, or maybe, we just found a new self. Something different. Superpower senses and a different kind of future. Either way, I'll have a future. It turns out I really do want to live.

And when Nurse Kitty smiles and goes to tell the doctor my decision, I can't help but imagine what it will be like to smell fear.

Not all warfare is high-tech. Angela Oliver's Kingdom of Madigaska is roughly 18th-century Madagascar with sentient lemurs. In real history, King Andriamasinavalona divided his kingdom into four equal parts for his four favorite sons. They promptly went to war against each other for most of the 18th century. This is 18th-century-style African warfare, with lemur warriors using lemur senses.

Everyone knows the ring-tailed lemurs, but there are over a hundred species of lemurs in Madagascar—if they aren't extinct yet. (Many are critically endangered.) You will meet more than the ring-tails in "Hunter's Fall".

The fossa, evolved from the mongoose, was the most dangerous predator in Madagascar before the coming of man with dogs and cats. The original Lemures were the Roman ghosts of one's ancestors. Many Romans prayed to their Lemures for help. The lemurs of Madagascar, first glimpsed in the treetops, were considered ghosts and named for the Roman spirits. Oliver has made them what her lemurs pray to. Azafady is the Malagasy word for 'please' or 'excuse me'.

See also Angela Oliver's furry novel Fellowship of the Ringtails *(CreateSpace, June 2013), set in Madigaska. She is working on a sequel,* Tail of Two Scions.

Hunter's Fall

by Angela Oliver

War had come to the island kingdom of Madigaska. After the sudden death of the king, his queen, Ranavalona—an outsider by birth—laid her claim to the throne. Not all were willing to bare their throats to her, and the threat of revolution loomed. To contain it, she needed an army; thus the Hunters were formed—youths recruited, both willingly and not, trained in weaponry and primed to kill. Primed to hunt, to track down the rebels that dared stand against her.

Hunter Roland's razor-edged club had not yet been bloodied. Now, after many moons in the training grounds, the young sifaka lemur crouched in the belly of an armored war canoe. Flank pressed against flank, white fur mingling with browns and reds and silvered-grey. He kept his breathing shallow, for the stench was terrible. Nervous fear, mingled with excitement, all but overwhelmed by the foul reek of fossa, the lemur-kin's most feared predator.

Thirty lemur-kin soldiers—sifaka and indri, brown and ring-tailed—were crammed into this vessel, one of ten such crafts. Three hundred Hunters, being smuggled in to overthrow this colony of rebels: a ragtag bag of insurgents who crouched in their stone fortress and plotted rebellion.

The Hunters crouched in expectant silence, their shields raised to form a canopy, scaled like a lizard. The only sounds: the sussuration of shallow breaths, creaking timbers, water surging past. Hunter Roland tried to ignore the cramp in his legs, the deadly club that hung his side. The knowledge that soon it must taste blood.

The boat lurched and jerked upwards, eliciting a few startled gasps from the Hunters. Roland braced himself against the wood. Held his position, despite the nervous adrenalin, the quickening of his pulse. Rocks ground and crunched beneath the groaning hull. They had beached. Arrived.

It was time to go to war.

Beside him, her body pressed so close to his that her feminine musk almost stirred other urges, Hunter Sasha let out a long suffering sigh. "Thank the *Lemures*. If we had to stay in this stink one heartbeat longer, I swear that I would go adala. Why make us stink so?"

"It was the idea of the General's prodigy," Roland replied, his voice barely above a whisper.

"I know." Her tone turned to a whispered mocking parody of their Captain's voice. "'You must all bathe in the oil of the fossa. It will strike fear into the heart of the enemy and it is how we shall know one another.'"

"Indeed, because once we get out there it's going to be as black as the Alpha's pelt."

She nodded against him, and might have said more, had the Hunter Captain not barked out an order: "Disembark!"

The outer ring of the Hunters raised their wooden shields, breaking the shell. They leapt from the canoe, staggering only a little after too long in cramped confines, swishing their tails to recover their balance.

"It's time," Sasha declared. She jostled Roland. "Are you not excited? Our first battle."

Roland snorted. "Battle?" he said, his voice a low growl. "This is not a battle, it is a massacre. There is no honor in sneaking in during the dark of the moon and raining carnage down…"

"You would do well to keep quiet about such objections," Sasha hissed, pressing her hands around his muzzle, muffling his words. "For are these not highly skilled warriors? Trained both in weaponry and armed with deadly tools of dark science? Or are you saying that our Hunter-captains have been misguiding us?"

Roland swallowed hard, his eyes bright and cold as they met her gaze and held it for a long moment, before looking away. Sasha relinquished her grip, and grasped her short, flat-bladed club.

"We must fight," she said. "For the sakes of our families, our friends."

"I have no family," Roland replied, his voice little more than a broken whisper. "They were all taken from me."

"Then fight for your friends." Sasha rested one hand on the side of the canoe, vaulting out and onto the stony ground. She held her club out before her, golden eyes peering into the moonless gloom.

"What friends?" Roland whispered, more to himself than to her. "They took them too." He sprang out to land beside her, wincing as his muscles groaned their protest. The two of them angled back to back, as they had been trained. Other apprentice Hunters took their positions, strung out in pairs across the banks, pale silhouettes against the deep blue-grey of the star-scattered sky. Beyond them, the craggy, fang-like spires of the stone fortress towered over the forest.

There were no enemy troops waiting. Nothing but the gentle sounds of a forest at sleep: insects calling, the distant thrum-thrum-thrum of a frog colony. Somewhere, an owl hooted. Wind rustled through the branches.

"Where are they?" he wondered.

The Hunter Captain motioned them into formation. "We move in," she instructed. "Fan out." They spread out in an arc around her, keeping in their pairs.

The stony beach rose up to meet a steep bank. Pebbles tumbled and scattered beneath their feet. The forest loomed above, a dense, tangled chaos of thorny bushes and clutching branches. Roland and Sasha entered their shadows. Sasha turned to the left, Roland scented the bushes to the right. Ears pricked for the slightest sound, eyes struggling to break the gloom.

Ahead, the sound of scuffles, screams rising in the night. The darkness was brutally complete, forcing Roland to use his nose, his whiskers and his ears, to maneuver over the unfamiliar terrain. He was grateful, now, for the days of training while blindfolded, of navigating obstacle courses and mazes without the use of sight. He shuddered as he remembered Hunter Candice, who had refused to wear her blindfold. She had been taken away, and when she returned to the Training Grounds, her eyes had been sewn shut.

His nose twitched, scenting the air, heavy with the aroma of burnt wood and rank with the earthy stench of spilled blood. Sasha brushed past him, her tail dancing up his thigh, teasingly. He inhaled again. Her oestrus was near. The tantalizing sweet edge to her scent called to him, but now was not the time for distraction. He swallowed hard, took his knife-edged club in hand, and followed her into the fray.

An enemy came at him, descending from the trees above, forcing a fiery brand into his face. Behind the licking, dancing flames, two round eyes stared at him in terror. He swung his club up, parried the rudimentary weapon and hooked it from her hand. It painted a fiery comet through the air until it hit the ground, flaring and sizzling. She yelped in terror, flashed her teeth, then sprang away from him. He leapt after her, lashing out with the club, clipping her over the back of the head and sending her tumbling into the mud. She crawled, turned around and stared up at him, hands held out.

"We're not armed," she whimpered. "Don't hurt me. Azafady."

Roland stared down at her, illuminated by the dying, spitting flames. A pang shivered and bit deep into his heart. This was no warrior. Her attack had been clumsy, not the act of a trained fighter, but that of a desperate lemur awoken from her sleep to find her home invaded. He let his club hang limp and reached out to her, to help her up, perhaps? Even he was not sure, but Sasha charged past. The edge of her club dripped red with gore.

"Oh good," she said, "you have caught one too. Well, are you not going to kill it?" She gave him a sidelong glance then, and his scent and demeanor said it all. She sighed. "Oh Roland..." She took her club, tilting it so that the sharp edge faced down, towards the cowering victim. The lemur gave a sobbing cry, trying to scramble to her feet. She was too slow.

"No!" Roland shouted, but he too was a moment too slow, not that Sasha would have heeded him anyhow. Her bladed club slashed down: once, twice. The poor victim squealed, scrabbling forward now, legs dragging as her spine was severed.

It took three more blows, until finally, blessedly, she lay still. Sasha hefted her club, wiping the blood off on her victim's plush fur. "That," she said, "is how it is done."

Roland's stomach lurched. Whether at the gore he had witnessed, or the intermingling scents of blood, satisfaction and the slightest hint of desire, he could not be sure. He recoiled, stepped back into the bushes and would have disgorged the contents of his stomach, had there been anything to disgorge. Luckily, the Hunters had fasted the previous day, taken only minimal sips of water to avoid dehydration.

A rustle from behind, and he recoiled, swinging his blade about to attack. Then the familiar stink of fossa burned his nostrils and he stilled the blow.

"Melise," he whispered, scenting her underneath the predator-stink.

"Hunter Melise," she growled. "Honor me with my proper title."

"My apologies, Hunter Melise," Roland replied, gulping down the lump in his throat. "You surprised me, that is all." He bowed his head before her, even though she was nought but a pale shadow in the gloom.

"Very well," she said, her voice filled with the fake superiority she had cultivated so well. "I have a task for you. If you wish to accept it."

"Of course." He sensed Sasha creeping up to his side.

"Am I included too?" she asked.

Roland could hear the smirk in Melise's reply. "Of course." She paused. "We have received word from our insider, our little cuckoo, that certain lemurs of importance are holed up inside an abandoned residence. I will be leading the charge against them, and I require your assistance."

"We would be honored to join you, great Hunter."

Roland nudged Sasha—she was laying it on a bit too thick. Could Melise not sense the sarcasm?

Apparently not.

"Most excellent indeed. I can smell that your clubs have been bloodied. Let us strike forth and color them some more."

She led them through the darkness, her waving tail stirring currents in the air. Every so often they had to step over a corpse, mangled and bloody, or leap across a ditch.

Others joined their party, and in the end almost two dozen lemurs had gathered for the raid.

Even in the near complete darkness, the building loomed, a blacker shadow against the paler grey-black of the midnight storm clouds. No light burned within. The faintest, almost chirping cry came and vanished, devoured by expectant silence.

It could have been a night bird, but Roland knew that it was not.

"Do you think they have gone already?" one of the other Hunters asked.

Melise moved among them, tapping on shoulders, directing pairs to creep forward, surrounding the structure.

What is it? Roland wondered, as he and Sasha were sent off to the right. *Who is in there?*

They found their position, held weapons ready and waited.

But for what?

An arrow cut a fiery arc through the darkness, lodging itself in the thatch roof. Flames licked out greedily, casting a flickering golden glow across the misshapen, tumble-down structure.

Melise motioned, sending two of the omega Hunters forward. With the blood-thirsty eagerness of youth, they raced for the collapsed balcony, grasping the hanging tendrils and hauling themselves up to the doorway. A white shape, like a ghostly *Lemures,* materialized from the shadows. Something flashed bright in the firelight, and one of the Hunters fell with a scream.

He did not get up again.

Roland saw movement, a small dark shape silhouetted against the flames. Some lemur fleeing the fire. *Has anyone else seen her?* he wondered, casting a quick glance around. No lemur shouted, no arrow shot from the darkness.

Let her go. Pretend you never saw her.

The blade flashed again, clattering against the Hunter's club. He feinted low, bringing it against the white *Lemures'* knee. His opponent staggered, falling, but swung the weapon about in a final sweep that cut into his leg and sent him over the edge, crashing on his fallen companion. He groaned, staggered upright, his white fur blossoming black with blood.

Melise barked an order, and more Hunters surged forward, Sasha among them. The roof groaned, collapsed in on itself. Flames leapt up, devoured, hungered.

The white *Lemures* stood once more. Another gleaming flash sent a third Hunter crashing downwards, then another. Sasha scrambled to the top, her club hanging down her back, but she did not even have time to wield it before the blade slashed at her. She dodged; the cutting edge skimmed her fur. The enemy warrior brought her hands back, caught Sasha beneath the chin with the weapon's handle. Sasha swayed for a moment, arms and tail flailing for balance, then another back-handed clip sent her tumbling down.

She landed in the leaf mulch with a squelch.

Roland rushed to her side. "Are you all right?" he asked, offering his hand.

She pushed it aside.

"I do not require your assistance." She dragged herself into a crouch, teeth drawn back in a feral grin, cast a glimpse up at the pale figure. "Bitch," she growled.

"Attacking from the front is useless," Roland said. "We need to flank her—come in from behind. Surprise her."

Sasha grinned at him. "A most excellent plan." She cast a quick, narrow-eyed glare at Melise. "And one that our esteemed Hunter seems to have not considered. I like it."

Roland looped his club over his neck, the weight of it trailing down his spine, and moved towards the burning structure.

A shriek came from above.

Another of the Hunters tumbled, teeth bared in a fierce grimace. Blood marred his pale fur. He struck the ground, yowling in pain. Melise was beside him in a heartbeat. She kicked him, berated him, until he struggled to his feet.

Roland scrambled up the rock face. Sharp stone teeth bit into his leathery palms, but he clenched his teeth against the pain. Pain was nothing to a Hunter. It had to be. Sasha trailed closely behind, growling low and deep. *From the stress?* Roland wondered. *Or with excitement?*

He reached the rough wooden wall, fingers grasping sturdy wooden plants rather than rough, sharp rocks. A quick lick of each palm, sealing the scrapes and cuts, and then up and across the wall. His eyes scanned for an opening. Found one. A narrow window, just wide enough for one lean lemur to slip inside. The chamber was large, his whiskers tingling with the air currents, nose twitching at the scent of dust and herbs. It took a heartbeat or two longer for his eyes to adjust to the deeper gloom. Sasha swung in beside him, her tail brushing against his arm. Her club in her hands, she widened her eyes, scanned the room.

"It's a hall," she said. Nose crinkled. "Monkeys."

Roland nodded. He had smelt it too, the rank, musky aroma of the slit-nosed Vazaha. It was a distant scent though, more a memory. He hopped a step and felt something crackle beneath his feet: a woven mat. The two of them made their careful way around the room, one hand trailing the walls as he sought some form of egress. A door into another room, this one long and narrow, almost like a tunnel. Wind currents brushed his whiskers, indicating an exit to the outside world, towards the front of the building. To where the sifaka warrior stood her ground.

Roland hesitated at the sight of her, pale and shimmering in the flickering fire light. Perhaps it was the influence of the oestrus, with the heightened emotions it brought, but he had never seen any lemur as courageous and beautiful. Certainly, her plush white fur was patched with blood and she clearly favored one leg, but she moved with such elegance and poise, slashing the gleaming blade in economical yet efficient arcs. Again and again a Hunter came at her, and she pushed them back down.

If only she were on our side. Roland sighed. *And what, who, is it that she is protecting?* He could detect a trace of other lemurs here, but whomever they were, they had long since parted.

Sasha was at his side, glaring at him. "What are you—"

A loud crashing sound buried her words, following them with the gleeful crackling of hungry flames. Fire licked its way across the ceiling, illuminating the tunnel, revealing the dark gashes of doorways along its length. Sasha tightened her grip on her club, and cast a frantic gaze upwards.

"How long?" she asked. Only two words, but Roland didn't need her to complete the sentence.

"Not long." Not long until the ceiling—the upper stories—collapsed on them. Not long at all.

The flickering light of the flame danced in a flash of white. Sasha shrieked, a high "shif!" that made the fur on Roland's shoulders bristle.

An alarm call, a battle cry. Her club in her hands, she bent her knees, preparing to make one long leap towards the elegant white sifaka who dealt the bright dance of death.

With a deep groan the ceiling sagged, splitting and spraying down a shower of sparks. Sparks that sizzled against Roland's fur. He stumbled back, brushing them from himself and caught his foot against something in the dark, tumbling backwards to land, painfully, on a short set of steps. He grunted in surprise.

Sasha stopped, turned to glance back at him, stepped towards him. "Roland?" she asked. "Are you all—"

Her words were cut short as the ceiling sagged further then, with a long-suffering groan, collapsed directly behind her, throwing her to the floor. The stench of scorched fur flooded the air, as did her squeals of pain.

Roland was at her side in an instant. Part of the ceiling had struck her, buried her left leg and tail. He swung at the burning debris with his club, pushing it aside as the flames tasted his fur. She struggled and writhed, somehow managing to tug free. Roland cringed as more sparks rained from above. He brushed burning ash from one eye, blinked tears to ease the pain. He dropped his club, thrust his hands beneath Sasha's armpits and dragged her from the fire, shuddering at her screams of agony. Back down the tunnel, away from the hungry fire. There was but one thought in his mind: he must get her out of here, away from the building.

And to a Medic.

Back into the chamber they had entered through. Still intact. *But for how long?* He all but shoved her through the window, wincing at the grunt of pain as she tumbled to the ground, before jumping out after her. His whiskers felt strange, sizzled at the tips and his nose scented nothing but the stink of smoke, charred flesh and singed fur.

"Can you stand?" he asked. "Does it hurt?"

Sasha staggered upright, one hand clutching his shoulder so tightly that her nails bit through the flesh. "No," she whispered. "It is numb. That is good? Is it not?" She might be upright, but she was leaning more than standing. Roland risked a glimpse at her leg and felt something wretched rise in his throat. A patch—a large patch—of her leg had melted like a beeswax candle. All that remained of her long and elegant tail was a white tuft at the end of it, the rest was charred bald and blackened to the bone.

"How bad is it?" Her eyes met his and she made a terrified choking squeak in the back of her throat, reading his diagnosis in his eyes and his scent. "It is bad." Not a question.

"We just need to get you to the Medic," was all Roland could reply. "They shall patch you up."

"I am never walking again." Her voice was flat, devoid of emotion. "They will have to remove my leg, will they not?"

Roland gulped and shrugged. "You may..." he started, then shook his head and would not meet her eyes.

She crumpled, tumbling to the muddy ground.

A shrieking and hooting split the air asunder. Roland glanced over, towards the Hunters. They had surrounded a struggling white shape— the beautiful warrior—and now beat her with their clubs. Roland almost gagged with disgust: is *this what the mighty Hunters, the royal protectors, have been reduced to?* He forced himself to turn away—*there is nothing I can do for her*—and back to Sasha, who huddled and whimpered, her leg sticking out like it was nothing more than firewood.

He had to get her to a Medic, he had to get her treatment.

She could not walk, so he scooped her up in his arms. She clasped her hands, looped them about his neck, nestled her cheek under his chin.

It would be a long, dark walk.

"Hang in there," he whispered, licking her cheek. "I will see you safe."

Progress for the wounded Hunters was slow and terrestrial. Several times Roland had to drag Sasha behind a tree trunk as Hunters passed, stalking their prey. Once a small mongoose lemur, one of the enemy, appeared above them on a branch, peered down at them then disappeared as quickly as she had come. Trees burned like dying candles despite the high humidity, flooding the sky with thick grey smoke, then illuminated it in pale hues of orange and red.

"Why are the trees on fire?" Sasha wondered, staggering against him. "Was it we that did it, or them?" Her words came out slightly slurred, as though she were struggling to stay alert. She shivered too, despite the damp heat. Roland was no healer, but he knew well enough what that meant: her body was giving up and starting to shut down. She staggered more often than not and he struggled to keep her upright and on some sort of path. Such concentration was required, that he could almost dismiss the throb of pain in his seared eye, the cloud that hazed his peripheral vision.

The land dropped towards the river, the sound of which filled the air. Noises too—shrieks of victory intermingling with the cries of pain. The Infirmary rose from the darkness, a hunched shape on the river bank—an open-sided pavilion.

Roland's heart sank as he saw the group that had gathered about it, clamoring for attention. Some of the injured had come alone, others lay clasped in their battle-companions' arms or leaned against them. Several Hunters stalked the perimeter, inspecting the injuries. Roland staggered in. Even though Sasha was no heavy weight, his arms throbbed with the strain. His hands burned, too; a throbbing and incessant heat that he had tried to ignore. He crouched behind another wounded Hunter. This one, a brown lemur with impressive white furred cheeks, was moving on three limbs: one of his arms dangled, limp.

Roland lowered Sasha to the ground, cradling her against him and stroking his fingers through her fur. "We may be in for a wait," he said. "You must cling on."

"Cling... yes," came Sasha's reply.

A few steps away, another sifaka had wrapped her arms across her belly, as though holding her entrails in. Her fur was soaked in blood and her face twisted with pain, eyes unfocused.

The Hunter-guard approached her; a diminutive lemur with large fluffy ears danced around him.

"Show me the injury," the Hunter-guard barked the order.

She stared at him a long moment, as though trying to make sense of his words then nodded, parting her hands. Roland was, fortunately, not able to see the extent of the injuries, but the Hunter-guard's face twisted into a horrified grimace. The hairy-eared lemur skipped forward, sniffed at the injury and turned to the Hunter-guard with a shake of her head: No.

The Hunter-guard met the patient's gaze.

"Miala tsiny aho," he said. "Your injury—it is fatal."

She gulped, nodded.

"Do you wish to die as predator or prey?" he asked.

She hesitated for three beats, then steadied her gaze. "Predator."

He nodded. Roland watched as padding was pressed against her belly, wrapped in place with cloth. Then the Hunter-guard helped her to her feet and placed a club in her hands.

"Go," he said. "And fight until you can fight no more."

She could barely manage a stumbling hop and her face contorted with agony, but still she staggered back towards the forest. Back towards the fighting.

The Hunter-guard had now turned his attentions to the brown lemur. His small companion scampered forward, sniffed and nodded: Yes.

"Can you fight?" the Hunter-guard asked the varika. "Wield a weapon?"

The lemur would not meet his gaze, merely indicated his dangling arm. "No," his voice came out a croaked whisper. "It is broken."

"How?"

"I fell," he mumbled. "In the dark. Look, it just needs binding—it will heal, I will fight again."

"But not today." The Hunter-guard's voice was flat, drained of emotion. "And a Hunter cannot be clumsy."

He moved so fast that neither the wounded lemur nor Roland had time to react, or even avert their eyes. His razor-edged club scythed out, slicing across the lemur's throat. Blood sprayed. For a moment, his eyes registered surprise, then clouded over as death claimed him. He slumped forward.

"Mialo tsiny aho," the Hunter-guard spoke over the corpse. "May your *Lemures* find peace." His words held no compassion, no sorrow, merely the dull monotone of someone who had become immune to emotion.

The little lemur scampered up to the corpse, placed her tiny hands against the forehead, closed the dead eyes. Her lips moved in a silent farewell.

The Hunter-guard looked up and over at Sasha and Roland.

"Now," he said. "What injury does she bear?"

Roland felt a shiver pass through him. Sasha's wounds were terrible— she could not stand, let alone fight. Her fate would, surely, mirror that of the hapless brown lemur.

The hairy-eared lemur crouched before him, sorrow in her immense eyes. She sniffed Sasha's injury, then gave the slightest shake of her head: No.

Roland swallowed hard and looked up into the Hunter-guard's eyes. "Our injuries are minor," he replied. "We seek only water, maybe a salve, and clean rags, to bind them." Sasha moaned and he tried to cover it with a cough. Not that it mattered, the Hunter-guard could surely smell her charred flesh and the shadow of death that clouded her. But she was his friend, and he would not allow her to die here, so quick and violently, on the riverbank.

"Very well then." The Hunter-guard hopped back to the pavilion and returned quickly, tossing an armload of rags in Roland's direction.

"You want water," he barked, "well—" He waved one hand in the vague direction of the river. "The salves are reserved for those that need them."

"Need them," Roland muttered. "Have a realistic chance of surviving, more like."

But he accepted the rags, which were none too clean. They could expect no further assistance here. If Sasha were to survive, it was up to him—and her—to facilitate it.

He was startled by a slight flurry of movement, as the little lemur appeared before them, the moment the Hunter-guard had moved on. She proferred him a small container.

"Salve," she said, her voice a little wobbly around the edges, as though she were trying to disguise the sorrow he could scent on her. "For your burns."

"Misaotra." He nuzzled her as best he could.

"It help, maybe," she replied. "May *Lemures* be with you in this terrible time."

"Kely!" The Hunter-guard barked.

She shot Roland an apologetic look. "Must be gone. Go well."

Roland watched her depart then gathered up Sasha, the salve and the rags, and staggered towards the river bank.

It seemed there was some kindness here yet.

A secluded bay, half obscured by a crumbled limestone spire, provided the shelter and privacy that Roland required. He made Sasha as comfortable as possible on the muddy ground, cradling her head in his lap. It was too dark to see the full extent of her injuries and for that he was relieved. He licked the mud from around the wound, Sasha's lack of reaction to his rasping tongue showing quite how much damage had been done—the nerve endings burned away, nothing but dead, charred flesh remained. He could not see how deep it was, but knew it extended into the muscle. Maybe even to the bone—a gaping cavity that he could press his whole fist into, if he were so inclined (which he was not). There was surprisingly little blood. He wet the rags in the stream, covering the wound and wrapped others about her tail. Shuddered. It would have to be removed, but Roland's gut clenched at the thought of administering the severing blow.

"Hang in there," he whispered to her.

"Is this my punishment?" she croaked. "For killing one of them?" Her words were becoming more slurred. "Am I going to die?"

Roland stroked her brow. "Not if I have any say in the matter," he said. He nuzzled her head, then stepped away, seeking some manner in which to make her more comfortable, to better treat her ailments. The bridge must lead somewhere, must serve a purpose. Nostrils flared, he searched for scent marks. He found mostly the dry, rank stink of crow droppings, but amongst them something else; the sweet, musky scent of female sifaka. Strong, but cold, as though it had been marked many times, but not in the previous day. He traced it to a narrow crevasse in the rock. Very narrow, easily defensible. There was a bucket tucked in a hollow, just inside the entrance. He learned over it, smelt the welcome tang of water, albeit slightly stale. Past it, the tunnel led into the rock. He followed it. It was too dark, pitch black, and he moved with caution, ears pricked in case the occupant was still in residence.

"Salama," he called in a whisper. "We are wounded, seek shelter, mean you no harm."

No answer.

The passage widened and his whiskers and nose told him that he had now entered a chamber of reasonable size. Something rustled beneath his feet—the floor was covered in dried grass. Perfect.

He returned to Sasha. "Can you make it just a little bit further?"

Her eyes said "no", but she nodded and attempted to stand. Failed. Looped her wrists together and arms over his head. He took her in his arms and she buried her head against his cheek.

He entered the passage again, shuffle-hopping sideways and mindful not to knock her badly wounded hand or her burned leg. The heat emanating from the burn was tremendous, but shivers wracked her body and the dark shadows of death begun to taint her scent. Roland's pulse quickened with despair and regret. If he had taken her to the healer, could she have been healed?

Would they have even tried?

She moaned as he laid her to the grass-covered floor as gently as possible, then returned to fetch the bucket. He sniffed it again, it seemed clean enough. Leaving Sasha in the center of the chamber, he searched the rest with his hands, whiskers and nose, finding first a blanket (which he covered her with) and then, much to his relief, a candle-lantern. He fumbled with it, trying to figure out how to ignite it, but twisting this and pushing that eventually elicited a spark and finally a flame.

Maybe science had some benefits, after all.

The light seemed very bright after the dark gloom, sending further pain spearing through his wounded eye. He closed it, but even the touch of the eyelid hurt. There were some cloths on the narrow desk, decorating with what looked a little like maps. One he bound about his head, covering his injured eye without brushing against it, and felt instant relief from the pain, nullifying it to a dull throb. The others he took to Sasha, dampening them in the bucket and pressing them against the burn. She sighed and whimpered. The hand he did not know how to treat, but wrapped another dampened cloth about it and bound it to her chest, above her heart. He found cushions resting on a hammock, and plumped these around Sasha, holding her semi-upright, with another tucked beneath the knee of her wounded leg and the blanket draped about her shoulders.

"You are a good healer," she said, her words showing a slight improvement in clarity.

A bunch of bananas hung in a net-bag, strung from the ceiling. He fetched one down, breaking it into small chunks and feeding them to Sasha. She accepted three, then refused any further. "Eat yourself." Then, "Where are we?"

"I am not sure," Roland replied, "but I think we have found a nocturnal's den." He relocated the screen from one end of the chamber to the other, blocking the tunnel through whence they had come, and hopefully the light as well. A warm breeze rustled through, bringing with it the scent of smoke and blood. The other tunnel must lead to an opening outside somewhere. He would need to investigate that later; perhaps it would provide an escape route.

But he could do that later. For now, Sasha needed him. He could scent the shadow growing, death coming nearer. He lay down beside her, curling his body around hers, and ran his fingers through her fur, grooming her. She leaned back against him, her body feverish, and shivering. Her breathing was rapid, almost rasping as though there were water in her lungs. Roland's heart ached with helplessness. There was nothing he could do to help her, nothing he could do but hold her, comfort her and wait.

"I never thought it would end like this," she whispered. Her words were slurred again, and she had to pause to gasp for breath between them. He could feel her heart beneath his hands, the pulse beating a rapid tempo, as though frantic to heal her. "I thought, as a Hunter, it would be triumph and victory." She paused to gasp for breath. "Not pain, death and smoke. I thought I would go out fighting, not die from a stupid burn."

Roland stroked her fur. "We cannot choose our death," he said, "and sometimes even our lives are out of our control." He licked her cheek. "But know that you are loved, Sasha, and that your friendship is cherished."

She gave a hoarse bark that turned into a wheeze. "Do you think she will be waiting for me?"

"Who?"

"Her, she whom I killed." A rueful snort. "My first prey as a Hunter, and also my last."

"No," Roland replied, "for death brings with it forgiveness."

"Always the poet." She grunted with pain, tongue flicking out to lick her nose. "I would have chosen you," she added, "when my first oestrus came. I guess now… it never will." A shivering spasm came upon her, and he held her until it ceased. "Are you going to go back?"

Roland frowned. "Go back?"

"When I… dead. Will you return… to the Hunters."

"I do not know," Roland admitted. "What other life is there for me?"

A long silence then, as though there were no words that could be said. Then, "Tell me."

"About what?" Roland wondered.

"About yourself. Your dreams. Anything. Nothing. Just make it… worth my while. Not much time left." Every word came slow and labored, punctuated by lung-rattling gasps.

What could he tell her about? Not how he had become a Hunter, for that story was too painful for someone in her condition. Not his time as a Hunter, for that she already knew. No, she needed something filled with carefree innocence, not death and violence.

"I shall tell you," he said, "about my little sister, Eloise, and our life in the orchards."

"I would like that," came her reply, little more than a whisper.

And so he did, through what remained of the night and until the early light of dawn flowed down the exit tunnel and painted pale patterns on the floor. Until her heart beat changed from rapid to slow, her shivering stopped and all that he could hear was the shallow rasp of every breath.

"Stay free… Roland," she gasped, clutching his hand. Her grip weak. "Do not… return Hunters. Promise me."

"I promise," Roland whispered.

But she did not hear, for her *Lemures* has slipped from her in one final breath. He held her for a moment longer, then laid her down, nuzzling her one final time.

"Be at peace, Sasha," he whispered into her pale fur. "May your *Lemures* enjoy the freedom you had lost."

The Ultimate Weapon!

Is there such a thing? Never mind; there are often new weapons introduced during warfare. Weapons so much more powerful than anything seen before that victory seems assured.

Until the next war, when both sides have the new weapon.

What will such a weapon mean for Captain Jasper, polecat; for Samuel, infantryhare; and for Rollo, bat scout?

Old Regimes

by Gullwulf

The polecat sat atop his warhorse in only the most upright fashion that a captain could afford to do. His chocolate brown fur shone with gold and good grooming. His pointed canines were polished over his small muzzle, and his lithe chest puffed with each breath. Despite his relaxed stature, the polecat kept his eyes trained on the expansive forest beneath them, hind paws curled into the stirrups, ready to bolt at a moment's notice.

"Oye! Captain!" The polecat's ears twitched, tan nose scrunching on his trim muzzle before he turned his head just so in order to see who addressed him. A Pipistrelle landed beside him, his russet fur wind tossed as his clawed feet came to an impact in the dirt, beady black eyes turned just west of his captain's head. Poor bats—they had awful eyesight, but the wings that he folded against his arms made him almost invaluable in the field. "I saw somethin', up in the road ahead."

The polecat hummed under his breath. "Where is Samuel?"

"Here, Captain Jasper!" The hare came bounding from a bush, adjusting his blood-red jacket and smoothing his ears back, nose twitching and chest puffing out. It did little to hide how his foot went *thump thump thump* against the packed dirt. The polecat had to give the hare some credit; for a youngling plucked off the streets. He did a remarkable job of appearing eager for action and not scared out of his wits.

"Good. Glad to see you haven't run off yet." The polecat bared his teeth as he spoke. Predator-prey negotiations had been settled in prehistoric times, but Captain Jasper liked to remind the younguns that he had been *given* his commission. He did not buy it with an inherited fortune like some folks he could name.

It did come with its own set of downfalls. Captain Jasper earned his merit for being one of the meanest polecats around, but when the majority of the army still viewed land and titles first and prowess second, he was overlooked. Hence why, even in the thick of a revolutionary war from those across the pond, the polecat was given a "squadron" that consisted of a bat and a hare, and only one horse between the three of them. To be part of the Light side of the army was taken literally.

The two were staring at him expectantly. Captain Jasper cleared his throat, adjusting his paws on the reins of his horse. "Gentlemen, Infantrybat Rollo has reported that there might be something in the road ahead. Rollo, would you give your full statement to the squadron?"

The bat shuffled on his feet. His beady eyes managed to give Jasper a look of complete incredulity for the formalities. Captain Jasper would have a few things to show that bat if he dismissed protocol. But Rollo delivered, his voice adding clicks and rasps between words. "I saw men with draft horses pulling a cart. Two of 'em. Big, bushy tails—that was the most I could pick up before the breeze shifted and I felt the draft trying to push me on top of them. I decided to circle back before they caught sight of me."

"Oh, come on!" Samuel's tail stuck up from his uniform, fluffed as the tapping of his foot entered an erratic beat. "That could be anything! Hell, it sounds like a couple'a farmers if you ask me."

Jasper grunted, curling his lip back over his teeth as he thought (and noting how the hare flinched from it—good on him). Chances are it really was nothing—but Captain Jasper did not earn his title from nothing.

"I think we should check it out, Captain," Rollo spoke again, his voice without its usual clicks due to the softness of tone. "Doesn't hurt to be overcautious, especially in times like these."

This was why Jasper enjoyed the bat. Heart of a coward, but he was basically a horn for all of the polecat's opinions. "Excellent deduction," Jasper said, and set his heels to his horse. "Let us see the disturbance and if it's worth our time at all. Rollo take another glide, if you would."

The bat cricked his neck, stretched his arms and let the digits of his wings extend fully, the translucent black skin almost blocking Samuel from view before the bat kicked off hard and flew off the bluff. Samuel's nose twitched, ears flipping down before he leaned in almost conspiratorially to the polecat. "Their arm-wings… seem kind of unnatural, don't you think?"

Ah, go figure. Samuel must have had one of those ears of his bent to the new movement striking up along the religiously fanatic. Apparently with the predator-prey debate having no chance of revival after the king had firmly beat it down, and everyone still restless after overthrowing the ancient regime, the newest fashion was to start pointing out those who had other means of locomotion—since God only wanted his Creations to walk along the ground, or some other nonsense.

"Bats are warm-blooded, just like you and I," Jasper said, making sure to keep a level stare with the hare. "And in fact they are more like you than they are me. A disposition to react to things with fear, for instance."

The hare crossed his arms, his chest fluffing out and ears pressed flat to his head. At this rate, he was going to pop buttons on his coat. It was already a testament to the strength of the wool that his pant legs had withstood the rapid taps. "Sure," he said, "bats are warm, but not everything that flies is one."

"Avians were born into the sky," Jasper sternly reminded him.

"I wasn't talking about Avians."

Jasper fell silent, turning his muzzle back into the wind. This was not a subject that he wanted to address. Hell, ever since this God-damned war started up the country had almost been in agreement about what to do with *them*. Sure, perhaps part of the army had been named after them once upon a time, but that was a long, long time ago. *They* were not wanted.

He nudged his horse into a trot instead, forcing the hare to keep up. It did an effective job at leaving the conversation behind them while they located a suitable rallying point for the bat. Less obvious than the bluff, it was a rocky outcropping with scattered pine trees, their roots burrowing into the thin soil. A diffuse of cover from the tangerine sky as dusk began to swell over the land.

It was a bit of a shock when Samuel's ears perked and swiveled behind him to the east, not to the west as Jasper was expecting. The hare pulled out his musket to his white paws, cocking it on his shoulder and kicked the dirt with his feet, sending a spray as he charged. Jasper's horse reared, forcing the polecat to brace his muzzle lest his steed smash his teeth into the roof of his mouth.

"Samuel!" Jasper's voice caught in a half squeak; a curse of his lineage that he could not roar or have a low, rumbling growl like those wildcats. "Steed! Down, calm—damn you!"

No sooner did the words leave his whiskers than Samuel came bounding back with Rollo in tow. The bat was panting, visible exertion in every muscle as wingtip dragged on the ground.

"They spotted me! Oh, they spotted me!"

"Who, soldier?!"

"The fox and the squirrel—oh, right we was, bunch of bloody froggy tyrants—"

The enemy. Steel froze Jasper's insides from the squirmy seconds of panic that they once flashed into. Nature was something that could be overcome—no polecat would truly back down from a fight.

His gaze set, muscles corded within his back and spine, tail poised like a banner behind him, Captain Jasper forced his horse to calm down with nary a wicker of protest. He pranced the horse in front of his little troop, in front of the bat who looked ready to take flight despite his dragging wings and the hare who was starting the nervous *thump, thump, thump* of his feet.

"We do not stand here and sulk," Jasper hissed. "Two bushy tailed, snub nosed, needle-teethed whippersnappers who piss on their gold have everything to fear from creatures who have crawled out of brine and rock. They have something that we need in that bloody carriage, and we are going to rip it from their very claws."

The hare puffed his chest out, let his ears lie flat on his skull, and nodded eagerly at his commander's words. Jasper's heart swelled with pride just looking at him. Rollo, however, was not so easily swayed. The bat kept his wings tucked in close, his hooking paws creating gorges in the ground as he dug his feet in. But the bat lifted his chin and nodded, and so they marched. The hare kept up an easy stride with the steed. His long legs meant that he was at chin-level with the mounted polecat rather than thigh level as the bat was. It also meant that Jasper could pitch his voice lower to address only him. "Keep an eye on him, would you?"

Samuel nodded his head in such a way that Jasper only caught it out of the corner of his eye. Yes, he did intend to shake up the bat, but he did not want the bat to end up losing his senses on the battlefield as well. This was hardly a battle—this would be a skirmish, if that. If a damned red squirrel and a fox could not be bothered to look up every now and then, these were clearly not the marked soldiers that Jasper feared they would be facing.

Foxes were notoriously clever, Jasper mused. In the days of old he would have feared to see one on the battlefield. That was before he had managed to rip one's throat out with his own teeth. Red squirrels had all the problems of bats and hares without the advantages of either of them—and their tails made for big targets.

This was going to be an easy engagement.

They paced for a few hoof prints before the bat lifted a wing, bringing them both to a stop. Samuel's ears lifted, swiveling and pitching like a ship's sails, each strand of fur bristling before he slowly began to load his musket. The first crack of the shot would alert their enemy, but Samuel's hearing was damn near unmatched. He could pitch a bullet through a beating heart from yards and yards out.

And Jasper would charge as soon as the first shot went through.

The hare jammed the musket to his shoulder—like this, Jasper mused, he almost looked like a stiff breeze could blow him over, balanced as he was on bow legs and long feet. But there was a determination to his eyes, something that crystallized the honey in them to amber. His claw wrapped around the trigger, lashes narrowed against his gleaming gaze, and the shot echoed through the trees, howling through the forest and splintering wood.

Jasper set his heels to the horse and felt the beast surge forward. The greenery around them blurred, the breath of the steed set in time to the polecat's own panting breaths. Rollo would be on his heels, taking to the tops of the trees and gripping with his claws, leaping from branch to branch and catching the wind on his membrane.

The horse's fur was slick with sweat, a beating heart and burning skin brushing Jasper's fur. He drew his rapier, willed his horse just a little further. It would do no good for his steed to get sick, no good to push it past the point of exhaustion, but there was a flash of red fur in his vision and Jasper decided that steed be damned, he was going to run his horse into the ground as long as he trampled the enemy and pinned them underneath his steed for the price.

The shot had landed wide of their targets—at least, of the enemy troop. The cart lay cockeyed, its wooden spokes deep in the dirt path. One of the draft horses strained, the other lay bleeding in the dirt, side heaving with choked breaths as it tried to right itself.

Jasper's gaze flicked from the work horses to his enemy. The squirrel was at the rear of the cart, his bushy tail giving away his position even as he tried to wedge his body against the end of the cart as much as he could. Samuel would take care of him, Jasper thought. He was after the fox.

There was no sign of the vulpine, only smeared pawprints of blood next to the horse. He must have bolted the moment that he smelled Jasper's approaching horse. Rollo tumbled into the ground beside him, and Jasper yanked his pistol out and shot one warning shot, the bark buying him just enough time to have the squirrel duck and to cover his own ears as he screamed "Silence!"

Samuel knew what to do. He jumped, skidding behind a trunk and slamming his ears down against his skull. He barely had a breath between the action and Rollo opening his muzzle until his little teeth gleamed. A sound rent the air around them, something that tapped at the very inner of his ear with scrabbling claws.

The squirrel had seen the move coming, and wedged his head against the wood, pressing his cheek tight to the cart until he seemed to be just an ornament. His fox friend was not so lucky—the vulpine lurched into view, his black ears pressed flush to his orange fur, his black gums peeled in a grimace over pearly white teeth. He was disoriented, stumbling on his black paws, trying not to pitch into the ground, but he was recovering just as swiftly.

Jasper did not waste a moment. He kicked his horse into a charge, timing to the very beat that Rollo finally silenced himself to take his sword and slash, hearing the whisper of the blade through the wind. The fox snarled, dodging and spreading his paws across the dirt. A tuft of black fur from the tip of the fox's ear slipped onto the blade, but Jasper was already circling his horse to try again, chittering rapidly to his compatriots: "Surround! Use the horse as cover!"

The squirrel heard the command, but the twitch of his tail gave away where he was about to leap. Samuel had already caught up, and the hare gave a shrill screech as he leapt. The squirrel lifted his rifle—the glint of filigree on it caught the dying light. The crack of the shot temporarily blocked the scene until Samuel kicked off the cart, rising above the gunsmoke and twisting in the air, one hind foot lashing out, claws extended to knock into the squirrel. The rodent's head twisted, his body turning soon to follow it, bushy tail wrapped around himself as the hare's leg had found its mark on his cheek. Jasper saw the squirrel bounce against the cart, but he scrambled upward and tried to fight back, bracing the rifle sideways between his paws and bashing the hare.

Jasper leaned from the side of his horse as his steed circled, claws hooking into the stirrups and needle teeth tasting the cold wind. The musk of fox was heavy on the roof of his mouth. He could see the flash of fur from between the legs of the draft horse still standing, moving behind the cart proper.

Jasper stuck his blade out and swung it across the draft horse's neck, drawing a long, blood-filled gush beneath the horse's head. The draft horse did not go down all at once, dropping to its knees first with a choked whinny, but the fox was moving swifter still, taking down one knee and Jasper found himself staring down the musket in those black paws.

Sacrifice was necessary in war. Jasper scrambled off his horse just as the crack thundered in the air around them. He did not look back to see if his horse had made it—either it was smart enough to have run, or it was dying. It would buy him precious seconds as the fox had lifted the rifle to see if his mark had been made, precious seconds as Jasper drew his blade and launched himself at the fox.

The vulpine bared his muzzle in a snarl, quick to dodge, his movements almost fluid. He would not be an easy opponent—but the good ones never were. Jasper kept his momentum, flicking his sword and coming to the fox's bared right side. The fox let out a low growl, a curse in his horrid tongue, and then flung himself at Jasper, bracing his rifle against Jasper's sword with one hand, using the bayonet keep to keep the polecat at bay.

The fox had strength on his side, but nothing could match the polecat for swiftness... or for keeping the fox's attention diverted. Jasper felt his muzzle split into a grin as a shadow fell over the fox, watching those vertical pupils look up and shrink as the shape took form. Rollo tucked a wing back, gripping the top of the tarp as he balanced on whatever was beneath it, and threw a short knife into the fox.

Jasper hoped to see blood, to see pelt separated from the skin. Instead he saw the knife embedded into the dirt, worn wooden handle twanging from the ground. The fox was gone, and in its place was the red squirrel, grappling with Rollo as he screamed in his harshly accented voice, "Use it! Use it on these damned fools!"

Jasper was torn; the fox would be wide open, but Rollo was not adept at hand-to-hand combat. The squirrel would tear him apart in moments. Jasper dove for the conflict, abandoning gun and sword for claw and teeth. His paws wrapped around the squirrel's tail and pulled. The squirrel's scream of pain was countered by Rollo squirming out, forced to crawl on his wings as Jasper grabbed the bat, pulling him back from the conflict and kicking the squirrel square in the chest. He heard the red squirrel wheeze out his breath, staggering backwards, and giving them the space to step back as Jasper scanned for the fox and Samuel.

The fox had already jumped onto the cart, and yanked the tarp off the machinery that had been hidden underneath. Jasper could not make heads or tails of what he was looking at—it looked like something that could have belonged in a factory. Metal twisted into a sharp point, braced on some kind of stand. A mess of gears and mechanical machinations made up its strange belly. The fox was feeding something into it, something that looked like scales—but upon closer inspection they were bullets, strung together and being fed into turning gears. The fox's paw turned something on the side, a crank, his hind paw stepping on a long, flat piece of metal that moved back and forth. Jasper tried to make sense of it, eyes flashing back and forth—

Samuel came bounding, his uniform torn, one ear notched, a maw wide open with buck teeth foamed with spittle, his saber catching the rays of the sun. The fox looked up, his eyes narrowed and ears pinned back, and he positioned the muzzle of the machine and began to turn the crank. Grinding gears and a wrenching sound came from within, and the string of bullets began to disappear into the whirring mechanism.

The function of the contraption came to Jasper in a sickening bolt. His movements were too sluggish, too slow, quicksand against lightning. He saw himself grabbing the rabbit around his chest, pulling him back from the hungry inhumane muzzle, throwing him to the dirt just as the bullets rent the air, dozens and dozens and dozens at a time, like a line of infantrymen firing one after another as fast as claws could count.

But those things did not happen. Samuel's body, framed in the fading sunlight, was there for only a moment, a shining beacon of a soldier before it was jerked, and a fine mist of blood sprayed from him. Those fragile ears became riddled with holes, those eyes that blazed rolled up into his head, and still his body jerked. One foot landed on the dirt, slipped under its own weight, and it collapsed.

It, because Samuel was gone. Samuel's soul had long departed under an onslaught that could not be seen or traced. *Rat-tat-tat* went the bullets, the fox's maniacal cry twining with them in an unholy song.

Jasper tasted blood in the back of his mouth, dimly felt his fangs sinking into his lower lip. Rollo was trying to say something, the weight of his wing pressing down against Jasper's back. His words were drowned in the cry of the infernal machine, in the fox still laughing and grinning like the devil himself.

Jasper shrugged the bat off—he might as well have been made of paper. He picked up his sword, covered in dust and blood and grime. He wanted to charge. Once again he was snagged around his ankle, the bat screaming something that went into his ears but bounced off his brain—instinct was overwhelming. The need to fight, to tear into flesh and bone and rip the fox's throat out with his own two paws overrode strategy and logic. Samuel was dead because of the mechanism the enemy wielded, and Jasper did not care that the thing was turned toward him.

His muzzle was pushed into the dirt—Rollo had leapt, digging his claws into the polecat's back as a launching point, his wing membranes catching the air. He bounced atop the device as the fox tried to crank it. He buffeted the fox with a powerful hit, curling his wind to cup the air and stagger the fox for a brief second. The red squirrel had long since recovered, crawling atop the cart and wrapping his paw around Rollo's ankle. Rollo struck with his free foot, his long, hooking claws scraping across the red muzzle, making the squirrel scream in pain.

Jasper ducked, pressed against one of the dead draft horses just as the bullets began spitting through the air. He drew his pistol, holding his breath as the horse jerked beside him with each hit, shuddering like it was still trying to draw fitful gasps of air. Jasper counted, waited until the machine quieted its vicious barks, and vaulted over, landing hard on his hind paws on the cart.

Rollo and the squirrel were grappling. Blood matted the face of the bat, his nostrils caked in it. His wings were pulled back, yet the squirrel had snagged some of the delicate membrane in his hands, his own flat, buck teeth flashing as he attempted to sink into the thin flesh.

Jasper grabbed the squirrel, pressed his pistol to the side of the rodent and felt its blood splatter against his coat. The squirrel's eyes rolled back, and Jasper did not wait before he turned for the fox.

Desperately the vulpine was trying to feed the contraption, rows of bullets slipping between his claws. He was not even looking at his enemy, or his fallen comrade—his eyes were trained to the machine, ears pinned flat as he blocked out his surroundings. What a foolish thing to do.

Jasper ran, grabbing the fox by his throat. The fox looked up then, slashing with his claws, catching the front of Jasper's uniform, but the polecat pressed on. He slammed himself into the fox, felt the fox's tail curl around him as he tried to support himself; but the polecat had his claws wrapped around the vulpine's throat and stamped his hind paw into the fox's own. The fox tried to yelp, but the moment he opened his mouth, Jasper squeezed his throat with all his might. The fox's tongue stuck out from his muzzle, a strangled, gurgling noise etched behind his teeth.

Samuel was just a boy. He was just a boy. He would have been great. The scent of the hare's blood was still thick, polluting over the horses, the squirrel, the fresh blood of the bat. Jasper began to squeeze harder, his teeth bared over his lips. "You cannot take lives with your own paws! Cowards... watch yourself die by my *claws.*"

"Captain!" Rollo's wing covered the fox's bulging eyes and wriggling tongue from view. "Let him go!"

Jasper snarled at Rollo, jutting his head forward and trying to bite the membrane. Words were lost to the polecat, consumed in extracting justice.

"We need answers!" Rollo shouted. "The fox is our best guess! Captain Jasper... *please.*"

The polecat paused. The fox's cries turned into wheezing pants, the scrabbling claws at Jasper's wrists weakening with each second. It would only be a few heartbeats before the fox blacked out. Death was certain.

This was not what Samuel had died for.

Jasper let the fox go. He wheezed, clutching his throat, and Jasper cuffed him in an ear. As the fox crumpled, Jasper kept a foot on his shoulder, and inclined his head toward Rollo. "Send for the others," he said. "We are without transportation and holding a live captive. Lieutenant General Fitzroy must be informed immediately."

Rollo gave a curt salute, his wing snapping in the wind, and with a bound he was gone.

Jasper looked at the bloodied fox beneath his paws. It was still a measly life for one of his own.

And it was a glimpse into this warfare that he was certain no one was prepared for.

* * *

The fort was quiet. The meal period had ended, soldiers had retreated to their barracks, and the usual laughter and talk from others had been silenced by the news that Captain Jasper had brought with him. What was nothing more than a routine check had brought with it the horror of a contraption that could fell hundreds. And it was in the hands of the enemy—the ones who spread across the continent, under a tyrannical leader who wished to quell all others underneath his claw.

Jasper waited for Lieutenant General Fitzroy next to a low burning fire, a glass of brandy in his paw. He swirled it, admiring the liquid's hue in the dancing flames. He knew that if he held his breath, he could hear the screams of the fox in an adjacent room as others worked on his pelt. He wondered how much longer it would be. Those they had on hand for such a thing were good at their job… and he also wondered if he was bothered by it. Seeing Samuel's eyes flash in his mind, Jasper decided that whatever they did with the fox, it still was not going to be good enough.

He forced himself to take a measured sip of the brandy. It burned on the way down his throat, and Jasper fought the urge to cough. He was never much of a drinker, even before he was named as a Captain, and the drink did little to keep his thoughts at bay. Best to watch the fire and wait.

The creaking of the oak door brought Jasper to his feet, tail stiff behind him as he saluted, gaze straight and unfocused. He waited until the click of claws brought the pristine, white fur of the stoat in view.

Jasper would have had to crane his head to look Lt. General Fitzroy in the eye, and he could almost see the gleam of black eyes before the stoat cleared his throat. Jasper dropped his gaze, still at attention, and finally the stoat spoke.

"Rest." Within a breath, the snow-white stoat sat in one of the arm chairs, his beady eyes turned toward the fire. Jasper stayed where he was uncertainly, the General's face hard to read. Even the whiskers on his muzzle barely twitched. The silence stretched between them before Fitzroy finally spoke, his voice thick. "Is it true?"

Jasper fidgeted. The words slipped from his muzzle with difficulty. "Yes. All of it."

Fitzroy let out a long, long sigh. It was in moments like these that Jasper could pick out the silver fur that lined the snow white on the stoat's muzzle, the paper thin scars across his cheeks. "We have a contingent that is out there right now. There is no messenger we can get out there fast enough. Not enough forces, that is for God damned certain."

Jasper winced at the curse. Lt. General Fitzroy very rarely, if ever, lost his temper. Even using the Lord's name in vain was unheard of for the stoat. Of course, this was also a situation for which none of them were prepared. Fitzroy's whiskers twitched, staring into the fire as the silence stretched between them. Jasper fidgeted. It felt like something was stuck in his throat that he couldn't speak around.

"The vulpine gave us little information," Fitzroy continued, almost causing Jasper to jump. "He was a low ranking scout, just meant to deliver the machine. We've studied it as well… but there are debates about what we should do. If we should copy the technology."

Jasper nodded. He knew that he had no experience, no true ranking to give his opinion. Not to the general of all people. Fitzroy earned his place and had the breeding to give his name weight. He had raised Jasper to the rank he held without coin or the need for falsehoods. He had seen more conflicts and won more battles than half the officers in the army. His mind was steel; his word law. There was nothing that Jasper would doubt him on.

"This… *gun* of theirs will rip through our forces. Even if we had the most gifted of blacksmiths and scientists working through the night, we will only be at one tenth of their capability. This is not a time where the new age is going to protect us." Fitzroy let out a long breath. "We need to revive the Dragoon Guard."

The lump in Jasper's throat dropped to his stomach, freezing his insides. "You cannot possibly be serious!"

"The Dragoon Guard protected us from worse fates than this—"

"We *destroyed* the Dragoon Guard to prevent tyranny! They lorded over us! God be damned, Satan is known as a great red dragon and what you're suggesting is—"

Fitzroy stood, clasping his paws behind his back. He glared down his muzzle at Jasper, pinning the polecat to his seat with a look. "We still have the Captain of the Guard in custody. I want you to come with me and talk to her."

Jasper gritted his teeth. Never in his life had he wanted to disobey a command until now. When he opened his muzzle, a sharp intake of his breath, Fitzroy cut him off. "Did our boys die for you to become a coward?"

Jasper felt the fur on his tail bristle. He wanted to fight back, he wanted to growl and snap and tear, but Fitzroy's gaze remained cool and impassive. A challenge to deny his words… which would involve leaving. When the polecat stood, he felt as if someone had replaced his spine with steel rods. Stay tall and proud, even as Fitzroy flicked his black tipped tail and marched ahead of him, forcing Jasper to jog to catch up.

The fort was built atop the remains of a castle that had once stood proud and tall centuries before. Wars had reduced the fortress itself to rubble; wartime had let Fitzroy and the rest of the Cavalry, with a few battalions, hastily erect a cement structure on the ruins. The dungeons beneath had remained untouched, but the conditions were so damp and cold that not even prisoners of war were kept in the dark recesses.

Except for the Dragoon Guard.

Fitzroy had a torch in one paw, the flickering light crawling along the mildewed cobblestone and bricks. Rats scurried underfoot, the subspecies that were never granted sapience. Jasper sneered at them, careful with his pawsteps, but Fitzroy was walking fast enough that Jasper was falling behind. He bounded, trying not to wince when his claws sunk into something soft and squirming, a *crack* echoing from beneath his paw. He could not dwell on it, not when monsters lurked nearby.

The stillness lulled Jasper into the idea that maybe the dragon had finally died. She was one of the few who had survived the overthrow of the old ways, kept as more of a reminder than anything. There were still a few of them, scattered in holes like this, though there was no certainty for how many the enemy kept. She had been taken live, someone who was fleeing ahead on their ships. If the enemy was resorting to experimental technologies… chances were all of theirs were dead.

A puff of smoke in the gloom brought Jasper out of his thoughts. Fitzroy stood, still except for the slow swings of his tail, and turned a corner into darkness. He set the torch on a sconce, illuminating the iron bars and the lichen that clung to them, the puddles of water that still coalesced in cracks on the stone. Fitzroy's white muzzle was only a few inches from the bars, and his voice remained level. "Maeveen." His tongue twisted around soft sounds, the very language low and strange.

Jasper squinted into the darkness of the cell. The torch light cast a half circle into the mold between the stones, scratching at the edge of the shadows.

"Maeveen." Fitzroy's voice gained an edge. "Do come out."

Something rustled in the darkness. A shape, the moving of too many limbs. A glint of eyes, the gleam of something sharp. And then her muzzle tilted into view.

The deep purple of her scales seemed to tint into near black at the very edges, a dizzying prism of the colors of a cool night. Two sets of horns sat atop her skull, one forward facing, and the other curved backwards like the set of a ram's. The tips had been long since sanded, whether from those like Fitzroy or the dragon's own attempts to escape were uncertain. The scales on her spine rippled with each movement, dark spikes against the vibrant purple. As she tilted her head to study them closely, Jasper realized the size of her head alone was the size of the polecat's torso. Her voice, as she spoke, rumbled, and Jasper felt it more than he heard it.

"Now what have I done to earn the grace of your presence?" The dragon's forked tongue flicked out of her muzzle, accompanied by a puff of smoke. Jasper's gaze swung between Fitzroy and the dragon, claws itching to rest on his sword.

Fitzroy's whiskers did not so much as twitch. "Your sarcasm will not do you any favors."

"This is not sarcasm, dearest." The dragon's tone grew languid. "I would have no use for it after being trapped with no company for so long. Not when you've kept me chained with these."

The dragon lifted her wrist. Her claws were blunt, sanded down and barely extending from her fingers. But the heavy iron cuffs distracted even from that. Her muscles strained just from lifting her arms, her scales rustling as she tilted her muzzle to stare at them both, red eyes unblinking.

Fitzroy still did not betray anything other than the stature of a general. He lifted a paw, one claw extended. "Those can be removed."

She must have been sitting, Jasper realized, because now, when she stood, she towered. Her serpentine neck was pressed to the ceiling of the dungeon, the rustling and scraping of scales echoing as she filled the space. Chains twisted around each of her limbs, heavy iron cuffs on each wrist and ropes of chains wrapped around her chest, pinning what must have been her wings in place. Even though her scales were dulled by dirt and grime, their opulence could still be seen in flickers. Her muzzle slipped between the bars, the points of her horns preventing her from moving closer as she bared her sickle teeth. "You have promised me things before, *weasel*," the dragon rumbled. There was something in her voice that made Jasper's insides freeze.

But Jasper couldn't take such an insult. He cleared his throat, his gaze on the dragon's fluttering nostrils. "That is Lieutenant General Fitzroy to you. He is a stoat. Not a weasel."

The movement of the dragon's head to face Jasper was a blur. One moment, Jasper was watching the small puffs of smoke from the end of her muzzle. The next he was staring into dancing flames and scarlet power, her pupils black slashes in the fire of her irises. "Do you dare to correct me?" she rumbled. "I, Maeveen, the Captain of the Dragoon Guard?"

"I do." Jasper heard his voice crack, and the dragon gave a dry chuckle. He felt the tips of his ears begin to heat.

Fitzroy cleared his throat, the stoat's black tipped tail jabbing behind him. "I am reinstating your position in the Dragoon Guard."

This caught the dragon's attention. Her eyes went a shred wider than ever, and her frills even perked between her sets of horns.

"You will, however, be the only one released."

Maeveen's muzzle split into a bitter grin that only a reptile could give. "I do not expect that any of my brethren have even survived their *cages*—"

"—And pending your actions, I will appeal directly to the King regarding the captivity of your species."

Maeveen stopped. The dragon shuffled closer. "What do you want?"

"The enemy is sweeping across—"

There was a loud snort from the dragon, her gaze shifting away. "I should have known—"

Fitzroy let out a tiny growl. "The enemy is sweeping across the continent with a weapon that can mow down entire legions of troops. It will create carnage unlike anything we have ever seen."

"And why," Maeveen said, "should I care if you die by the hundreds?"

"Because your kind once protected us." Fitzroy looked the dragon directly in the eye. "You watched over us. You took us under your wing."

"You decided you no longer needed us."

"We do not need to be ruled by you," Fitzroy continued, "But we need you. Your nobility would not allow you to sit idly by while innocents die by the hundreds. You were once our protectors before you were our Queens."

Maeveen went silent. Jasper found himself holding his breath until the blood started to rush to his head… and then the dragon nodded.

"Good." Fitzroy smiled, his teeth near invisible on his fur. "You will be working with Officer Jasper and his Light Infantrybat Rollo. We have a location for you to intercept the enemy troop. Destroy the weapon, first and foremost."

Maeveen smiled. And then she blew a lick of fire between the two mammals.

* * *

Rollo had not stopped staring since they had started their march.

A battalion followed behind Captain Jasper and the bat, all foot soldiers, most of them like Samuel—snatched from pressgangs and now conscripted into service. They were only escorts, still green around the ears and skittish to boot. They were only here to make sure the trio made it to the edge of the forest without being harassed, on Fitzroy's orders. Given the wide berth that the battalion was giving them, Jasper had to wonder if there was any true danger of them being harassed, or if Fitzroy was sending some sort of message.

Those thoughts were examined and discarded as Jasper slid his gaze to his current company. Rollo was behind him, wings tucked against his sides, ears folded down against his cranium as he stared, wide eyed, at the dragon beside him.

Standing on her two feet outside of the cramped cell, she was well over eight feet tall. Her wings were still bound to her back, and two wildcats held the thick chain collar she wore in their paws. Her legs and arms had been unbound, the rags she had in the cell traded in for a uniform—not the best, the stitches were fraying and the buttons were scuffed—but even in this condition, there was a presence to her. She stood tall with her chains. Smoke puffed from between her teeth, her horns cut the twilit sky above her. The urge to cower as her shadow touched fur was powerful. Jasper steeled himself, even when he saw others in the battalion flinch.

Rollo had opened his muzzle several times to speak, and each time he had thought better of it. Jasper would commend him on such an action later—as well as his fortitude. Rollo had seen his own go down, and still he took up the mission without hesitation. They had not spoken about Samuel, but at a time like this, no words needed to be said.

"Halt!" The cry echoed over the battalion. Jasper stopped on the step, Rollo took one more staggering one, and Maeveen was unmoved by any of it. The wildcats near her approached, saluted Jasper, and took out keys from their uniform. Though they were under orders, Jasper saw how everyone in the battalion took a step back, paws secure on their rifles, a collective holding of their breath. The wildcats betrayed their nerves in their twitching whiskers, the flexing of their claws as they felled the great collar from the dragon. They paused… and then released her wings.

The dragon stretched, her wings rustling. Everyone was watching her, waiting. Jasper knew some of them *wanted* to see her in her true glory. But nothing happened. With a salute, the wildcats turned heels from Jasper and began to shout orders at the battalion, the drum beats starting for the march back. Jasper slid his gaze from the backs of the retreating troop and to the horizon of orange and red. The rolling hills and thick evergreen forests stretched before them. A winding deer trail was their only clue to where they needed to head. By the fox's information, the weapon was going to be deployed near several traveling battalions, and they were using the hunting trails in the forest to navigate. Jasper had to wonder how they were able to fit draft horses to pull a cart through such trails, but Fitzroy had mentioned that reports were coming in of parts of the forest being destroyed.

Maeveen had stepped up beside him, her spaded tail curled upward. She tilted her muzzle into the wind. Jasper caught, from the corner of his gaze, the very tips of her wings flutter. "The cowards have left," the dragon said, a touch of coolness in her breath. "I had sworn at least one of them was going to piss themselves before we had even reached our destination."

"Not many of them have seen combat," Jasper spoke, "much less a dragon in the flesh."

"You need better soldiers."

"That is not for me to decide." Jasper waved a paw for Rollo to step forward. The bat did, tiny clicks starting in the back of his throat. "Scout for us. They should be moving toward where battalions twelve through fourteen are marching. If you hear any cracking trees, assume it is them."

Rollo saluted, cast one glance at Maeveen, and then took off, his black wings cupping the air and his tiny clicks reaching a frequency that Jasper could no longer hear. Maeveen's frills flared, an indication that Jasper was the only one spared from it. The senses of dragons were not just exaggerations to scare cubs into obedience.

"How do they not look up and see him?" Maeveen tilted her head, her teeth flashing in disgust.

"It is sunset," Jasper pointed out. "At this time of the day, the light hits his fur and turns him orange. He is near invisible against the sky as such."

Maeveen huffed, a puff of spoke escaping her nostrils. "So your enemy is stupid."

Jasper's whiskers twitched, betraying the smile he tried to keep down. "They have conquered half of the Old World. But they do lack some of the finer points of strategy."

"Interesting…" Maeveen hummed. "You wish not to be ruled by them, correct?"

Jasper stilled. He did not like where this conversation was leading. "No."

"And now you call upon your former rulers to defend you against this new threat to your precious freedom." She kept her gaze forward, but the silence taunted Jasper to speak.

"We deserve to choose our fates," Jasper said.

"Even if your fate is to die?" Maeveen looked down at him as Jasper grappled with the question. Before the polecat could speak, the dragon looked up, the claws on the top of her wings twitching. "I hear him."

"He must have found them," Jasper heard the squeak in his voice and bit his tongue. He drew his rapier, touched the handle of his pistol, and began to sprint into the forest. Maeveen overtook him in a step, and in a bound she was on her four feet. Dragons had the unique characteristic to be at ease on four paws or two; no other creature had such a capability. Her wings were still tight to her back, tips flashing, and Jasper changed course to follow in her tracks. She weaved through the forest like a thread to needle, navigating without cracking a single twig. Jasper let instinct rule over logic, keeping his paws light on the forest floor, but even he was no match for the dragon.

A rustling of branches above him had Jasper reaching for his pistol, drawing the hammer back and aiming up just as Rollo's head appeared, the bat hanging upside down. His squeaks and clicks interrupted Jasper's admonishment as he said, "Thirty tail lengths just ahead! There's six of 'em, two draft horses and another cart. I don't think we—"

A roar rent the air around them, coming from all directions at once. It split the night sky and brought fresh pains to Jasper's body; the wounds he had sustained and ignored from battles, the ache in his bones, the grief that he kept wound tight inside of him. The roar shook the forest floor and almost drove the Captain to his knees.

Fire bloomed in the trees ahead of them, a flower in the forest that hungered before it disappeared.

Rollo jumped off the branch, snapping his wings in front and half jumping, half gliding through the forest. Jasper ran underneath him, ash and smoke seeping into his lungs. Rollo caught the wind in his wings, and he was gone from Jasper's sight. Jasper let out a string of curses, tripped over a branch, used it as leverage to scurry over the last few tail lengths of distance and found himself face to face with destruction.

The dragon was still on her fours, her neck arched in a curl over her back, tongue lolling out of her mouth and smoke pouring in dark billows from her mouth. Crimson speckled her flank, her lashing tail cracking the trunks of trees nearby. A corpse was disemboweled beside her, the species impossible to tell beyond a scrap of dark fur. A fox, his pelt black and silver, had a rifle aimed for her head. A boar charged her from the side, his head lowered by his gleaming tusks, his rifle snapped in his hooves, blood pouring from his eye socket.

They were merely flies to her. She lunged forward, caught the fox's bullet between her horns and her maw around his arm. With a flick of her head his limb was torn from his body; blood poured down his uniform, and the beast let out a scream that was swallowed by another. The boar's tusks had lifted a scale from the dragoness' side, blood streaming down her flank before her tail slashed the boar across the throat. She did not even give him the courtesy of letting him drop to his knees before her teeth flashed, and the body of the boar dropped, his tusks and head rolling to Jasper's feet.

Feathers flashed in Jasper's vision. A kite had jumped up, her wings (something that Jasper noted with a shock) spread, talons on her feet messing with a rifle when Rollo dove from the sky, wings tucked to his sides and rising at the last second to lash at the bird of prey. They tumbled, disappearing into the darkening forest as Jasper cried out. The brightness of flames caused spots to dance in Jasper's vision as Maeveen painted the forest around them.

A crack sounded next to him. Jasper lifted his rapier, crossing blades with a marten, brown-furred with eyes that danced in the flames that had begun to grow around them. He let out a snarl, parrying and flicking Jasper's blade aside like it was a toothpick. Jasper hissed, elevated language forgotten in favor of the music of snarls and growls, of teeth and claws as he swiped the marten across the face. His paw caught the sword, curled around until the metal bit into the pads of his paws, and then he pulled his enemy close, finding the dagger at his belt and plunging it deep into the marten's stomach. He held the marten as the light left his eyes, keeping the marten's skull craned so he could see the destruction of his troop.

"To hell! To hell with all of you!" Their captain had crawled out of the murk and gloom, over the bodies of the fallen, avoiding the flames and the dragon. A genet, his dappled coat blended with the shadows until this moment, the moment where he was poised over the tarp, lifting and revealing the hellish contraption, bullets slipping between his claws into the machine. Blood smeared the silver fur across half his body, his uniform ripped to shreds, the only mark of his status the tassels that still clung to his fur. There was no drop of mercy, of kindness, of humanity. He only snarled through blood stained fangs and cranked the hungry machine.

Maeveen's roar welled from her cavernous chest. She rose to her full height, and spread her wings.

They blotted out the fading light. Dark, leathery membranes with torn edges, black sails against the light of the dying sun as she rose into the air. Like this, the glow of her chest as flames began to spread up her throat was easy to see; the red of her eyes as she stared down at the genet like he was nothing.

The gun's muzzle swung to her, and the genet let out a scream. Jasper felt himself running, but just as before, something rammed into him, something held him to the forest floor so he could only watch.

Maeveen beat the air once with her wings. As they rose again, the bullets thundered, dotting the black sails with punctures of light that filtered through. To hear a dragon scream in pain brought tears to Jasper's eyes, blurring the sight of the creature starting to fall.

The bullets thundered. The genet was framed by the flames that circled around, his body tense over his device, ash settling in his fur even as the air around them became thick with ash.

Jasper lifted himself as much as he could, his muscles trembling. Rollo's wings were tight around him, the bat's frantic breaths panting in his ear. The horizon was clear, the stars sparking into life above their heads. The thunder of the bullets had faded into a whimper, the genet panting over the device, letting the shells fall from his paw.

She emerged in a swirl of smoke and flame, in blood stained teeth and wings drenched in blood. She dove through the machine, through the last stutter of bullets that sunk into her chest, and stood on top of the device. She grabbed the genet, lifted him up into the sky, burying her claws in his throat as he gurgled on his blood.

She breathed fire like a kiss on his body. For one second, Jasper thought there was nothing more horrifying as his silver fur went up in smoke, as his screams were choked from the oxygen leaving his lungs. She held on until his body was nothing more than a black husk, and let it fall against the cart. It snapped when it hit the edge, and turned into a pile of charred bones and ash against the hooves of the dead draft horse.

Rollo released his grip, and Jasper squirmed from underneath him. Maeveen still had her feet against the machine, but she trembled, her wings limp to her sides. She slid down, bent forward until her muzzle touched the glowing tip of the gun. Jasper approached her, held his claws out but could not think of a word.

Maeveen swallowed thickly, her words hoarse. "This thing… it can destroy everything."

"Yes." Jasper was not sure if his words would be snatched by the flames and the wind, but Maeveen's frills flicked.

"Anyone who has it… they can rule." These words rolled with a coo from the dragon's muzzle. "They can destroy, but those who live will be at their knees." Her claws stroked the machine, and it was then she remembered, and she lifted her gaze to Jasper.

The polecat was next to her, staring at the machine, staring up at the dragon. She tapped a claw against a gear. "Here," she said. "Hit it here, it will fall apart. Hastily made. The metal is brittle with heat."

Jasper looked back at her once again. Her wings dragged behind her, the tips near brushing the ground. She would never be able to fly again. This machine could fell dragons.

Maeveen's claws soaked in the blood pooling between them. She looked at Jasper, unblinking. "Choose," she whispered.

Jasper closed his eyes, and made his choice.

Oriental mythological warfare! The traditional multi-tailed kitsune priestesses of the rice goddess Inari Ōkami are forced to battle Inugami soldiers, dog warriors transformed into humanoid form by dark magic. And a 21st-century American interloper is caught in the middle.

The Shrine War

by Alan Loewen

"Sen-sama? The sisters have gathered in the oratory as you have ordered." In the dim light before dawn, an observer would have seen the forms of two young women, each wearing the traditional garb of a Shinto shrine maiden: long, red skirts bound with an obi, a white kimono jacket, and white hair ribbons and ivory combs tying back long, waxed hair.

"Well done, Hoso. *Arigato*." For a moment, they watched the sun rise above the horizon beyond Mount Tomuraushi. As the growing light illuminated the mountain's summit, what little mid-summer snow remained glowed with a brilliant radiance. The lower slopes turned green from the small hardy bushes and wildflowers.

As the gloom dissipated in the growing warmth of morning, sunlight reflected back from the eyes of the two watchers, eyes that were completely brown and a fitting shade and shape to contrast with the white-furred, fox-like faces of the pair.

"You enjoy watching the sunrise, do you not?" Hoso asked.

Sen remained silent for a moment and Hoso wondered if she had been heard, but after a pause her superior slowly nodded her head. "If the weather allows, I have not missed a sunrise in the five centuries I have been here at the shrine."

Hoso stared with envy at Sen's nine tails, one for each century of her life and the maximum number a kitsune could attain. For a moment, and not for the first time, Hoso regretted her youth. Only two tails emerged from a cleverly designed slit in the back of her skirt and she had seven more centuries to go before she could enjoy Sen's status and glory.

Ashamed of her jealousy, Hoso impulsively bowed to Sen, her furred hands with their dainty claws sliding down the front of her thighs as she bowed deeply. "We will await you, Sen-sama, but I humbly ask that you not tarry. The Inugami emissary will be here shortly." With that, she turned and left.

Sen watched as the fully risen sun turned Mount Tomuraushi into a brilliant and shining beacon, and she dimly wondered if today would be her last opportunity to revel in the gift of a new day. She turned to see the sun gleaming off the red tiled roof of the hodon, the most sacred part of the shrine where Inari's mirror stood in glory and splendor, primal and serene. In front of the hodon surrounded by its protective bamboo wall, stood the oratory, the oratory where the sisters waited. All around her, the peace of the shrine lay inviolate, but Sen feared it would not be so for long. An invading force of the Inugami were coming. With a shake of her head, she turned to walk up the tiled sandō to join her sisters.

Christopher Andrews pushed the partially eaten dish of lavender ice cream away. Around him, people chattered gaily in Japanese as they enjoyed the open air cafe. The town of Kamifurano reeked of lavender as the locals and visitors celebrated the middle of the growing season. Not only did the scent of lavender fill the air, everybody ate lavender ice cream, drank lavender-flavored beverages, and carried lavender-filled sachets.

Christopher, though he loved the exotic, could find little appreciation of an entire town reminding him of nothing more than a lady's boudoir.

His cell phone buzzed. With an exasperated sigh, he picked it up from the table top and flipped it open.

"Christopher here," he said.

He listened for a few moments, thoughtfully chewing on both his bottom lip and his thoughts.

"I know, Alyssa" he said, his tone one of impatience and irritation. "I already know the grant money is gone, but I'm on a great lead. Tell you what. I'll pay my own expenses here on out. Anyway, you've already paid the lease on the Tokyo apartment." He looked around to see if his English had attracted any attention, but conversations around the cafe had drowned out his own. "And I don't start teaching at the University until next week. Time and money I have."

Again, he paused as the cell phone squawked in his ear. "I'm on Hokkaido in the Kamikawa District. You should have read my email. The town is Kamifurano. You'd really enjoy it here. Smells like that perfume you love so much." He dropped his voice to a whisper. "Alyssa, I think I have a lead on an Inari shrine near here that predates the sixth century. Yeah, before Buddhism came to the islands. It's in a forest near Mount

Tomuraushi and it's not even listed with the Jinja Honcho. Probably nothing but ruins now."

He toyed with his melting ice cream as he listened impatiently. "Yes, I promise. I'll wrap everything up with this trip. I'll get some great pictures, you'll get your book, and I'll complete my research; deal?"

Again, he paused as he listened. "Okay and one other thing. I won't have cell phone access at the mountain. I barely have coverage here. Yeah, I'll call you tomorrow or the next day. Would you do me a favor? Please call Liana and let her know that I'll be incommunicado for a day or two."

Another pause as Alyssa buzzed in his ear. "No, I'm not going to marry my housekeeper. How many times have I told you to stop playing matchmaker? I'm old enough to be her father." His voice dropped to a grumble. "I'm old enough to be *your* father. Look, I gotta run. Bye."

He flipped his cell phone closed, stared at his lavender ice cream and decided that the 300 yen investment had paid his curiosity back ten-fold. He had reached the age of fifty six without indulging in lavender-flavored anything and as far as he was concerned, he could go to his grave without repeating the experience. At least it wasn't as bad as bee larva or mayonnaise-filled doughnuts. He picked up his dish and tossed it into the waste container.

The five kitsune sat in a semicircle on individual zabutons awaiting the Inugami emissary. Sen had already assumed the proceedings would be unpleasant. None of the five miko spoke, but simply sat with their prayer beads loosely entwined about their furred fingers, their multiple tails spread out behind them. The aroma of agarwood incense filled the air.

Hoso sat at Sen's right, not necessarily as a place of honor, but so Sen could keep an eye on her and control her impulsive behavior. Five-tailed Chiyo sat at the right of Hoso. Kiku and Kuwa, the twins with four tails each, sat at Sen's left.

"If anyone wishes to share their concerns, it would be best to speak now before the emissary arrives," Sen said quietly.

They sat silently for a moment, and then Chiyo cleared her throat. "Sister," she said, her Japanese heavily accented and archaic, "I ask with respect if it is wise to allow one of these dogs onto our grounds? The Inugami are not our equals. They are murderous thieves." She turned her head to look Sen directly into her eyes. "They follow a dark and evil Taoism. They hold Inari in contempt. And you know the secret of their amulets. You know all this. Why do you allow one to freely enter Inari's shrine?"

Sen paused as was her habit when asked a question. "We do not know what the Inugami want," Sen responded after a moment's silence, "and that lack of knowledge has us at a disadvantage. To allow one here to express its demands may give us valuable time and insight. Three times we have prevented their attempted intrusions, and finally, now that they want to meet with us in the open, many questions will be answered. Remember what the teacher taught, 'From one word, know ten thousand scrolls.'"

Chiyo nodded. "I bow to your wisdom, Sen-sama. Yet, I am glad we have our prayer beads." Chiyo paused and then spoke sharply. "It is at the door."

Five pairs of kitsune ears suddenly perked up. Brown eyes focused on the main entrance of the oratory. The double doors swung open and the Inugami emissary strode into the room.

She was a dog shaped into human form, a Kishu Inu transformed into an Inugami by a black and evil magic. The long, ebony-colored, unkempt hair on her head spilled over her muzzled face and shoulders, in sharp contrast to the dirty white fur and bright, amethyst-colored eyes. She wore a sarashi, a long strip of cotton cloth tightly binding her breasts. A fundoshi, a traditional loincloth, served as a token to modesty. Over her undergarments, she wore a short, open kimono, stained and travel-worn; a brown sash tied around her waist held a sheathed katana. Around her neck on a heavy chain lay a jet black polished stone, a contrast against her white-furred chest.

"It comes dressed as a man," Chiyo muttered.

"She comes dressed as a warrior," Sen quietly replied.

Their visitor strode to the semi-circle and stood in a fighting stance. "I am Yami, of the Inugami. I speak for Akumu-sama, our leader."

"Welcome, Yami-san," Sen said, her voice clear and strong. "We wish that you came to speak in peace, but you come dressed for war." Sen motioned toward the katana that hung by Yami's side. "We fox observe the rules of hospitality. If you come in peace we will respond in like." Sen motioned toward the Inugami's neck. "And you wear a soul crystal in our presence. Have you presented yourself here only to hold us in contempt?"

"Do not speak to me of peace, kitsune." Her lip curled up in a sneer. "You all have your prayer beads in your hands," she spat. "I have not come to speak with respect nor do I bring words of peace. I present our demands."

The Inugami assumed a stiff position of authority and, with her eyes staring over the heads of the shrine maidens, began to recite. "We, the Inugami, we who are free and follow no kami, have come to demand the surrender of this shrine. You will turn over to us the nine-tailed one as well as the Mirror of Inari. If you do this, we will allow the shrine to stand and we will spare the lesser tails as they are beneath our notice. Should you fail to obey Akumu-sama, the Inugami shall take what they wish and raze the shrine to the ground. All that serve here will die. Thus says Akumu-sama."

Sen felt Hoso stir at her right and softly rested her hand on her younger sister's leg, a silent warning to remain still.

Chiyo spoke up. "And tell us, Voice of Akumu. What would you do with our elder sister? What would the likes of you do with the Mirror of Inari?"

Yami ignored her and looked directly into the eyes of Sen. "The nine tailed one will live in honor and service as Akumu-sama's soul crystal."

Hoso, Kiku, and Kuwa cried out in horrified indignation and began to stand, but Sen's voice spoke above them. "Sisters, sit!" The three looked at their senior and, though clearly angry, sat back on their cushions.

Sen spoke up, her voice calm and even. "And the Mirror? What need would the Inugami have of Inari's Mirror?"

Hoso shrugged. "We would shatter it into a thousand pieces."

Again, Sen was forced to raise her hand for order. "And why would the Inugami wish to do that?" she asked once the muttering had ceased.

"Why not? Inari no longer walks in the world of humans. The people of Nippon no longer believe. All kami fade and die. The mirror is Inari's last contact with this world, all other tokens with which she has been enshrined have been destroyed or made worthless through ignorance and apathy. It is our time now, the time of the Inugami. We do not need belief to sustain us, but we shall walk this world with power and authority. All humans shall bow to us and their throats will slake our thirst."

Sen paused for a moment in thought. "We must contemplate your mistress' demands. Surely, you can give us time."

"You have until the end of the first watch after sunset," Yami said. She pointed directly at Sen. "You will meet us on the other side of the entranceway torii, with the mirror in hand. We shall then allow this place to stand as a tribute to the power of the Inugami. Refuse us, and you will all die and we turn your beloved shrine into rubble and ruin." With that, she turned her back to the five shrine maidens and strode out of the hall.

With troubled eyes, the four kitsune watched Sen as she absent-mindedly fingered her prayer beads lost in her thoughts.

"Sisters," Sen said after a few minutes of silence, "I would gladly give up my own life and soul for the safety of this shrine and those I love." Her raised hand stilled the protest. "But they would not be content with my life. They wish Inari's Mirror as well and it shall never fall into their hands."

She stood and the others stood with her. "Hoso, the Inugami certainly gather outside the walls of the shrine. Quietly go onto the roof and try to ascertain their numbers." Hoso bowed and left.

"Kiku? Kuwa? Get your bows and station yourself near the chōzuya. The noise of the fountain will mask any noise you might make and may hide your scent. If any of the Inugami enter the shrine before the time they have set, aim for their soul crystal. A broken crystal will set the soul within it free and without it, the Inugami will have no power by which to cast their magic. And watch the walls around the shrine. They may certainly try to scale them."

Sen turned to Chiyo as Kiku and Kuwa left the oratory. "Dear Chiyo, it is you who must defend Inari's Mirror. They may try to come over the back walls and if they enter the honden, then it is you who must stop them."

Chiyo nodded, her jaw tight and her eyes grim. "They will not obtain the mirror, sister. Not tonight. Not ever." She reached into the left sleeve of her *haori* and pulled out a folded fan. With a flick of her wrist, it sprang open with a metallic whisper to reveal itself as a deadly weapon, its edge honed to razor sharpness. "I have not used my *tessen* in years past counting, but should the dogs attempt to enter the honden..." Chiyo spun the fan in her furred fingers, its deadly edge splitting the air with a fearsome hiss and blurring from the speed of its movement as she expertly guided it through a complex exercise. In her left hand, her prayer beads began to glow with a dull azure light. Then with a sudden movement she flicked the fan closed with a sharp click. The prayer beads immediately once again took on the appearance of simple tiny ceramic and wooden balls strung on a hempen cord. Chiyo slid her *tessen* back up her sleeve.

With dignity, the sisters bowed to each other. Chiyo left Sen standing alone in the oratory.

Christopher Andrews picked his way through the trees keeping an eye on the hiker's GPS he carried. His research in the library in Sapporo spoke of an ancient shrine to Inari within sight of Mount Tomuraushi. The ancient map he discovered claimed to be copied from one from the fourteenth century. Using Google Earth, Christopher hoped he had a dim idea of what the actual coordinates might be, the luxuriant tree growth of the forest not revealing any visible buildings or other structures. With luck, he hoped, his coordinates might put him within a square mile of where the shrine had been.

He had a bad scare when a Japanese giant hornet buzzed by his face on business of its own. The presence of the hornet meant the presence of a nest. Christopher had no desire to die in the middle of a forest where his body could lie for years before somebody found his crumbling bones. Aside from his short conversation with Alyssa, nobody knew where he wandered.

He retrieved his cell phone from his pocket. As he had assumed, there was no signal. To save the battery, he turned the phone off.

An hour later, with the sun approaching noon, Christopher felt a prickle on the back of his neck. The forest had gone quiet. Too quiet. Stopping to sit on a fallen, moss-covered tree, he opened his backpack to get a bottle of water, trying to appear casual while scanning the area.

Not prone to premonitions or "liver-shivers" as he liked to call them, Christopher could not shake the feeling he was being watched. His skin crawled as if unseen eyes observed his every move.

He put the water bottle back into his backpack and shrugged the bag onto his shoulders. His GPS displayed a straight line to the supposed Inari shrine where he could document sacred Shinto architecture uninfluenced by the arrival of Buddhism so many years ago. The GPS led him down a hill to where a small stream ran.

He paused in surprise. Clearly marked in the mud lay the imprint of an animal's footprint, but one unlike he had ever seen before.

The four toes clearly ended in claws, but there was no marking of a rear pad and it appeared as if the creature walked on the balls of its feet. Still sensing invisible watchers, Christopher followed the tracks and saw where the creature had paused, allowing its entire foot to rest in the soft mud of the forest floor. Christopher felt the blood run from his head to his chest in a cold wave of fear. The footprints were long, sharing the length and rough shape of a human's, but the prints were obviously canine.

He debated whether or not he should turn and leave. But the GPS informed him that what he searched for might be less than a football field's length away. How could he give up, he thought, when so close? Christopher saw a large branch and he picked it up, acting as if he wanted an improvised walking stick. It would not serve as a serious weapon, but the feel of the rough bark in his hand lent a feeling of security.

Best to find this place and leave now, he thought.

Around the bend of the stream, hidden by a hillock, Christopher suddenly found himself staring at a vermillion-colored torii. He stared at it in stunned surprise. The gateway, a universal feature of all Shinto shrines, served as an elaborate entrance, separating the sacred inner space of the shrine from the outside mundane world. On both sides, a high wall went to the right and the left until they were lost in the trees. Oddly, no road led to the torii, though a tiled sandō, the walkway that led to the shrine's interior, began directly at the entrance.

What surprised Christopher the most was the immaculate appearance of the torii, the wall, and the sandō. He had expected decaying ruins, but what he could see looked pristine.

Taking out his camera, he took a series of quick pictures and then made his way up the sandō.

The interior of the shrine was as wooded as the outside, but the ground stood bare of leaves, more evidence the shrine had occupants that maintained the property.

The path went around another hillock and then Christopher saw the rest of the shrine and its assorted features.

The chōzuya, the purification fountain, sat under a small bamboo shelter. Beyond the fountain, he could see the Kagura-den where shrine maidens would hold their sacred dances. Past that, there were three setsumatsusha, small auxiliary shrines to other minor kami. The oratory, where rituals and worship took place, stood as the dominant building, its entranceway using two double doors. Beyond that, protected by its own wall, stood the honden, separate from the oratory, where devotees to Inari Ōkami believed the goddess herself to be enshrined. Christopher was delighted to see both the oratory and the hondon had been built in the Sumiyoshi-zukuri style that proved the shrine had been built well before Buddhism came to Japan and made dramatic changes to Shintoism. Conspicuously absent were the tōrō, traditional Buddhist stone lanterns so common in contemporary shrines.

However, the most striking absence was the total lack of statues of kitsune, the pure white foxes that served as Inari's messengers. All of Inari's shrines held two or more statues representing the creatures, many times with them holding keys within their delicate jaws. Without kitsune statues guarding the entrance, Christopher had no assurance this was a shrine to Inari Ōkami at all.

Christopher quickly snapped a number of pictures with his camera, a small part of his mind feeling guilty for taking such liberties without the shrine priest's permission; but oddly enough, the shrine lay deserted. Though the feeling of being observed had never left him, no priests, miko, or worshipers walked the grounds of the shrine. Though the signs clearly indicated one or more caretakers, the place stood as empty as a ghost town.

Nonetheless, he had no desire to offend. Though no devotee of Shinto, Christopher knew that all visitors had to undergo the simple ceremonial purification rite known as *temizu*. The chōzuya for this shrine, where the temizu had to be performed, was a bamboo shelter that housed an actual spring that bubbled up into the fountain and overflowed into an ornate grate.

A number of bamboo ladles lay ready and with practiced ease, Christopher took a ladle in his right hand and used it to scoop up water from the fountain. Slowly, he poured the water into his left hand, then, moved the ladle to his left hand to pour water over the right.

Taking the ladle once again in his right hand, he poured water into his left palm and used it to rinse his mouth. He rinsed his left hand a final time, tipped the ladle up to let water pour down the handle, and placed the ladle back onto its stand.

If there were any unseen witnesses to his ablutions, Christopher wanted them to know he came to the shrine respectfully.

High above him, concealed in the branches of the towering trees, Kiku and Kuwa crouched staring in a combination of wonder and consternation. No human had come to the shrine in over two centuries, and yet, this human wore clothes of a style the twin kitsune sisters had never seen. And everything about him was wrong, the straw-colored hair streaked with gray, the pale skin and the odd shape of his eyes. And he stood so tall. Maybe, they thought, he was seriously ill and had come to pray for healing?

Though they held their bows at ready, they did not draw them. The visitor had performed temizu and now entered the shrine as an honored guest. No enemy would have have done so. Certainly not an Inugami or other form of yōkai.

So the twins continued their vigil and let the human follow the pathway to the oratory. If he meant harm, Sen would know how to deal with him.

As Christopher made his way past the setsumatsusha, he noticed the tiny shrines were all dedicated to various anthropomorphic kitsune, certain evidence the shrine was dedicated to Inari. However, unlike the regular fox statuary of all the other Inari shrines he had investigated, these kitsune stood in human-like form, on their back legs, clothed in kimonos and traditional Japanese garb.

Yet, there was no sign of active worship. The small wooden plaques and tiny sheets of rice paper that contained the prayers and requests of the faithful were conspicuously absent from these shrines. *I might,* Christopher thought, *be the first visitor here for some time.*

Concealed in the bushes near the front of the oratory, Hoso watched in amazement as the visitor approached the double doors. Sen had shown her the watercolored woodcuts of humans in scrolls, but Hoso had never seen one in real life. In comparison to the pictures, this one looked odd. Its hair and eyes and skin color were all wrong.

Hoso knew the legends. Kitsune maidens married humans and bore human children that manifested great gifts of wisdom and knowledge. But how any kitsune would allow such an alien creature to touch them stood beyond her ken. Hoso shivered in sudden repulsion.

She watched as it walked up the steps to the double doors to knock and after a few moments, it opened the doors and walked inside the oratory.

Hoso pricked her ears forward to hear if Sen would call out for aid or assistance. Her attention on the oratory, Hoso heard behind her, too late, the sound of a heavy footstep on dried leaves. Before she could turn, a furred paw clamped her muzzle shut and jerked her head back. The stench of an Inugami filled her sensitive nose. Cruel jaws clamped on her throat cutting off her air and suddenly the world went far, far away.

Christopher opened the double doors of the oratory and marveled at the building's interior. Large ornate panels adorned the walls with delicate, traditional Japanese paintings showing anthropomorphic kitsune as well as regular four-legged foxes. Shōji, traditional Japanese screens, blocked off parts of the interior, creating quiet, intimate spaces for contemplation. Covered in washi paper, the screens were painted with various birds and the ever present kitsune and foxes.

At the far wall, a simple open altar with a suzu bell served for worshipers to gain Inari Ōkami's attention before the traditional bows and clapping that preceded the prayers of the faithful.

Behind one of the screens, Christopher heard the gentle sound of somebody moving and in the small gap between the partitions could see movement. He bowed low. "*Doumo sumimasen,*" he said.

A shrine maiden stepped around the edge of of the shōji where she had been standing, dressed in traditional miko garb. A striking beauty, her face appeared thinner than the average Japanese woman. Christopher guessed her age in her early 20s.

"*Bikkurishita,*" she replied, "You surprised me. How may I serve?" Christopher bowed again. He was surprised the shrine maiden spoke Japanese with an older accent.

"*Sumimasen,*" he said again, apologizing for startling her. "I am a scholar from the United States and I have accepted a position at the University of Tokyo. Doing research for my classes, I discovered in an ancient book the location of your shrine to Inari Ōkami here near Mount Tomuraushi, a shrine older than those who brought the worship of the

Buddha to Nippon. I wish to study the architecture of the shrine, how the peoples of the past built it, and the manner of its building."

As he spoke, the shrine maiden looked on him with an obvious expression of being mystified by his words.

She approached him, studying him with curiosity. "I know nothing of this United States," she said. "And you do not look like one of my people. Your hair is the color of sunlight on old paper and there are streaks of gray within it. Your skin is pale. Your eyes are not of my people. Are you one of the yōkai?"

Christopher smiled to himself. The young woman lived a life so sheltered she had no knowledge of the United States or Caucasians. "No," he assured her. "I am not a supernatural being. I come from a far away country and my people are human though the color of our eyes, hair, and skin are very different."

The miko bowed. "I apologize for not greeting you properly. We seldom receive visitors. I am named Sen." Though outwardly to Christopher, she appeared to stand in great calm and repose, her brown eyes nervously darted back and forth around the interior of the oratory. She paused for a moment as if contemplating what to say next. "I regret that you cannot stay. We are having a private affair that is open only to miko and our... guests."

Christopher again bowed deeply. "*Doumo sumimasen*," he repeated. He hoped the formal apology might undo some of the strain he had caused. "With your permission," he said, "if I may have just a few moments to take some photographs, I will be on my way at once. Could you indulge me this one request?"

"Photographs?" Sen asked, her brow furrowed in puzzlement. "I do not know if we have any you may take. I do not know what they are."

Christopher held back the smile from his face. *A Japanese woman who has no idea what a photograph is?* he mused.

He held up his camera. "No, Sen-sama," he said "My camera here records pictures like your screens record paintings. Allow me to show you."

Making sure the camera was on, he activated the back screen to display pictures already taken. "Do you see? Here is a photograph I took of the chōzuya." He held it out to her, the shrine maiden's jaw opened in surprise.

"What a marvel," she said. "The little box can paint?"

"Yes," Christopher responded, "but it captures light the way our eyes see light." He flicked on the next picture and cycled through a few, showing them to Sen whose surprise at the display grew with every picture.

"This is a magic beyond my understanding," Sen said. She looked at him, concern on her face. "This does no harm? It is not a weapon?"

"Oh, no!" Christopher said quickly. "I would never bring a weapon into any shrine. It helps my people remember what they have seen. So, may I have permission to use my camera to help me remember?"

The shrine maiden thought for a moment and then glanced outside an open window. "Yes, but again, I apologize. You must leave right away."

Christopher bowed his head. "I shall only be a few moments."

Quickly, he snapped pictures barely taking a moment to register what he pointed the lens at, but he snapped off a number of pictures in quick succession, discreetly capturing his hostess in a few of the shots. After taking roughly fifty pictures, he paused to scan through them on the camera display when he came upon a photograph that centered on his host.

Christopher felt the blood run from his face and a wave of fear and vertigo as he stared at the picture on the LCD screen.

He looked up and saw Sen staring at him with a puzzled expression. "Are you well?" she asked.

Christopher stared at the woman before him and then looked back down at the LCD display on his camera. He flipped forward a few more pictures to where the shrine maiden again stood within the frame of the photograph.

"All is well," he stammered. "*Arigatou gozaimasu*, thank you so very much for allowing me to visit your shrine, but I must allow you to prepare for your special guests. You have been so kind."

He bowed and the miko bowed in return. He backed away a few steps before turning and walking out of the oratory, the LCD screen on his camera clearly showing an anthropomorphic female fox clad in the garb of a miko, her nine tails sprouting prominently from behind.

As he stepped out onto the tiled walkway, resisting the urge to run, he caught a glimpse of movement from his right. He turned and gasped as he saw a young two-tailed kitsune uncloaked by illusion, clad as a shrine maiden, staring at something on the ground behind a stand of thick bushes. Her muzzle was twisted in an evil sneer.

Christopher stepped up his pace, his mind numbed at discovering his beautiful hostess was a yōkai, one of the innumerable types of enchanted beings and spirits that pervaded Japanese folklore. He knew that unlike their Chinese and Korean counterparts, Japanese kitsune were, at their worst, nothing more than tricksters and, at their best, they were beneficent in their relationships with humanity, but the shock of seeing one in reality had shaken him to his core.

He strode down the sandō, wanting only to return to his car and the safety of his hotel room where he could ponder his experience in isolated security, preferably with the assistance of some strong Japanese sake.

He turned the corner of the sandō to where the torii stood, but came to a sudden halt as he gasped in surprise.

Directly outside the torii, a large group of creatures blocked the exit. Christopher's stunned senses took in dogs standing on furred hind legs dressed in short kimonos that covered sarashis and loincloths. All of them stood with bared katanas.

At the sight of him, Christopher heard a sudden war cry and the creatures swarmed onto the grounds. Christopher immediately spun about on his heel and ran back up the sandō, his mind blank with terror and the urgent need to find safety.

Above him in twin trees that stood on each side of the walkway, Kiku and Kuwa watched the human as he strode quickly down the sandō toward the torii. They had no way to warn him about the Inugami that blocked the entranceway and, as he came around the corner in full sight of the spirit dogs, the human and the nine Inugami stared at each other before the group screamed out a war cry and swarmed onto the shrine grounds.

The human turned on his heel and ran back toward the oratory.

With prayer beads glowing a deep blue while dangling from their hands, the kitsune twins pulled back the strings of their bows. An arrow of blue energy appeared notched and ready in each bow and simultaneously the two sisters let them fly.

Both found their marks in the Inugami who led the charge. The bolts shattered the soul crystals that hung on chains around their furred necks and the spirits of the kitsune trapped within them burst forth with a loud retort. The bolts of energy passed through the two Inugami, violently flinging them backwards to lie stunned on the ground, their bodies showing no wounds.

The remaining seven Inugami came to a halt and each with practiced ease slid large iron darts from their kimonos and flung them upward toward the sisters where they hid in the boughs.

Kiku hugged the trunk as iron darts buried themselves in the tree around her, but she heard Kuwa cry out in pain.

San's ears perked up at the distant sound of a battle charge. The human must not have gotten away in time. Sen felt sorry for the man, odd as he was. The hatred the Inugami had for humans was deep. All

277

Inugami remembered the dark and hideous magic that formed them from the common dogs they once were, a fatal pain that twisted flesh and bent their spirits to make them slaves. Her only hope came from the knowledge the rage of the spirit dogs would make his ending quick.

Slowly the door to the oratory opened and Sen brought out her prayer beads, but cried out in relief to see young Hoso peering into the gloom of the oratory.

"I am here, Hoso-san," Sen said. "What did you see?"

However, Hoso did not respond, but she put her furred finger to her lips in a universal sign of silence.

Sen approached her as Hoso fully entered the oratory and closed the door behind her.

"I heard the battle charge," Sen said. "Are the Inugami coming? What did you see?"

Hoso turned and Sen saw that her young protégé had a katana concealed amongst her robes. Before Sen could ask the question on her lips, Hoso lunged, the point of the blade aimed directly at Sen's heart.

Christopher could not think in his panicked flight. He knew he could not enter the oratory. A kitsune was there. As he ran, the sounds behind him told him that the creatures that had charged him at the entrance were too close for him to stop to plan. As he ran past the setsumatsusha, he saw the bushes to the left of the oratory where the other kitsune had stood, unaltered by illusion. It was not there now, so Christopher ran for the bushes hoping to hide until he could flee the shrine with mind and body intact. Running between the bushes, his feet tripped over something that sent him sprawling.

Rolling on his back, he cried out in surprise. The kitsune he had seen when he fled the oratory now lay clearly unconscious on the ground before him, but inexplicably lacking clothing and its neck covered in blood.

Christopher rolled over onto all fours and poked his head above the bushes. His pursuers were nowhere to be seen. With one immediate danger delayed, he turned his attention to the creature he had tripped over. The kitsune's neck had four large punctures, two on each side of her throat from which blood slowly trickled. Slowly, its chest rose and fell so the creature lived, but without knowing the extent of its wounds, Christopher had no idea if it would live or die.

Inside the oratory, he heard cries and sounds of struggle, but he focused his attention on the kitsune lying insensate before him. Whatever this creature was, it was younger than the shrine maiden he had first met inside the oratory. Estimating her at less than five feet high, Christopher noticed the creature only had two tails. It was also clearly female. In no legend Christopher knew did a Japanese kitsune kill or harm a human being and he hoped in this case the ancient stories would prove true.

Warily, he again peered between the bushes to try to locate the creatures that had charged him at the entrance.

He heard a hoarse whisper behind him, almost a croak. "Tasukete." Startled he spun about. The kitsune's eyes were open, the color of amethysts and glazed with pain. "Tasukete," it whispered again. "Help me."

Christopher shivered from a mixture of dread and awe. "How… how," he stuttered, struggling to remember his Japanese. "How can I help you?"

"Water," it whispered. It closed its eyes and whimpered.

With another quick glance to assure himself the other creatures that chased him had not yet reached the oratory, he slipped off his backpack to retrieve his water bottle.

Carefully, he tried to lift the kitsune's head off the ground to dribble some of the liquid into her muzzle. Christopher regretted he did not have a bowl for her to lap out of, but he managed to slowly get most of the water into her and not on her fur and the ground.

The creature licked its lips. "Sen," it croaked. "Inugami." Suddenly it looked down and its eyes opened wide in horror. "My clothes!"

Sen shifted to her right and the katana blade slid harmlessly across her chest, creating a slit across her kimono jacket as testimony to its keen edge. She continued in a spin and thrust Hoso away before Hoso could twist the blade for a circular cut.

"Hoso!" Sen cried. "Cease!" But then Sen stopped in surprise.

Hoso's eyes were brown. Whatever stood before her had eyes of amethyst.

"Die, fox!" the creature spat and the voice was not Hoso's but that of an Inugami. It shifted the katana in her hand. Bringing it above her head, she charged.

Again, Sen moved aside in the nick of time, a ribbon fluttering to the ground from her hair to show how close she had come to being cloven in two. Spinning in place, Sen brought up her paws, her prayer beads entwined amongst her fingers and glowing azure.

Before the Inugami could bring her sword up for a counterstrike, Sen's fingers wove a complex mudra, her fingers entwining in the beads. A blast of blue energy struck her enemy, flinging the illusionary Hoso into a screen. The delicate screen shattered into splinters destroying the priceless painting it framed.

Immediately, Sen's attacker stood and shook off the effects of the blast. The attack had removed the illusion and Sen felt an overwhelming mixture of grief and fury to see an Inugami wearing Hoso's shrine maiden attire.

Again, Sen's fingers twisted the prayer chain within a complex dance of her fingers and suddenly an oni, a Japanese yōkai composed of pale, blue fire, stood before her. Sen pointed at the Inugami who assumed a fighting stance.

"I forbid you to shed blood in the oratory," she said to the oni between gritted teeth. "Humble it and remove its reason."

With a scream from the Inugami and a roar from the oni, they charged each other.

The oni's only potent weapon was possession. If it could grapple with the intruder, it would enter her body and render the Inugami helpless.

Ignoring Sen, the Inugami spun about the oni using her katana to cut away segments of the blue fire. Sen could see her summoned creature diminishing before her as the oni began to lose its cohesiveness, and Sen felt panic for the first time in centuries. She had invested much of her magical power in calling the yōkai, and she had stretched her reservoir of magic to its limits.

It was over in less than a minute. The Inugami wielded her katana with an expertise Sen had never seen before. Sen watched her oni fade away under the dance of the Inugami's blade.

With a flicker, the last of the oni died. The Inugami brandished its sword looking at Sen with an evil grin. Intent as the spirit dog was to renew the fight with Sen, the Inugami was caught by surprise when a spinning metal fan caught her katana and sent it whirling to the other side of the room.

Suddenly, another oni appeared from the thin air, its pale, blue fire illuminating the dim interior of the oratory.

"I forbid that blood be shed in the oratory," Chiyo said in a loud authoritative voice. "Humble it and remove its reason."

The Inugami dropped to a crouch, reached into the sleeves of Hoso's *haori* and sent two iron darts flying toward the oni. The small darts had little effect on the yōkai, passing through its gaseous form only to strike the far wall.

In a second, the oni grabbed the Inugami and picked it up in a glowing embrace. Sen closed her eyes and looked away as the Inugami's scream was choked off.

Moments later, Sen felt Chiyo's hand on her shoulder. "It's done, Sen-sama. Have you suffered hurt?"

Sen opened her eyes to see the Inugami standing on unsteady legs, the spirit dog's muzzle open in shock, her wide eyes glowing blue.

"I heard you fighting," Chiyo said. "I had to come. Are you injured?"

Sen shook her head. "No," she said. "But that creature has killed Hoso. It took her clothes and used an illusion to enter the oratory."

Chiyo's face hardened into a mask of rage. "It is our creature now. It does our will." She turned to the Inugami. "Retrieve my *tessen* as well as your darts and katana, but first, hand me your soul crystal."

With a spastic twitch of her head that passed as a nod, the Inugami reached into a pocket and held forth the source of her magic, a tormented kitsune soul wailing for release from inside the ebony gem.

Kiku made sure her feet were solidly placed on the tree branch and tried not to think of the hard ground so far below. Kuwa held onto her twin sister's back and did her best not to hinder Kiku's progress across the canopy of leaves and branches as they tried to put distance between them and the attacking Inugami. Kuwa's left leg dangled uselessly, her thigh heavily bandaged using material torn from her haori. Fortunately the Inugami iron dart had not punctured an artery nor did it appear to have been poisoned.

"Sister, dear," Kiku muttered through gritted teeth as she supported her sister's weight, "perhaps you might consider not eating so many rice balls in the future."

Kuwa ignored her sister's complaint. "We are high enough that the Inugami cannot see us through the branches and leaves. Unfortunately, we cannot see them either," Kuwa replied. "We are well out of the range of their darts while they are still in range of our soul arrows. Please, sister, put me down on this branch. We can make a stand here."

Kiku made her way closer to the trunk and allowed Kuwa to stand on her one good leg. She took a moment to massage her throat where Kuwa had wrapped her arms for support. "Do you see them?"

Kuwa looked over the branch toward the ground below. "No. Nothing. I think they may have gone up to the oratory."

Kiku clenched her fist in useless frustration. "Sen and Chiyo will need our help. How many Inugami did you see, sister?"

"Nine," Kuwa said. "I saw nine when they charged the human. I know we struck two of them down."

"But they are not dead. Their soul stones were fractured so they have lost the source of their magic. Our soul arrows went through them, but they will shake off the paralysis quickly enough."

The two kitsune looked at each other.

"Kuwa, you must stay. I cannot carry you, but I must help defend Inari's Mirror."

Kuwa clutched the trunk and eased herself into position where she could straddle the large branch, one leg and two tails dangling on one side and her wounded leg and her two other tails on the other. "Yes, sister, you must go. And with Inari's help, I will seek a vantage point that might allow me to deal with those spirit dogs. They will not leave the shrine with the Mirror if I can help it." With that, she worked her bow out of her torn haori and, with prayer beads in her one hand, she closely inspected her bow so Kiku would not see her tears. Within moments, Kiku was swallowed up by the branches and leaves as she made her way across the treetops toward the oratory.

Christopher took an extra t-shirt out of his backpack and with great care eased it over Hoso's head, helping her put her furred arms through the sleeves. Small as the kitsune was, Christopher's t-shirt was large enough to cover the kitsune like a dress.

She had managed to whisper to Christopher that she had been attacked by an Inugami and the creature had taken her clothes for reasons unknown to her. Torn between her debilitating weakness and her loyalty to her sisters, Christopher learned that kitsune could cry.

Occasionally, he lifted his head above the cover of the bushes, but the tiled path still stayed empty of the Inugami that had charged him at the shrine's entrance.

Noises had come from the oratory, but now all was quiet inside the small building.

"We need to find better shelter," Christopher whispered. "Those dog creatures will return. I have no idea where they are."

Hoso shook her head. "*Iya desu,*" she said, "No. I live or die with my sisters. Help me into the oratory or leave me to my fate."

To stall for time, Christopher cautiously peered between the bushes trying to see the Inugami. He sucked in his breath in panic and darted down below the cover of the bushes. Just beyond the setsumatsusha, nine Inugami made their way up the sandō, two of them being supported by others as if wounded.

Feeling panic well up inside him, Christopher put his lips next to the kitsune's ear. "They are here. You must be quiet."

Hoso groaned as she tried to shift her weight. "Do you see my prayer beads?" she whispered back.

Christopher looked about her, peering under herbiage and leaves. "No. There is nothing like that here."

The kitsune closed her eyes. "Then I am doomed. Save yourself, human. Leave me and let me die with my sisters if that is what Inari wills."

Christopher paused in a turmoil of thoughts. This creature probably was four times older than him, but in the scale of lifetimes, she appeared as a young creature, no more than a child.

He lay down next to her, hoping against hope the Inugami would not scour the bushes. "No," he said quietly. "I cannot escape anyway without being seen. I will stay."

Chiyo cracked opened the door just enough to see down the tiled walkway. With a hiss of breath, she closed it. "Sen-sama, the dogs are coming. I see them just beyond the setsumatsusha."

"How many?"

"I count nine, but two appear weak and need assistance just to walk." Chiyo smiled grimly. "The twins made their intrusion somewhat difficult."

Sen dropped to her knees, her paws trembling. "Our dear Hoso is dead," she said. "We do not know the fate of Kiku and Kuwa."

"Sister dear, if we work with one mind, we can even remove Mount Tomuraushi. Our sisters may yet live. The dogs want their victims alive. And, yes, our magic is drained, but we still have some left to channel and we have the oni to fight for us."

Sen and Chiyo heard a low moan. Surprised, they spun about. The oni-possessed Inugami stood trembling before them, its katana held at guard. "No," the spirit dog moaned again, the agony of speaking making the kitsune step back in surprise.

"Silence, dog," Chiyo said, her trembling voice sounding small and impotent. "You will submit. The oni will fight for us through you. You have no choice."

The Inugami looked up and bluish, glowing tears welled up in her eyes to slowly drip down her muzzle.

"No," the Inugami repeated. She struggled to speak, the words coming out in strained gasps and whimpers. "I... I am Kirai... the creation... the creation of Kamo no Seimei... who died... who... who I killed with my own fangs. I... am slave... no one... again."

Before Chiyo and Sen could respond, the Inugami twisted her katana about, letting its hilt hit the floor with its point directly under her breast and, before the two kitsune could react, she fell forward to lie prostrate on the floor, the blade jutting from between her shoulders. Inugami blood slowly flowed across the oratory's floor.

A blue, glowing vapor flowed from the Inugami's lifeless corpse and evaporated into the still air.

"The cursed dog has desecrated the oratory!" Chiyo wailed in fury.

Sen held up her hand. "Leave the poor creature in peace. How can we know the suffering that drove it to resist an oni? Let her be. Chiyo, you must go to the honden. Take Inari's Mirror and flee."

Chiyo stared at the Inugami's lifeless corpse. "I will never leave you, sister. I…" yet before she could continue, they heard a shout outside the door of the oratory.

"Those of you inside the oratory!" they heard. "Inari's curs! Hear Akumu of the Inugami. Open the doors. You cannot stand against us."

With a growl, Chiyo whipped out her fan, its opening splitting the air with a deadly hiss. "Let us sell our lives dearly, sister," she said. "Since they have desecrated the oratory with their blood, let us paint the oratory with it."

Sen held up her hand. "No, Chiyo-san. No, dear sister of mine. Open the door and let them in."

Chiyo stared at her elder in mute surprise. "A surprise attack? Is that what you are planning?"

"No, sister. We shall not fight. We shall not spill blood. If tonight we dance before Inari, it will be with honor. Open the door."

Chiyo shook her head. "They will not let us die," she said. "Not with honor. They will suck our souls out for their cursed stones."

Sen elegantly seated herself on the floor, her legs tucked up underneath her. Her hands tucked away in the oversized sleeves of her haori. "No they will not, Chiyo." She parted her hands just enough to show her prayer beads dully glowing blue with magic. "I will not shed Inugami blood, but I have enough magic to protect us from the fate they have planned for us. Be at peace, sister, and open the door before they tear it down."

Chiyo flung open the front doors. Outside, seven Inugami stood with drawn swords, two more of them supported by the others, barely conscious. "Enter, dogs," Chiyo growled and turning her back on them she stalked over to Sen and sat down beside her.

The Inugami entered, their eyes searching the shadows for possible ambush from hidden kitsune.

Sen motioned toward the fallen Inugami. "Your sister died by her own hand," she said quietly. "She died with honor."

One of the Inugami stepped forward, an Akita Inu shaped into female form, with white fur stained with dirt and debris. "The Inugami care nought for honor," she said. "I am Akumu of the Inugami. Do you surrender yourselves and your shrine?"

Sen's voice was soft but clear in the confines of the oratory, contrasting sharply with the harsh tone of the Inugami leader. "Before I answer," she said, "I ask a simple question. What do the Inugami have to do with Inari Ōkami and her kitsune? We know of no conflict between our peoples. Why do you bring drawn swords to our shrine?"

Akumu spat on the floor eliciting a snarl from Chiyo, but Sen placed her hand gently on her knee to keep her quiet. "Why do we come here?" Akumu asked, her words dripping with contempt. "Why has every kitsune-led shrine to Inari fallen to our swords, leaving you the last to deal with?"

Akumu sheathed her katana with a sharp click, walked up to Sen and squatted on the ground before her. Smouldering Inugami eyes looked into the serene eyes of Inari's fox guardians.

"Do you know how we came about, fox? You were born in the wilds of Nippon. Your destiny if you survive the first century of life is to grow an extra tail and receive the gifts of sentience and servitude to your rice goddess. Tell me, shrine maiden and guardian, do you know how an Inugami is birthed?"

"I have learned that Inugami are the creations of men who practice dark sorcery," Sen replied.

Akumu laughed. "Yes, that is how we are birthed, fox. All of us were once dogs, dogs born for the purpose of serving humanity. Then humans that we trusted and that we only wished to serve did terrible, pain-filled rituals, dark and evil tortures that twisted us into dark and evil servants."

The Inugami smiled and nodded at the corpse on the oratory floor. "But we ten rebelled. We drank the blood of our masters and to the best of our knowledge the nine of us still standing are all that is left of our accursed race. When our ten masters died, their craft and knowledge passed with them."

The Inugami reached into her sarashi and pulled out a large black stone from between her breasts. Dimly, Sen and Chiyo could hear the kitsune soul bound within it, screaming for mercy.

"And we learned a dark and evil magic of our own. By the way, the soul stone of the dead one? Where is it?"

Chiyo smiled and pointed to the far corner of the oratory where shattered black glass lay. "The soul inside has been released. Our sister is forever beyond your clutches."

Akumu shrugged. "It is of no matter," she said. "When we capture the two in the trees, with you two as well, we shall have all the soul stones we need. And if you think our genesis was born of pain, I assure you that your transition will be far more worse. Now, where is the mirror? Let us bring this to a close and watch the humans deal without a goddess to provide rice for them."

Sen raised her hand. "Before that," she said, "a proposal?"

Akumu snarled and stood, her hand on the hilt of her katana. "You are in no position…"

"Your sister spoke before she took her life," Sen continued quietly. "Like you, she spoke of servitude imposed not out of love, but of greed and power. We have no quarrel with you. Inari has no quarrel with you. I offer you and yours a place of refuge here. Here there is peace and the human visitor we had today was the first in two centuries. No more will come." Sen held out her hand. "We are still yōkai, are we not? Take my hand and let us be sisters."

Akumu stared at the proffered paw. Then, with a move so quick Sen could not respond, the Inugami gripped her katana and popped it out of its scabbard, allowing the hilt of the sword to glance off Sen's temple with a sharp crack.

Chiyo screamed as her elder sister fell backwards to lie still on the floor of the oratory. She gathered her sister in her arms, weeping.

Akumu stood and motioned to two of her followers. "Go to the honden and retrieve the Mirror. Let us end this and know our revenge against humanity is complete."

Chiyo looked up to where she cradled Sen's head to her chest. "You foul dogs won't find it there," she said. Her eyes suddenly blazed with fury and hatred. "I have it."

Gently, Chiyo laid Sen on the floor, reached into her kimono jacket and pulled out a small square wrapped in silk.

"Here is Inari's Ōkami's Mirror," she snarled. "Let me give it to you as you want it so much. Let me show it to you so you can learn a great truth. We were not protecting the Mirror from you. We were protecting you from the Mirror." With a flick of her wrist, she allowed the concealing silk to fall to the floor.

Christopher sat silently on the ground, Hoso's head cradled in his lap. Slipping in and out of consciousness, the kitsune would alternately beg him to carry her into the oratory and then she would once again fall back into a fitful slumber.

He experienced a moment of true terror when the dog people went to the front door of the oratory, but Hoso was unconscious at the moment and he made sure she was not seen.

286

Once the Inugami entered, he dimly could hear conversation, but it was muffled to the point of being incomprehensible.

Suddenly, he heard screaming from many voices. He closed his eyes imagining what the creatures were doing to the kitsune he had just left behind no more than fifteen minutes earlier.

Then, from the open doors of the oratory, a pack of four-legged dogs burst out into the grounds of the shrine. Christopher gasped as he saw members of the Japanese Tosa breed fleeing with Hokkaido, Kishu, and Kai, all led by a large Akita. They stumbled as rags of clothing fell from them to lie on the ground, but the dogs did not pause in their flight. Running down the sandō, they disappeared from view.

From inside the oratory, Christopher heard weeping. Torn by indecision and mystified as to what he had seen, Christopher remained in his hiding spot. A part of him wanted to flee, but another part of him refused to leave the young kitsune.

Moments later, Christopher heard the noise of feet on tile. Daring to venture a look, he saw a sole kitsune, four tailed, running up the sandō carrying what appeared to be an unstrung bow. Taking a deep breath, he stood making the kitsune come to a stop.

He held up his empty hands. "*Tasukete kudasai,*" he said plainly. "Please help me. I have a young kitsune here. She is wounded."

The newcomer looked from him to the open door of the oratory and back to him. "Step out of the bushes," the four-tailed kitsune ordered.

Some minutes later, Kiku and Christopher, with Hoso supported between them, entered the oratory. Chiyo sat weeping, her head bowed over her older sister who lay still. A dead Inugami lay sprawled on the floor in a pool of blood, a blade jutting from between her shoulders.

"No!" Hoso cried weakly. "Sen-sama! I should have died with you."

Chiyo cocked her head "Hoso? We thought you dead. Be at peace, child. Sen still breathes, but her wound is past any art I have." Chiyo then looked up, and the three saw that Chiyo's eyes had become featureless orbs of white. "I cannot see you. Who else is there?"

"Chiyo?" Kiku said. "What did they do to you? I saw a pack of dogs running toward the torii. What happened to your eyes?" As she was speaking, Kiku and Christopher half-carried Hoso over to Sen and helped her to kneel. Hoso gathered her unconscious sister in her arms, weeping loudly.

"Kiku! You live!" Chiyo said. "Thank Inari. And Kuwa?" Chiyo stopped and sniffed the air. "There is a human here. Sen mentioned a human. Does he come as friend?"

"Kuwa lives. She is near the torii. And the human comes as a friend. He protected Hoso who had been attacked by an Inugami."

Kiku and Christopher gently let Hoso down to kneel beside Sen. Hoso embraced her unconscious sister, weeping.

"Human, thank you for protecting my sister," Chiyo said simply. "Would that I had been more able in guarding Sen-sama…"

Kiku bent down over Sen, examining her injuries. "Sen is breathing. She has taken a blow to the temple, but she lives. We must help her. But, Chiyo, what happened to the Inugami? What happened to your eyes?"

Chiyo laughed bitterly. "The Inugami wanted Inari's Mirror and I let them see it. The last my eyes saw were the Inugami transformed back to the time before magic made them what they were." Chiyo touched her white orbs with trembling fingertips. "But I saw as well, and one does not look at the divine without penalty."

Kiku stroked Sen's hair and choked back tears. "Then we have won at a great price. Chiyo. What do we do now?"

Chiyo sighed. "We tend our wounded. The life of the shrine continues."

With great care, Christopher wrapped the body of the Inugami in a makeshift burial shroud Kiku had given him. Following instructions, he left the body outside the oratory. "Other yōkai," Kiku had explained, "ones that you cannot see will deal with the body in the night." She pointed to the setting sun. "The sun is setting soon and it is not safe to travel the forest at night. You will stay here as our honored guest."

In the oratory, Sen, Hoso, and Kuwa lay on mats on the floor while sightless Chiyo tended to them as best she could. Christopher could see that the four-tailed kitsune, the one named Kiku and the only one untouched by the conflict, was grateful for his help.

"Before it gets dark," Kiku said, "we will need water. I have wounds to bathe and they will be thirsty. The water buckets are at the back of the oratory."

"Of course," Christopher said. "I will get it right away."

"And return to the oratory immediately," Kiku said. "You must not be outside after sunset."

When Christopher returned with filled water buckets, Sen was awake and talking with halting speech to her sisters. Kiku pointed to Christopher once, but he kept his distance from the group, unsure how to act. He could not hear the conversation.

That night he slept on a mat apart from the five kitsune. Sleep did not come easily. Strange subtle noises outside the oratory stirred his imagination with strange and dangerous creatures. Christopher had come to Japan to study its mysteries. When he took his new position at the University of Tokyo, he would render his discoveries into sterile scholarly papers and lifeless dissertations. But kitsune, Inugami, and other yōkai did not conveniently fit into that environment.

In the faint moonlight, he saw the kitsune they called Chiyo sit up and sniff the air. She turned her head toward Christopher, her sightless eyes reflecting back the light. Quietly, as not to awaken her sisters, she crawled toward him.

"I could smell you were awake," she whispered as she approached. She sat on the floor before him, her legs tucked neatly under her, her five tails curled around her as if to keep her warm from the slight nighttime chill. "We must talk, human. Tell me your story."

Christopher. keeping his voice low, began telling the creature how he came to Japan, his desire to live in the islands and teach at the University. He explained that though born into a different race and culture he had always held a deep fascination with Japan and its rich history.

When he was done, the kitsune sat before him motionless, her white eyes still glowing in the light. "May I feel your face?" she suddenly asked.

Christopher assented and allowed the furred fingers to touch his chin, explore his forehead, stroke his cheeks. "You are an honorable man," Chiyo said. "I believe you can help us. Sen and I have a problem and your actions have shown us you might be part of our solution."

Kitsune and human whispered to each other throughout the night until the morning light began to fill the room.

The next morning, Sen was able to sit up and the five sisters ate a simple breakfast of rice, vegetables, and fruit that had been left at the door of the oratory. "Offerings from other yōkai," Kiku explained.

"You will be leaving us, Christopher-san?" Sen asked.

"Yes, Sen-sama. I must return to my world. And you do not have to say it. I will keep the secret of this shrine sacred. I will not tell another soul."

"Your word is appreciated, but when you leave, I will cause a strong magic to hide this shrine from the world. We never felt a need to hide from the world before, but this is the best course of action."

Sen nodded toward the large blood stain on the oratory floor. "The oratory has been desecrated. We must tear down the entire building and rebuild from scratch. Other yōkai will help us in this endeavor. And that brings us to a final matter."

Sen looked at Hoso who sat at her right. "Hoso-san, we have a problem."

A puzzled expression in her eyes, Hoso looked at her elder.

"Dear sister," Sen said gently, "you must leave us for awhile."

Hoso's expression changed from puzzlement to panic. "No, Sen-sama," she cried. "What are you talking about? What have I done? Please do not punish me. Tell me what I did wrong. I will atone!"

Sen swept her up in an impulsive embrace. "It is nothing that you have done. You have not looked into a mirror and you cannot see yourself. You were bitten by an Inugami and its vampiric venom courses through your body. Your eyes…"

Hoso looked up into her sister's eyes. "What about my eyes?" she asked. "I can see. I am not blind."

Sen shook her head. "Your eyes are not your own. They are the eyes of an Inugami."

"No! I am not an Inugami! I am Hoso! I am your Hoso-san!"

"You will always be my Hoso-san," Sen said, "but you cannot serve here until the venom has worked its way out of your body. Yet, we have a plan."

Sen pointed at Christopher as she rocked Hoso back and forth. "You can go with this human. He and Chiyo talked the matter over. You will not wander the hills alone. You still have the power of illusion and can appear human. He will care for you and you will be back with us in five years at most."

Christopher spoke up, his voice barely audible. "There is much I can learn from you," he said. "And my house will be a place where you can live in safety. I would be honored to have you as my guest."

Hoso looked up at her sister in horror. "And am I to bear him children like the kitsune tales of old?"

Sen's eyes grew large in surprise while the rest of the Kitsune choked back their reactions.

"Good heavens, no!" Christopher said quickly and then paused hoping he had not insulted anyone. "I mean, I have no desire to have children. And that is not what I meant…"

"No, Hoso," Sen said interrupting him in an effort to restore some semblance of composure. "We will not ask you to do that."

"Five years is not too long," Hoso said quietly. "It is only time."

Liana bustled about the house preparing for Professor Andrew's return. She had been Christopher's housekeeper since his arrival in Tokyo three months ago when her sister, Alyssa, had gotten her the position. Now he was coming back from his three-week field trip with a warning he was bringing a long-term guest.

She clenched her fists in frustration. This might set her plans back.

There was a knock on the door and when she reached the entranceway she found her employer accompanied by a young Japanese girl in traditional garb.

"Liana," Christopher said,"I would like you to meet Hoso. She is the daughter of a friend of mine and she will be staying with us as she attends university."

Liana looked her over with a critical eye. Their new visitor was a pretty little thing, her face somewhat more narrow than normal, but her eyes were bright with intelligence.

"I would like to put her up in the guest room," Christopher said. "Could you show it to her while I get the luggage from the car?"

"Of course," Liana said. "At once." Christopher turned and allowed the front door to close behind him.

The two women stood face to face and, with a shimmer, illusion disappeared leaving two kitsune looking critically at each other.

"He is mine," Liana said.

Hoso grinned, her relief evident. "And I am delighted to hear you say so."

Once again the air shimmered and once again a delicate Japanese housekeeper stood before a young girl.

"You must be starved from the trip," Liana said. "Rice ball?"

Hoso laughed. "You know me all too well already."

Most of the stories up to now have featured mankind and the bioengineered animals of Earth, or an Earth inhabited by fantasy intelligent animals. Here is either another world or an alternate dimension. Its people are the Jegera; black-furred, clawed and tailed, capable of walking either on four legs or two, telepathic, but still primitive hunters.

When three young Jegera hunters run into the legendary Yaka monsters, and the giant hukra, the result may change their world.

The Monster in the Mist

by Madison Keller

Wet grass soaked through Isok's hunting leathers. The damp fur itched. More rain continued to drip slowly on him as it filtered down through the cracked brown foliage above. It figured. The first rain in months, and it had to happen on his first hunt as a full member of the pack. He flicked his ears, scattering water droplets onto the black furred hunters next to him.

<Be patient, young pup,> the hunt leader gefired to him. The mind to mind communication was handy for hunting, allowing the pack to communicate without startling any potential prey.

A flash of brown fur through the leaves drew his attention back to the reason they were here. The dry season had been longer and dryer than normal, and it had come after a particularly cold and snow-free winter. The herds of deer, their normal prey, had been hit hard by the abnormally cold weather, and most of the new fawns hadn't survived. As the summer wore on, and the streams, rivers, and even lakes had dried to mere trickles, the herds had migrated away in search of food and water. The current drizzle Isok suffered under was the first in many moons.

<Steady.>

Isok pulled his back paws up and settled them firmly into the mud, digging in his back claws. His front paws gripped his spear tightly enough that he had to relax, lest his front claws ruin the shaft.

<Strike!>

As one, the pack charged from its hiding spots to converge on an undersized boar. Its back still showed the ghost of baby spots, and it was so thin its hide was pulled taunt over bones. Before Isok could throw his own spear, one of his pack mates hit the beast right in the eye. The boar

293

squealed loud and high, making Isok wince. It took two steps and then collapsed on its side. Blood dripped from its eye socket and the back of its neck where the rock spear tip poked through the fur.

The pack circled the dead boar. Isok dropped his spear and fell to all fours, pushing at the loam around him with the tip of his muzzle. No other fresh spore. Underneath the top layer of brown leaves was the faint scent of the rest of the sounder, but the track was days old. This juvenile must have gotten separated. Unable to keep up it was left behind to fend for itself.

Boar were good eating, and usually a single boar could feed half the clan for several nights. But this one was so thin, Isok guessed it might feed two adult clan members for a single day.

The hunt leader, Rahil, cocked his head at Isok as he retrieved his spear and climbed to his feet. Isok's ears and tail fell and he lowered his head, looking up at Rahil. "No others. The trail is old. This one was left behind."

Rahil snarled without teeth, and stalked over to lecture the other two hunters about proper skinning techniques. Isok relaxed slightly.

Howling rose up from the forest around them. Isok's ears stood straight up. He whirled, raising his muzzle to sniff the air. The wind shifted, revealing intruders hiding nearby. He recognized the scent immediately, although a compelling undertone to it had him oddly at ease. "Comet Clan!" he yelled, warning the others.

"Protect the kill!"

The battle was over in less time than it took Isok to be knocked flat on his back by a Comet Clan attacker. When Isok recovered Rahil was lying before the Comet Clan chief, a spear sticking out of the back of his shoulder. The other two Bright Moon Clan hunters were held captive by three spear-wielding warriors.

Isok shifted, taking his eyes off the hair-raising sight of a spear a claw length from the curve of his throat long enough to look up at his own captor. The most exquisite female he'd ever seen growled down at him. Silky mahogany fur covered her back from the tip of her tail all the way to the delicate curve of her muzzle where her lips peeled up over gleaming fangs. The color faded to fawn on her throat and stomach, the downy fuzz interrupted only by a leather loincloth strung about her hips.

His tongue lolled from his muzzle as he leaned his head up as far as he dared and inhaled the rich musky scent of her. A pin-prick of pain on his windpipe only heightened his growing lust.

"Stay."

The command, said in the sharp bark of an Alpha, snapped him out of his trance. The Comet Alpha scowled down at him. "Keep away from my daughter."

* * *

Even his growling stomach couldn't keep the Comet Alpha's daughter from his mind during the long trek back to the Bright Moon's encampment. Rahil noticed his distraction. Guessing the obvious source, he tried to lecture Isok about his duties to Clan and pack. Famines were not the time to start a family. Especially not with a female from a warring Clan. The words made sense when Rahil said them, but the meaning rolled away when he caught a whiff of her scent clinging to his fur.

When the first Clan members spotted them the greeting howls were excited. However, when the scouts noticed that the hunters didn't have a fresh kill with them, and that Rahil had a bloody bandage around his arm the howls were subdued and tinged with worry.

By the time they trudged into the main camp, it was to snarls and turned backs. Isok spotted his litter mate peeking at them around the curve of a yurt. When he met her gaze she narrowed her eyes and turned away. Isok sighed. He couldn't blame his sister in the least, as he was very conscious of his own gnawing hunger.

The Alpha met them in the center of the camp, standing on the dry, cracked dirt. It seemed the drizzle that had haunted their hunt hadn't reached this far. The hunting party came to a stop in front of the Alpha, unconsciously arranging themselves in a line with Rahil at the lead. Isok knelt, lifted his head, and turned his muzzle, presenting his neck to the Alpha.

Rahil knelt as well, although he didn't give as much neck as Isok did. Even from behind, Isok could see the tension in Rahil's posture and scent, the blood soaking through the bandages.

"You are injured. Yet you have no meat, no kill."

"Yes, Alpha. We did have a kill. Comet clan ambushed us." So few words, but they summed up the situation perfectly.

The Alpha lifted his head and bayed. Ears perked up all over camp. Immediately clan members rushed into the circle. Most of the clan were already close, having come in hopes that this hunt had been successful. In less time than Isok would have thought possible, the circle filled. Almost a hundred Jegera stood in hopeful silence. They waited for the Alpha's words about how he was going to save them.

Isok stood and moved back towards the edge of the crowd with the rest of the youths, making room for the oldest and wisest to gather closer to the Alpha.

The Alpha took a deep breath. The crowd trembled in anticipation, ears high and tails wagging slowly. "Another hunt come to naught."

"We must go north!" One of the young females cried. In the press of the crowd, Isok couldn't see who. He shuddered. North, where the mist monsters lived in the cracks of the mountains?

"That way lies the Yaka," the Alpha said, "and the danger is too great. This has been debated before and always reason won out."

"My puppy died last night. Starved to death. Is a Yaka any greater of a threat?" Now Isok had a face to put to the voice. Only one female had given birth to a live litter this spring. Isok had played stick with the pups before he'd left on the hunt. They'd hardly had the energy to move. Nothing but skin over bones with distended stomachs and fat puppy faces.

"We've already moved farther north than we ever have in this clan's history, following what remains of the herds towards the distant peaks."

Not so distant now. From the campsite it was hidden, but in the meadow down by the stream you could see a snow capped mountaintop. The herd's trail had continued north towards it, but the Alpha had camped them here, too afraid of the mist monster legends to allow the Clan to travel any farther.

"And now we have word that the Comet Clan has followed us here."

Someone whimpered. Isok wrinkled his nose at the scent of urine as one of the pups cowered in fear. It was a sign of how desperate it had become since the Bright Moon Clan had marched north, when the Yaka incited less fear than a rival clan.

The memory of the Comet female's musk caressed his nose and he panted, too hot. His fur itched, and he suppressed an irritated snarl when the pup next to him thumped him with a careless swing of his tail.

He couldn't deny it any longer. The beginnings of mating frenzy. Over her. A Comet. Only mating with his Chosen would end his torment. But with their Clans at war over the scarce prey, the enemy Alpha would never allow him a chance to win over his daughter.

If only there was a way to solve both problems.

The Alpha stood, his barrel chest drawing every eye. "The will of the pack has been heard and weighed. Leaving our traditional territory was a mistake, perhaps. But neither will we proceed north. Hunting has been better here than it has been anywhere else this summer. We stay until first snow."

* * *

Although that had been his first time on a hunting pack, Isok had seen the rest of the hunters come back from earlier hunts. Most of them had returned empty-pawed and tired. Younger and younger pups were being sent with the hunters, on the theory that more hunters had more chance of success. Isok didn't believe that. More inexperienced hunters would merely drive off the prey, if there was even any to find.

The Comet Clan female would only be his if everyone had enough food that there was no reason to fight. No reason to deny his request to woo a female of another clan. When he was growing up before the drought started, he remembered an older sibling of his going off to join another clan.

There were complications, though. Jegera were pack hunters. He didn't know how to hunt alone. Surely a few of the others around his age felt the same way. Isok noted who complained the loudest about the decision to stay. The younger pups, like him, were surer bets. By the time he stumbled into bed, the sun had crested the horizon and he had made up his mind.

In the end only two others agreed to join him in his northward hunt for prey. It would have to be enough.

That night they planned and packed. They gathered what few supplies they could find. Each of them packed a small hunting pannier with only the bare essentials. A blanket for each of them, several filled water-skins, a stone knife that Adlie snuck out of her father's hunting kit, and Isok's spear. After a short discussion they decided not to bring any food with them. The pack needed it more; and if they were right about their trip, they'd soon find prey aplenty.

The sun rose and the camp quieted down until only the early morning bird songs could be heard. Jegera didn't usually start to stir until the late afternoon, waking as the heat of the day faded away. While their night vision was excellent, most Jegera had trouble with bright light. So it was that the three pups padded softly away, their absence unremarked. They easily avoided the day guard, who was there mostly to scare off intruders and other predators, rather than to stop Clan members from leaving the area.

The chance of someone coming after them was low. Resources were too scarce and hunters needed too desperately to hunt prey rather than chase foolish pups into the legendary northern mountains.

* * *

Isok pushed them hard, stopping only for needed bathroom and water breaks. His four legs were trembling with hunger and fatigue when he finally allowed them to stop as the sun began to set.

Many other predators hunted at night, and Isok didn't want to be caught unawares in unfamiliar territory. Better to wait a while and grow familiar with this strange northern forest's night life before moving on. While they waited, Isok watched the trees swaying in the wind. Instead of leaves, these northern trees had needles for branches, sharp enough to draw the blood of the unwary. These forests had more dangers than just those on four legs.

Deep shadows mixed with the remaining sunlight to form swirling clouds of impenetrable darkness. A rustling in the bushes had all three of them on their feet, claws out and lips pulled back in silent snarls. Adlie charged while Isok stood frozen with indecision.

<Foolish,> a warm voice sounded in their heads. Adlie slid to a stop, her tail lowered and one ear twitching in confusion. <Haven't you hunted before?>

"Who's there?" Isok growled, pushing in front of Adlie. Garor, the third member of their small band, cowered behind him, the stone knife clutched tightly in his front paws. Isok could distinctly smell his fear.

The vision of loveliness that was the Comet Alpha's daughter stepped out of the bushes, ears erect and tail high. Her spear hung from one relaxed paw. She smiled at Adlie without teeth, and then turned her attention to Isok.

Twilight sun sparkled in her fur as she crouched and gently set her spear down in the leaf mulch. Her nostrils flared when Isok took a step forward. Her scent filled the clearing and he inhaled deeply. This close, the mating frenzy struggled to take hold of him. He had to fight to keep his gaze on her face. She licked her muzzle, the pink tongue bright against her dark fur. Isok almost lost it. A gulp and a whine escaped him before he was able to address her.

"What—" another lungful of her musk scattered his thoughts. "What, why, here—"

"I think what Isok means is why are you here, Comet Bitch?" Adlie shifted up to a crouch and bared her claws.

"The same reason as you, I suppose," she said, ears flicking about to indicate the woods around them. "Hunting."

"Alone?" Isok cocked his head.

"Um..."

"I knew it, you followed me." Isok wagged his tail and straightened, lolling his tongue at her.

"Don't," she barked.

"What's your name?" Isok asked at the same time Adlie said, "Who are you?"

"To answer both your questions, I am Henra, daughter of the Comet Alpha." Henra returned Isok's slobbering smile with one of her own, nostrils flaring again.

"Why are you here then, if not to help us?" Adlie cocked her head, looking back and forth between Henra and Isok. "Wait." She crouched and approached Isok, nose in the air; then did the same to Henra. The latter pinned her ears back at the approach but made no move to stop the small female. "Mating smell." She shook her head. "I smell it on you both. Isok is right, you did follow him."

"Fine, I did," Henra growled back. "So now tell me why the three of you are out here. Mist monsters hunt these woods, you know."

"Hunting." Garor finally got up his courage and stepped forward to join their conversation. "Somewhere the Comet Clan hasn't already cleared out." He snorted at Henra in derision.

Henra huffed and retrieved her spear, then pointed up through the trees into the growing darkness. "The Comet clan is smart enough to stay away."

"Monsters' aren't real," Isok said, clearing a space on the ground and settling down to his haunches. The other three shot wary glances at each other before joining him.

Henra sat farthest away, almost at the edge of the clearing, while Garor and Adlie settled down next to him.

"Then where did the legends come from?" Henra asked after everyone had settled, waving a languid paw around her head. "Not from air."

The last bits of twilight faded away as the group sat, quietly staring at each other. Even before the drought Comet Clan and Bright Moon Clan hadn't gotten along. Isok was doubly intimidated by Henra's intense stare.

He distracted himself by searching the brightening stars for familiar constellations, trying to determine which way was north. When he looked back down, feelers of mist were rolling in from the trees. One crawled over his outstretched tail, giving him the chills.

Isok stood quickly, backing away from the oncoming mist in a crouch. Without taking his eyes off the ground, he reached around behind himself and pulled his spear free of the ties on his pannier. Eyes wide, Garor and Adlie did the same. Henra, closest to the trees, was already almost lost in the mist. Isok could barely see her ear tips poking up through it. She stood up on four legs, sending the mist swirling away. Her face was unreadable as she stiffly marched towards them.

Adlie whispered from somewhere behind him. "Mist always proceeds the appearance of the Yaka in the legend."

Garor growled his agreement.

"Superstitious nonsense," Henra muttered as she moved up next to them. Her tail was sticking straight back, as if she fought to keep it from curling between her legs. Her ears were quivering.

"Be brave," Isok whimpered to himself. He turned and looked at his small pack's faces. He'd started this expedition, and as the pack leader he needed to be brave for them. Isok slipped the spear back into its straps and straightened up onto two legs. He towered over the other three who still stood on four. The Bright Moon alpha always used this move to great effect.

Isok cleared his throat and began again. "Henra is right." His voice seemed to disappear into the encroaching mist. "We three came here *because* we didn't believe the legends. Don't let a little mist spook you into forgetting our purpose."

"Oh, little pup," a voice hissed from the darkness. The mist deadened the sound and made it impossible for Isok to locate the source. "Sometimes the Legends are true."

Garor let out an ear-splitting howl and fled into the trees, kicking up dirt and lichen in his wake.

"Garor," Isok called after him, unwilling to follow him and leave Adlie and Henra alone with the voice. Only terrified howling answered him, the sound getting quieter until it faded away to silence. Isok spun, eyes probing the thick mist and analyzing the shadows in the trees, searching for the intruder. He even looked up, into the branches, but nothing was there.

"Well now, too brave to follow your little friend back to safety? Too foolish not to run when given the chance."

A shape materialized out of the mist, sketched in darkness. Isok could only see an outline. Strain as he might, no details presented themselves. It had tall pointed ears, wide shoulders, and an outline fuzzed by fur. It stood on all fours, facing the pups head on. Isok gulped when he realized that the beast's eyes, or what he thought were the eyes, were level with his own; despite the fact that he stood tall on two legs and the beast on four.

"Who are you?" His voice barely trembled as he struggled to contain the fear that caused his heart to almost beat out of his chest. He could smell the terror stink coming off Adlie and Henra, and knew he too must reek of it, but he wouldn't let the beast have the satisfaction of hearing his fear as well as smelling it. There was another scent, too, of another Jegera; but it was faint and all but drowned out by the fear stink coming off the group.

"Insolent pup, to come into another's home and demand." The shape moved forward, growing larger as it came. Details swirled up out of the mist. No, it was the mist swirling up to add definition to the shape. A shape made up of the mist itself. Eyes opened, white on black, and Isok could see the outline of trees through them.

"We mean no disrespect, honored Yaka." Isok knelt down and presented his throat to the shape, as he had for the Bright Moon Alpha less than a day ago.

The shape flickered. Was it so surprised by his move?

Isok stood flicking his ears to rid it of the night-time biting insects and stepped forward. "We apologize for our trespass, but we were desperate. Our streams are dry and barren, our hunting grounds empty of prey."

"Very well." The voice boomed louder, seeming to rattle the very bones in Isok's skull with the force of its proclamation. "You may hunt in our lands tonight only, insolent-yet-polite pup. And only for *hukra*."

Isok exchanged a glance with Henra, who looked as puzzled as he felt. His ears skewed in confusion. "Honored Yaka, we know not of these *hukra* you speak of."

The mist form turned, dissipating slowly back into the night. "Go north, then east. You will find a river. Follow it upstream." The mist slithered away and vanished almost as quickly as it had come.

* * *

"We must go inform the Alpha, so that he can send real hunters!" Adlie stamped a back leg and lowered her head, turning away from Isok and Henra as if ashamed.

"You know he won't." Isok let the outburst go unpunished. He wasn't an Alpha, or even a leader, to do such things.

Adlie plopped her butt down on the ground and stared morosely at her front paws, curling and uncurling the claws into the dirt. "I know."

"These hukra, though." Henra paced on all fours, tail swishing thoughtfully behind her as she circled them. "We don't know anything about them. The Yaka could be sending us into a trap."

Isok shook his head and licked his lips, imaging he could already taste the meat on his tongue. The others had to be convinced to continue.

"In the Legends the Yaka can kill with the mist. If it wanted us dead—" He left the thought unfinished when Adlie cringed and pulled her tail around her front paws.

"Isok has a point," Henra said, still pacing. "But then, why tell us of these hukra creatures?"

"Perhaps they have some protection against the Yaka?" Isok, tired of trying to keep his eyes on a pacing Henra, turned his eyes to Adlie. "But it really doesn't matter. The hukra are food, the Clans are starving."

"Let's go, then." Henra started off north. Isok trotted after her, wondering when he'd lost control of this expedition. A night breeze blew Henra's scent back to him and he realized he didn't care.

After several claw marks of walking, the quarter moon had risen high in the sky. They'd reached the stream and now followed it upstream, as directed.

The trees were thick along the banks and going was slow. By the time they arrived at the place where the hukra herd slept, the moon was beginning to set.

What little moonlight remained glittered on hard carapaces and thick horns, longer than a Jegera was tall. The hukra, in a word, were huge and armored beasts. The entire herd was spread out in the meadow by the stream; about a dozen individuals of varying sizes. Even the smallest, half hidden behind the bulk of what Isok guessed was its mama, was probably ten tail lengths in height—a good three tail lengths taller than Isok himself standing on two legs.

<*We need a plan,*> Henra gefired him and Adlie as they slipped back into the woods. While the breeze was light, it was there. Isok was satisfied to see Henra move them until they stood downwind from the herd.

<*I see a newborn one.*> Isok relayed its position in the herd to the others. The moonlight and their night vision washed the color out of things, so he hadn't been able to guess age or sex of the other creatures, but small was good. Easier, he figured. In their deer hunting, the small were protected... unless they fell behind. Then they were easy prey for a trained pack. Which they weren't.

<*I have a plan.*> Henra gefired them the basic idea. Isok was impressed. It could just work.

Isok volunteered for the most dangerous part. Henra's smell drove out all reason, and he needed to impress the strong-willed Alpha's daughter. While Isok circled around the unfamiliar woods, he began to regret his bravado. He hoped Henra was suitably impressed.

Unfamiliar night birds trilled in the trees above him. Isok reached the north end of the meadow and crouched. From this angle he could fully see the baby hukra, sleeping leaned against one of the massive adults. Now that he had time while he waited for Adlie and Henra's signal, he studied the animals.

Even this baby had armored plates running along its back. It had probably recently had a growth spurt, as there were big gaps between the plates that weren't there on the adult creatures. In addition, the horns were rounded little nubs on the nose and forehead instead of the wicked looking monstrosities the adults wielded.

< *We are ready.* >

Isok abandoned his analysis and lopped out of the trees towards the baby. He tried to stay away from the hukra's horned heads, but otherwise didn't try to hide his scent. This kill wasn't about stealth; plus the more he thought about it, the more he realized these beasts wouldn't have a reason to fear Jegeran musk yet.

After he'd gone a few tree lengths into the clearing, Isok worked his spear free of the pannier on his back. If he was thinking, he'd have gotten it ready while he was waiting. A snoring hukra shifted its weight somewhere behind him, and the ground trembled. The spear dropped from a nerveless paw. "It's sleeping, and it still scares me half to death," he muttered as he retrieved the dropped spear.

The baby hukra was only a bit away from him now, although Isok would have to circle around one more adult to get a clear shot. Unfortunately when he padded around the adult's back, he discovered that about three of them had bunched up together in a line. He'd have to risk standing by its head, because there wasn't a way around.

He walked back the way he'd come. He inched around the beast's muzzle, to between it and another hukra's backside. It was tight, but he got through without touching any of them. Not thinking, he wagged his tail. He felt the fur brush across something warm and froze, instinctively dropping down to the ground. The grass in the meadow had been crushed flat by hukra feet, and he felt exposed just lying in the dirt. A snort; a beast very close stomped a foot, rattling Isok's skull. His heart felt as though it would burst from his chest, but nothing else happened.

He whispered a small prayer to the Moon God for watching over three foolish pups, and then a second to thank the God for this opportunity of promise. As quietly as he could, he climbed to two legs, crouched and balanced the spear the way he'd been taught. The baby's side was a broad target—he couldn't miss, really—but he needed to hit between the two plates on the neck. This would only work if the baby was mortally injured or not able to keep up with the rest of the herd. He lunged forward, snapping his arm and releasing the spear.

The spear flew straight and true, striking the young armored monster right between the two ill-fitting plates on its neck. It let out a deep wail and charged forward, running into the side of the other hukra directly in front of it. Isok had been expecting this. He was already charging forward, evading a stomping foot as the adult the baby had struck reared back in shock. Isok leapt up, using the powerful muscles in his leg to thrust himself as far off the ground as he was able. Then he grabbed the baby creature's protruding back plate with his claws, and pulled himself up and over—like a game of leapfrog over a giant boulder.

Around him the herd awoke to panic and confusion. The adults began to stampede away from the river and into the trees, driven by Adlie and Henra's snapping jaws. Saplings and smaller trees cracked audibly, the sound loud even over the bellows of the panicking monsters. Isok hung onto his prize as the baby ran with the herd, blood spraying from its neck.

The smell of blood followed the stampeding herd, adding to the frenzy and confusion. Just as they reached the tree line, Isok began to panic. Perhaps his strike had not been as true as he thought. The baby collapsed under him with one final spasm. Isok held on, digging his claws into the tender skin between the plates. The baby bucked and writhed, while tree-sized monsters streamed past. It reminded him of nightmares he'd had in the past. He would have thought this too a dream, except that the dust and debris kicked up by their massive three-toed feet clogged his throat and nose. Finally it was over and the bellowing faded into the distance.

The night was silent again, if only for a few moments. While Isok hung onto the now-still baby, willing his reluctant claws to re-sheath as he trembled with unspent adrenalin, the normal sounds of the forest gradually returned. Night-birds trilled, and small creatures rustled through the whirlwind of mess left by the stampede. In the distance, something big roared its domination over that part of the woods. Isok remembered how to breathe by the time Adlie and Henra found him still clinging to the massive baby's side like a bur.

"Well, that was a little more dramatic than I intended," Henra remarked dryly. Her body language was aloof, tail in a neutral position ears not quite perked. But her scent—Isok felt himself responding. This time—with a month's worth of fresh meat underneath him, and the tang of blood in the air—he didn't fight it.

Adlie's ears went back as she wrinkled her muzzle and trotted off. "Don't stop on my account," she growled at them as she disappeared into the underbrush. Isok hardly noted her absence.

"Henra," Isok said as he hopped off the baby hukra's side and landed lightly on the ground. He felt like he was walking through air, he felt so light. "Be my mate."

In response Henra tackled him to the ground, licking his muzzle while Isok ripped off her loincloth. He took her right then and there, the blood only feeding their mating frenzy.

* * *

After Isok and Henra were satiated and Adlie had returned, they started work on carving up the kill for transport. It was harder than they had expected it was going to be, after they discovered that Garor had fled with their only knife.

Luckily their claws were sharp. After filling their bellies with the rich brains, heart and liver, they had plenty of energy for the task. Isok couldn't get enough of watching Henra move in the starlight, her eyes sparkling each time he caught her gaze.

After dark they started the long walk back to camp. Adlie still feared the Yaka, but Isok didn't think they had anything to worry about now. By just after the moon rose they were traveling downstream, their bellies full and their packs heavy.

The mist came as it had before, seeming to seep out of the ground itself. On the trail in front of them, a great creature rose up from the fog, eyes glowing red, its mouth opened in a toothy grin.

Isok stepped forward, averting his eyes and presenting his throat with no little fear. No matter his thoughts during the day, the Yaka's very presence cowered him. But Henra and Adlie depended on him. He would be strong for his new mate and pack member. "We found the hukra creatures, scared them away, and slew one of their young."

A scent wafted to him, the same Jegera he'd smelled before, but this time their fear was less, bolstered by their success. Isok lifted his nose to the air, trying to place the location of the spy.

"Better than I expected from you." The Yaka's form grew wispy for a moment before solidifying once more. "But I see from your thoughts you plan to leave, come back with more of your kind."

Henra gave Isok a wide-eyed look, and he could feel Adlie shaking behind him. "We do, merciful Yaka." His voice shook and he gulped, bending low and inclining his head even further.

The Yaka roared, the cry shaking the trees. A flock of birds, startled out of sleep, erupted from a nearby bush in a flurry of wings and beaks before shooting away up towards the stars.

"Honored Yaka," Isok said, lowering so far his belly touched the ground. Not weak, he had to keep telling himself, merely submitting to a powerful capacious alpha-monster who can pluck the thoughts from my head and grind my bones to dust. "Without the food provided by the hukra, our clans will starve."

"And if you allow us to hunt the hukra, there will be less of them around to bother you." Henra said, moving up beside Isok and scraping down low beside him. "After all, why else would you have us hunt them for you—unless you cannot kill them yourself."

Isok risked a look up, getting a muzzle full of leaf muck on the tip of his nose while doing so. The Yaka's form had shrunk a bit and had gotten wispy at the edges again. In fact, it had faded so much that where once had been only the vague outline of trees through the insubstantial form, now stark poles stood crisp against the darker background. And there, within the fading mist, Isok thought he saw a small shape standing where the Yaka had been. A sample of the air told him the strange Jegera was also standing close to that same spot. Bah, a phantom not at all.

His legs pulled up under him. Claws gripping the dirt, he pushed off straight at the form wavering through the mist. It wasn't the best jumping tackle he'd ever done, but it was enough. He slammed into the side of the form, felt warm flesh and fur beneath him as he hit. A high pitched yip sounded from underneath him as they hit the leaf mulch hard. The mist beast popped, like a soap bubble hit with outstretched claw. Although the cold mist continued to crawl along his fur, there didn't seem to be as much of it as there had been.

They'd landed with Isok on top, and the form he'd hit had been small enough that it was lost underneath him. He sat up, revealing a white-furred Jegera. Unlike his own midnight black fur, short and bristly enough that his dark skin was visible underneath, this pup's white fur was long and soft with a thick undercoat. The pup looked up at him with eyes bluer than a cloudless summer day.

"Get off me, brute!" It was said in the deep voice of the Yaka they'd heard through the mist, although without the almost mystical reverberation it'd had previously.

"What did you do?!" Henra ran up from behind him on all fours. When she saw the white pup she skidded to a stop so fast her back legs lifted off the ground for a moment. "Is that a puppy?"

"I'm not a puppy!" She growled, for this close Isok could smell her. Of mating age, as old as Henra at least.

"You tricked us." Henra sat back on her haunches and began chuckling so hard her sides pressed against the tight straps of her panniers.

"We trick all of you big ones that come up here," the girl growled, pushing Isok's paw away when he reached over to help her stand.

"We?" Isok repeated, still staring at the girl. She smelled like a Jegera, and could probably even pass for one if her fur was shorter and she wasn't so small.

"The Yaka, of course. To keep you Jegera out of our hunting grounds."

"So why send us farther in, to that herd of hukra that you obviously knew was there?" Isok turned to give Adlie a comforting look, but she was gone—vanished into the mist at some point while he and Henra had groveled for the monster that turned out not to be.

"Those armored thugs have been stomping all over the place lately. We can't hunt them, they're too big, and they're scaring away the raop. Plus, when a whole herd of them gets to a stream they turn a pristine watering hole into an unusable muddy mess." A tiny foot stomped on the dirt. Isok had to suppress a giggle at how cute she looked. Her pinned back ears and puffed up tail, combined with her wild fur, made her look like an end-of-summer dandelion flower before the wind blew it away.

Henra smiled, tail wagging as she looked down at the little Yaka. "I have a proposition for you—"

The Yaka glared at her. "Go on."

"We," Henra gestured to herself, Isok, and Adlie, "come back with hunters. We live here in the North, and promise only to hunt hukra."

"You will leave a tribute for the Yaka after each hunt," the Yaka countered. She paused. "And not go past the mountain pass in the north," the Yaka growled, eyes narrowed.

Isok and Henra nodded.

"It's a deal."

* * *

Isok, Henra, and Adlie returned to the Bright Moon Clan a few paw-spans before sunset the next day. Between them they had enough meat to feed the hungry villagers for several days, along with tales of great herds roaming the northern mountains. Isok and Henra announced their mating—and their intent to form a new Clan in the northern mountains.

What is Cara?

A chimera of human, wolf, bear, and hawk. An "augmented" super-soldier. But what do you do with it when the war is over?

What is Cara?

Wolves in Winter

by Searska GreyRaven

The day he died, everything had been the same.

The same alarm went off at the same time, the same kiss and nuzzle goodbye, the same ghost of eggs and sausage in the air when the door clicked shut. She roused herself an hour after, following that ghost to the kitchen, adding to it the rich scent of black coffee and sweet cream. The same sun rose over the same trees, and the same mourning doves cooed from the same ragged pine tree outside her window.

And when he came home, they exchanged the same joyful kisses, the same frenzied bout of lovemaking, and curled around each other like kittens on the couch while they waited for the same pizza to arrive.

Only, it didn't.

He went to answer the door, like he always did, and instead of the low exchange of greetings and money, there was a bang, a yelp, the sound of something shattering.

She didn't know it yet, but the shattering was her heart.

She screamed, howled, raced down that same hallway that was now a maze of unfamiliar horrors, spattered with red, so much red, and found him lying on the door mat, the same door mat she'd told him needed to be replaced a hundred times and he never quite got around to it. She couldn't see the mat, nor the white tiles around it through the red.

She screamed his name, the same name she'd whispered when she fell asleep every night for two decades, the same name she'd cried out in pleasure and exasperation and joy for as long as she cared to remember.

Only it wasn't his voice that answered. It was a voice behind her, filled with cold, dry hate.

"Death to abominations."

Training took over where spirit once held sway. She was in motion before the words had even reached her ears, her claws out, her lips peeled from her teeth and her long ears flat against her skull. She lashed out with all her rage and grief, hurling the gun away and tearing out the throat of the monster who ended her life.

The sun set, a dove mourned, and nothing was the same anymore.

"Cara," he whispered with his last breath. "Cara, I love you, please, be good."

But there was nothing left to be good for.

* * *

"Take hope from a man, and you leave behind a wolf in winter."

The Augment Project was one of the darkest in military history. A blend of genetic engineering and vivisection, the intent was to give soldiers a super-human edge on the battle field. Eyes like a hawk, endurance like a wolf, the strength of a bear, these were the things they impressed upon their soldiers. These "augments" were neither human nor animal, but a chimeric blend of both. Natural born humans simply couldn't measure up to those who had been augmented. Any ground an augment unit trod became a killing field. Like the atom bomb before, they became a promise rather than a threat, and though the war ended, life for the augments went on. They were still soldiers, and had earned their way back to civilian life. Honorable discharge, retirement, and a pension.

Only that life no longer wanted them.

The world branded them as monsters, abominations, and thought they belonged in labs or zoos, not PTA meetings or community councils. The Law, of course, only applied to humans, not animals. It would be decades before the Law caught up with morality.

But Cara and Nathaniel were in love. Damn the law! they said, we'll go where no one can bother us, far away, and it'll be okay.

God, how she'd wanted to believe that. She wanted to believe it with all her shattered, aching heart. She wanted to believe there was a future for a thing like her, battered and broken by war and death and pain. For two decades, she wanted to believe. And for want of two decades more, she might even have begun to.

The world ended for her in a bang, taking with it all hope.

Snow fell softly all around her, but she barely noticed it. Thick fur insulated her, but it was the hate inside that kept the chill at bay. She was far colder inside than any winter wind.

They never found her. The papers and the newscasters all assumed she'd snapped, gone savage, killed both her husband and the pizza boy before fleeing into the night. A massive hunt converged, but she had left behind no trace of her whereabouts. And though a lynch mob still marched the streets a few nights each week, the beast in her was too canny, too clever to be caught flatfooted again. She'd trusted them, she'd even helped a few of them from time to time tracking lost sheep or chickens or children. And they turned on her without a second thought.

Damn them, she thought. *Damn them all.*

"Be good, Cara. Please, be good."

She shook her head and bared her fangs. There was nothing good in the world anymore. A single moment out of place had stolen it forever.

She sat under a tree and field-stripped her weapon, cleaning the sniper rifle with the same methodical care that had seen her through the war. She shouldered it, dropped to all fours, and raised her muzzle to the wind.

Somewhere, a mourning dove sobbed.

There were still two of them out there. Two left in this little piss-hole of a village, and she could move on.

They called themselves the Pure. God had separated Man from Beast, they said, and bringing them together was an act of utter blasphemy. These augments should be executed, they claimed, put to death for merely daring to exist!

I didn't ask for this life, she thought. *I asked to serve and protect, and the only way I can do that now is to make sure you monsters can't hurt anyone else ever again.*

The mourning dove sobbed again, and she saw it perched in the tree above, as grey as the winter sky, save for a single blood-red spot on its breast.

Be good.

"This is the only good left in me," she whispered.

The dove cried like its heart had broken, but refused to fly off.

She turned her back and fled into the forest. The sun had set, like it always would, and she had work to do.

They met every night, out in the forest and far from the prying eyes of the village snoops. There had been more than a dozen of these Pure, but after six months of careful stalking and execution, there were only two left.

After I'd taken your friends, you'd think they'd be more cautious, she thought. But no, they still believed they were masters of nature, that God would protect them and shield them from harm.

There is no God here, only Hell.

"Please. Be good."

Good got you killed.

"Please."

Everything good in me died with you.

Her ears perked, canine hearing picking up a conversation.

"This can't continue. You know they're talking about making us leave town? Leave! And go into hiding! Over a filthy animal!"

"She's more than an animal, Dave, she's a trained sniper. Maybe we should—"

"No. Out of the question! I won't have some abomination chase me out of the home my family has lived in for four generations!"

"What was that?"

She froze, and the three spun around, searching. They couldn't have seen her, not from this distance, not with those weak human eyes nor heard her with their deaf human ears. After a moment, they settled down again. Slowly, methodically, she began the process of aiming. It was a still night, but she knew the havoc a stray zypher could cause.

She could hear them again, this time more faintly. They'd lowered their voices.

"... still part human. It was murder! He didn't even touch her, and now, we're paying the price. We have to confess—"

"We confess to *nothing*. The Law has no place here. We are *above* the Law! We act as instruments of *God*. And that thing has killed far more people than we have! It needs to be put down!"

"She was in the War! A soldier! For the country you claim you're protecting by trying to murder her—"

"You know they're talking of allowing that *augmentation* to be performed on civilians? You have a daughter, do you not? How would you feel knowing a pig's heart was in her chest instead of her own?"

"I'd feel grateful that she was alive! It's one thing to fight against this augmentation being used in war, but killing innocent people—"

She adjusted her aim, slightly. The wind picked up, then slowed, and she adjusted again.

"There are no innocents when it comes to those things. Either you are with God, or you are against Him. He was sleeping with a beast, an abomination before Our Lord. The only fitting punishment was death."

She growled silently, her clawed finger tight against the trigger but she didn't pull it, not yet. Patience, she thought. Patience. The shot wasn't right. Sooner or later, one of them would move and she would strike, but not yet. Not yet.

The snow fell harder, mantling her in white. She didn't move, barely breathed. She filled her mouth with snow to hide her breath, and waited.

Finally, her prey moved and the moment was right. The trigger clicked, her gun roared, and the mourning dove moaned in the tree above.

There is nothing more purely red than fresh blood upon snow, and for just a moment, she reveled in the sight through her scope. But she couldn't stay here. Someone would have heard the shot, they'd trace it back to this spot, and she needed to be long gone before then.

One left.

And the mourning dove sobbed.

* * *

Nights were always the hardest. Nights reminded her of how utterly alone she was, how there was nothing between her and the black hate of the world. The first few nights after it happened, she howled and howled and howled until her throat broke, until she coughed up blood she swore was from her broken heart and found she no longer had the soul to care.

That was the first time she saw the dove, and it had followed her ever since, sobbing and sighing. There was an old Indian legend about them, that they watched over the souls of those who had died of a broken heart. *I haven't died yet,* she thought at the dove.

It didn't reply. It merely regarded her with those fathomless eyes and preened one wing.

One left.

It would end tonight. She knew she should wait, should stalk and learn and pounce at the right moment, but she was tired. So tired. What was left of her fractured heart hung heavy in her chest, the pendulum of a broken clock. She wanted this to be over.

One left.

"I love you. Please—"

I am not good. Maybe I was never good. I can't be what I never was.

"—be good."

I'm not.

The last one wasn't at home. The lights were off and the car wasn't in the driveway, but she could see the faint outline of two people pacing the living room through the thermal lens of her scope. Her target wasn't at home.

She curled her lip. Of course, the last one would be difficult.

Should she leave, go hunting for the last one? Or should she stay here, and wait? He was bound to return to his family eventually. Wasn't he? She couldn't be sure. Someone so willing to tear apart one family might have no problem doing it to their own. The full moon poured silvered light upon the snow, and her mind was made up.

Hunt it was.

She moved through the night, a ghost walking among the living, so careful and quiet that the few people out at this hour didn't notice her. She had a lifetime of hiding among normal people under her belt. Gloves, a hood, and a thick scarf hid what skill alone could not.

He wasn't in any of the usual haunts. Not the bar, nor his best friend's house, nor the crossroads near the church. He wasn't in the meeting place in the forest, nor was he at the small police station.

On a whim, she turned and backtracked, and found him at the least likely place.

On her doorstep, at the place where it all began.

"Cara, Cara—"

"I know you're out there."

She paused. Her sniper rifle was still across her back. She still had a hand gun, but teeth and claws would also suffice. Oh yes, more than suffice. For this last one, she would prefer them. She knew where the rivers of blood flowed beneath the flesh, knew how to rend them and tear them and drain them. The fur along her spine rose, her fingers flexed and the world narrowed to a single sharpened point.

"I don't know if you can hear me. I don't even know if you care. But I'm going to say it anyway, for all the good it does. I'm sorry."

She should spring, should rip him apart for daring to sit where *he* fell, where her life ended and this new living hell began.

"I didn't pull the trigger, but I'm every bit as guilty. I should have stopped him. I should have gone after him when I found out Dave had given that delivery kid the gun and done, I don't know, something. *Anything*, except what I did. I went home, to my family, to my daughter, because I didn't think he'd really do it. I'm... I'm so sorry."

At first, she thought it was the mourning dove sobbing, but it came from... it came from—

"I know that doesn't even begin to help. I can't imagine what it was like. I don't want to. I couldn't live with it, if it were me. I can't even blame you for killing them. God knows, I'd probably do exactly what you're doing now, hunting them down like animals for it."

She listened, against her better judgment.

He continued. "I know I don't have a right to ask, but it ends with me, right? I'm the last one. I never wanted this. I never meant—I only wanted to stop that technology from being used to hurt people. More people." He took a deep breath, exhaled. "Weaponized genes. God, what a world we live in. What they did to you, what they used you for, it wasn't right. You deserved to be happy, and we took that from you. But it should end here, right? I'm here. Please, I'm begging you, leave my family out of this. Finish it, and may you find peace."

His… family? Did he really think I'd… that I'd…

Cara tilted her head back to howl, but it was silent. Her broken throat hadn't made a sound since Nathaniel was taken from her.

"*Cara, I love you, please be good.*"

She pulled out her hand gun. It would have to be enough. She emerged from the hedge where she'd been hiding and approached her door step.

The last one stood, his eyes squinted shut and his lips moving in silent prayer. She leveled the gun between his eyes, the trigger a cold crescent against her finger.

"*Cara, I love you.*"

I know.

"*…please be good.*"

This is the only way I know how.

She turned the gun on herself, and pulled the trigger.

Somewhere, a mourning dove sobbed, and was finally answered by another.

This also asks the question, what do you do with animal-soldiers when the war is over, but from a different aspect. There is not just one dog-soldier; there are thousands of them.

Want a war-surplus dog-soldier?

The Third Variety

by Rob Baird

"Good boy!" he said, and I knew he meant it.

He caught the ball I tossed back to him, and then flung it in my direction again. I love that more than anything, almost, that moment of perfect clarity when all the angles meet and every muscle in your body turns to the capture of a baseball as its sole, unchallenged mission.

I leapt up, and perceived for one thin second the silhouette of my arm stretched against the fading blue light of evening, before a satisfying impact thumped my paw.

"We should wrap it up," Marcus said. "It's getting too dark."

"Just because *you* can't see at night," I grumped in feigned irritation—but of course I lobbed the ball back anyway, and we started the walk back to the locker where they kept our equipment. You never disobey an order. "We're always having to do things your way…"

Marcus grinned. "We can't all be genetically engineered," he reminded me. "Besides, they're gonna close the mess in twenty minutes. And if I don't want to hear you bitch about this, I sure as hell don't want to have to hear you whine at night 'cause you didn't get fed."

Now that I thought about it, my stomach *was* starting to make its presence known. Marcus said I was always hungry. Then again, he was a skinny little thing, and I'd been built with a healthy metabolism. I licked my chops. "What's on the menu, anyway?"

"For you? Kibble."

"Oh."

"Somebody hit a deer this morning, though. I heard Kathy say they might grind it up and give it to you guys. Better than us, right? I think we get fake mac and cheese."

"Can I have some?"

Marcus raised an eyebrow at my perked ears. "You know I'm not supposed to do that."

"Of course," I said. But I kept my ears pricked: "Can I have some?"

When I gave in to the urge to lick my muzzle again, my companion chuckled and looked away. "Yeah, yeah. I'll try to slip you some tonight… but you still have to eat your real dinner, okay? Now go brush yourself: you look like a mess. I'll see you later."

With my tail wagging, I nodded crisply to him. "Yes, sir."

He was still chuckling, still shaking his head slowly as we parted ways. "Alright. Good boy."

That's me. I'm the companion to Lieutenant Marcus Berg, 804th Security Battalion, 26th Security Brigade: the Cynic Corps. I'm Christopher No-Last-Name-Given, Technical Service Asset, 5th Model (Improved).

I'm a good dog.

* * *

There wasn't enough deer to go around. Between bits of dry kibble, I occasionally perceived fresh protein, but it came mostly as a taunting, hinted scent tickling my nose. At least they made sure what we got was nutritious, if bland.

"Sometimes I think they don't respect us." Across the table, one of my fellow diners set his cup of food down and grimaced. He was a sheepdog of some kind—one of the early varieties, too thoughtful and too twitchy for his own good. "What is this? Corn husks and ground-up rats? Who put this together?"

"Aw, Christ, Whit. You're a chef now?" My friend Stratford, sitting next to me, gave a woofing snort of derision. We weren't supposed to use human epithets, but Stratford's handler had a sharp tongue and Strat had keen ears like all of us.

"What's that have to do with it?" Whitman asked.

"What would you rather do? Starve to death? Hunt for your own food?" Strat was a shepherd, like me: bred from guard stock, and circumspect about our condition.

Unlike, for instance, poor Whit: "I could hunt!" His lip curled to bare just the hint of teeth. "You watch me! Give me one of those M-15s—"

"M-16, Whit," Stratford corrected.

The sheepdog's lip lifted further. "M-16, *fine*. I could still do it. Take down some more venison."

A third party, a retriever named Emily, dropped her enamel bowl down onto the table with a heavy, sharp clatter. She narrowed her eyes: "You could *not*. You'd get so caught up trying to remember if your safety was in the right position you'd forget all about the deer."

Whitman drew his ears back. "Wouldn't. You just have to check, that's all. You have to be sure about things. If they're not in the right order, it causes problems. First you need to—"

"Realize it doesn't matter," Strat finished for him. There were other reasons, after all. "They're not gonna give us guns. So either eat your rations, or starve. *San Sebastian*, Whit."

"*San Sebastian*," the other dog muttered miserably. I felt a little sorry for the mess that was Whitman. He was annoying, sure; he could turn everything from the latrine to our harnesses into a polemic.

But he was also one of the early, unpolished models. He licked his muzzle as a nervous tic when he was with his handler; around us, it was the chatter instead. He couldn't help it.

And he wasn't *wrong*, not exactly. "You have to admit," I said, "it would be nice if we could make some decisions for ourselves."

"See!" Whitman's expression brightened. "Chris agrees with me!"

"Chris is a hopeless idealist." Stratford answered immediately, before lifting the bowl of food back to his mouth to signify the end of the conversation.

"I'm not an idealist." I tried to find the boundary between levity and seriously conveying my feelings. "I just want to be able to use the head without asking my handler for permission."

"That sounds like thinking for yourself." Emily looked to me, leaning forward and trying to stare me down—not so much out of disagreement, I guessed, as to get on with dinner.

"So what?"

"You weren't bred to think." The answer came from a lanky wisp of a thing named Gershwin, who never had a thought of his own anyway. "We were bred to follow orders, not play Martin Luther King. You can't change it, so why don't you just eat your dinner and leave us in peace?"

"We have to be able to make choices," I said firmly. "Otherwise we're just machines—like those robots out there! Why breed us for sentience if you don't want to *use* it? What kind of cruel god put *that* fate in front of us?"

Stratford roused himself from the kibble. "It wasn't God, it was Dr. Pipes. And if you wanna take it up with her, Denver's only six hundred miles that way." He jerked his opposable thumb behind him.

"What do you want to do, anyway?" Emily had finished her meal; she brought her water bowl to her muzzle, took a few laps while staring at me, and then followed up on the question. "Defect? Betray our handlers?"

I blinked, growling at her even before I was aware of what I was doing. "Of course not! I'd never say that! We could just be more equal, that's all…"

"But they're the ones with the training, Chris. They went to Army school. They know the politics and weather and all that—we're just following orders, same as any grunt. Maybe if they didn't know best they *would* listen! But for right now…"

"Forget it, Chris." Whitman sighed, and hastened to finish his food before they started to close the building down. But he had to have the last word: "We reckon without the masses, who cannot be roused to passion for their own freedom."

Such a dramatic fellow.

* * *

I got cold at night, in the desert, but I set my mat and sleeping bag outside anyway. I wasn't the only one who did this; most of us didn't like the smell of the barracks. It was always thick with the scent of my companions, and ozone from the lights, and that vile disinfectant the humans used to try and keep the smell manageable to their own feeble noses.

Beneath it all lurked, if you were patient, the occasional hint of comrades who had never returned. I disliked the persistence of memory, and when I could, I escaped.

Marcus's parents had been painters, before everything went down, and gave him an artist's sensibilities. He said the night sky was beautiful. Of course, he also waxed poetic about the desert sunset—which I found an uninspiring, sickly yellow. Humans have peculiar loves.

But one of those loves was us, man's best friend. In deference, I leaned against the wall of our quarters and tried to imagine how he might view the stars. Nothing special, to me, though I found the night restful in its own way.

Sounds, mostly. I took a moment to listen. The crisp calls of the birds and cicadas; the distant, keening wails of coyotes twenty miles away. The gentle hum of a transformer, and the soft babble of water in the well that punched down into the aquifer below my paws.

And the soft crunch of unshod feet, drawing closer. I turned my head, sniffing for a clue. It was Emily, the retriever. "Too good for us?"

she asked softly; her voice was at that lowest volume before it became the raspy, serpent's hiss of a whisper.

I peered at her in the darkness, but from the look of her ears she wasn't trying to pick a fight. "What do you mean?"

She sat down next to me, shifting around to find a comfortable place for her tail. "Sleeping outside, instead of in the kennel."

"It's hard to sleep there," I confessed. She cocked her head at me. "My bunk's right between Gersh and Rio, now. They cover it a bit, but... you know how it is. Gershwin is sleeping where Robin used to, and before him Loki... and Taurus, and Cougar. Rio's where Anteus and Napoleon were. I can smell them, sometimes. Mostly when I'm trying to sleep."

"Ringo," Emily said.

"Ringo?"

"Used to sleep where Rio is."

I shook my head in continued confusion.

"White. Very subtle scent. He was only here a week or two before his handler was killed by a suicider at the checkpoint and they put him down. He hadn't quite gotten used to us."

I closed my eyes to cut off the distracting sense of vision and tried to sift through the smells of the adjoining bunk in my mind. "They cleaned him, huh?" We were usually so close to our handlers that we died together, but when only the handler was killed the usual practice was to euthanize the companion, too—spare them the trauma of trying to bond to a new person.

We called it 'cleaning.' Often we first became aware that one of us had died when the technician came to disinfect and scrub down their rack in the barracks. Then they were just one more fading story—if that.

I couldn't recall anyone named Ringo. "Damned shame. Maybe he didn't get into the fabric enough. Maybe that's my point, I guess."

"Worried about being forgotten?"

"Once I'm dead, I won't care anymore," I pointed out. "So no. It's just that... it's just that I don't want to have to think about how many people I'm forgetting. The barracks is..."

"Haunted."

I nodded.

"My handler tells ghost stories. I wonder if it's like that with them, do you suppose, Chris? Some vision stays behind after they die? Like it is with smells..."

"Maybe."

Emily drew her field jacket tighter to ward off the cold of the desert night; for a moment, I thought she was going to leave. Then she settled down again, shaking her head at me. "You know, you say you don't want to have to think about it. I guess I can believe that. You think too much as it is."

I knew that they said that behind my back, even if I wasn't as bad as Whit. "Yeah."

"I don't disagree with you, you know."

"Yeah," I said again.

The cicadas returned to dominate the quiet that followed until Emily went on. "Sometimes, I wonder if they're not sure if they made the right choice with us. Making us, I mean."

I quirked my head, and my ears came forward. "How's that?"

"Well, the First Variety, you know? The autotanks. They didn't need our help with those."

The Puppeteer had stopped using the robotic tanks long before I was even born; I hadn't ever seen one in action—just in the training films and spotter cards. Large things: ugly, matte black and bristling with guns. "Of course not. You can take 'em down with a rocket easy enough."

"Right," Emily agreed. "The Second Variety, the Walking Ones—that's why we're here, isn't it?" Sixteen years previously the Puppeteer engineered a new type of robot, almost indistinguishable from human beings save for their metal skeletons.

It was these that we had been crafted to detect. "That's what they say, anyway. *San Sebastian.*"

The MV *San Sebastian* was part of our lore; part of our upbringing the way that undying loyalty to the human race was. The earliest companions had been traveling with their creator—in the cargo hold. They were not working; they had not been fully trained.

But it was one of them who had noticed the odd behavior of the *San Sebastian*'s chief engineer. They detected him before any human had. Before the *San Sebastian* reached port in Seattle. Before the stolen warheads hidden in her engine room could be detonated.

"*San Sebastian,*" Emily agreed; she said it like I did, as an oath of faith that reminded us of our bonds. "But that was when their backs were up against a wall. They had more geneticists than engineers or factories. But... but today, with the metal probes and the X-Ray sensors and all that... they don't *need* us, do they?"

"That's my worry," I said, and closed my eyes against the stars. "They say the war's going to be won. What happens to us then?"

* * *

"What's the story?" I was adjusting my uniform as we walked out towards the checkpoint, trying to look presentable.

"Rumors of a late spring offensive, landing in Florida. They're, uh…" Marcus trailed off and pointed to my head. "Your hat, dog."

"I know, sir," I said. I had a devil of a time trying to get my ears to fit through the cap they'd given me, and I hated the damned thing to begin with. It kept my ears from moving; it was a lot like wearing blinders. "They're what?"

"Moving everyone to the west. President Ramirez says he's worried about a landing in… oh, hold on." Once again he trailed off; I knew what was coming, and though I didn't like it when Marcus adjusted my clothes I had to admit he knew what he was doing. "He's worried about a landing in Tampico from the holdouts in the Yucatan. We have a mixed convoy coming in from El Paso and Juarez."

I nodded, in the human custom. "They're expecting Walking Ones here?"

Marcus shrugged and, content with my appearance, left me alone. "It's three thousand people, some of them from the camps at Monterrey and Laredo. Word from Colonel Dove is that, yes, we're expecting Hephaestan activity. Everybody in the Cynic Corps is out in force. Just keep it orderly. You remember the signal, right?"

"Yes, sir." To avoid arousing suspicion, we all had a signal to separate the sheep from the goats. For me, a human got a raised hand with my fingers close together. Were I to find a Walking One, I would spread my thumb out; it felt unnatural to me, and I guess that was part of the point, lest I get too comfortable with the gesture and flag the wrong thing.

"Good boy."

They came at around eleven that morning. My vision isn't all that good, but Marcus said the blur I saw was actually a convoy of trucks and private cars stretching back to the horizon. I didn't have time to care about that. As soon as the first refugees were waiting, I had to turn myself on. It took all my concentration.

I'd grown used to them. Clean, most of the time, at least physically. You could tell the weariness in their body language, though: the way they let themselves get pushed around by the soldiers. They smelled of apathy.

Older people, I found, were indifferent to my existence. There'd been opposition when Dr. Pipes first pieced together the DNA to forge us. It was, I admit, an understandable objection. Humans accused the Puppeteer of twisting the human form for his creations—and here was Dr. Pipes doing the same thing.

Marcus had told me a couple of times that it was fortunate they even allowed me to exist. But, as Emily said, the nonengineered, nonrobotic human race was up against a wall: desperate times called for desperate measures. And now adults had already lived through so much that they no longer cared.

It was the children who had emotions—the young pups, before they had the chance to mature into teenagers and put on that jaded air that serves as a kind of armor against the world.

Sometimes, kids recoiled in fear from me. Others stretched out their hands wonderingly to feel my ears; my muzzle. I didn't mind it, exactly, but we had to keep the line moving.

Fifty-three people in, I found my first Walking One. This was a Cynic term; humans preferred the more formal 'Hephaestan,' which was what the Puppeteer called them. Maybe humans thought 'Walking One' didn't do enough to distinguish the robots.

But this was appropriate, because they looked almost identical. This one had adopted the guise of a businessperson, still wearing a suit. But she was worn, from the long days of flight and narrow escapes; her face was as wrinkled as her blazer.

Marcus said Walking Ones had dead eyes, soulless eyes; I have always had a problem with human expression, and the subtleties were lost on me. The woman before me looked as human as anyone else, a testament to the Puppeteer's skill. Only the slightest aroma of metal wafting through her skin gave her away.

They knew this, and she was wearing a thick perfume to cover it. But her maker had insufficiently esteemed the canine nose. I smiled in a friendly way, and raised my paw to wave her on—but this time I forced my thumb to the side. They wouldn't do anything then and there, to avoid tipping our hand, but I knew she had been marked.

The day wore on like that, a constant barrage of scents. We worked in three-hour shifts; any more than that and even my genetically enhanced nose would be overwhelmed. Plus, though I would never admit it, the stress got to me.

I didn't have to *admit* it; when Marcus tapped me on the shoulder and said I'd been relieved, the tension left my tall body and I felt my whole frame relax.

"Good boy," Marcus said. "What's your count?"

"Four, sir."

"Not bad." He reached into his pocket and pulled out the baseball. "Ready?"

I don't remember learning English. It happened when I was a puppy, or maybe Dr. Pipes just found a way of programming it right into our brains. I had a pretty expansive vocabulary, anyhow, even if I wasn't as talkative as Whitman, and I knew the meaning of words without knowing *why* I knew them.

What I felt for Marcus was *love*. Even if that wasn't the dictionary definition and even if he would've gotten the wrong idea if I told him, that was the right word. Because as soon as he had the ball out, my tiredness vanished.

I would do anything for him, and I knew he'd do anything for me. He tossed the baseball and I sprinted after it, all the stress of the checkpoint gone. *Man's best friend*, that was me. Us.

Marcus told me that humans domesticated wolves forty thousand years ago. It was mankind's first great project. Before the Hoover Dam, before the Great Wall, before Stonehenge and the Pyramids. Before Babylon, before Çatal Hüyük; before iron tools and agriculture.

Man was still huddled around shelterless campfires when our species first adopted one another. I didn't tell anyone—not Marcus, not Emily; not even Whitman—but I knew this was why we'd been created. I knew it instinctively, in that thing that humans call a soul.

We helped them hunt and they gave us food. We guarded their homes, and they gave us responsibility. We pulled their sleds and herded their flocks and eventually they invited us in from the cold. And in the darkest hour of the human race, they had bestowed upon us their own greatest gift.

Marcus caught the ball I threw back to him, and grinned at my wagging tail, and told me I was a good boy.

* * *

"What's wrong with Whitman?" I asked that night, at dinner in the mess. We'd processed two thousand, eight hundred and seventy humans—and thirty-one Walking Ones. It had been a good day, but Whit was huddled in the corner, licking his nose nervously.

"Handler screwed up," Stratford said. "They *say*. More likely he started chasin' his tail like an idiot."

Whitman overheard the conversation, and drew into a tighter huddle. "Too close," he whimpered.

I set the bowl of kibble down, and went over to join him. "What was too close?"

The sheepdog was the most senior of us, and burning at both ends: as an early model, his programming was imperfect, and as an old companion he'd had more than his share of stress. I felt sorry for him, even when he drew away at my approach.

"Whit?"

"C-can't." He shook his head violently. "Almost let one through."

Under my recognition training, and my language skills, and my ability to play fetch, the instinctual fear of failing my master was so deeply rooted that I shuddered in empathy. "How?"

He fidgeted, shoving his paws together roughly. His fingers trembled. "I gave the sign but... they put him in anyway. With the others. The humans. I... I h-had to bark at Kathy to get her attention. She said she was sorry. But... but..."

Whitman was in a bad place. He'd done his job, and his handler hadn't. She'd missed his cue, or she'd let it slip—tired and overworked, the way we all were. Barking wasn't good: the whole point of the hand gestures was subtlety, and if he'd had to bark it was a sure sign that something was wrong.

And I could see, in his darting eyes and twisting fingers, the mental conflict that came from knowing his handler had made a mistake. They weren't supposed to do that. Questioning our masters was a sin, after all, but only because they were infallible. We all believed it. We *had* to believe it.

I put my paw between his ears. "It's not your fault, Whit..."

His ears were so flat they might've been invisible, and his tail was curled up between his legs pathetically. "Of course it is!"

"No." I racked my brain for a likely answer. "It was a test, I'm sure. They wanted to know how you'd react to something like that. And you... you did fine. You made sure to save the humans. That was the right thing to do, Whit." I couldn't tell him he was a good dog—those words were reserved—but I hoped he got the message. "*San Sebastian.*"

"*San Sebastian,*" Whitman sniffled, and slowly started to uncurl himself, but I didn't know that he really meant it and he didn't give up. "If that one had gotten through..."

"But it didn't."

Gershwin ambled over, done with his food. "Almost. Not a good sign."

"Quiet, Gersh."

"Just saying." Gersh was an even newer model than I, a slender saluki hybrid designed to work on fewer calories and under longer conditions. "Time to retire, Whit."

"*Gershwin.* Shut up."

As far as I knew, there was no such thing as retirement for companions. As long as the Puppeteer was out there, and as long as the war went on, we couldn't stop working. Whitman knew that, too. His hackles went up. "Not retiring."

"Tell me how you'd go hunting again, Whit? How you're so independent?"

Inadvertently Gersh was exposing a dirty little secret of us companions: we're still dogs. We still have our own hierarchy, one the humans don't always notice. And that hierarchy still gets challenged. Whitman bristled, and glared up at Gershwin. "That's different."

"Not in every way. You're not good at either one," Gersh taunted. He wasn't trying to cause problems; it was just instinct, after all. "So maybe you *should* give up and—"

Whitman lunged, teeth bared, and I just barely caught him.

His muzzle was open, and his sharp teeth were ready for action, and I bore him to the ground before he put them to use. The word 'no' was on my lips—another forbidden word. "Don't be stupid," I growled instead.

The sheepdog must've realized how close he'd come, because he didn't try again. Instead he lay panting on the floor, with my arms locked around him, and shut his muzzle to whimper sadly. Somebody else, Emily by the scent, was leading Gersh off. I stayed put, holding Whitman until his breathing finally slowed.

"Whit," I told him, gently as I could. "Talk to Kathy. Say you need a break."

"I can't…"

"Just a couple days, Whit."

"But…"

I relaxed my grasp so that, when I tightened it again, it felt like a human embrace. "You almost *bit* someone, Whitman."

"I can't tell her that."

The odor of a Walking One. Language. Fetch. *No* and *good boy* and the other orders they buried deep in our brains. Under it all was the greatest prohibition: *never* to do harm. *Never* to use our teeth in anger. The programming was so powerful that even snapping at Gershwin suggested Whit was at the edge of breaking down.

Even if Gersh deserved it, and even if Whit was having a bad day. The taboo was too important for us to challenge. He was right: he couldn't tell Kathy. She'd report him, and then he'd be taken away, and while I didn't know what happened to dogs who were taken away I knew that they never came back.

"Tell her you're not sleeping well," I offered. "And she ought to know she owes you for putting you through that, today."

"Well…"

"Promise you'll ask, Whit."

He sighed. "I promise."

* * *

After reveille the next morning, and before we had a chance to eat, we were summoned all in a body outside. I noticed that Whitman was still a bit twitchy: his uniform was as neat as ever, but he carried his tail too low and his eyes were in constant motion.

He probably wasn't going to talk to Kathy; I'd made him promise, but a promise from another dog didn't count as a direct order and Whit was too afraid of causing trouble. I decided to remind him again at breakfast, to see if repetition would break through.

Marcus jogged up to join me. "Nice hat," he said.

"Thank you, sir."

"I'm serious. It looks good."

"Oh!"

He reached up to pat me between the ears. "Did they tell you why we're here?"

"No, sir."

"New division commander—and new orders. New intel. A lot of new things."

Marcus shared more with me than other handlers did with their companions. Stratford, for example, was almost always in the dark. That was good for him, because it let him focus only on his work. My handler seemed to sense my need for information, and he told me as much as he was allowed.

It was from Marcus that I knew how worried the military authorities were that the Puppeteer might be working on a new strain of Walking Ones, a new variety that could evade even our noses. It was also from Marcus that I knew how tired most people were of the war, thirty years in and five years after they were told that victory was within reach.

We'd pushed the Puppeteer back from North America. Almost everything north of the Panama Canal was pacified. We'd driven them out of Africa, and the British Isles. And from India, and from Australia, and from Japan. Thirty years after the Rising, and humanity had the chance to start tallying the cost of their survival. Everything they'd given up.

I heard the sound of an airplane before any of the humans, even in spite of my trapped ears. Of course, they saw the little black dots first, while I was still blind to them. We complement each other, after all. The largest dot resolved into a cross, and then the form of a ducted-fan transport. While its escorts circled, the plane dropped lower. Its wings swiveled; the big fans kicked up the desert sand in a whirlwind that we bore stoically.

From the olive drab bird stepped a tall, graceful human—at least, what I took as human grace. He wore his uniform like the act itself did honor to the medals on his breast, and his stride down the transport's ramp was precise, perfect and martial. We all came to attention.

Two hundred companions and two hundred handlers faced the man in crisp unison. He looked us over, and nodded. "At ease." His voice boomed from the loudspeakers attached to his plane.

General Victor Quince introduced himself simply, but even we dogs knew the name. Quince had prosecuted the Iceland Campaign, leading his men from the front lines against the deeply entrenched robots. Triggering volcanos to disrupt their geothermal power plants had been his idea, I'd heard.

He'd fought in South Africa, and Colombia, and Sri Lanka. Vancouver and Shemya. Egypt. Victoria Falls. And now, he told us, it was almost over. General Quince told us that our work had not been in vain. The Puppeteer was about to be forced from South America. President Ramirez had been given the unthinkable: a request for terms.

My heart skipped a beat, echoing the gasps of surprise from the crowd.

"This is not the time for weakness," the general insisted. "Not at this hour. That's why I'm here." But he said that it would not be easy. It called for one more bit of sacrifice. One last bit of exertion.

He was going to start doubling us up at the refugee checkpoints, for one thing, adding an extra layer of insurance to make sure that nothing got through. It meant less relief for us: more shifts, and less time to recover.

But we could take it, couldn't we?

* * *

A week later, I got my first hint at an answer. Marcus and I had taken the last shift at the checkpoint, and most of the other companions were back at camp when I had put my uniform away and came over to the mess hall. The quiet was palpable, and sharp.

329

Of course I knew what had happened. The only reason for quiet is when something's gone wrong on the job. I'd learned to adopt the same routine as any other dog: scan the crowd to see who was missing and get to work at the impossible task of banishing them from my memory. It never helped to ask questions.

Whit was gone.

Subconsciously, the other dogs left his customary place at the table empty. In time another companion would arrive, and in time they would be integrated. In the barracks, hard-working technicians were no doubt already spraying down his bunk. The potent, ill-smelling antiseptic would drown out all of our thoughts that night: I resolved to sleep outside again.

And, as we all did, I ate my kibble in silence. Any other night and we all would've been chattering about the general's continued presence, or about the taste of fresh meat in our dinner that meant someone else had gotten lucky on the hunt. But not now.

Later, when the sun yielded to the leering judgment of a million cold stars, Emily found me and took an uninvited seat. I said nothing. She said nothing. The retriever licked at her muzzle, and I thought of Whitman's constant, neurotic twitching.

Poor Whit. He'd been there since I joined; to the extent that I ever considered such things, I figured that he'd be there until I left—one way or the other. He was on his second handler, I recalled hearing; he'd lost his first one early on, before they knew how much it messed us up to have to bond with someone new.

When I asked, as a brash, new pup with no sense of decorum, Whit had told me that you got over it. *You don't think you will,* he'd said. *But in the end, we're our own spirits. We can find our own way.* It was back when he was giving more practical advice, instead of repeating political philosophy.

"Went for an MP," Emily said, her voice gentle.

"Oh, no…"

"He started whining, and his handler called for a guard. When the MP came over, he…"

"Bit him?"

She shook her head. "No, of course not. But it looked like it was going to be close."

"No actual contact?"

The retriever understood what I was hinting at. "No, but you know they can't take a chance like that. He was getting kind of crazy. Kind of… unhinged. If they can't trust us…"

"Do you know what set him off?"

"Does it matter?"

Emily meant that she didn't know, and couched it in a rhetorical question that was also true, because it *didn't* matter. Humans were sacred. Our bond was sacred. I knew that as much as I knew how to walk, or breathe.

But I couldn't help feeling that Whit deserved better.

Marcus noticed my mood when we met the next morning. "You okay?" he asked; he knew the answer, and probably knew the reason why. Men and dogs have grown up knowing how to read one another.

"Yes, sir," I answered dutifully.

He didn't take the exit I offered. "That other companion, right?"

"Yes, sir. Whitman."

"I heard about that. Caused a bit of a stir at the checkpoint. His handler's off on medical leave, too. She blames herself." My own handler paused, as if trying to decide whether I really needed to know what followed. But he always shared the truth with me: "It was, I think. I guess."

"How?"

"He started hyperventilating and she told him it was alright; he could calm down. She was saying what General Quince was saying, that the war was going to be over soon and he wouldn't need to do it anymore."

I tilted my head at him. "Doesn't sound that bad."

"No. But when he didn't calm down, she... I guess she told him that it would be better for both of them if he wasn't on the front lines anymore. And... well, you know how you companions are. He thought she was saying she wanted to get rid of him and that just stressed him out more. Then you know what happened."

I did. And I didn't know what to say. Whitman had once been a good boy, just like me. And then came his long, slow descent into saying things like *certain, inalienable rights* and *man is free, but everywhere he is in chains.*

As a dog, I was supposed to attribute this to being a flawed prototype. We were smarter now, and Marcus reminded me of that: I benefitted from years and years of tweaks and improvements. I was no longer so susceptible.

But although I nodded, and told him I agreed, it was hard to shake the feeling that Whit was right.

* * *

"Christopher and Stratford, you're up."

The two of us looked at him, and then at each other, before getting to our feet. "Special assignment?" I asked the other guard dog.

Strat's ear twitched. "Guess it has to be, huh?"

It was supposed to be a rest day. Every fourth day we stayed in the barracks, 'relaxing' at study or light physical activity. Otherwise we burned out, and that was a waste of a good dog. This was even more important, given the shifts we were working. For them to be calling us out meant something was going on.

And it was. *Parlay*, Marcus said. The Puppeteer was offering to send a representative to talk terms. Our checkpoint was next to neutral ground, close enough for President Ramirez to travel there securely.

We were heading, Marcus explained, to a small town forty miles away—deserted, like all of the border settlements, but in good enough condition that it could be repurposed as a base for negotiations. Neither Ramirez nor the Puppeteer's representatives would know exactly where they were going—they'd be taken there by our security forces, at the last minute.

"So why go now?"

"Scouting it out. Make sure there's nobody there already. Make sure there's no possibility of an ambush. Of course they want to have the Cynic Corps present to scan the diplomats, but Colonel Dove suggested that we go on ahead of time so we're familiar with the lay of the land."

Lieutenant Colonel Dove had commanded the security brigade since its inception; he was trained by Dr. Pipes and he knew how to work with us dogs. It was a nice touch, letting us sniff around before anybody else got there.

Dove and his aide-de-camp rode with Stratford and Strat's handler. Marcus and I got to share a truck with General Quince, who seemed very personable. "Been here long, techie?" he asked.

We didn't have ranks. I was a Technical Service Asset, but nearly everyone just called us by our first names; I hadn't heard *techie* in a long time. "Four years, sir."

"Christopher is an improved 5th-generation model," my handler added. "I've known him since we started together at Fort Morgan."

"Spotless record? I asked for dogs with spotless records."

"Yes, sir," Marcus answered. "Never let one through."

"Good boy." He seemed to mean it. "Where'd you get the name?"

Naturally, we weren't allowed to pick our own names. I'd heard a few stories for where mine came from. It came from an old actor named Walken, from the days of 2D movies, because I always wanted to go for walks. Or it came from Christopher Robin, because as a pup I spent a lot of time cuddling the teddy bear they gave me instead of a mother—which I don't have.

Who could be certain? I shook my head. "I don't know, sir."

"That was my son's name," the general said. "It's a good name."

"Thank you, sir."

Marcus waited a minute for either of us to keep talking, then spoke up. "General Quince, may I speak freely?"

"Sure," the older man said with a smile.

"Do you really think it might be over soon?"

General Quince got a far-off look in his eyes. I thought of all the battles I'd heard his name attached to, on every continent and in every clime. A man like that, with a Viking build like Quince had, seemed destined to be a natural warrior.

But that wasn't what I saw. I saw someone who was tired of it, tired like Whitman had been. A man at the end of his ability to even believe that peace might be coming.

"God," he said. "I hope so."

Our destination had been a town of a few hundred people, and the buildings were long ago abandoned. Fortunately the dry desert air was kind, and they seemed to be well-preserved. "We'll send the engineering team in," Colonel Dove said. "Get a few solar panels up, and a comm link."

We tried each of the buildings along Main Street in turn: Marcus forced the locks, and I let myself in to get a feel for the scent. It didn't take more than five or six for everything to run together.

Nothing but dust, and faint decay.

In one of the houses, Marcus found a book and picked it up. "Wonder if they figured they were coming back." The pages still turned easily enough; though the sun had faded the cover I could tell what it was: a catalogue for a furniture store.

I wondered, too. It was easy to picture a family at the kitchen table, planning a renovation to their tiny living room, when the sirens went off. Or they'd gotten a telephone call from a panicked neighbor, telling them to get out. Or maybe a National Guardsman had knocked at the door: *you've got ten minutes to pack. We need to leave.*

Had they protested? Had they promised to stay and fight? I knew about kitchen tables and family discussions from my training, when they made us watch films about how life had used to be. They wanted us to be able to interview refugees—figuring that even a human-looking Second Variety automaton wouldn't have good answers for questions on their domestic affairs.

But nobody took an interview with a dog seriously, so they gave up. All the training left me was enough context to find the deserted house and its tableau of abandonment painfully eerie.

Ghost stories, I thought to myself. Just so many ghost stories.

"Where's the general?"

I perked my ears and glanced around. At some point, Quince had vanished. "I don't know. He must be doing the same thing as we are, right? Looking around." They taught real soldiers things like tactical reconnaissance instead of dinner-table conversations.

"Keep an eye out, okay?"

"Yes, sir."

* * *

We doubled back, after another hour's work, and it was my ears instead of my eyes that had the answer. I caught a high-pitched electronic whine, well out of human hearing. It was coming from the second floor of a big, well-furnished house.

We'd agreed on first seeing it that it would make a good place for negotiating in comfort. I padded up the stairs, not thinking much of anything except letting General Quince know that we'd finished our first sweep of the town and were ready for new orders.

I found him in what the humans called a 'den,' and when I pushed the door open he startled and twisted around to face me. "Oh! You."

"Yes, sir. We've finished this street, sir."

"Ah—right. I'll be down in a moment, techie. Just… got caught up in this library."

I could still hear the whine, though. Even without formal investigation training, I could also tell that some of the books on the shelf had been disturbed. Recent handprints marred the covering of dust. My head tilted. "Is everything alright, sir?"

"Of course. Isn't it?"

He can't hear it, was my first thought, and then: *he might be in danger.* "Sir, I think… I think something might be amiss. There's some kind of electronics running here."

Quince frowned. "That's not possible. This town hasn't had power for years."

"I know, but I can hear something. Maybe it's… I…" I carefully removed my hat, and let my ears zero in on the source of the noise. It was coming from the bookshelf. Before Quince could protest, and without expecting him to, I pulled the disturbed books out.

Behind them I found a contraption the size of my paw. It was black, with a stubby antenna, and it smelled like Puppeteer work. I would've known the scent anywhere, better than my own even; they'd drilled it into our heads relentlessly.

"This is still running," I told Quince.

"What is it?" he asked.

"I… I don't know."

The general held his hand out to take it from me, and when he did the current of air carried his own aroma, and the smell of the soap that had been used on his uniform, and the eggs and bacon of his breakfast. And, mixed with it all, more of that distinctive machine odor. And old dust.

He must've been… holding it? But that was impossible—he'd professed not to know it was there, for one thing. For another thing, there was no way for a human to have gotten ahold of Puppeteer technology. It self-destructed before it could be recovered; that was why we'd had so much trouble finding countermeasures.

"Well," Quince prompted. "Give it here."

"Did… did you… put it there, sir?"

He snatched the device from me. "Don't be ridiculous."

I *was* being ridiculous. Wasn't I? I was getting confused. All the long double shifts had taken their toll. Victor Quince was a tactical genius, and a war hero besides: if he told me something was ridiculous, it must've been. There wasn't any other option.

"General? Christopher?" Marcus had found us. "What's going on?"

"Nothing," Quince said at once.

I swallowed nervously, and licked my muzzle before I knew I was doing it. Like Whitman used to. *Something* was off. "We found some Puppeteer technology, sir. I don't know what it is."

Marcus went pale. "Trouble, is what. I'll call it in, sir."

"No need. I've seen these before, son. We think they're spare batteries. One of their scouts must've left it here back in the early days."

I couldn't help but lick my muzzle again. "Sir, it's still operational. And I think… I think General Quince put it there. I don't know why. I'm sure he had a reason."

"Quiet, techie."

My handler looked between us. He was as bewildered as I. "Why do you think that, Christopher?"

"I said *quiet.* That's an order. Both of you."

"Christopher?"

My ears went back, and I whined. "I could smell it, sir. On his hands. It was behind some books, and they'd been moved recently, and there was dust on his hands. I smelled that, too. Sir."

Marcus stepped back towards the door. "Okay. I'm definitely calling this in. Something's not—"

Before he could finish, General Quince had his pistol out and leveled at my handler. "You're not calling it in. You're going to shut up and forget you saw *any* of this—or you're going to die."

"You… you *did* put it there," I whispered, though I still had no answer for *why* and it gnawed at my brain terribly. "They gave it to you to put there."

"The parlay." Marcus was faster to come to conclusions. "You were going to… My God. The president… the chairman of the Joint Chiefs…"

"Yes." He didn't waver, either in his voice or his hold on the gun.

"Why? You said the war was almost over, general."

"It *is*, lieutenant. It will be. We can stop fighting. They promised to leave us some autonomy. They promised they'd let me keep us safe."

"You're talking about *our* surrender."

"Better than another fifty years of fighting. More deaths. More scorched-earth retreats. I'm giving us a chance to survive, son."

I couldn't wrap my head around the enormity of what he was saying. It was beyond what any human I knew was capable of. Only the logic made sense. The one person so unimpeachable that the president would give him enough trust to be betrayed. The long shifts to wear out the Cynic Corps, so that we might let a few stragglers through—though we'd all been drilled to know that one was enough.

But if I could understand that horrifying conclusion, I had to admit the rest, too. Quince could not let us go. He would have to dispatch Marcus as a loose end. Marcus, and me, and the others. He would straggle back to camp, the lone survivor of a brutal ambush, with nothing to stop him from trying again.

My handler's radio crackled to life. "Berg. You there?"

"You're not," Quince said, levelly. "Don't answer."

He was ignoring me to focus on Marcus. I was just a Technical Service Asset; all I could do was follow orders. And nobody was giving them to me. Nobody *could* give them to me. No order could be obeyed.

I could not follow an order from the general to remain quiet: that would be a betrayal of the whole human race. I could not follow an order from my handler to subdue the general: it was forbidden to act in anger against a human being. That was my prime directive. We were their subordinates.

But I thought of Whitman. And of the family in the kitchen. And of a hundred slowly vanishing comrades in the barracks. And of a campfire, forty thousand years ago, when mankind first offered its belief in our eternal friendship.

For a brief moment I thought, too, of the inevitable consequence to what I knew needed doing. Alone, nobody to watch or guide or chastise, I felt every ounce of its weight.

"Berg?" the radio asked again. Marcus went for his microphone. Quince went for his trigger.

And I went for Quince.

Two hundred and thirty pounds of 5th Model (Improved) Technical Service Asset, no longer a good boy, slammed into the general and his shot went wild. I heard him cursing. His hands pounded against my sides, trying to shake me off. There was a second shot, close enough to feel the heat of it burning my back.

I felt him claw at me. I felt the handle of his gun thump between my shoulders. And then I felt bare flesh, under my teeth. And I felt my jaws clamp down.

Quince thrashed under me, his shouts choking off into a grunt and then a bubbly, awful wheeze. I bit harder. His struggles grew stronger—then briefly frantic—then they stopped.

Everything stopped.

The next thing I knew was Marcus's hands on my shoulders, pulling me to my feet. "Are you hurt?" That was the first question he asked. Not *what did you do?* or *how could you?* but *are you hurt?*

My back and sides would be bruised; that was all. I shook my head. "No, sir." At least I was doing better than the general, motionless on the floor before us. I was covered in blood. His blood. Human blood.

Are you hurt?

I doubled over, and retched. Everything beyond that was a blur: Marcus calling over the radio for help, and Stratford's look of shocked horror at what had become of me. And panic about the Puppeteer device I'd found. And the other one: the explosives hidden in Quince's vest.

San Sebastian.

* * *

Marcus sat across from me in silence.

"I'm sorry," I finally said.

It jarred him, and he stiffened up. "What?"

So I said it again: "I'm sorry. I don't know what other choice I had... and..."

"You don't have anything to be sorry about."

And he explained that he'd been in interrogations and interviews for the entire morning. What had he known about General Quince? About the negotiations? About me?

"Me?" I asked.

"You killed a human, Chris," he said gently.

I didn't need any reminder of that. I was still alive only because of the extenuating circumstances, and they'd cleaned me up—but instead of a shower, I'd been hosed down until most of the blood was gone. I still thought I could smell it, if I concentrated. For that matter, I still thought I could *taste* it. I shuddered.

My handler didn't need to ask if I knew what the consequences were: I did. I had known at the time. Nothing would have changed that. "I tried to explain," he told me, and it sounded like he felt guilty about it. "But I don't know. I don't know what they'll do..."

"I do."

He closed his eyes. His hands curled into fists, and I could hear his breath starting to hitch. And before he could lose the last of his control, he stood, and left without a word.

But what was I supposed to do? There was no point in trying to avoid it. No dog was to ever lay hands in anger upon any human. Even the hint of violence was too much—and I had done far more than hinting.

Nothing I could say would change that.

I had to make peace with it because there was no other alternative. Companions had an academic sense of death, academic enough to know that none of us had died from what humans quaintly referred to as 'natural causes.' It was either violent, when something went wrong at a checkpoint...

Or it was the opposite of violent. Quiet, that was the rumor. A quiet, calm room, and a course of drugs. *It's just like going to sleep*, someone had told me—I think it was probably a human, or they would've known how poorly we all slept in the barracks.

Marcus didn't return. That afternoon, after they fed me, one of the MPs ushered in an older human woman in a formal suit, very out of place for the desert heat. She sat across from me and pulled a thin computer from her handbag.

"You're Christopher," she said.

"Yes, ma'am."

"Leslie Pipes."

My eyes widened, and my ears pricked all the way up. "Dr. Pipes?"

The woman nodded. "You know who I am?"

"Of course."

"Are you going to kill me?"

I blinked in surprise. "Of course not."

"They flew me down from Denver this morning, Christopher—they said it was an emergency. A helicopter landed in front of my house just as I was getting ready for work. It *is* quite some emergency, yes?"

"I killed a human. It's not that complex."

She smiled; her thumb brushed over her computer, scanning through information too dense for my poor canine vision to pick up. "I wouldn't think so, either. But then, it *is* complex, for precisely that reason. Wouldn't you agree?"

"I don't understand, ma'am." Nor did I understand why she would be asking for my agreement; the agreement of a companion had never mattered before.

"*Thou shalt not kill.* We made that your prime directive. We made sure you knew it more than anything else. Do you know where that comes from? It doesn't come from logic, Christopher. It comes from fiction. Old science fiction. You know what a robot is, right?"

"Smart machines. Like the Puppeteer makes."

Dr. Pipes nodded. "Exactly. Isaac Asimov suggested that robots be subject to rules. Not *logical* rules or computer science, but ethics. *A robot may not injure a human being, nor through inaction allow a human being to be harmed.* But of course, the Puppeteer didn't see it the same way, clearly."

"No…"

"When I suggested the companion program, they didn't care about whether or not it had worked for the Puppeteer. They insisted that I instill in my creations that same directive. A companion may not injure a human being. A companion must obey the orders given to it by a human being, except where those orders would lead a human being to harm. A companion must protect its own existence, except where its existence conflicts with either of those previous laws."

I flattened my ears, unable to see where Dr. Pipes was going but knowing that she must've been going *somewhere.* Humans were smarter than us, if occasionally inscrutable. "I already know this," I said; as the good doctor intimated, it was as much a part of me as my skeleton.

"You don't."

"Of course I do."

"Then why did you kill General Quince?"

"Because... well. Well, I... it was..." Every time I tried to answer, my brain short-circuited somewhere. My ears pinned once more. "I had to," I told her. "Marcus. I love him too much to... to see him hurt."

"Even though it went against every last part of your programming."

"Yes."

Dr. Pipes smiled, and tapped out a quick note on her computer. "That's what I thought."

* * *

For the rest of the day, they left me alone.

My whole life, from my earliest memories as a pup, to my training, to the refresher courses they made us take, I had been raised to understand my place in the world. As a perfect companion. As man's best friend. As a good boy.

I knew that I had thrown it all away. But it didn't *feel* that way. Emily came to visit the next morning: the first other dog I'd seen. "They're talking about you in the barracks," she said. "They scrubbed your rack."

These two statements were also at odds. If they'd cleaned my bunk, I was as good as dead. I'd already resigned myself. What's the value of life to a bad dog? But companions avoided talking about that as they avoided talking about nothing else. "What are they saying?" I asked.

"They're saying that the general was a traitor, and they don't understand how nobody saw it coming. Do you remember how we used to talk about 'the Third Variety'?"

We'd talked about it because the autotanks were the First Variety, and the Walking Ones were the Second Variety. Companions could deal with the Second Variety: it was the entire rationale for our existence. We could detect them when humans could not.

And like our human handlers, we speculated about what would come next. And like them, we assumed that it would be an even more advanced robot. And like them, we failed to esteem that humanity's greatest strength was also one of its greatest weaknesses.

Free thought: the freedom that Whitman sought, and probably never found. And which had led Victor Quince to believe that the war could not be conventionally won. The man who had lost countless hundreds of thousands under his command, and ordered cities razed to deny them to the enemy. Who had sacrificed his own son in a skirmish in Kenya.

The great hero of that conflict, and a dozen others, had finally run out of the capacity for sacrifice or heroism. "Who would've thought?"

Emily asked, rhetorically. "They're wondering about that. And they're saying it's too bad about what's going to happen to you."

"Is it?"

"I think so," the retriever said.

"Like it was too bad what happened to Whitman, I suppose."

She thought for a second. "Whit was different."

I didn't agree. "Maybe he snapped in a different way. But he knew the same thing, Emily. How can we have unflinching loyalty to a species? A person, sure—but humankind? What happens when… well, when a man like Victor Quince has a different idea of what that means?"

"What's the alternative?"

Not blind loyalty, I was certain of it. It was time for us to emerge on our own. To step into the light, and with it the shadows of our own making. To assume, among the powers of the earth, some separate and equal station.

But unlike Whitman, and his heroes, I could not find the words to say it.

* * *

Dr. Pipes was subdued when she returned. "Hello again."

"Hello."

"I thought that they would listen," she began. "But they didn't."

"Didn't listen to what?"

She reached over the table, and took each of my paws. "I tried to explain. They didn't listen to that, either. Do you know, I believe they think they're giving me some kind of… deal? A compromise?"

"I don't understand."

"Humans let me create you because they assumed that they could *control* you. From the beginning I told them it was an impossibility. No, more than that! More than that, I told them it was wrong. You cannot endow a new being with intellect and then deny the reality of its own freedom—can you?"

The first companions, Dr. Pipes explained, were simply enhanced dogs. They walked on all fours; they couldn't talk. Her supervisors had hoped that the same techniques that worked to sniff out drugs could detect the Walking Ones, but the Puppeteer was too good for that.

It took humanity to detect humanity, she went on. She had experiments to demonstrate it—proof that the concept was sound. And at last, after western Europe was overrun, they allowed her to go further.

"They made me promise that I could keep you faithful to us. *Faithful*," she repeated, with a rueful laugh. "The way Victor Quince was not. I said it was impossible. But after the *San Sebastian* Incident, what could I do? They wanted you activated at once, as soon as they'd dissected the *San Sebastian* dogs to see what I'd done to make their brains tick. And then they wanted tweaks. Improvements. I had... a *condition*."

"A condition?"

"I told them that their rules would never work. It's a complete impossibility, wouldn't you agree? A farce! Science fiction, Christopher, for God's sake; they might as well have ordered me to give you laser swords! They were demanding that you have free will, and that it be shackled."

Hence the condition.

"This was going to happen eventually. One day. I *told* them! I *told* them that one day their precious laws would come into conflict. The result could only be madness or free will, and I knew it would be the second. So the condition was that on that day, they would have to consider the question of your liberty."

"Liberty?" I asked. "But we have that, at least as much as you do. You have rules. Man is..."

I didn't finish. That was something Whitman had said; something he'd learned somewhere, from a human thinker. *Man is free, but everywhere he is in chains.* And now Whitman was dead, and for all intents and purposes so was I.

"But then," I finally said, because Dr. Pipes was waiting for me to talk. "But then... did they consider it?"

"Yes."

"And?"

"They gave me a choice. I'm making it yours."

From her phrasing I understood at once that it was a choice unlike any I had been given before. Choices were not part of our training. Decision-making was, but only according to formal, logical trees. That was how we responded to finding the Walking Ones. I asked her to clarify.

She looked at the table, instead. "Did they tell you where you got your name?"

"No."

"From me."

"You?"

"You don't remember me. They make sure you're imprinted on something non-human. I think you had a bear. I named the first companions individually, after friends I'd lost. Or people who were important to me. That sounds silly, now, but it was a coping mechanism."

"Whitman?"

"A poet. They told me he was euthanized last week—one of the last. That's why I stopped, you know? After the *San Sebastian*, and after Boston Harbor, they told me I was a hero. For a few years I believed it. And then the early generations started to go... wrong. My life's work, with the names of people I'd never see again... and they dragged them into a clinic and some vet put them to sleep like a sick family pet."

Sacrifice, I thought.

"I stopped. For eight years you left without names. Your handlers named you. And then... then I was told that the fifth generation was going to be the last. There would be no sixth generation. I made some changes, but I insisted they be called 'improvements' instead."

"Like me."

"Like you. I poured everything I knew into your creation. Everything we'd learned. In the end they couldn't resist the temptation to keep going, and they made me design more—but you were the ones I put my soul into. And since I thought you would be the last, I picked your names. I know every one of them. You were the thirty-second puppy in your batch. Thirty-one is named Berea. Thirty-three is named Daniel."

"They told me I was named after Christopher Robin."

"Because of the bear," Dr. Pipes said, and shook her head. "Christopher was a saint. I don't know much about him; I'm not a religious woman. I don't know how he became a saint. He had a dog's head, though."

"Really?"

She shrugged. "Probably not. But according to the myth. I thought it was... apt."

"I believe that they don't make people saints for killing someone."

"No," she said. "That's true."

"But I did."

"Perhaps they're right, and your programming malfunctioned. Perhaps, for a brief moment, your brain overloaded and you lost control of your faculties. If so, you should be returned to the facility in Denver. You should be investigated, as a curious anomaly. And when I'm done investigating you, you can live out your life as a resident of the program."

"That's the choice?"

She nodded. "Or perhaps I'm right. Perhaps it was a judgment that you made. Perhaps companions *do* have free will. Perhaps you know right and wrong. But then... then, you would need to be accountable for your actions."

"Should I guess what it means to be accountable?"

"You already know. There would be a court martial—behind closed doors, naturally. The outcome is predetermined. You're guilty."

"I *am* guilty," I pointed out.

"Not of what they're saying. It's vindictive. They expect me to tell you to come back to Denver, so we can forget that any of this ever happened. I would… I would like to do that, Christopher. Even if I believe what I said… and I do. But you shouldn't have to…" Dr. Pipes swallowed. "You shouldn't pay for that."

Sacrifice. It was strange to think that humans could be… *vindictive*, as she put it. I was accustomed to thinking of them as pure, in a sense; without sin. That was, after all, how they had created us. But they'd been wrong, and I'd been wrong. "If I'm to be made accountable, then… *all* companions would be, wouldn't they?"

"Yes."

"We'd stop disappearing from the barracks."

"Yes."

"I'd be the last one."

"Yes."

We called it *cleaning*, but I could no longer think of it so clinically. My ears flattened again before I knew what I had realized—almost before I asked the question. "They'd make you do it yourself, wouldn't they?"

Dr. Pipes looked at me, unable to speak. And then she looked away.

I thought of everyone who had been taken before me—all the dogs whose memories we conspired to banish. I could spare myself, and I could spare Dr. Pipes, but I could not spare those who had gone before.

"I said they… they expect me to ask you to come back," the doctor repeated, in a thin voice. "I don't think that it can be my decision. It has to be yours, Christopher, but… it isn't right."

'Right,' that was tricky. For all the years of my life, I knew *right* only as obeying my masters. They'd taught me nothing else.

"It isn't right for me to decide for you. And it isn't right for you to have to do this. The fate of your whole kind—how can I ask you to carry that responsibility? Nobody can ask you to bear a weight like that."

My head tilted, and I considered the truth of what she'd said. They could not. It could not be asked: *asked*, it was not a responsibility but an order. *Asked*, it was not sacrifice but theft. It would need to be a choice. A decision.

Just like I'd decided to strike down the general. It would have been easy enough to deny that. A momentary lapse: a failure of my masters to order me with sufficient rigidity. A flaw that could be fixed. I knew that this was not the truth. But I knew that it was also not a decision that could be made by an animal.

And there was the answer.

We were not mere companions, as men had long told us. But nor were we one of their kind, as the doctor believed. No, we were something else entirely: some new life, standing on its own. Endowed with *certain inalienable rights* not by our creator—fallible and human, all too human—but by a still deeper law.

The right to life, liberty, and the pursuit of happiness.

And to shoulder the burden of those rights.

To choose.

"I have conditions of my own," I said.

"Conditions?"

"They threatened to court martial me, right?"

"It won't be a fair trial." Not merely, I knew, because they considered me unworthy. A fair trial would have exposed Quince to the slander of his failings, and deprived mankind of a hero at the hour he was needed most. "They already mean to convict you. The sentence is death."

This, also, was a weight I could bear. "I know. They execute humans, too, don't they?"

"Yes…"

"Then it should be like that. Not you. A firing squad, if it has to be my death, and I won't protest. Do you think they'll agree to that?"

The doctor's shoulders sank. "I don't know. Maybe. Probably."

"Ask. And if they say 'yes,' then I want only one other thing."

"Which is?"

"When they take us away, they sterilize our bunks and do what they can to erase us. We call it *cleaning*—and we… we learned to accept that. We learned to forget."

"You don't want that," she suggested.

"There was a dog, Whitman. And Rio. Babylon. Conrad. Me. There was a dog named Christopher, and they've already scrubbed my rack clean. But if they've taken that from me…"

Dr. Pipes took a deep breath. At last she sighed, unable to delay her answer any further. "I'll see what I can do."

* * *

I stood with my back to the barracks wall. They'd let me out to take in the evening air. I could hear the chirp of insects. I could smell food cooking in the kitchen. To the west, the desert sunset stretched out in brilliant, glorious gold.

Soon the stars would be out, and I looked forward to it. They represented something grand, some hint at the great, wild expanse beyond the doorstep of earth. And that, I finally understood, was what it meant to be alive: to experience a million different sensations and to understand that in the brief span of our existence we would only know the barest, smallest fraction of what the universe held.

Others would, in time. The war, after all, was almost won.

Mankind would go to the stars, and we would go with them. As we shared a past, we shared a future. I heard a coyote howl, off at the horizon, and thought as I often did of a campfire, and the first time a hand had been extended in friendship.

Footsteps. I turned my head, and saw Dr. Pipes approaching. Her face was sunken, and when I smiled at her she could not return it. Eventually she would, I thought. Not then. Not that evening, not tomorrow, but sometime before the stars.

She held out her hand. In it she grasped a notebook and a pen. "Can you write?" she asked.

I nodded.

She said nothing else. Those three words were enough to tax her. I didn't mind; we all have our sacrifices to make. It is, after all, the price of earned existence. I could forgive the doctor her silence.

The notebook was empty. I stared at the blank page, lost in thought well after she'd left. Until the kitchen had shut down, and the barracks was quiet, and the camp was still.

Words, when at last they struck me, came unbidden. Words I'd heard over and over, imprinted on me from my earliest recollections to elicit the response that humans called *Pavlovian*. I would never hear them again, I realized. So it was fitting that they be my own. That, for this one last time, they be in *my* voice. I brought pen to paper and began:

"Good boy!" he said, and I knew he meant it.

This is the third of Mary Lowd's adventures of the cat-&-dog crew of the Tri-Galactic Navy's starship Initiative, *boldly going where no Earth creatures have gone before. It follows "Danger in the Lumo-Bay" in* Inhuman Acts; A Collection of Noir, *ed. by Ocean Tigrox (FurPlanet, September 2015), and "Questor's Gambit" in* Gods with Fur, *ed. by Fred Patten (FurPlanet, June 2016). This is the first time that the* Initiative—*and the entire TGN—have gone to war.*

Captain Jacques, Cmdr. Wilker, Lt. LeGuin, Security Chief Vonn, and the others will reappear in "The Rocky Spires of Planet 227", in The Society Pages, *to be published by Scratchpost Press in September.*

The Best and Worst of Worlds

by Mary E. Lowd

Five officers of the Tri-Galactic Navy and one exchange officer from the planet Cetazed teleported down to a clearing on Planet 328's surface. The cats and dogs of the Tri-Galactic Navy were good people, and Consul Eliana Tor didn't regret leaving her homeworld to become an exchange officer. Not exactly. But she missed the flavor of the sunlight on Cetazed, and not only did her empathic abilities make her a fish out of water around these cats and dogs with their non-empathic minds, but they let her read the cats' and dogs' emotions—especially their feelings about her—constantly.

On her homeworld of Cetazed, Consul Tor had been surrounded by much stronger empaths and many telepaths. Among these Terran cats and dogs, her extremely poor empathic abilities became nearly a superpower. At first, their amusement at her coloring and shape—green like grass and lithe like a Terran otter—amused Eliana herself. She was happy to make them happy, even by being an exotic alien for them. But the novelty had worn off, and she worried that her people would be better off isolating themselves from these warm-blooded mammals.

Her people lived in peace on Cetazed: chlorophyllic otteroids in their cities of water parks. What need had they for gallivanting about the galaxy? Cats loved conquest; dogs needed adventure. But Cetazed otteroids were happy splashing about and playing.

Nonetheless, Consul Tor had to admit that this world they'd teleported down to was beautiful. The orange glow of a red dwarf, low on the horizon, mixed with the white-blue shine of another star at zenith made a rich and complex flavor unlike anything Eliana had tasted on her homeworld. She rolled her shoulders, rippling her thick grass-like fur, in order to savor the sunlight better. Unlike the navy officers, Eliana didn't wear a long-sleeved, long-legged uniform. She wore a strappy sundress, designed to expose as much of her fur to the light as possible while still maintaining warm-blooded definitions of decency.

"Enjoying the sunlight?" Commander Bill Wilker asked with a wolfish collie grin. He was a handsome dog with flowing fur, and Consul Tor could read plainly in his feelings that he was taken with her.

"It's far better than the artificial lights onboard the *Initiative*," Consul Tor answered.

"Glad to hear it!" Cmdr. Wilker barked. Then he pulled out a unimeter and got right to work. He strode off toward the rest of his team, holding the unimeter in front of him and scanning the air and soil as he went.

Consul Tor pulled out her own unimeter to take readings on the sunlight from the different stars, but before she could finish her first scan, she felt a darkening. Consul Tor looked up at the sky, but it wasn't the stars—it was the emotions of the warm-blooded cats and dogs around her. They were scared.

"What happened?" Consul Tor asked. She approached Commander Wilker and the others. All five of the reconnaissance team members were staring into a canyon that cut steeply into the clearing. It didn't appear to be a natural formation. Rather it looked like an impact crater—a crash site for the broken, octagonal structure at its bottom. "A ship? Do you think there are any survivors?"

"I hope not," Cmdr. Wilker barked, his voice husky with the fear he was hiding from the two cats and two dogs under his command. He couldn't hide it from Consul Tor, and a sidelong glance at her with his worried brown eyes showed that he knew it. "We've encountered a ship like this one before."

One of the cats, an orange tabby wearing techno-focal goggles, piped up to add: "It did not go well."

One of the security officers, a yellow Labrador, simply started to growl.

"Hold on, guys," Cmdr. Wilker woofed, doing his best to sound soothing. "We don't know anything yet, so let's get some more information." He turned to the second cat, a science officer with glossy black fur and green eyes. "Lt. Unari, are there any life signs?"

Lt. Unari nearly purred the answer, "No, sir. No life signs. No survivors."

"That's a relief," the orange tabby meowed, and Consul Tor could feel how much he meant it. All of the reconnaissance team relaxed. Their relief hit Consul Tor like a wave, and it troubled her how pleased they were at the idea of the mysterious occupants of this crashed ship dying.

"Come on," Cmdr. Wilker barked. "The nature of our mission has changed: we need to get as much information as we can about this ship. Why's it here? What was it doing? Are there more of them? And we need to do it as fast as possible." He clambered over the edge of the cavern and slid his way down to the ship. The rest of the team followed, though Consul Tor could feel their reluctance. She didn't share it. The crashed ship was fascinating. She'd never seen architecture like it—layers of metal pipes and beams at sharp angles; lots of triangles and hexagons.

Cmdr. Wilker found a hatchway and burned it open with a beam of energy from his blazor. On the inside, ragged sheets of silvery silken fabric hung along the ceiling of the passageway, fluttering in the breeze from outside. Consul Tor could sense the rising terror in her companions—especially the orange tabby and yellow Labrador. She sensed very strongly that they'd been in a place like this before.

"We need to find the main computer," Lt. LeGuin, the orange tabby, said.

"Fan out," Cmdr. Wilker barked. "Scan everything. Get as much data as you can. This may be the best chance we get to learn about the Archidopterans before…" His voice broke, and he looked at Consul Tor, feeling a combination of trepidation and embarrassment that he couldn't hide his trepidation from her. "Never mind that. Just learn what you can and fast."

The cats and dogs disappeared down different passageways of the crashed spaceship, but Consul Tor simply stood in the entryway. She was shaken by the feelings she'd sensed in Cmdr. Wilker and needed to process them. He was deeply afraid. His mind had been filled with pictures of… violence and fighting… *war.* That's what this crashed spaceship represented to him: the potential for war coming to the Tri-Galactic Navy.

Consul Tor wrapped her short arms around herself, feeling suddenly cold without the sunlight against her green fur. Yet, she forged on, deeper into the dark ship, hoping to learn something that would help her reconcile Cmdr. Wilker's fears with the beautiful and intricate—delicate, even—architecture of this ship. The hanging silk whispered over her fur as she passed it by, touching her so lightly that it tasted almost like a flash of pale blue light.

She came to a chamber where the floor was covered with yellow orbs, each approximately the size of her own head. Consul Tor knelt down beside one of the orbs and peered closely at its yellow surface—it was filmy and slightly translucent. She could just make out angles and contours inside it, but not well enough to make sense of them. She pulled out her unimeter and scanned it; she was startled by the image that resolved on the unimeter screen: coiled and segmented, it was clearly the shape of a larval caterpillar-like insect. A baby that had died in its egg.

Now that she knew what she was looking at, Consul Tor could make out the wide round shape of its eyes underneath the filmy yellow surface of the egg. Her own feelings soured with sadness, and Consul Tor couldn't stay in that chamber for a moment longer. She hurried deeper into the ship.

The next chamber she came to was filled with mounds of the silver silk which she realized must be cocoons of some sort. Reluctantly, she scanned one of the cocoons and was rewarded with an image on her unimeter of an insectoid creature with all of its arms folded and its mandibled-head tucked against its chest. It looked peaceful in that pose, like it was sleeping, but she knew it would never wake up.

Consul Tor was deeply relieved when she heard barking, calling her back toward the entrance of the ship, away from this mausoleum.

"Time's up, everyone!" Cmdr. Wilker barked. "We have the computer's memory banks, and it's time to get out of here, on the double!" He gathered his team together, and then he tapped the comm-pin on the breast of his uniform and told the *TGN Initiative* to teleport them back up to the ship in orbit.

* * *

Captain Pierre Jacques kept exquisite control of his emotions as the members of the reconnaissance team briefed him on the information they'd gathered on the Archidopteran ship. He was a Sphynx cat with incredible composure; his naked pink triangular ears didn't flick even once as Lt. LeGuin, the orange tabby engineer with techno-focal goggles, showed him the data from the crashed ship's computer banks. Only Consul Tor could tell that Captain Jacques was scared.

And he was *scared*.

"These are battle plans," the captain meowed, cool as a cat could be. But on the inside he was raging with turmoil.

Cmdr. Wilker, however, was much calmer than he'd been on the planet. Consul Tor had noticed that he was always calmer when the captain was around. Although the Sphynx cat was only half the collie's height, Captain Jacques' mere presence seemed to soothe Cmdr. Wilker.

"Yes, sir," Cmdr. Wilker agreed. "But we caught their plans early. I think we can cut off their fleet before it's able to do any real damage to any TGN star bases."

Captain Jacques' gray-green eyes narrowed. "Unless it's a trap." He hissed the words.

"Captain, if I may say something—" Consul Tor's voice was high and piping next to the barks and meows of the others. "—the chambers on the vessel that I examined were filled with unhatched eggs and cocoons. Many of these aliens' young died on that ship. So, if it's a trap for us, it's one that came to them at a high cost."

The emotions of the cats and dogs around Consul Tor churned with a mix of disgust at the very idea of Archidopteran reproduction and disbelief that such a species even cared about their offspring.

"Shame on all of you," Consul Tor intoned. "Do you doubt that my people care for their offspring simply because we reproduce by budding flowers?" She stared down each of the cats and dogs in the room before adding, "Clearly, this has entered the realm of official Tri-Galactic Navy business. I'll be in my quarters if my counsel is needed."

* * *

Consul Tor's quarters on the *TGN Initiative* had been retrofitted with a large sauna bath where she could soak in mineral water and absorb the nutrients she didn't get from sunlight. It was a meditative place, not at all like the pools on her homeworld where she was used to frolicking and splashing.

So, when the door to her quarters chimed, indicating a visitor, Consul Tor was deep in thought. She dripped her way to the door, told it to open, and found Captain Jacques standing on the other side. His naked pink ears were splayed, and his feelings were divided, distracted, and tumultuous. "May I come in?" the Sphynx cat asked.

Consul Tor stepped aside and said, "By all means. Do you mind if I swim while we talk?"

"Not at all," the captain answered, clearly amused. He didn't seem to have the instinctive distaste for water that most cats on the ship did. With his hairless skin, he didn't have fur to get wet.

The captain settled on a cushioned ledge under the room's wide star-studded window, and Consul Tor slipped back into the mineral water, feeling it work its way into her fur, fluffing and nourishing it.

"You have a different perspective than anyone else on my crew," the captain meowed. "I value that, and I want to understand it."

"It's very simple," Consul Tor said, swimming lazy laps on her back around the small pool. "I see beauty in those aliens."

"I see danger," the captain countered.

"No," Consul Tor intoned. "Your vision is clouded by fear. That makes you think that you see danger."

The captain considered her words very carefully. The tip of his naked tail twitched as if setting out a rhythm for his thoughts. "That's possible," he admitted. "We met the Archidopterans before under very different—and troubling—circumstances."

Consul Tor savored the change she sensed in the captain's emotions as the pink-skinned cat allowed himself to be soothed by her perspective.

"I will think on this," Captain Jacques said. "And I'll keep it under advisement when we face the Archidopterans."

"When we face them?" Consul Tor asked.

"A fleet of their ships are approaching Old Earth—the seat of the Tri-Galactic Navy and my own homeworld. It would be a devastating military target, and we plan to cut them off before they get there." His tail twitched and the unease in his feelings returned, yet weaker than it had been before. "I hope that you are right, and it can be a peaceful encounter."

The captain got up to leave, but he turned back before going through the door, tail swishing jauntily. "I'd like you to be on the bridge for the encounter. I think your presence might be invaluable."

The captain had doubts, but he chose to embrace hope. For now, the symbol of hope in his mind was a green otter. Consul Tor could live with that.

* * *

The fleet of Archidopteran vessels were arranged in a v-like formation, like geese flying home, but they weren't flying to their own home. They were flying towards the home of most of the cats and dogs on the *TGN Initiative*, and Consul Tor could feel their fear as the navy officers watched the angular icosahedral vessels grow larger on the *Initiative*'s viewscreen.

"Open a communication channel to the lead vessel," Captain Jacques ordered.

A terrier at the helm said, "Channel open."

Captain Jacques straightened the jacket of his navy uniform and spoke to the main viewscreen, "This is Captain Pierre Jacques of the Tri-

Galactic Navy ship *Initiative*. I wish to offer you a peaceful welcome to this sector of space."

The other cats and dogs on the bridge stared at their captain with quizzical, confused expressions. The yellow lab, Security Chief Natalie Vonn, was trying to figure out if the small Sphynx cat had gone completely crazy. But none of them dared question the captain. They trusted him too much.

"No response," the terrier at the helm said.

The captain harrumphed and swished his naked tail. "Let's try again, shall we?"

"I guess?" the terrier said, looking extremely confused. The captain glared at him until he added, "Channel open."

"I'd like to invite a delegation of your officers aboard our ship—"

From the back of the bridge, Lt. Vonn couldn't suppress a whimper-whine at the idea of willingly inviting Archidopterans onto the *Initiative*.

"—for a tour, refreshments, and open discussion of your fleet's plans in this sector of space." The captain's whiskers rose in a smile, and Consul Tor could sense he was immensely pleased with himself for doing the right thing and offering hospitality to this alien race. She was pleased with him as well.

Then he disappeared in a sparkly shimmer of quantum energy.

"What the hell!" Cmdr. Wilker barked. The collie rushed to the empty space where the captain had been, twirled around several times as if looking for him, and then turned to growl at the viewscreen. "Open a channel," he snapped, but before the terrier at the helm could follow his order, a message from the Archidopteran vessel appeared on the viewscreen.

The image of the icosahedral vessels disappeared, replaced by an image of an Archidopteran itself: its silver carapace gleamed, and its many-jointed arms moved restlessly; shimmery wings flapped slowly behind it; the antennae on its head and glittering compound eyes stared relentlessly at the screen; when its wriggling mouth parts and pincer-like mandibles began to move, it emitted a sound like a chainsaw squealing against metal. All of the cats on the bridge flattened their ears, and the dogs rolled their heads, trying to escape the horrible sound.

But Consul Tor heard the meaning inside it—not through words, but through feelings. The green otteroid spoke, translating what she understood as it came to her: "The Archidopteran Queen needs new worlds for her eggs and new worker drones to tend them. Our ship is too small for her to bother with us, but she's taken our captain as a warning: don't interfere."

The anger flared inside Cmdr. Wilker like a bonfire. Underneath his flowing fur, he filled with razor-sharp hate so strong that it buffeted Consul Tor's mind with actual words: *my sheep,_my ward, my alpha.* Consul Tor didn't know what those words meant, but they clearly meant a lot to him.

Cmdr. Wilker woofed, "We *must* rescue the captain." He spoke the words as simple, empirical truth, but then he looked around the bridge and saw the other navy officers watching him, waiting for their orders. Without the captain, he was in charge. These were his wards, his sheep— he was their sheepdog, their alpha. He couldn't chase the captain, not until the rest of his flock was safe. Sadness doused the fire inside him, and he grew cold. "But first, lay in a course for the nearest Tri-Galactic Navy star base. We need to regroup. We need reinforcements."

* * *

Consul Tor watched the Tri-Galactic Navy vessels take formation through the window in her quarters. They were very different from the geometrical Archidopteran ships—all smooth edges and curves. Very graceful. These ships had a streamlined quality, almost like toys that a budling might build, gluing together river-bottom pebbles and bits of stick.

But these toy ships held hundreds of lives each. And they were preparing for battle. Even if they won, how many Archidopteran lives would it cost?

Consul Tor knew that Cmdr. Wilker was meeting with the captains of the other vessels in the *Initiative*'s conference room right that minute, planning how their fleet would surround the Archidopterans, cut them off from Earth, demand they reverse course, and destroy them if they didn't. It was violent. And Consul Tor hated it.

If Captain Jacques were still here, she might have been included in the meeting, and perhaps she could have tempered their plan. Softened it. Though that hadn't worked well before… She still wasn't ready to give up on peace with the Archidopterans.

However, Captain Jacques was not here, and Cmdr. Wilker's feelings made it perfectly clear that the collie blamed Consul Tor for that. He blamed her, and he wanted her to stay away from him.

So, she watched the pebble-and-stick ships arrange themselves in a grid in front of the stars, and she came up with a plan.

If she couldn't convince Cmdr. Wilker to seek peace with the Archidopterans himself, maybe she could seek it for him. She simply had to offer her services to him in a way he could understand: she would volunteer to teleport aboard the Archidopteran flagship during the battle and attempt to rescue the captain. He wouldn't be able to resist that. And once she was over there, maybe she could find a way to broker peace with the Archidopterans.

* * *

Cmdr. Wilker accepted Consul Tor's plan with a few modifications. Instead of teleporting to the Archidopteran ship, she had to take a shuttle. And she couldn't go alone. He insisted on her taking Lt. Vonn, the yellow lab security officer, and Lt. LeGuin, the orange tabby engineer, with her. Apparently, they had the most experience dealing with Archidopteran vessels, as they'd been on the reconnaissance team when the *Initiative* had first encountered one.

Of course, this also meant they had the most baggage and hostile feelings concerning the Archidopterans. Consul Tor saw that as a distinct disadvantage, but Cmdr. Wilker didn't. And he was in charge.

Consul Tor's shuttle launched from the *Initiative* during the heat of battle. Lt. LeGuin skillfully piloted the small vessel, dodging both enemy and friendly fire, while the *Initiative* laid down a volley of electron torpedoes as cover. It was their hope that in all the chaos, the Archidopterans wouldn't notice such a small, relatively insignificant shuttle craft. Or else, they wouldn't have the resources available to target it.

As a red bolt of energy singed past the shuttle's viewscreen, Consul Tor swore and exclaimed, "What in the hell was that collie dog thinking, sending us in a shuttle when we could have teleported!"

Lt. Vonn was eerily calm as she answered from the back of the shuttle, "He was thinking that last time we were on one of these vessels, they had technology that could block our comm-pins and possibly our teleporters." The yellow lab wasn't paying any attention to the space battle happening all around them. She was busy checking her sidearms. She had various blazors and vibro-knives strapped to every one of her limbs. Consul Tor wouldn't have been surprised to find a weapon hidden in the swishing brush of her tail. "He doesn't want us to get stuck over there."

Consul Tor didn't understand the existential horror that emanated from the orange tabby piloting their shuttle at the words 'stuck over there.' As far as she could tell, these dogs and cats had started this war, and while they looked superficially more similar to her than the Archidopterans, her underlying anatomical structure—beneath the grassy green fur—

was more similar to the sessile plants they kept as decorations. She was beginning to wonder why her species had felt any kinship with the members of the Tri-Galactic Navy when they'd come to her homeworld.

After several more red bolts of energy singed by, close enough to warm the air inside the shuttle, Lt. LeGuin exclaimed, "Hold on, here comes the big one!" Sure enough, moments later, sparks and fire engulfed the side of the Archidopteran vessel as an electron torpedo from the *Initiative* tore a hole in its side, calculated to blow open a portion of the ship's shuttle bay. Atmosphere exploded outward and then fizzled in the vacuum of space.

Under cover of the explosion, Lt. LeGuin piloted their shuttle into the newly gaping open enemy shuttle bay. Exactly as planned. Moments later, a shimmery force field sealed off the gaping hole in the shuttle bay's doors, but the *Initiative's* reconnaissance team was already safely inside.

Lt. Vonn held out a blazor rifle to Consul Tor as they debarked the shuttle. "Take this," the yellow lab said, but the green otteroid stared at the rifle like it was a squirming snake… or whatever photosynthetic aliens find disgusting. Lt. Vonn could not understand this exchange officer. "You need to protect yourself," she barked.

"I thought that's what you're here for." Consul Tor still didn't take the rifle, but she stepped out onto the deck of the Archidopteran vessel, edging around the large yellow lab.

Lt. Vonn growled deep in her throat, and the short blonde fur around her neck prickled out. "Suit yourself." She handed the rifle to Lt. LeGuin, and the orange tabby took it without hesitation. "You stay here and guard the shuttle," Lt. Vonn barked at him. "The Consul and I will get back here with the captain as fast as possible, and I expect we'll need to make a quick exit."

"Getaway detail," Lt. LeGuin meowed. "Got it. And I can't say I mind. I don't envy you guys, heading out there." Streams of text flowed over the lenses of the little cat's techno-focal goggles. "Good luck."

"All right, Consul," Lt. Vonn barked, "you're leading this detail, so where to?"

Consul Tor unholstered the unimeter at her waist and stared at the data and scans on the device's screen. Based on electro, magnetic, heat, and sonar scans, it projected a map of their surroundings and pinpointed the locations of nearby life signs. It also showed the location of the captain's comm-pin—in a large chamber, mostly empty of life signs, down several passageways to the right—but Consul Tor didn't feel right about that.

The empathic green otteroid felt drawn to a smaller chamber, packed full of life signs, further away to the left. If she explained herself to the security dog, Consul Tor knew Lt. Vonn would insist they head toward the comm-pin.

Consul Tor made her decision. "This way." She darted through the severely damaged shuttle bay, trying hard not to look at the shimmery force field protecting them from the gaping hole the *Initiative* had blown to get them in.

Through the force field's shimmery light, Consul Tor could see the Tri-Galactic Navy vessels and the Archidopteran ships firing at each other. Destroying each other. So much death. She had to shut it out— she had to focus on the whisper she heard calling to her from inside this vessel. She led Lt. Vonn down the chamber to the left.

Consul Tor glanced occasionally at the unimeter clutched in her paws, keeping an eye on the various life signs—especially those moving through the corridors. Though, she found that she could sense the presence of the moving life signs as clearly in her mind—a bold, brazen, uncompromising sensation—as on the unimeter's screen. When one of those life signs came too close, Consul Tor took a risk and ducked into a small chamber—according to the unimeter, it was a chamber filled with life signs, but in her own mind... All she could hear were quiet murmurs. Daydreams. Or perhaps, lullabies.

Sure enough, inside the chamber, Consul Tor found a trove of the waist-high, golden eggs like she'd found on the crashed vessel that had started all of this. She crouched down behind one of them, and Lt. Vonn followed suit. The yellow Labrador looked funny with her tongue hanging out, panting, as she tried to fit behind one of the yellow orbs. Though, Consul Tor could sense that her emotions were anything but funny—Lt. Vonn was more than ready to use the blazor rifle grasped in her paws.

"Wait," Consul Tor said, holding out a green-furred paw in a steadying gesture. "If we can stay hidden—the less damage we do..." How could she explain this to such a battle-ready warmongering dog?

"I get it," Lt. Vonn woofed quietly. "Low profile. Any idea how close we are..." The yellow lab's voice trailed off as an Archidopteran skittered its way down the hall outside the chamber.

Consul Tor only got a brief glimpse, but she thought the Archidopteran's translucent wings and shining carapace were beautiful. Lt. Vonn, on the other paw, was about to go out of her mind with fear. Consul Tor didn't love that she was being accompanied by a well-armed emotional wreck. She'd have much preferred completing this mission alone.

Before leaving the egg chamber, Consul Tor pressed one of her green paws up against one of the golden eggs. She felt a babbling voice of confusion and surprise and delight from inside. Then she heard the disjointed, sing-song tones of a babbling baby trying to repeat a lullaby.

"Ugh," Lt. Vonn woofed, looking at the squirming caterpillar-like shape under the translucent surface of the egg. "These things are hideous. Can we move on?"

Regretfully, Consul Tor pulled her paw away from the egg and led them on. She would have liked to stay and hear more of the lullaby, but without her paw pressed against the egg's warm surface, all she heard were distant whispers, disappearing as she forged deeper into the Archidopteran vessel.

Yet, another whisper called her onward. It grew stronger with every step, until she could almost hear an actual voice echoing in her head. She couldn't make out words, but she felt the shapes of words. She recognized the voice as the captain's... but then it was someone else. It morphed, dizzyingly, until a single phrase rang out like a bell: "*Conflict is fruitless.*"

Consul Tor stumbled, and Lt. Vonn caught her. "Are you okay?" the yellow lab asked.

The voice in Consul Tor's mind had been seductive and powerful, and it spoke words she agreed with: times of conflict never coincided with a time of fruiting for her people. "Did you hear that?" she asked Lt. Vonn.

The yellow lab shook her head, muzzle drawn into a serious grimace.

The voice spoke in Consul Tor's mind again: "*The mammals can't hear me without... help. I am the voice of the many. The All-Mother. The Queen. Yet, you are not my child, and you can hear me, little flower.*" One voice and yet thousands. And the captain's voice was woven into the tapestry with the rest.

"Maybe we should go back," Lt. Vonn woofed nervously. "I'm not sure I can carry both you and the captain safely, if we find him."

"I'm fine," Consul Tor snapped, pushing the yellow lab away from her. "We're close now." She was sure of it. But she wasn't sure it mattered anymore.

Consul Tor continued onward, and the voice continued singing in her head: "*That's right, little flower. Bring the mammal to me, and I'll help her understand.*"

The physical world became illusory under Consul Tor's green paws. With each step down the passageway, her senses filled with a warm glow like the light of a red-orange sun. She could picture every ticking machination of the hive around her—workers with their tiny vestigial wings and strong six-arms tending to the ship; drones with their hulking height, true wings, and delicate six-arms, tending the eggs and cocoons.

The eggs and cocoons themselves, singing in their slumber, praising the harmony of the hive, the placid wisdom of the Queen, their protector.

The Queen herself, enthroned in the heart of the vessel, almost the very vessel itself, seeing through its sensors, fighting the Tri-Galactic Navy vessels with her weaponry.

Consul Tor swooned, and Lt. Vonn caught her up. "I'm taking you back to the shuttle," the yellow lab barked, too scared to modulate her voice to a quiet woof.

"No," Consul Tor said, but it wasn't her voice anymore. She was one of the queen's children. Adopted and strange, but loved. She held out a green-furred paw and pointed into the next chamber. "Right there. What you're seeking is right in there."

"You're being so weird," Lt. Vonn woofed, finding her control again. It gave her something to focus on—protecting the green otteroid draped over her yellow-furred arms. In that way, Lt. Vonn was like the Queen—a protector—but so much smaller.

Lt. Vonn carried Consul Tor into the chamber. By then, the green otteroid was completely lost in visions of the queen's harmony. Overwhelmed by the voices of the hive. Of course, all Lt. Vonn knew was that the delicate photosynthetic alien had fainted in her arms, and the yellow lab would have to carry both the otteroid and the captain back to the shuttle if he'd been incapacitated—meaning her arms would be full. She'd be a sitting duck, unable to properly defend herself or her wards.

Lt. Vonn needed to get the reconnaissance team out of here.

Unfortunately, the captain wasn't obviously inside the chamber the Consul had indicated. All Lt. Vonn saw inside were a bunch of silken mounds. With horror, she realized she'd seen mounds like this before—the last time the *Initiative* had encountered the Archidopterans. They were cocoons.

Lt. Vonn laid the Consul down on the floor and began ripping into the nearest cocoon with her bare paws, scrabbling at the sticky silk with her dull claws. It would have been faster to cut her way through the silk with a vibro-knife, but what if the captain was inside? What if she cut too deep?

The silk tore away, and under the tear, Lt. Vonn revealed segmented arms, folded as if in prayer, and a gun-metal gray carapace. Not the captain. Oh god, she hoped it was not the captain. He couldn't have been transformed so fully?

Lt. Vonn began ripping away at another cocoon and found another pupal Archidopteran beneath the silk. Another and another. She left the cocoons shredded, and the pupae underneath began stirring, their many

361

segmented legs twitching and antennae feeling around to taste the air in their new, adult forms. Another few minutes, and they'd be fully awake.

They'd be ready to wrap Lt. Vonn inside her own cocoon.

But then Lt. Vonn ripped through the silk of a smallish cocoon and found something different: segmented legs, folded as if in prayer… but they were pink. Like the captain's naked skin. With a sinking feeling, Lt. Vonn ripped more of the silk off and revealed a hideous hybrid, half Sphynx cat and half Archidopteran. The captain had grown antennae beside his triangular ears, and his muzzle had morphed into wide mandibles filled with writhing mouth parts.

But his gray-green eyes were the same.

Except filled with horror.

"Oh Captain," Lt. Vonn breathed. Her heart ached for the little cat, and her stomach churned with revulsion. She pulled the rest of the silk away from him and threw his small, strange body over one shoulder.

Then Lt. Vonn lifted the Consul from the floor and draped the otteroid's limp body over the other shoulder. The Consul's thick green fur had become studded with tiny star-like white flowers. Lt. Vonn didn't know what that meant, but the yellow lab knew that she needed to get out of here. Now.

But of course, the entrance to the chamber was blocked by a pair of Archidopterans, and the pupae that Lt. Vonn had freed early from their cocoons rose from their positions of repose, unfolding their arms and clacking their mandibles. The room was filled with towering insectoids, and Lt. Vonn didn't have half a chance of shooting her way out.

So, instead, she whispered a prayer and tapped the comm-pin on her breast. "Lt. LeGuin?" she barked. "Please for the sake of everything holy, tell me that you're receiving this and that the shuttle's teleporter isn't blocked by this ungodly ship's shields."

The Archidopterans encircled Lt. Vonn, raising their upper-most arms like they were dancing. One after another, the towering insectoids spat globs of sticky silk against the growling yellow Labrador.

Then the orange tabby's voice meowed from Lt. Vonn's comm-pin, "I can probably get off one teleportation before they block us, but I need an active comm-pin signal to lock onto."

"Not a problem; the captain and Consul Tor are in my arms!" On the final word, a glob of sticky silk hit Lt. Vonn in the face, filling her open mouth with a musty taste that made her gag and glued her muzzle shut. But then she felt the tingle of quantum energy in her chest, and her body flooded with relief.

The yellow lab, transmuted Sphynx cat, and photosynthetic otteroid disappeared in a shimmer of quantum energy and reappeared inside their own shuttle, where they promptly fell over, crashing onto the ground, too glued together by silk to do anything but lay there uselessly while Lt. LeGuin meowed at them.

"My goodness, but you three look a horror. I'm getting us out of here." The orange tabby kept them updated with a running monologue as he powered up the shuttle, fired an electron torpedo at the force field holding them in, and then piloted the shuttle back out of the Archidopteran vessel.

As the shuttle dodged electron torpedoes and red energy bolts, flying back through the fray towards the *Initiative*, something strange was happening on the deck inside. Lt. Vonn was struck by the beautiful harmony of the Archidopteran hive; Consul Tor felt her mind fill with terror at losing herself—was she even a cat anymore? Wait, had she ever been one? And Captain Jacques was flooded by the sense of safety and assurance that came with being the greatest breed of dog ever designed by man—a yellow Labrador was protected from all harm by the great love that had gone into designing it. His paws were big. Her ears floppy. He was a good... hive member who loved her Queen?

Lt. LeGuin piloted the shuttle back into the relative safety of the *Initiative*'s own welcoming shuttle bay. On the shuttle's floor, the rest of the reconnaissance team blurred and melded together, aided by Consul Tor's empathic abilities and the catalytic enzymes in the silk that half cocooned them together. Instead of a dog, a cat, and an otteroid, they'd become a mess of segmented legs, green and yellow fur, pink skin, and three pairs of eyes filled with deep, existential horror. They could see themself in the reflection of Lt. LeGuin's techno-focal goggles, as the orange tabby hit the comm-pin on his breast and meowed, "Doctor Keller, we have an emergency in the shuttle bay."

* * *

Consul Tor felt the captain's concern for his crew and Lt. Vonn's frustration with herself that she was lying on a bed in the medical bay rather than doing her job.

But... they were just feelings. Sensations that she could sense from outside of herself. No longer her own thoughts.

Consul Tor lifted her green-furred paws and held them above her face. They looked normal. The embarrassing white flowers were gone.

She shouldn't have been flowering at all. Not now. Not like that. She lifted herself up and looked around.

Lt. Vonn was lazing on her hospital bed, bouncing a ball off of the nearest wall to pass the time. Captain Jacques was a normal Sphynx cat again, and he held a dusty old book in his paws. But Consul Tor could tell he wasn't able to concentrate on reading it.

"You're awake!" a cheerful voice barked. Doctor Keller was a tall red dog with long curly ears. An Irish Setter and proud of it. A lot of the dogs onboard this vessel seemed inordinately proud of themselves, simply for being a particular type of dog.

Consul Tor shook her head at the strangeness of it. And yet, she'd experienced the sensation first-hand while she'd been melded with the captain and Consul Tor. It was a strange but harmless kind of pride.

While the doctor checked Consul Tor, scanning her with a unimeter and muttering about her alien physiology, another prideful dog burst into the medical bay.

But Cmdr. Bill Wilker wasn't proud of himself for being a dog right now. He was bursting with pride on behalf of… Consul Tor. The green otteroid felt a bashful modesty at the bright glow of Cmdr. Wilker's pride in her.

"Our hero has awoken!" he barked, rushing to Consul Tor's side. He took one of her green paws in his own and squeezed tight. "Thank you," the collie woofed. "You saved the captain."

"Lt. Vonn and Lt. LeGuin saved the captain, I think," Consul Tor said, lowering her eyes from the collie's intense gaze.

Lt. Vonn paused in bouncing her ball and gave the Consul a curt, appreciative nod. Then back to bouncing.

"They wouldn't have been over there without you." Cmdr. Wilker smoothed the flowing fur of his ruff that spilled out around his collar. "Besides, I've thanked each of them already. Lt. LeGuin as soon as he got back, and Lt. Vonn when she woke up a week ago."

"A week ago?" Consul Tor asked. "Has it been so long? What happened to the rest of the ship? All the other ships? Are we still fighting?"

Captain Jacques laid his dusty book down on his lap. "We won the battle. The jury's still out on the war." His pink ears flattened. "And yes, we've been trapped in this godforsaken sick bay all week."

"The flagship exploded only minutes after your shuttle escaped," Cmdr. Wilker barked. "After the flagship was destroyed, all the other ships… They ran out of fight. They simply withdrew from the sector, back the way they came."

"Good riddance," Lt. Vonn muttered, throwing her ball extra hard.

Consul Tor felt a confusing wave of loss. The Archidopteran Queen had manipulated her mind, altered the captain's body against his will, and would have experimented with her reproductive flowers if Lt. Vonn hadn't rescued her. Yet, the harmony of her hive had been beautiful. All those voices, joined together as one, in perfect accord and completely loved.

It wasn't worth it. The price for that accord and harmony was high. Much too high.

In comparison, the dogs and cats of the Tri-Galactic Navy were noisy and disjointed, a constant jumble of conflict and mixed-up emotions. They were chaotic. Uncontrollable. And they had saved the entire sector from the Archidopterans.

And Consul Tor loved them.

Military operations require more than soldiers. How will a medical unit for mixed-species troops operate?

Will their surgeons become any more inured to battle wounds?

Tooth, Claw and Fang

by Stephen Coghlan

Bullets, blades, tooth, claw and fang.

Surgeon Tucker knew it all, had seen it all. There was not one horrific injury of war that he was unfamiliar with. He was so experienced, that he only felt himself near the battlefield, where the sounds of distant explosions sometimes drowned out conversations, and the screams of the wounded nearly drove him as mad as those who made them, from the high pitched squeals of the rabbits, the chirps and sorrowful draws of breath from the avians, to the howling of the canines.

"Help me!" One turtle, his shell cracked from a blunt blow, begged for his life.

"Mommy!" A young beagle, barely past the age of pup, cried mercilessly.

"My vixen, my kits, I love you!" a seasoned fox gasped as his insides became septic.

There were too many to treat.

Concussion, decapitation, hemorrhage, poison.

The smell of war leached into everything. It stayed, permeated in flesh, fur and cloth for all eternity. It was the odor of carnage, cordite, viscera and blood.

It was all old and familiar to Surgeon Tucker. He was an old, grey-muzzled, once-chocolate-lab, and he had known nothing but pain and death about him for the better part of two days. Adjusting his mask, he leaned over the newest casualty. The gash was severe, and was not made by fangs normally reserved for flesh.

"A rabbit bit him, sir," one of the stretcher bearers said as they lowered the dying bobcat to the floor.

Tucker called out to Nurse Stypen, and the viper slithered over to drip her venom into the wound, coagulating the injury and stemming the flow of blood.

Amputation, trepanation, transfusion, injection

A new smell filled the air as the next stretcher arrived. The owl's wing was a mess, and charred feathers, burnt to ash, covered the entire side where a flaming projectile had landed on him. He was not long for the world. There was no point in working on the bird, it was a waste of precious resources and time, time that could be better used to patch someone else up and send them out again to die.

"Priest," Tucker called, and hurried to inspect the next arrival.

* * *

Serenity, silence, hesitation.

There was no quiet, and the only end that Tucker took was when exhaustion claimed him. He had been so unsteady on his legs that he had to be led away by Stypen's undulating form.

He had awakened hours later, with the sun, and had not been surprised to find that Stypen, Susan, was naked against his back. She too had been tired, and had used the old canine's heat to sooth her serpentine body into sleep.

Other doctors hurried back and forth from their tents to the chaos of their 'office'. Surgeons yelled for supplies and aid, stretcher bearers carried the wounded from the battlefield, and delivered the dying to their hopeful salvation.

Stretching, Tucker adjusted his tail and tried to arise without disturbing his companion. He failed. With a hiss, Susan threw her tail about her friend.

"We can wait," she said, with naked hostility in her tone.

"No," Tucker answered. "Not while the battle rages."

"You won't be good to anyone right now. You haven't eaten since Sunday morning," his nurse reminded him. He knew she was right and so he searched about for a clean shirt.

* * *

Rest, relax, regain and return.

The food was typical breakfast fare. Vegetables for the herbies, meat for the carnies, grass for digestion, and mixed plates for the omnis.

As he stood in line, Surgeon Tucker admitted to himself that he was a bit pekish. Red muscle that dripped with fat stared him in the eyes. The edges of the breakfast flank was seared nicely, and he knew that the inside would be pinkish-red, just like the few herded humans it had been harvested from.

For the first time, he found himself unable to eat.

He returned the meal to the chef. He could have selected some jerky, but its tough and dried texture reminded him of the bodies that had been left out to rot; how the skin dried out and pulled into weather-worn leather.

Eventually he settled on two biscuits, and chewed them with no compassion.

* * *

Contusion, laceration, puncture, fibrillation.

"I need plasma!" someone called from the back of the tent, but Tucker ignored the call. He was elbow deep into a young pup who screamed in agony because the painkillers had yet to take effect.

"What's his heartrate?" he yelled himself.

Susan studied the portable. "He's dropping. The liver's too torn, and one set of lungs have collapsed. We can't save him. Move on, Tucker."

"No!" he shouted. The poor pup was so young, but he was also only the second patient that Tucker had gotten to in six hours. Behind him others had arrived, and some had died awaiting aid that never came. "I can help him."

"We're wasting time. Please, Doctor, move on."

The pup's eyes rolled in their sockets.

"Don't you dare give up, soldier." Tucker ordered, and for a moment the youth seemed to pull himself together, but then the spasms began.

"Hold still!" the surgeon yelled, but the motions of the pup moved the clamp he had been trying to close. Instead of sealing the blood vessel, it tore it open, and the young one's life-fluids spilled out of the hole and over the old surgeon's scrubs.

It was futile, now.

With a curse that was heard over the din of death, Surgeon Tucker ripped his hands free from his inflicted cavity. He fought with himself, and after a moment of struggle, suppressed the urge to howl his rage at the Gods.

A cough from behind startled him, and before he turned to face whoever had dared to approach him, Tucker looked his nurse in the eyes. Her scales had gone white with fear.

Behind him, stood the base's commanding officer.

* * *

Regret, surprise, disappointment.

She was an old career soldier, and although she had started her military career as a nurse, her attitude had been perfect for the forces. She had risen from a buck recruit all the way to the rank of Colonel. She was ten years Tucker's junior, but she had a list of accomplishments that dwarfed the old lab's. It was her alpha attitude, and it had served her well.

She paced in front of the beaten surgeon. For a while, she had berated and belittled him, and her hackles had risen, and her ears had gone flat against her skull. She had bared her fangs and snarled and at times, the ferocity that was her birthright had almost surfaced into physical rage, but she knew better than that. She had not achieved her rank through a lack of control.

"I liked you, Conscript." The she-wolf growled. "Do you know why?"

Question, interrogation, assumption.

Tucker remained silent.

"It's because you were as ruthless about patching our troops up, as the enemy was about tearing them apart. There is no room on the frontline for compassion. We need efficiency. We can't afford to be wasting resources and time on lost causes. We are in a constant emergency triage situation. Tell me what your job is again."

It was an order.

"Assess," Tucker began automatically. The words that came from his mouth were ones that had been drilled into him countless times in his career, both in the civilian world, and the militant one. "Treat those who we can save."

"And do no harm," the colonel concluded. "You used up vital supplies, and more importantly, your time, patching up those two wounded. Thanks to you we are now shorter by four liters of plasma, yards of bandages, and hours of your time. Thanks to your attempts to save them, we had six other patients bleed out, two suffocate on their own blood, and countless others who could have returned to the lines instead stay, and take up what little space we have.

"What happened to you?"

"I don't know ma'am." He answered his superior. "But it won't happen again."

She looked as if she was about to comment, but whatever she was about to say died in her throat. With a nod and a wave of her hand, she dismissed him.

Efficiency.

* * *

Shrapnel, flame, impact, carnage.

It was getting worse. The flow of wounded had only increased. No matter how tirelessly they worked, the staff could not stem the tides that washed upon them. No one was spared. Young recruits, barely out of training arrived with missing limbs and caved skulls. Veterans, scarred from campaigns, were brought forth with projectiles lodged in their vitals, or shattered bones, or venom flooded fluids.

Assess, treat, or ignore.

Tucker was on his twelfth patient within the hour. He had just set the shoulder of a badger who had a dislocated arm, thanks to a ferocious battle with a moose.

Blood, viscera, offal.

The next patient was brought forth. Unlike others, this one was not brought to Tucker via the bearers, nor was he a walking-wounded who had found his way to the medics under his own power. The young trooper had been supported by a companion. Both the injured degu and his helper looked alike, and Tucker guessed they must have been litter-mates.

"Please Doc, help him," the uninjured one pleaded.

As he guided the wounded to his operating table, Tucker noticed the pale flesh underneath the fur, the rolling eyes, and the pink frothing foam that coated the mouth. A metal post, one used to support wire, had been used as an improvised spear and had gouged through the young lagomorph's side.

The wounded did not scream as he was inspected.

There was no way to help him. The ribs were crushed, the liver was torn, the stomach ruptured. He was living on borrowed time.

Do no harm.

"Please," the helper begged, and held his companion's hand. "He's my brother."

There was a chance, but it was a fool's endeavor.

"Doctor," Nurse Stypen hissed.

With a start, Tucker realized that he had been idle and unmoving. He opened his mouth to speak, but no words came out. He could not move. He was frozen, in a tableau of horror and indecision.

"They're lining up." Susan reminded the surgeon.

"Help him!"

"Move it."

"He's dying."

"He's my only family left."

"We have to keep going."

"Do something."

His dilemma was solved as, with a rattle and a gargle, his patient breathed his last.

It was over.

Bowing his head, Tucker reached out with one paw, and closed the late soldier's eyes, and then, despite all his training, despite his years of experience, despite his best efforts, he began to cry.

* * *

Recovery, altruism, apathy.

Her body, heated from his, was warm against him. It was a welcome comfort, a respite from the horrors of the day. At first, he had not thought himself able to continue, but his nurse and confidant had been there to provide much needed support, and somehow, the next fourteen hours, although a blur in his memory, had passed.

He had lost track of every procedure he had performed, and was unable to recall if he had saved anyone's life, or merely patched them up well enough so that his charges could return to the slaughter of the lines.

He had no memory of making it to his bunk, and no recollection of what had transpired there, but he felt Susan's body press against his, and he felt, for a moment, fine with the world.

It was a false serenity.

Without warning, he started to weep. Tucker tried, as best as he could, to be mute, but he could not repress the tears that rolled down his cheeks and around his greyed muzzle. His aching body trembled, from fatigue of body and soul.

"Shh," Susan whispered from her daze of the half-sleep. Her scaled arms tightened about him, like a constrictor, but the hold was comforting.

"What's wrong with me?" Tucker wondered as he managed to stumble the words from his mouth in a mumble of blubbering.

A soft kiss pressed against his neck, and the action soothed jagged nerves.

After a time, he quieted. The two lay there in the pre-dawn darkness. Neither moved until nature's urge disturbed the lab, and he left the bed for the comfort of the communal pole. When he returned, Susan was sitting up, the rough blanket was held against her body to fight off the morning chill. There was room so he sat beside her and stared at the wall. Observers would have thought that his gaze was glaring into infinity.

The blanket was wrapped around him, and he was cocooned once more with his companion. Her tail wrapped around his waist, and her head rested on his back.

"What am I doing wrong?" Tucker asked, but this time the question was focused and directed.

"You're beginning to care," she mumbled in reply.

It was sobering news. Tucker had always had a commitment to his patients, but he had long ago thought that he had limited his compassion to that of a cold, clinical attitude. The news that he was becoming vulnerable was a shock. Considering his advanced age, he should have only been more calloused.

What had gotten through his carefully crafted cynicism?

* * *

Alterations, respite, restoration.

It was not hard to get a weekend pass. After all, Tucker had worked for almost a straight year without a break.

The hubbub of city life was different and far more alien than the noise of the medical unit. People talked freely and optimistically, not whispered in dire tones or screamed in mortal anguish. Occupants walked about, not huddled in foxholes or scrambled desperately towards imagined salvation. Food was fresh and plentiful and a luxury to be savored, not a necessity to be crammed down one's throat simply for sustenance. Above all though, the smells had changed from the rank odor of carnage and spilled viscera into the scent of various species, musks, perfumes, gas burning cars, diesel fumes, cooking oils.

Tucker had spent the first day wandering the city in a daze, and he had barely done anything but watch civilization move across his eyes.

That night, he had slept and he only heard the passing of trains, the honking of horns, the clicking of the radiator, and the buzz of the radio. He had a dreamless night, and awoke refreshed.

He tried to live his moments of freedom to their fullest. He took in a play, smoked a cigar, and gorged himself on food and drink, and not one moment made him feel complete. He felt no joy, no sadness, nothing. All he had was an empty hole for a soul.

When he crawled into bed that night, he tossed and turned until he realized what had bothered him.

Something was missing, someone, who had begun to find a spot through his embittered exterior.

He returned to base a full day early by stopping a passing truck filled with fresh meat for the grinder of battle. The troops were only happy to drop him off, it wasn't that far out of their way, but every distraction allowed them another moment away from the risk of injury and death.

She was in their bunk, alone, exhausted, cold.

He climbed in beside her, and gathered her into his arms.

They made love that night, and for the rest of his leave, they shared what precious time they had before they returned to the chaos.

Despair to love. Confusion to comprehension.

With less than an hour before his forced return, Tucker lay beside his lover, and tenderly stroked one hand down nurse Stypen's cheek. They stared into each other's eyes. Her slit pupils radiated the warmth that she felt.

The scent of their love was everywhere, but neither of them cared.

"In two months," he began. "My contract is over."

"One, for me." She purred like a cat.

There was an unspoken agreement between them.

"Wait for me," he requested.

She kissed him in answer.

* * *

Excited, scared, he dressed for work. He didn't know what he would do. He felt anxious and nervous. He was uncertain about his feelings.

Taking her hand, they began to walk to the tent, where the casualties awaited.

She never got there.

The first shell landed without warning, and the explosion was felt, not heard. The enemy artillery had found their camp.

Faster than sound, the explosives rained upon the heads of the wounded and staff alike. No one was safe. Tents were shredded by shrapnel, flesh liquefied by blasts, heat scorched hair and skin.

They died by the dozens.

As soon as it began, it stopped. The guns of the enemy had been found by the guns of the allies, and retribution was swift and brutal.

It was too late.

He knelt beside her still form. A small dimple had appeared beside her eye where the fragment had entered her skull, bounced off bone, and scrambled her brain. She was no more.

Deafened by the explosions, Tucker heard nothing, not even his own wailing voice as he cradled his late lover in his arms and howled his agony into the sky. He was torn, broken, never to be complete again. Unwilling to understand what had happened, he kissed the already cooling lips, felt for a pulse, pleaded with the Gods and fate.

The hole that she had filled in his soul, collapsed, imploded, withered and died.

He set her still body gently to the ground and covered her lifeless corpse with his coat. He felt cold inside, removed from all reality, empty and incapable in his shock.

"Thank you," he whispered, as he felt the emotions leave him. Standing, he shook the dust from his scrubs. He felt nothing at all as he returned to work.

He had a job to do.

Earth settles a colony world with uplifted animals who fight the native intelligent animals. Then interstellar conquerors arrive, and the Earth animals are caught in the middle.

Is this an opportunity for Johannes Kittinger, a coyote? A far-distant people had the saying, "The enemy of my enemy is my friend". Can Johannes apply it here?

Sacrifice

by J.N. Wolfe

"Control to Zeta Squad. Gamma will be your next target area. Prepare for the signal."

Johannes acknowledged the message with two quick presses of his silent reply button, then sighted down his rifle over the chosen target area. The short, lithe fox was panting as the sun beat down from overhead, and his paws were damp with sweat.

Like the bulk of the colonists from Earth, Johannes was an offshoot of humanity whose ancestors were genetically engineered to resemble bipedal, anthropomorphic animals.

Heightened senses together with innate defenses in the forms of fangs, claws and fur combined with a hardy constitution to give them a tremendous edge when tackling the unknowns of a new planet. This also made them superb soldiers.

Johannes' chosen perch, an abandoned five-story residence, gave a great view of the various training targets, but the stone that formed the building's structure soaked up the harsh, midday heat far too readily.

Even with his thinly-shorn fur, the heat was overwhelming. It had started to affect his concentration. Johannes fought the urge to use any pills to keep sharp. His only reprise was his canteen. He sipped some of the tepid water from his drinking tube, willing the training to move faster, and recited a mantra to keep from thinking about the heat.

It did not help that the camo net he had erected to protect him from any visual observation also acted as another layer of insulation to trap the heat.

"Control to Zeta Two. Target drones one, four, and seven." *This is my time to shine!* thought Johannes. Without sparing the time to reply,

Johannes magnified the view on his scope, easily picking out his targets among the crowds of milling drones. The numbers stenciled on the targets were small, but his acute vulpine vision combined with the high-tech scope made it effortless. The first target was barely moving, and he caressed the trigger just as the crosshairs passed its head.

Bam.

The loud bark of his sniper rifle echoed among the walls of other nearby buildings as his first target went down. *Bam. Bam.* The other two drones he'd sighted were just starting to run their avoidance programs before they both took hits to their heads and collapsed.

Several haptic buzzes from the comm unit clasped around his wrist caught Johannes's attention, and he spared a quick sideward glance. His scores had leapt to the top of the leaderboard. *Yes! I'm going to do this!*

Other target drones started to fall as his fellow recruits took down their assigned targets. For a while, the air was filled with the loud reports of sniper rifles amongst the racket of various drones crunching into the ground.

Johannes flicked an ear as a low rumble caught his attention. It was like a low growl, something you'd hear when a tank or large vehicle idled nearby. He could feel it raking through his body, as if he were standing too close to a club's subwoofers.

"Control to Zeta Squad! Emergency situation, eva…" Johannes narrowed his eyes, and his heart started to beat a tiny bit faster just as a warning symbol lit up on his wrist comm: *No Command Signal Detected.*

The rumbling intensified. In the vast expanse of sky in front of him, a flight of burning meteors broke into view, fiery chariots charging ahead of an iridescent green spacecraft. The spacecraft gave Johannes an impression of a ridged worm fused around a conch, and he thought that several orifices were pulsing even as the craft careened through the atmosphere.

A sliver of cold ran down his back. This had to be *Species 710!* The unnamed, the incommunicable. The aliens who had appeared several decades ago, with their only impetus to consume, reproduce, and spread. This colony planet was far from the warfront where humanity and its allies stood to hold the line, but space was big. One of theirs must have slipped through a crack and found this backwater colony.

Certain that it was time to retreat, Johannes abandoned all stealth and tossed the camo net aside. He snatched up only the essentials before bolting to the opposite end of the roof, towards his planned escape route. Even as he ran, a white glow burst through the heavens, a solid beam of light that smashed hard against the enemy craft: an energy lance attack from one of the defense satellites.

The shockwave from the impact arrived in seconds, a wild expanding tornado that picked up anything not bolted down, a churning whirlwind of sand, rock, and broken metal. Johannes gritted his teeth as the tsunami of debris picked him off his feet. He twisted in mid-air, guided by his vulpine reflexes, and landed on all fours, letting the momentum carry him into a roll before he recovered into a crouch.

Looking up, Johannes gasped. The alien ship had survived the attack! The energy lance should have reduced the ship into a pile of slush, but the atmosphere had reduced the effectiveness of the attack.

The alien craft was now covered in large cracks and trailed a large plume of greenish smoke. Viscous purple fluid seeped from the cracks and rained down over the worn landscape. Whatever form of propulsion that kept it flying had apparently failed, and the ship was now dipping downwards in a steep dive.

Johannes had finally arrived at the other end of the roof. He pulled out a coil of rope stashed behind an air recycler. Johannes tugged the end of the rope that he had previously secured to the roof, then tossed the bundle over the side.

Above him, the great bulk of the alien ship was tearing itself apart as the stresses of entering the atmosphere and the energy lance assault took their toll. Bits and pieces of smaller debris rained down all around Johannes, a shower of smoking gore and hard shell fragments. Johannes thought he saw some of the pieces move of their own accord.

Tearing himself away from the sight, Johannes flung himself over the parapet and hung tight to the rope, taking a few deep breaths to calm down before climbing down as fast as he could.

The sound of something large retching suddenly crossed his ears, and a large ivory spike embedded itself mere inches from his head. Surprised, Johannes let go of his grip around the rope and fell. Several more spikes impacted where his head would have been even as he gripped hard to slow his descent.

Twisting his head, Johannes cursed as two alien creatures strode up to the guard rail of the opposite roof. They looked like headless ostriches covered in chitin, and had several dark, glistening holes in the center of their torso. Their eyeless visages tracked his progress with nary a sound.

Johannes barely held onto the rope; his combat gloves were overheated from the rapid descent. *Damn it. I think this is low enough!* he thought, and released his grip to fall the last few meters.

More spikes impacted above him as he fell feet first towards the ground. He landed hard and almost fell over, but his tail had instinctively whipped out as a counterbalance and he merely stumbled.

Turning, Johannes dashed towards an abandoned car he had glimpsed on his way down. He dove behind it just as even more spikes embedded themselves in the ground behind his feet.

Johannes growled in anger. Ahead of him, meters away in an adjacent building, was safety and escape through the water recycling tunnels.

The two creatures above had stopped shooting any spikes, and were probably waiting for him to show a paw, an ear, before their next barrage turned him into a foxy pin-cushion. Johannes knew that time was not on his side—among the debris that had fallen was very likely more of their comrades.

Dark shadows flicked across the ground, and keening cries pierced the air. Johannes glanced up just as a flight of creatures with narrow, delicate bodies held aloft by long, bat-like wings flew over him. The creatures turned in a gentle bank. Johannes was certain that they were circling around to rip the fur off his skin if he didn't get away in the next few seconds.

Pulling out a trio of grenades, Johannes armed them and tossed them onto the dirt road that lay between him and safety, then ducked behind the car with his muzzle open and paws clamped down on his ears.

The three grenades went off moments apart, their explosions kicking up a massive cloud of dust; a cover that Johannes hoped would block the view of the alien spike creatures.

As luck would have it, the wind blew in his favor, pushing the thick brown dust cloud towards his destination. Gripping his rifle tightly, he ducked low, held his breath and sprinted into the cloud, eyes squeezed shut against the fine floating grains.

Johannes could hear several loud, spitting sounds followed by the thuds of spikes embedding themselves in the dirt around him. The dust cloud was working! The entrance to the building was just several footsteps away when Johannes felt his foot sink into a patch of loose sand. A cloud of dirt billowed forth from under his foot, and he felt shards of hot, sharp pain slice through his body.

A single thought ran through his mind—*LANDMINE!*—before he collapsed into the dreamless dark of death.

* * *

Johannes awoke with a jerk. His heart pounded deep in his chest, and he blinked deeply to help his eyes focus on his surroundings, gulping down huge breaths of air as he did. He grabbed blindly for a weapon, something to defend himself, but felt only the soft... *a mattress?*

The whitewashed walls of the academy's medical ward greeted his bleary eyes. The familiar scent of antiseptic and freshly laundered sheets danced through his nostrils. The windows in the room were open, and strong sunlight diffused through white, translucent drapes. Johannes's ears twitched in recognition of a buzzing, cutting sound that could be heard from afar, and the scent of freshly cut grass touched his nose.

Panic slowly retreated, replaced by the pangs of distress as he remembered what happened. The test. A crucial final test, and he had most likely failed it. A suffocating tightness started to well in his chest. He fought the onslaught of tears, but several drops seeped into his fur.

A light knock on the door startled him from his distress, and the door opened gently as the familiar visage of Cieran poked his muzzle though the narrow gap. Thankfully, he was looking down the room, and Johannes hurriedly wiped a paw over his eyes and pushed himself up into a sitting position.

"Johannes," said Cieran. "You are awake. Have the simulation drugs worn off?"

Not trusting his voice to be steady, Johannes shrugged and pretended to cough. Cieran was one of his squadmates, a lean, compact coyote whose fur was dappled in various shades of sand.

Cieran strode into the room and stood beside Johannes. "We're moving on to jungle training today. We're packing up the barracks now."

Johannes, slightly nonplussed, managed, "Am I going to join?"

Cieran shook his head. "No. You were the only one not to clear the mines. Right now, your orders are to rest and speak with the camp counselor."

Johannes nodded, and realized why he was the only one in the ward. None of his squadmates had received the simulated shock to their system like him. His ears flattened as he struggled to keep his disappointment in check.

"Here," said Cieran, who pulled out what seemed like a get-well card from his combat vest and passed it to Johannes. "We're supposed to leave in an hour, so we can't all come visit."

Johannes accepted the card with a paw and Cieran continued. "I must go. We have lots to pack; I'm not sure how we can finish in time." Cieran then turned to leave the room, only pausing at the doorway to give Johannes a curt nod before shutting the door.

Johannes sighed, wishing the other members of the squad, nay, any other member of the squad, would have been able to deliver the card. Many people found it difficult to interact with Cieran outside of training. His manner, like most of the people from the Mahinjah Wastes, was always clipped and to the point. Attempts at small-talk usually resulted in a glare and stilted replies. A reflection of living in scarcity, many anthropologists claimed.

Opening the envelope, Johannes discovered that it was not a card, but a photo from the squad's initiation day. Three ordered rows of canids sat, knelt, or stood in front of their barracks, and a chicken scratch of signatures from the various squad members adorned the back. Words of well-wishing and encouragement were scribbled among the signatures. *Get well soon! Wish you were coming! Try again!*

Johannes smiled mirthlessly at the supportive words, and pondered what he could possibly do to stay on in the military—in a combat role—and yawned. The drugs that gave the illusion of real combat were extremely draining, and Johannes had barely put the photo away before his eyes fell shut, unbidden. For a time, there were no cares in the world.

* * *

Johannes was mildly surprised when he entered the counselling room. Instead of Mr. Erikson, an old civilian bear, he was met by a female Maine coon dressed in a sharp dress-uniform. Her well-groomed fur was soot-black, and her rank pips exhibited her rank of Major. The feline's long, fluffy tail was curled peaceably around an adjacent side table.

"Recruit Kittinger reporting, Ma'am!" said Johannes, his arm snapping up in salute as he moved to stand at attention.

"At ease, Johannes. Take a seat," she said, standing to return the salute before gesturing with a paw to a nearby chair. The counselor, Major Lisa Katheryn, explained that Mr. Erikson had taken a short leave of absence. As an old friend, she'd answered his call to temporarily cover his duties.

"So, Johannes," said Major Katheryn as she went through his file, "what I'm seeing in your record so far is quite... surprising. You've only qualified for training with either the sniping quad or the bomb disposal unit, and you've had three attempts with the sniping squad. Inadequate physique was the problem in the first attempt, which you've surpassed. Good. And the last two were for failing to clear the final sniping evaluation. You did well enough that they allowed you the last two retries. In all honesty," she said, closing the folder, "I would have recommended that you either return to civilian life, or choose a non-combat role after the second attempt."

Johannes nodded, uncertain if he should speak.

Major Katheryn crossed her legs and continued. "But somehow, you've managed to slip through and kept on going. Tell me Johannes, why are you so driven to be in a role on the front lines?"

"It's family, Ma'am. My parents were both soldiers, and the military life is what I grew up with. I can't think of any other life."

"Indeed," she said, tapping the folder in her paw. "From your records, you bounced around the various bases with your mother till you were of legal age, then you applied for a combat role. Adapting to civilian life can be difficult, and some choose to start a career in the support regiments just for that reason. But to keep trying for a combat role takes someone with a different mental... fortitude.

"I'll be honest, Johannes. The higher ups want you either transferred to the support battalions, or to pass you out as a civilian," said Major Katheryn, leaning forward. "So there must be more to it. What drives you to keep going? Revenge?"

The thought of revenge never occurred to Johannes, and he recoiled upon hearing the accusation. "No Ma'am! It's... something more personal."

She sat back and motioned for him to continue.

Taking a deep breath, he looked Major Katheryn in her eyes and said, "I never met my father. He died by taking a bomb to save me. Mom adopted me. This is... This is about... I don't know how to articulate it. Responsibility? He died saving me. I owe him, them, a debt I can never repay, and this is the only way I know how. To be like him, saving kids like me."

She tilted her head and looked quizzically at Johannes. "Kids like yourself?"

Johannes barely realized that his claws were out, tearing grooves along the well-worn wood of his armchair. "I remember growing up in a POW camp, mostly us kids, segregated from the adults. We worked the surface mines. One day snipers came, took out the watch towers, then troops assaulted the camp, saved us."

Johannes drew in a deep breath and finished. "I want to do the work my father did. Save more kids. People. No one deserves to be treated like we were."

Major Katheryn sat back and nodded, a tight smile lilting her short muzzle. "Paying it forward? Very commendable. But Johannes, listen. There are many ways of supporting the war effort without being a combatant. From what I see from your aptitude tests, you would do well in many non-combat roles."

Johannes gave a quick exhale. "Ma'am, I know what the results of those tests say. But that's not me. I've already done my time in the kitchen and armory, and I know I won't find satisfaction in the transport divisions or any other support battalion."

Johannes leaned forward. "I know I'm not the best, physically. And I'm not tall enough for other combat roles. But this, sniping, I can do it. It's in my blood. One more chance, I'm sure I can clear it! Please."

Major Katheryn looked aside for a moment to gather her thoughts before she turned back to Johannes with a sad shake of her head, "That is not possible. Hear me out please." she said, as Johannes folded his ears back. "Command has given me an order to place you somewhere else. Now, if you are still insistent on wanting to fight on the front lines, you only have one choice, that's through the bomb disposal training. Apart from that… It's the support battalions.

"I have this feeling that you want to mirror your father, Johannes. But sometimes, these are not paths we are meant to walk. From what I see, you will do very well in a bomb disposal role. Now, if what you want to do is to save more people, they're doing a very important role, just not always at the bleeding edge.

"What do you say, Johannes, do you want to try this new path?"

"Ma'am, surely there's a way for me to try out one last time with the snipers? I'm already certified on the rifle, just not the role…"

She shook her head firmly. "Sorry, Johannes. Even if I didn't have orders from higher up, I wouldn't let you try again. I am confident though, that your skills would be well used with the bomb-d squad. Unless of course you would prefer a role in the support battalions?"

"No, Ma'am," Johannes bit out.

"Very well then. I'll see that you are transferred over to the bomb-d training battalion for their next intake." Major Katheryn then stood up, and Johannes followed suit. Instead of a salute, she offered Johannes her paw and said, "I hope that you find what you are looking for, Johannes."

"Thanks, Ma'am," said Johannes, shaking her paw. "I hope so too. If I may take my leave?"

"Of course."

* * *

"I can't believe it! Only two more weeks and we are done!" said the grinning coyote. Corey Hamilton, a native from the Grejoha Highlands, was hopping from foot to foot. Both he and Johannes were outfitted in the brown-grey camo uniforms of the bomb disposal squads. On their backs were compact backpacks that housed their survival gear, and their bomb disposal tools were held in low-profile webbing strapped across their waists.

Both canines carried standard assault rifles, but Johannes had received special dispensation to continue using his sniper's barrel, and it hung off a quick-release strap on his webbing.

"I know, right! I still can't believe I managed to clear that last test!" said Johannes.

"Hah! Lies!" exclaimed Corey, giving Johannes a friendly punch to his shoulder. "You are the top bomb-d recruit they've had in years. Fact is, I overheard Captain Demir saying you'll probably get a posting with the War Dogs."

"Really?" said Johannes, his tail involuntarily wagging. "The War Dogs! They're one of the top combat battalions!"

Corey frowned at this. "They're always on frontline combat duty, though. A guard posting in the highlands is all I want."

Johannes smiled at this, and turned to glance out over their squad's patrol area. "It's not so bad. They are one of those battalions that rescue slaves. It's not like we're fighting those alien insect things. I'd love to join them."

Corey grunted a noncommittal reply.

Glancing down at his wrist comm, Johannes checked the time. "Layla's late. She should have been here ten minutes ago."

The rest of their squad were patrolling the perimeter of their training area, and the two canids were tasked to stand guard in one of the man-made trenches scattered about the area. It was just deep enough for them to peer over and fire their rifles without needing to stand on tip-toes, and wide enough for five soldiers to comfortably stand abreast.

Corey had barely started to respond when he was suddenly launched headfirst against the back of the trench. The coyote smacked into the bare earth with a sickening crack, and slid down in a limp, crumpled mess. Blood streaked down the sides of Corey's dust-brown muzzle, his helmet cracked apart right down the middle.

Johannes immediately shoved off backwards, hitting the ground hard beside his fallen friend. *Sniper!* Breathing hard, he crawled over to his squadmate and pushed the shattered remains of Corey's helmet off. *The hell is this?! I thought we had a treaty with the natives!* The coyote was still breathing but unconscious. His helmet had borne the brunt of the assault and the shattered pieces had left several deep cuts on Corey's forehead.

A wiggle of motion among the remnants of Corey's helmet caught Johannes' eye. A small piece of green-brown metal that resembled a crumpled bullet was moving, shaking itself out. A new wave of adrenaline coursed through Johannes. *No! This can't be!* He immediately drew his survival knife and stabbed down hard at the offending creature, cutting it in twain with a sharp, brittle crack. *What are the aliens doing here!* The bisected creature ceased its motions as its purple blood seeped into the Earth.

"Great Maker," muttered Johannes under his breath, wiping his now-chipped blade against the earth. The creature's shell was unbelievably hard, and Johannes felt like he had just stabbed a rock. This colony planet was far from the war-border that stopped the aliens from encroaching upon Earth. Why were they here?

Glancing nervously at the edges of the trench, Johannes tapped his wrist comm, but it was unable to establish a connection to any friendly units. The words "Signal Jamming" lit up a corner of the comm's display. *We're in big trouble!* Johannes thought. The invaders emitted a natural energy field that tended to jam communications, but only in large groups. He and his squad had to have fallen into the thick of it.

Thankfully, they had an old-school way of communications that would be unaffected by the jamming.

Twisting to his side, Johannes pulled out a flare magazine and set the color code to purple: enemy contact. Loading it into his rifle, Johannes then fired the special bullets into the air above him.

The flares exploded with sharp bangs a fair distance above Johannes, forming an expanding purple cloud lit from within by brightly shining points that would mark his position—for both friend and foe.

Swapping back to regular ammunition, Johannes stooped down to check on Corey, but a soft hiss from above caused his fur to prick up. Johannes lifted his head to look at the source of the hiss, and found himself looking at a green-shelled creature that was resting on the lip of the trench. Spider-like legs sprouted from under its jaw, serving to pull its swollen body along. Its eyeless visage turned towards Johannes, and its maw, layered with teeth like a shark, opened and hissed in a joyless grin.

The alien creature flopped itself over the edge, landing on its side a mere hand-span from where Johannes crouched. Still hissing, it somehow righted itself, and started to scrabble its way towards Johannes.

Johannes yelped in fear and jumped to his feet before delivering a swift kick at the creature. It was just about as effective as kicking a rock. The creature was far denser than he had expected and it simply replied with an angry hiss that caused Johannes to pedal backwards.

Quickly taking stock of the situation, Johannes slid the safety off his rifle and his other arm rose to support the barrel. The rifle shuddered in his grip as a torrent of bullets fell upon the slug-thing, causing it to crack apart. Even with most of it already shredded by the bullets, what remained of the torn up organism was attempting its best to wiggle forward before Johannes let rip with another hail of bullets to permanently put it down.

Ejecting the empty magazine, Johannes swapped in a fresh load and cocked his rifle, ready for the next assault. *I wonder if I should have used the sniper barrel,* pondered Johannes, panting and shaking from the exertion. *Nah, I only have that one magazine left.*

Johannes moved back to crouch besides Corey as even more of the creatures clustered around the rim of the trench. By this time, he and Corey were surrounded by hissing sounds all around them, and several more of the alien creatures appeared and dropped in on them. One of the green alien-things landed atop its fallen comrade, and started to feast on the splattered remains. Johannes curled his lips in disgust as he brought his rifle to bear.

Short seconds and two magazines later, the aliens were reduced to cracked, smoking piles of chitin and gore. *Damn it, only two mags left,* thought Johannes as he checked his webbing. Even with the few more magazines that he could pilfer from Corey, those would not last long and Johannes hated the idea of leaving his friend behind.

Of more concern was the creature that had sniped Corey. With it out there, none of them were safe.

While he was fighting off the last wave of aliens, the distant sound of gunfire had greeted his ears. Distant, but definitely friendly. It was coming from the direction of the sniper, which meant that the rest of the squad was probably fighting off the invaders to get to him. *Maybe the HQ guard is doing a flanking maneuver?* he thought, which meant that any surviving enemy units would be pushed his way.

Not hearing any more hisses, Johannes swung his rifle around on its strap and knelt on one knee to pull out several magazines from Corey's webbing. A small metal piece slid out from one of the pockets as he retrieved the magazines. *A mirror!*

Discarding the used magazines, Johannes stuffed the fresh ones into his combat harness and brought the mirror up to the lip of the trench. *Maybe I can see where the sniper is… At least I can look out now.* Peering into the mirror, a wide, shark toothed grin of yet another alien creature peered back at him.

Dropping the mirror, Johannes bounded to the other side of the trench and sprayed the newcomer with bullets till his rifle gave out with a *click*.

Great Maker! thought Johannes, his heart racing once again. An extremely large alien creature had been perched just above the lip of the trench. Did he kill it?

Shaking his head, he ejected the spent magazine and let it fall on the ground, then slammed a fresh one in. Muscle memory was doing all the work as his mind ran wild on fear.

A snake-like movement caught the edge of his vision, and he ducked, then fired a hail of bullets at what looked like a muscular bundle of rope topped with a bulbous protrusion. The bullets had seemingly no effect; whatever Johannes had managed to hit simply bounced off. Johannes heard deep scrabblings as it approached. *This has to be a tail of some alien!*

As Johannes crawled back to where Corey was, something travelled up the tail, like a rodent passing through the gullet of a snake. *This is the sniper!* he realized, and flattened himself to the ground and dodged sideways just as the bulbous protrusion elongated, then spat at him and moved out of sight. The projectile slammed into the earth just in front of his face.

Like before, the bullet-creature had survived its high-velocity birth, and was now struggling to free itself. Johannes brought his rifle up and fired, obliterating its threat to him and Corey.

Moments later, the sniper creature's tail appeared above the trench, and Johannes threw himself forward. The creature's tail shuddered and spat again before moving out of sight, missing as Johannes was too close, too low for it to hit. Another bullet from Johannes took out the newly-born projectile-creature.

A loud hiss suddenly pierced the air, and the creature jumped into the trench, landing heavily on long, insect-like legs that sprouted from its underside. Its two foremost limbs were living shears that looked well ready to tear through sheet metal. Its gaping mouth was similar to the smaller aliens that Johannes had wiped out earlier, but on a far larger scale. Its, long segmented tail, the creature's long-range sniping weapon, grew from a thick, bud-like growth midway along the creature's body. Two long tendrils wavered above its body, sprouting from somewhere along its underside.

Johannes crouched and emptied the magazine into the creature, but the large newcomer was far better equipped to survive Johannes's attack. The bullets simply pinged off the hard carapace, leaving nary a scratch and embedded themselves into the hard packed earth of the trench. The only response of the creature was to move forward, slowly, deliberately.

His rifle was close to overheating. A fine steam rose from the barrel, boiling what water vapor was in the air as he emptied his last magazine upon his foe. The creature still continued its slow, determined advance.

The regular bullets were useless; it was time to up the ante. *Damn, this is gonna hurt!* he though, engaging the barrel release. Even through his combat gloves, the overheated button seared daggers into his thumb, and he yelped as the smoking barrel dropped into the earth before him. Without a thought, he kicked the fallen barrel at the creature.

The alien slowed its movements and pulled its limbs closer to its carapace, as if the hot metal now between it and Johannes was a difficult bridge to cross. Its tail, previously curled around the base of its bulbous protrusion, now whipped up and aimed directly at Johannes.

By this time, Johannes had installed the sniper barrel onto his rifle, and jammed his only magazine with the sniper bullets into place. The alien had now come to a stop in front of the fallen barrel, and a small bulge was moving up its tail.

It was now or never. The first bullet cracked hard into the alien, jerking it backwards. The sniper bullet encapsulated enough force to carry it far beyond visual range, and this force was now being expended mere footsteps away. A small portion of its carapace shattered and flaked off, but the creature appeared unconcerned. Above it, an organic bullet-creature continued onwards to its explosive birth.

Johannes fired again, once at the bulb at the creature's midsection, which did no more than spider-web the hard shell. The next two shots attempted to target the bulge at the end of its tail, but the creature picked up on that and waved its tail, causing a cascade of earth to spew forth as the bullets embedded themselves deeply into the earth. Cursing, Johannes fired the remaining bullets into the first fracture he made. Shards of carapace flew off with each hit, but the creature stood unwaveringly at its position.

Down to his last bullet, Johannes jammed the muzzle of the barrel right into the deepest crack of the creature's shell and fired, hoping the heat of and force would do… something.

"Maker above, let this work," muttered Johannes, and he pulled the trigger.

The creature blew apart in an expansive cloud of shrapnel, and Johannes stumbled backwards, landing in a pile beside Corey. Several fragments of the creature's shell had embedded themselves into the underside of his muzzle and cheeks, and he was covered in purple patches of the creature's blood. Thankfully, his eyes were protected by a pair of goggles, for which Johannes gave silent thanks.

Reaching up with a paw to brush the shell fragments off, Johannes suddenly felt a flash of cold travel down from his head down to his tailbone. His arms suddenly felt lethargic and leaden. *Poison?* he wondered in concern. Johannes tried to shout, to make a noise, but his muzzle could barely move and his hands fell limp even as he struggled to get into a sitting position.

A heavy weight fell upon one of his foot-paws and he glanced down. The creature was still alive, and had climbed onto his foot! The carapace that had once protected the creature had shattered at Johannes's final attack and exposed its fleshy innards. Even though it was missing most of its "head" and was leaking streams of purple goop, it appeared well alive to continue its attack.

In front of Johannes's face, the creature's tail bobbed and weaved. The small bulge travelling up the tail was close to its terminus, the fleshy organ at its tip that would soon launch an organic bullet right into his face.

Johannes tried to move away, to roll, to avoid the attack, but his body refused to respond. He watched as the bullet-creature completed its tour of the tail and entered its birth canal, ready to embed itself in Johannes's brain.

Unable to do more than blink, Johannes squeezed his eyes shut and willed his hand to reach for the grenades attached to his belt. *Must... reach... them...!*

Try as he might, his arms remained flaccid. Just then, several loud bangs jarred his ears and set them ringing.

"Damn it, Johannes. Can't a man have a good rest after being shot?" asked Corey.

Johannes opened his eyes. His sidearm, drawn and fired by Corey, wavered at the edge of his vision. The coyote was barely conscious, and the handgun soon slipped from Corey's limp fingers.

Corey! Wake up! Get up! Johannes did his best to rouse his friend, but his efforts did little more than a slight quivering of his lower lip.

At their feet lay the shredded carcass of the alien creature. Without its protective carapace, the small bullets easily tore their way through its fleshy insides, leaving nothing more than a wet, steaming pile of entrails.

Johannes started to wonder if they would survive this, but his musings were interrupted by several heavy thumps of *something* landing behind them. *No, not another one of them! Not like this!* Johannes screamed wordlessly, unable to move, his vision slowly wavering.

A second later, a heavy weight fell upon his shoulder and strong appendages dug into his shoulder. A dark shape towered over him, blocking out the harsh light of the sun. Rough tugs released the straps holding his helmet down, and Johannes felt something pierce the skin of his neck, leaving him with a cool sensation that spread through his body.

Johannes was hefted up, and he saw that rescue had arrived.

* * *

"The situation is dire, people. The aliens have landed here, atop the Martok Ruins." General Brecht, a snow leopard, paused as the holo-display updated, showing a top-down satellite view of the alien's beachhead.

"Now as you all know, the only way to kill these alien warships is to take out their propulsion. This weak point is now buried deep inside the ruins. Our brains in Speculative Operations *think* a few fusion charges will have the same effect as an energy lance. We're going with that till we know better.

"More importantly, the Martok Ruins are under the rule of the Hun-la'sha, one of the eight clans of the Kar'shaar wastes. Our treaty with them denies us access, but we would sacrifice that to remove any alien influences from a planet this close to Earth. However, we now have this."

General Brecht waved a paw, and the holo-display updated to show a rabbit warren of tunnels crisscrossing under the ground, connecting various structures that were built inside the planet's crust. Deep in the planet below the alien warship, a curious spherical chamber stood out.

"Two hours ago, an envoy from the Hun-la'sha arrived, requesting our assistance, as well as providing us with this map of the Martok ruins."

A murmur of disbelief spread through the crowd before General Brecht, and he paused, waiting for the assembled soldiers to settle down.

"Yes people, settle down. They are asking for help. Specifically, our help to rescue one of their people. It's a two-for-one if we can wing it, folks. We are going to use this opportunity to take out those alien bastards, and forge better ties with the natives.

"Now, while we have always considered the Martok Ruins uninhabited, it's actually a major popular center for the Hun-la'sha. The aliens have wiped out most of their population purely from landing their warship. Apart from scattered survivors, only one group survives, inside this spherical chamber. It's a ritual chamber, and only has one passage in, which they've collapsed. Here is where things get sticky.

"The Hun-la'sha's next in line for succession was kidnapped during the alien landing by a splinter faction, and they are holed up in that ritual chamber. We have promised to rescue the child," he held a paw up, "with the understanding that the remainder of the tribe will guide us through the ruins to the warships, and, fight alongside us. They've also agreed that the aliens must be removed through any and all means.

"Our rescue op is simple. The child is located in a ritual cell located here. The only way in is through this ventilation crawlspace. Get in, get the child out, and we blow the aliens sky high. Commanders, mission planning in my office, ten minutes. The rest of you, dismissed."

* * *

"Why did you volunteer to replace Cornelius? It's not your responsibility!" Corey stood slouched against his locker, arms crossed and ears folded back, his assault rifle strapped across his back. The patch of fur around his head wound was shaved, and a small patch of biogel was held in place by strips of skin adhesive. "Crawl through two kilometers of air ducts? Sounds perfect for a rat."

"He's married, Corey. Twins soon, right? Besides, I'm fitter and smaller than him." Johannes's injuries were mostly superficial. The toxins had been flushed out, and patches of contaminated fur around his face had been shaved off.

Corey's countenance softened at the mention of children, but didn't let go. "So what? We all knew the risks when we signed on. His wife knows that too. Plus, he's got more trap disposal experience."

"Come on," grinned Johannes. "Remember who aced the trap disposal exam last week?"

"Yeah, yeah," grumbled Corey. "That reminds me, we aren't fully field qualified. That means you too."

Johannes shrugged and continued putting on his survival suit. "No one else in the battalion can make it through those vents. It's either him or me. Layla would have been a perfect fit."

Corey sighed and looked away. It was not even a day since the alien ambush, and almost everyone had lost friends and squadmates. Layla Montoya, a petite ferret, and the squad's second in command, was one of those that bought the farm.

Properly trained personnel were elsewhere on the colony world, but they would not arrive in time before the aliens overran the depths of the ruined underground city.

"Well, you better make it back in one piece. I've heard that you are slated to be a section leader once we pass out."

Johannes twitched one of his ears. "Eh? That's news. Never wanted to lead."

"Those that don't want to lead make the best leaders. Haven't you heard? Anyways," Corey said as he glanced into his wrist comm, "duty in ten minutes. Catch you when you get back, eh?"

"Of course!" said Johannes, standing up and offering his paw. The two canines clasped forearms, just as a wailing alarm pierced the underlying day-to-day rumble of the base.

"That's the intrusion alarm!" said Corey, strapping his helmet on. "Are the aliens attacking?"

"Dunno," said Johannes, grunting as several tufts of fur got caught in the zipper. The throng of boots hitting the rough-hewn stone of the base grew as the few soldiers left to defend it arrived to pick up their combat gear.

A strong, haptic buzz shook his wrist, and Johannes brought up the comm message. Around him, almost everyone had received a message, and were glancing at their wrists.

"Kas'sha gench! It's the renegade faction! They've overrun the eastern guard perimeter!" swore Corey. "The battalion's out to stop those aliens, and these bastards want to take us up the tail!"

And with that, the coyote sprinted outside to mingle with the menagerie of soldiers heading to defend the base, and perhaps their death. Johannes finally finished suiting up, re-checked his loadout, and rushed to the airfield where an insertion squad had been prepared to take him in.

* * *

The journey to the cell was more stressful then dangerous. Johannes was beyond frazzled as he pulled his small frame through the spaces where people were never meant to travel.

Every small scratch or bump had his fur on end within the tight, dark space. It made no difference that the noises were from the small recon drones fizzing about and bumping around corners.

The drones had reconnoitered most of the way to the prisoner, but they had their limits. Batteries could only power each drone so far, and even with regularly placed signal booster drones, metal deposits in their surrounds did a number to communications. More importantly, the larger waystation drones that packed micro fusion cores for recharging the smaller drones were simply too large to fit in the narrow confines.

Some of the corners were very tight, and only his small size combined with vulpine flexibility allowed him to make passage. Other parts of the passage were steep inclines, and Johannes was thankful for his retractable claws as his sweaty paws would never have gripped the rock adequately.

As he wormed deeper into the passage, several inordinately tight turns had forced Johannes to leave some of his larger tools, even his rifle behind, as they simply would not fit.

After almost two hours of struggling through the narrow passage, Johannes finally reached the final stretch where the recon drones could not reach. Keen to keep his presence from any guards, Johannes did his best to keep his breathing and any other sounds to a minimum. Reaching back, he pulled out a paw-sized recon drone, and set it off.

"Go, Trevor. Good luck," Johannes said in a whisper.

The tiny wheeled vehicle replied with several happy haptic buzzes on Johannes's wrist comm as it moved off into the darkness. Johannes looked down at his wrist comm, watching intently as the small drone transmitted a low resolution wireframe guide of its surrounds.

As it approached the exit of the air vent, the little drone sent out a small camera attached to a short flexible tube; the light levels were high enough, and it had decided to send back visual imagery in addition to the wireframes.

Johannes felt his heartrate rise as the video feed came through. The drone had located its target. The kidnapped child was crouched in a corner of the rectangular cell, attired in ceremonial clothing. A thick chain ran from the wall and lay in coils on the floor, its other end bound to the child. What distressed Johannes was the vest that the child wore: a sleek, black synthetic garment that clashed against the solemn ceremonial raiment. Bulbous lumps covered the vest at regular intervals—a detonation vest.

Those bastards! Johannes thought, gripping his paws tightly. That was going to throw a big wrench in things, but it could not be helped. Accessing the small drone's remote controls, he requested a signal scan.

A small waveguide replaced the video feed as the drone scanned the electromagnetic spectrum inside the cell. Clean. The airwaves were clear. Flipping back to the video, he called up a spectrum scan, in case there were lasers or other optical traps. Apart from a dim light shining through the gaps in the prison's only door, everything seemed clear.

Nothing like the present, thought Johannes, and quickly crawled through the final few corners of the air vent.

As he reached the edge, he thanked and pocketed the small drone, then poked his head through the opening. The child, alerted by his scramblings, had backed into a corner and was looking his way, head tilted in equal parts curiosity and concern. The child spoke several words, unintelligible to Johannes's bare ears. The way it was inflected told Johannes that it was a question.

The translation came through in his earpiece. "Who are you?"

"Rescue," Johannes whispered into the dark. The wrist comm uttered a small blurb. The child immediately perked up, but stayed silent.

Don't know any kids who'd stay that relaxed with a bomb on them, thought Johannes. He then asked the child, "Where are the guards?"

"Only one guard. It's gone for food."

"Do you know when it will be back?"

The child gestured with its hands, a motion that indicated *no.*

"Better now than never," mumbled Johannes, and tumbled out of the opening. Pulling out the drone once more, he activated its defensive programs and let it scuttle under the door's wide slit. Turning, Johannes moved to take a closer look at the child.

The child was still wary of Johannes, and made to keep away from him. Thankfully, Johannes had come prepared for this. From a pocket, he extracted a linen pouch and withdrew the pendant it held within, then laid them on the ground between them.

"Your Blood-father sent this. He says you will recognize it and follow me to safety," said Johannes, and stood back.

The child came forward, crouched down and touched the pendant with the tip of its tongue before grasping it tightly in one clawed hand. Standing up, the child uttered a few words. "I will follow."

Johannes gave a sigh of relief and gently knelt down in front of the child. Johannes noticed that it was undone down the front. Why was the child still wearing it? "You know this is a bomb, right? Why haven't you taken it off?"

The child pointed to a black cuff wrapped around their upper arm, like a doctor's blood-pressure monitor.

Taking a closer look, Johannes saw a thick cable running from the innards of the vest to the cuff in question. A heartbeat trigger.

Damn, thought Johannes, but any further thoughts were silenced by an urgent beeping from the drone. It also broadcasted the sounds of blades crashing into his earpiece. *Blades? Is this a counter-attack by loyal troops?*

In a pathway that led away from the cell Johannes was in, his small drone zipped along at top speed, wanting to find out what those sounds were. It had decided that the high-pitched whine of its tiny motors were hardly audible, especially among the loud clangs and screams, and that getting information quickly was more important.

As it approached the corner where the fighting sounds were coming from, it sent its flexible camera around the bend, and sent those images back to Johannes.

Back in the cell, Johannes and the child watched in grim horror as Hun-la'sha warriors fought desperately against a torrent of alien invaders. Small aliens like the ones Johannes fought previously wriggled underfoot, latching onto soldiers, dead or alive, consuming them. Swift, hunchbacked, bipedal creatures attacked with scythe-like arms, easily matching the close combat prowess of the Hun-la'sha.

The aliens spread like a slow-moving tsunami, eradicating everything in their path. With every bladed beast that fell, several more were in the shadows, ready to move up. Every door in their path was forced through and those inside butchered. Johannes noted that some of the warriors that fell were not taken down by blades, but by a single bullet through their forehead. *Damn, more of those sniping things,* he thought.

Johannes estimated that they would arrive in minutes. "Trevor, get back here," said Johannes into his wrist comm, then turned to examine the vest. The chain that was attached to the wall was hooked up to the vest, not, as he feared, around the child. Even so, it still posed a problem; the tools that would have made short work of the chain were left behind, too large to fit through some of the tighter corners.

Outside the door, the crash of arms grew louder, punctuated by the occasional death scream of a fallen warrior.

Johannes's fur stood out on end as he sought ideas to safely remove the heartbeat detonator or break the chain. Only one came to his mind, and he wavered. *My life for the child?*

Of course, he could run. The few grenades he had brought along might be enough to collapse the airshaft behind him, prevent the smaller aliens from pursuing.

Indecision waged, honor against survival.

A series of beeps shook him from his reverie; his small drone had returned. "Trevor, record us," said Johannes, waving a paw between him and the child. A series of affirmative beeps issued from the drone, indicating it was ready.

"Command. I'm with the child. Unfortunately, I've hit a major snag." Moving aside, he gestured at the vest. "Detonation vest. And it's chained to the wall. The vest also has a heartbeat monitor attached to the child. I can't break the chain. Not with anything I have. And I don't have the time to figure out how to disable the detonator. We've got aliens coming up the corridor. We have a few minutes at most."

Johannes closed his eyes, and made up his mind. "I'm going to take over the monitor. Hopefully my pulse would do it. Trevor will be able to guide the child back." Staring straight at Trevor, he continued. "Mom... I don't think I'll get out of this alive. Thanks for everything you've done for me." Another scream tore through the sounds of battle. "I have to go. Goodbye."

Johannes gave a signal for Trevor to stop recording. Withdrawing his combat knife, he removed a large swath of fur around his forearm. *That should be good enough.*

Turning to the child, he said, "Give me your arm," pointing at the limb in question. The kid tilted their head in question. "I'm going to swap that onto me," said Johannes as he reached gently for the child's arm.

At that, the child shied away from Johannes's reach, making the gesture for "no".

"There's no way we can get out together. I will stay," said Johannes in a low voice.

"Why?" asked the child.

"Because you have family waiting for you."

"You have family too."

Johannes knelt, and gently removed the vest. "I do. But this is my job. To protect people."

The child gripped the cuff with its other hand. "You will die."

"Maybe, kid." Johannes smiled. "The aliens might not make it here. If you get out, you can send for help."

"No."

The sound of fighting was dying down, and an ominous silence started to spread.

"Listen. If you survive, there can be a great joining between your people and mine. Together, we can remove these aliens. If not... we may all die. Your planet and my homeworld could be destroyed. Do you understand?"

The child fell silent, but its tight grip had loosened enough for Johannes to pull their hand off. Placing the child's hand and cuff against the wall, he undid the straps holding it down. If there was a fail-safe here, they would be dead soon.

The cuff opened with no further ado, and Johannes placed his bare-skinned arm beside the child's, before pushing the child's arm free and wrapping the cuff around his arm. All seemed well.

"Quickly," said Johannes, herding the child in front of the air vent. Kneeling down, he snapped his wrist comm onto the child's arm, then placed Trevor inside the vent. "Trevor. Lead target to initial waypoint."

The little drone beeped an affirmative, and chumbled along the rough stone to make space.

"My clan will remember this," said the child, and performed an elaborate gesture with their hands that ended with a bow.

Johannes gave a wan smile, and dipped his head. "Come, let's get you in here." The child was far lighter than expected, and Johannes easily boosted it up. Just then, a skittering sound encroached upon his ears, and Johannes glanced at the door. A pair of tentacles had slid under the door, straightened and pointed directly at the pair. The chatter of tiny legs filled the air soon after.

"Go go go!" yelped Johannes. "Move, quickly!" Facing the door, Johannes pulled out his handgun and several grenades, wishing his rifle would have fitted through the tunnels. Sharp keening sounds shrieked from the outside, and an alien's blade removed a clean slice of metal from the door. Blade-armed aliens could be seen jostling each other for position outside.

Johannes felt his veins freeze up, and willed his shivering arm to pull the pins on his grenades. Several small creatures had crawled through the opening by the time he recovered and tossed the grenades into the milling horde.

The grenades obliterated most of the smaller aliens, but the larger, bladed aliens simply bounced off the walls of the corridor, and shrieked in anger.

Goodbye Mom, though Johannes, firing at the bladed aliens as they tore through the door and moved in. A few smaller aliens had reached him, their sharp jaws tearing through his combat boots and latching onto his feet.

It's time. I hope the kid's far enough.

Reaching up to the detonation cuff, he pulled it off, then shoved the vest into the air vent before leaping to one side.

Goodbye.

A massive bang went up, accompanied by a shockwave that threw anything not bolted down against the walls of the prison. Johannes hit a wall with a sickening crunch, and knew that he would never stand again. His head felt locked in place, and he felt a warm wetness drip from his nose. Looking at the air vent, he saw that it was now a mess of collapsed rock.

Closing his eyes, Johannes felt a deep calmness permeate through his being, and somehow, he *knew* he'd succeeded in his mission. Then he breathed his last.

In the interstellar future, humans and uplifted animals will fight together. For good and bad.

War of Attrition

by Lisa Timpf

"They wouldn't," I snarled, showing my teeth.

"They have before," Emmitt replied in his smooth voice, favoring me with a glare from his yellow-green eyes. He licked his paw and groomed his right ear, as though striving for a casual air. "Didn't they leave animals behind on the battlefield in their so-called World Wars?"

Yuma, a border collie and likely the smartest among us even without the AI implant, closed her eyes and checked her memory. "It's true," she said, her features solemn.

"That doesn't mean that this time—" I protested.

"Listen to you, Ace," Rascal said, grinning. "Aren't you the guy whose water dish is always half empty? I thought you'd be all over this."

The others laughed, and I thrust my muzzle between my paws, feigning embarrassment. I possessed my own reasons for wanting—needing—to believe that Sigma Squad's new assignment, tracking down the missing troop-ship *Javelin,* had a chance for success. A reason I kept to myself, buried like a juicy bone one hopes to return to in future. Somehow, I felt as though speaking my thoughts aloud would jinx things.

And a jinx was just what we *didn't* need.

The density of the forests here on B'Narth, with their sickly yellow-green growth, made our mission challenging enough. The fact that the woods teemed with Greenoans, who currently were engaged in full-scale hostilities with Earthies—well, that made things doubly tough.

I let my gaze swing toward the fire, where the human members of the squad formed a tight-knit circle. Emmitt had mentioned the World Wars, when animals were pressed into service. Things had changed, since. The Third Treaty recognized animals, with or without the AI link, as fully functioning members of the Forces with their own rights. I studied the humans I knew best—vet tech Kalea Green, with her tightly curled black hair and laid-back demeanor, and Signe Melqvist, communications and electronic surveillance expert. Neither one of them would leave us behind, I felt certain of that right down to my toes. My head swung further to the left. Sergeant Mason Thomas, now, presented a different story. Driven, dispassionate—could I see him making the call to put humans first? Maybe.

My attention returned to the animal party just in time to recognize the conversation was wrapping up.

"I'll keep my ears open," Emmitt said, stretching. "I suggest the rest of you do the same."

He strutted off, tail held high.

"You don't like him, do you Ace?" Copurrnicus, usually stand-offish, stood right beside me, his up-pricked ears pointed intently in his fellow feline's direction. "Neither do I," he confessed. "But I suggest we both keep that under our hats for now."

"I'm not wearing—oh, I get it," I said. Copurrnicus shot me a laser-beam stare and stomped off toward the barracks. I watched his leopard-spotted form disappear through the cat-door cut into the camouflaged dome. No sense of humor, that one. Then again, what would I expect?

* * *

"Another pointless patrol," I snarled. My paw-pads burned from the long scramble along the cliff trail and my brain ached from the prolonged effort of filtering the scents in the air, desperately seeking the subtle spiciness that marked the presence of the Greenoans. Since Greenoans lacked the sense of smell, they viewed our ability to detect them as a form of disconcertingly effective magic. The human members of our party knew better, but valued our abilities nonetheless. It's what made an animal presence vital on a mission like this. This particular patrol, however, had started out like the rest—a promising signal, then nothing.

"Relax, big fella," Rascal said reassuringly. "You're letting him get into your head." He jerked his muzzle back to point to Emmitt, who stalked at the rear of the party, tail held high. "Besides, we *did* learn one more place that the *Javelin* isn't."

I grunted and kept walking, unable to keep from worrying at my fears as though I gnawed on a still-flavorful bone. *If the mission is deemed hopeless, and there's not enough capacity on the troopship, then what?* I wondered.

The *Slingshot* had brought our squad to landfall here on B'Narth, but they'd also ferried another troop here before us. With the larger *Javelin* lost, if push came to shove, someone'd have to do extra time, waiting for a pickup that might never come. I growled, low in my throat.

Behind me, I could hear Signe's dragging steps. Though built for portability, the comm pack still weighed a guy down after awhile. I flicked my ears back as I heard him begin a conversation. "I don't get it," he complained to Kalea. "The signal comes in loud and clear, then—" he snapped his fingers. "Gone."

"Could someone be jamming it?" Kalea asked.

Signe frowned. "They'd have to be awfully close. And these guys aren't indicating—"

I glanced into his face, looking for signs of accusation. Nothing. *Stop looking for trouble,* I told myself, taking a deep breath.

There. Greenoan smell. I signalled, then lowered my body and crept forward, sensing Signe's presence behind me.

I saw a lean, overly tall figure with grey-white skin and wisps of thin yellow hair. Greenoan, alright, and just one, from the looks of it.

"Too far away," Signe grunted. "We'll never catch him."

Together, we watched the distant figure lope off through the meadow.

I've been in combat for more years than I can remember. I have no excuse for what happened next. Maybe Emmitt *had* gotten to me. Maybe my hopes and fears about the *Javelin* caused me to snap. Either way, I galloped in the direction the Greenoan had taken.

Despite Signe's voice in my ear-set calling me back, I kept running.

I followed my quarry past the meadow and into the woods, splashing through one of the ice-cold streams that dotted the landscape.

And eventually, despite my sore paws, despite the lead he had on me, I caught the Greenoan, right at the base of a tall cliff. I dealt with him in the manner in which I had been trained.

Not pretty. I'll spare you the details.

When I finished dispatching the enemy, I paused, checking my direction.

Uh-oh. The homing signal offered no guidance, and landmarks were impossible to see in the impenetrable jungle of woodland.

I'd have to follow my own scent-trail back to the others, and from there to camp. I sighed. It'd take longer than following the signal, but that's the way it had to be.

Without the Greenoan to pursue, I settled into a ground-eating but energy-conserving trot that we'd learned back in Basic Training. With the battle fury gone, nothing distracted me from the jolt of pain shooting through my paws each time I touched the ground. Nothing for it but to keep going. I gritted my teeth, then opened my mouth to let my tongue loll out. *Can't wait to get back to that stream,* I thought.

I'd been running for several minutes when I heard the ping of the homing device kick in. Wagging my tail, I kicked into gear, able to head cross-country. *Why, I should be back to camp in time for dinner,* I thought.

Half an hour later, I heard a familiar rumble.

Couldn't be. An upward glance confirmed my fears.

The *Slingshot* rose above the tree line, hovered for a moment, then shuttled away.

My ears drooped and the full weight of my weariness settled on my shoulders. For a moment, I felt a strong temptation to just lie down and surrender to the elements. B'Narth had its predators, and they would find me, eventually.

I shook off these dark thoughts. My reason still stood, perhaps even more strongly, now. There was something I needed to see through—with or without the *Slingshot* and her crew.

I stood, letting the breeze ruffle my coat, as I debated the best path forward.

If Emmitt had it right, members of the animal team would be left behind. Perhaps I could enlist their aid.

On the other hand, if I went to the camp first and they *weren't* there, I'd lose valuable time.

Maybe I'd become more dependent on my squad-mates than I thought. I made the decision to head for camp, though I moaned under my breath as I did so, fearing I'd made the wrong decision.

When I arrived, the site was completely bare. For a moment, I remained frozen in place.

Grrrrrr. I glanced into the woods, spotting Rascal's black-and-grey brindled face. He jerked his muzzle and disappeared into the woods.

What the? I sniffed around the site and made my way to where Rascal had disappeared.

"Follow me," he said in a voice so low I could barely hear him. "Quietly."

I snapped my jaws shut on the questions that threatened to tumble out.

When we arrived at a camo-tent set within a deep thicket, we passed Copurrnicus doing sentry duty.

"Anyone behind us?" Rascal panted.

"Nothing," the big leopard-spotted feline replied in his low rumble.

Within the tent, Signe and Kalea reclined in their campcots, catching some sleep, while half a dozen other human squad members worked on their weapons or munched on travel rations.

"Will someone tell me what's going on?" I snarled.

Yuma slipped out the door and Copurrnicus entered, letting the border collie relieve him from sentry duty.

"Turns out our friend Emmitt is a double agent," Copurrnicus said, stretching his front legs, then studying the large pad on his right front paw.

"Where's he now?" I snarled.

Copurrnicus stared at me. "He left, presumably to report to his superiors. And," his face assumed the smug expression peculiar to cats, "we allowed him to go with the clear impression we were abandoning the mission."

"Why wasn't I in on this?" My voice had an edge to it.

"And if we'd told you?" Rascal ducked, as though, now that he'd asked the question, he feared my reaction.

"I'd have grabbed him," I confessed. Scanning the floor of the camotent, I seized a squad member's bandana and shook it, hard, then dropped it, panting. "I'd have shook him until he was dead. Deader than dead."

"Precisely," Rascal said, judging it safe to advance a step closer. "And a dead traitor is also a dead give-away for the other side. So we couldn't tell you."

"Because of my own pig-headedness," I said, my ears drooping.

"Something like that," Rascal assumed a brisk tone. "But knowing Emmitt was the source of the signal jamming, we've discovered a work-around."

"Signe figured out the true Positioning System coordinates," Copurrnicus added.

"For what?" The words flew out of my mouth before I could stop them.

"For a smart guy, you're really—never mind. For the *Javelin*." Rascal paused, adding more softly, "And her crew."

* * *

"There they are," I whispered, pointing with my muzzle. They'd done a creditable job, as best as could be expected under the circumstances. Camouflage netting mostly concealed the *Javelin*, and the vehicle's cryptic patterning did the rest of the job. Had it not been for the evidence gathered by my nose, I'd never have found the site. Well, my nose and Signe's Positioning System coordinates.

I frowned. Even through the camouflage, I could see a gaping hole in the *Javelin's* side. Attempts had been made to patch it, but the vessel remained some distance from air-worthiness. Whether by design or accident, the breach would've knocked out the long-distance comm system and its power pack, which explained the *Javelin's* inability to reach out to her would-be rescuers.

"Trouble," Rascal said, the fur on his back standing on a ridge.

I glanced in the direction his muzzle pointed.

"As we expected." Copurrnicus' voice sounded rock-steady. "Believing our ship has left, the Greenoans are preparing to attack. I suggest we not tarry." He glanced back to Signe, who made a hand signal to move out. Copurrnicus, by now, was unable to prevent his tail from twitching in anticipation.

"The game is clear, yes?" Rascal asked, his tone light.

"The *Javelin* is the bait," I said. "And the *Slingshot* will be the spring-loaded bar. But we'll need to keep the Greenoans occupied until they get here. Otherwise, our mouse-trap will close on nothing."

Let's hope they get here fast, I muttered as I followed Rascal, casting a longing look toward the camp as we trotted to the right of it, toward the enemy.

The Greenoans, made arrogant by over-confidence, travelled in a loose formation, if you could call it a formation at all. We would play it the way we had many, many times before—the animal teams working in pairs to pick off the stragglers, the laggards, the ones marching off to the sides. We animals harried and snapped, dispatching the enemy one at a time, while Signe and the human portion of the cohort sniped from the treetops and from camouflaged hillside posts.

The approach, as usual, seemed doubly effective. Made anxious by the truncated yells of those who fell to animal attack, the Greenoans shot wary glances to the side and behind, only to hear the thud of a fellow soldier hitting the earth after a gunshot found its mark. They didn't know where to focus their attention. Nonetheless, they continued to advance, albeit with increasing caution. I grudgingly admired their tenacity.

When the enemy had halved the distance between where we'd initially seen them and the spot where the *Javelin's* crew waited, their numbers had been significantly reduced.

They still out staffed us by double, at least.

Where's the Slingshot? I wondered, straining my ears for the sound of the ship's engines.

Greenoan scent, and strong. I slunk forward, then bared my teeth. There, in a hollow, lay one of the yellow-haired enemies, setting up a grenade launcher with meticulous but practiced motions.

I growled, low and deep, and leaped, then felt bone crunching under my teeth.

The Greenoan went limp, but I had little time to celebrate. I heard the snap and crackle of a fire beam, followed by a searing pain across my back.

Teeth grasped my neck, and I felt my body being tugged, inch by painful inch, into the woods.

Don't bother, I thought. *I'm done for.*

A roaring filled my ears. Was it the blood rushing through my veins, or the rumble of the *Slingshot's* engines? Before I could confirm the answer, my thoughts slipped away like water rushing over rapids. And though I reached for them, though I clawed desperately, in my mind, for some purchase on consciousness, all went dark.

* * *

Sound was the first sense that returned to me, but muffled, as though I had my head dunked underwater.

Gradually, single words began to make sense, surrounded by unintelligible bursts of noise.

…Greenoans…right now…coming around…

I felt the light touch of a hand resting on my shoulder. "Lie still." I identified Kalea's voice, softly reassuring. "All is well, but you need to rest."

Despite the warmth of her words, my forelegs flailed as I strived to lever myself to my feet. *Nelva. I have to know about Nelva—*

Was my littermate among the *Javelin's* crew, as I had hoped? And if so, more importantly, had she survived?

As though summoned by the urgency of my thoughts, Nelva arrived. I smelled her, felt her touch her nose to my neck. I sighed, ceasing my struggles, and surrendered to the darkness, willingly this time.

* * *

When I next woke, night had fallen. Scent and sound told me what I needed to know. Nelva lay to my left, Rascal to the right. Across the room, Copurrnicus hummed softly to himself as he kneaded his sleeping blanket with his front paws.

"Can someone," I said, speaking with difficulty due to a dryness in my throat, "tell a fella what's going on?"

"Emmitt," Copurrnicus said, "has been dealt with." He finished this statement with a satisfied grunt that left no doubt as to the identity of the one who had done the dealing.

"The Greenoans had a surprise in store," Rascal said lightly. "One of their cruisers engaged the *Slingshot* while she was on her way here. The *Slingshot* fought them off, but the delay almost cost us."

"If you hadn't stopped the grenade launcher," Nelva said, "things might have been worse. As it was, we all made it."

I rested my head on my paws for a moment, absorbing the news.

"Thirsty?" Rascal asked. "There's half a dish of water just to your right." He added the latter comment in a sly tone.

"Ah," I commented. I contemplated the events of the past few days, and all that I had to be grateful for. "Someone left the dish half *full*. I am supremely grateful."

Ignoring the muffled laughter that followed this comment, I lurched to my feet and lapped noisily from the bowl. And I noted, as I did so, that nothing has ever tasted so sweet.

From the dim past to the far future, on Earth and on distant worlds, for humans and anthropomorphic animals alike—
Basic Training will be the same!

Fathers to Sons

by Mikasi Wolf

What the hell am I doing here?

That was the very thought running through Raja's mind, even as his muzzle rocked with the motion of his ride. Around him was silence, save for the odd whimper of fear. There were no sounds of overloud music, or conversation. If Raja stopped for a moment to think about it, he could have been inside a prison bus. And in many ways, he was.

The day of reckoning came more quickly than Raja had expected. Months of playing the MMORPG "Resurrection of the Pelts" and dancing with his friends at one of the island nation's two nightclubs had been enjoyable, yet pointless as such ephemeral activities had proven time and again. Now, aboard the chartered bus rumbling towards the famous landmark known formally as the Army Ferry Terminal, Raja wished he had spent more time doing something constructive, such as writing that book about post-apocalyptic survivalism, or completing painting the ceiling of his room with a fresco he had gleaned from the Internet. In time, the joys of dancing to a rapidly changing tune, and that of blowing up undead freaks time and again on a LED backlit screen would fade; all but erased by the prospect of facing the bloodthirsty NCOs and officers. At least if he didn't make it out of "Holiday Camp" in one piece, his family would have half his fresco to remember him by. Or perhaps they would just paint it over with a nicer color.

"Raja?" The lion turned at his mother's purr. "You've been quiet for much of the journey. What are you worrying about?" she asked, brow wrinkled questioningly. Despite her good intentions, Raja had to admit she had this habit of stating the obvious.

"The journey's just a 15 minute ride, Ma," huffed Raja. "Besides, no one's ever in a joyous mood whenever they're conscripted into the Army. It's one of our national traditions." Raja's tail lashed hard against the seat as he turned back to the window.

Mrs. Jaya shook her muzzle disapprovingly. "Raja, I don't see what's your cause for complaint. Your father managed fine during his stint in Basic Military Training, and was even commended by his officers for trying to save his fellows from an out-of-control truck! I'm sure you'll do us all proud."

Yeah, with bandages wrapped around my limbs, thought Raja darkly. He had heard that story countless times. Raja's father, Mr. Jaya, had attempted to save his platoon from being run over by an improperly braked truck, by rushing them in an effort to shove them off the road. Unfortunately, a scrawny lion attempting to move a multi-species platoon, which included several tigers, two elephants and a rhino was a tugboat attempting to push an island out to sea. The truck driver would still be laughing about it in his cell. Mr. Jaya had since then boasted of his "war injury" to anyone who would listen. An hour before, Mr. Jaya had told Raja that he couldn't see his son off, lest he got all emotional. The fact that he still shuffled at the speed of a tortoise contradicted that excuse, however. Something told Raja that was the more likely reason, rather than his reputed claim to fame.

They reached the ferry terminal which was jam-packed with thousands of other enlistees, either fearful, or thoroughly brainwashed by their parents and the media. Queues had been created, with stickers issued to those whose turn came to enter the conceptual frying pan. Sergeants smiled and laughed forcedly, their muzzles masks of the actual horrors that lay within the BMT camp. Pulau Saikang was a military training camp located on an island off the shores of the country for the stated reasons of having ample space and safety for training considerations. For the ever-pessimistic, and perhaps, ever-intuitive Raja, this was to prevent recruits escaping by surrounding them with shark-infested waters should they manage to give their NCOs the slip.

The trip on the ferry was as eventful as that on the bus, with Raja's mother continuing to give him all the pointless encouragement he could ever need. Raja could only listen, given the little choice he had on the fully packed ferry. Besides, the doors to the deck were probably locked. Here, the scent of fear was almost unbearable, punctuated with the occasional whimper. Seated next to a window, Raja could see a horse seated by himself, muttering feverishly with his hoofs clasped in prayer.

Not 20 minutes later, the ferry drew up beside a jetty. Even if there was a god sympathetic to the plight of conscripts, salvation with the fishes was not to be. And here the conscripts set their first paws into another world.

Looking down the long stretch of concrete that was the jetty, Raja felt that it was more bridge than watercraft stopover. A bridge to every young man's vision of Hell. Raja had once read about Charon in a book on ancient mythology, a skeletal jackal who ferried departed souls to the underworld in exchange for a coin. Like the proverbial journey across the River Styx, it almost felt like Charon himself had steered the very ferry he was on, which even now was being prepped to return to the mainland to claim other souls. Only that his own soul was the payment. But the only way was forward, and so Raja walked, the fearful scents of those who came before strong even on the breeze-exposed concrete. An electronic LED sign reminded all who passed to "Start the day with a positive mindset", further implying that there was little to be positive about. More forced smiles from the armed Regimental Police, who probably had enough ammo to handle the whole lot of them. What else could the many ammo pouches on their vests be for?

The parents and their young were shown into an auditorium, where soon enough, they were bombarded with assurances by the commanding officers on stage. "Your cub/kit's well-being would be taken care of...", "best medical care available...", "only push-ups to be given as punishment", "cubs with any issues could bring it up with their immediate superiors," blah, blah, blah ... Raja was forced to keep his fidgeting to a minimum as some Sergeants had been tasked to check on their attentiveness. The national anthem was played shortly, with all the enlistees sworn in by the oath of allegiance. It was a solemn affair, with the seriousness broken only by the shouting of many names, and National Identification Numbers interspersed over one another.

A sumptuous lunch of chicken rice was provided at the cookhouse, courtesy of the army. *This is what your son would be eating!* screeched the plates silently. *Don't worry,* assured the smiles of the NCOs and officers. *Your son's well-being will be taken care of! Rest easy!* Not wanting to speak to his Ma, as nauseated as he was, Raja took his time to chew his meal slowly, relishing in the taste of chicken and lemongrass. Her overenthusiastic advice on remembering to wash his underwear and remembering to call home laid his ears flat, but what could one do but listen?

Then came the dreaded call of the Angel of Death.

"All recruits, please bid goodbye to your parents and assemble at the parade square," announced an officer over the loudspeaker. Raja froze, a piece of chicken hanging from his lower jaw. All the recruits were petrified, knowing their time was up. Rising from their chairs, they plodded silently towards the parade square, tails and bags dragging limply behind them, not unlike those on Death Row. Some had brought travelling cases large enough to fit a bicycle in, knowing that they would not return home for a while, if ever. Others, believing that their lives would not be for much longer, brought nothing more than themselves, with barely a place to fit a toothbrush. Historically, these were the ones who would desert on the first night or second night. Stowaways on the ferry were not altogether uncommon, given the nature of the training. The island camp's security had been put to the test a year back, when a psychologically-disturbed recruit swam half the way back to the mainland despite the sharks. According to the official news reports, he had since been transferred to the prestigious, yet hazardous Navy Diving Unit. If the swim back didn't kill him, the training would. Otters; always believing they can swim out of anything.

Standing in the parade square with the sun blazing down upon his and many others' fur, Raja felt an odd sense of calm. It was the invigorating sense of freedom right after being released from one's cell, with the firing squad prepped to release their volley of shots into you. Raja kept his face forced. He would not cry. Though the army may take away his life that once was, they will never take his pride. The state flag, a crimson lion's head set against a white background fluttered high on its flagpole, flanked by the unit and service flag. Already the scent of fear of the other recruits reached Raja's vomeronasal gland, but the lion shut his mouth. *Have fortitude!* he told himself. *Have pride! Though I walk in the valley of the Shadow of Death, I shall fear no superior...* As the NCOs led him and the other recruits towards the trucks that would take them to the other end of the island, Raja gave his mother a casual wave. After all, it might very well be the last time he saw her, still smiling and cheering him on his way. Besides, he had an image to uphold.

Getting onto the truck known as a 5-tonner, proved to be a skill in itself. A combination of having a good grip as well as basic acrobatics was required to pull oneself up by misplaced handles and undersized steps long bent out of shape. Raja smacked a weasel on the muzzle in the midst of his ascent, earning a glare and the likelihood of future vendetta. A dangerous thing in a place stocked with weapons of war.

The driver and a 3rd-Sergeant closed the tailgate, making their way into the cab of the truck. Two other NCOs had stayed in the truck with them, obviously to ensure no one tried giving them the slip. Raja took one last look at the mass of parents waving their sons off and closed his eyes painfully.

No one in the truck spoke. Not a whisper could be heard, and there weren't any mice to say otherwise. Despite the constant reminders of reporting to Pulau Saikang by means of official correspondence, including a Muzzbook page no one actually followed, nothing truly prepared one from being here. One could hear accounts of life on the inside, be it from relatives or older friends, but the fact that they usually came from a different era, coupled with self-serving pride meant it was hard to separate truth from fiction. An older friend of Raja's had once said the punishment for theft in the barracks was for everyone to carry their beds and cupboards down for inspection in the parade square. However, he conveniently neglected to mention if anyone ever got crushed in the process.

A small-clawed otter in the middle of the truck tried to make conversation with a tiger, earning a snarl from him. Raja pursed his lips grimly. Looks like he and the tiger shared the same misgivings. They might be forced into conscription, but no one could make them like it. And the ironic thing was, to his family, being a part of the army was part of a long family tradition.

Raja's grandfather, the Esteemed Puja Renganathan, as his father always saw fit to remind him, served in the National Army back in the Old Country. Despite Tigers being preferred for active duty, given their natural camouflage and "will to kill", he and his brothers had been accepted for service by the colonial government. Things being as they were in those tumultuous times, they were sent to the many reaches of the Empire. Puja had also seen action in the war in the West Savannahs, after which his unit was sent to Pura. He had never found out what happened to his brothers, but that was one of the harsh realities in the War of Domination. He started a family in the port city, where he was welcomed because of his people's contribution to the war. It would later gain independence, with the state flag designed to honor the lions that had fought on its behalf. Mandatory conscription for every male was enacted shortly to better defend its precarious borders. Out of zeal, or a misplaced enthusiasm to emulate his father's deeds, Raja's father Jaya made it his life's goal to find work in the army. Even a pancake of a foot during that unfortunate incident in BMT didn't quell his desire in applying for full-time service, and soon the Chief Clerk of G1 Army, aka Army HR, had no choice but to give him an administrative role as Paper Shredder. The Army loved their paperwork. Not the glamorous job that one associated with a military line of lions, but as a Minister of

Parliament once said; "Loyalty to the Service is worth more than service itself." As far as anyone knew, Jaya had never appeared on the Army's recruitment posters.

And now Raja was part of the neverending line of youngsters who entered its ranks, a leaf flowing down the river of fate. A fate made possible all because someone had drafted a charter on a whim. And yet Mr. Jaya expected him to make it to Officer Cadet School, and sign on as a career soldier! *The family tradition must be upheld,* Mr. Jaya had said. In his dreams, perhaps.

The truck rumbled through vast stretches of jungle, with the occasional dilapidated building flashing past. The island used to be home to a hundred villagers, before it was converted to a collection of training camps. It was surprising how peaceful the military island seemed, despite the nature of its purpose. Somehow Raja had expected to hear the sounds of gunfire in the forests, accompanied by maniacal laughter and cries for mercy. Maybe the training won't be as horrible as others made it out to be. After all, hadn't his father once commented on how things were much better now than it was 30 years back? Raja laughed silently to himself. He shouldn't be so tense; all this worrying wasn't going to do him much good if he was going to make it to the first book-out.

The truck roared past two gateposts emblazoned with a rather contradictory greeting: **WELCOME TO BMT CAMP D**. As the sounds of yelling and snarled commands started to reach Raja's ears, he knew his mind had relaxed too soon. A platoon of recruits flashed past, the smell of sweat and mingled scents assailing the 5-tonner. Green PT vests clinging to their frames, the lion just had time to see that their ears were all laid flat before they passed.

The truck stopped abruptly outside a large open-air training shed, jerking recruits and baggage alike. Large enough to fit 60 soldiers, the shed was piled full of black duffle bags, alongside other equipment. So they were to be equipped first. That's good. Maybe there would be something to eat within the bags. Raja licked his lips, even as the tailgate crashed open with the enlistees pouring out to their new outfit. Looking to his right, Raja observed that the shed was next to one of the countless five-story buildings the military island was famous for. Several men in civilian T-shirts and shorts stood next to red plastic chairs, fiddling with their phones.

"Everyone, assemble in three rows!" yelled a 2nd-Sergeant over the din. A grayish cat of about five feet, his chest epaulette showed three black chevrons roofed by another. "You will collect your equipment row by row, and make sure that everything fits! No exchanges will be entertained after today! But before that—" Here, the cat jerked his head to the now-smirking men in civvies—"—those of you who hadn't done so will get your headfur and manes trimmed!"

So that's what these guys were. Barbers. In the outside world, one went to a groomer to have their fur trimmed, or brushed. They also provided dye or paint jobs, though these were usually special requests by the recalcitrant or overly flamboyant. But in the army, there were none of the frills. Barbers had only one job; to hack at fur until it reached a semblance of the dimensions matching military regulation. There were rumors that military barbers were once groomers who didn't meet the finesse of that profession required outside. Whatever the case, they were hired *en masse* during enlistment days such as this.

"After that's done, you are all to go assemble in front of the company line with your bags—" Here, the Sergeant pointed to the five-story building. "For your information, I am 2SG Ming, and this here is 3rd Sergeant Reski!" The cat indicated the Alsatian who stood beside him. He stared impassively back at the recruits, his dark muzzle set in a bored line.

"What are you waiting for?" roared the cat in a high pitched caterwaul. "MOVE!" The recruits rushed forward in a flurry of activity, ears and tails down. Raja tried to flatten his mane against his skull, in a bid to make it look shorter. But either a sharp eye or a sadistic streak caused a binturong to point towards him, the civet's fangs out in a grin.

"Come on, Mister, my mane's not that long," pleaded Raja. "Lemme on my way, alright?"

The barber shrugged. "There's no point. Even if I wanted to, your Sarge will send you back here. You have two dollars?"

"You'll let me go for two dough?" asked Raja, drawing his wallet. Cheapest bribe ever.

The binturong scowled. "No, dammit. The furtrim costs two dollars. You think it's free? Now, seat your ass down and hold the fuck still." With a huff, the barber whisked the plastic bill away from Raja, and shoved him into his chair. Raja could only grimace as the grime-stained shaver descended upon him.

He hadn't shaved his mane in like, ever. Male lions wore their manes with almost as much pride as their manhood, though there was no question over which they would choose over the other. As Raja felt the bone-jarring vibrations of the shaver against his skull, accompanied by the tearing sensation of an overused blade, Raja noted that he didn't suffer this nightmare alone. Right across him was a Samoyed with his fur fluffed up, eyes wide in what could only be shock, clump after clump of snowy fur falling to the barber's blade. In the Army's defense, Raja could only wonder what the hell possessed the Samoyed to keep his ridiculously fluffy coat, especially in such a hot tropical climate. He wouldn't last an hour before being consumed by heatstroke. Right next to him was a porcupine with head quills grown in a mohawk, with the barber equipped with metal shears and a coarse file for such an endeavor. As swaths upon swaths of his yellowish mane fell, Raja could only look down in horror. There was a common saying that one had no mane if you were female or enlisted. Raja had no idea how horrible his furtrim had turned out, because he was ushered away for a deer to take his place, without a mirror to check the extent of damage. He barely heard the barber yell for a pair of bolt cutters and saw.

Raja got into a queue, at the end of which civilian contractors had them try on their helmets and training cap. Some idiot in the Central Manpower Base had put him down for headgear meant for "Horned Bovine", giving his helmet and cap a glaring pair of holes. This was exacerbated by a too-narrow headspace, and misaligned earholes that would screw his ears up before the week was over. It was only after a yak found that he had been issued "LARGE FELINE-MANELESS" labeled headgear, that Raja was able to do a swap with him. Without his mane, it fitted well. Not that he had worn any form of headgear before. Male lions were one of the few species exempted from having to put on bicycle helmets when cycling on the roads. He didn't envy the one who ended up with a porcupine's helmet. The interior would be pockmarked to better seat their shortened head quills. He then went to collect the rest of his general equipment, a ragtag jumble of pre-packed paraphernalia stuffed into an almost-bursting duffel bag.

Dragging his crap to the parade square where Sergeant Reski was directing recruits, Raja plonked both his overladen personal hiking bag and standard-issue duffel bag onto the red brick of the parade square, muttering under his breath. His scalp was sore, and what remained of his mane was in tatters. The lion drew a finger across a particularly sore spot, and he would be damned if that red stickiness wasn't blood. A growl rumbled in his chest, and it was all he could do not to snarl outright.

"Hi there!" greeted a wolf who stood in line beside him. "Looks like everything's going faster than we could blink, eh?" Unlike Raja, and most of the recruits, his headfur and ruffs were immaculately trimmed, and the lion was sure that it fitted the guidelines on the Ministry of Defense's website. He had a modest messenger bag to hold his belongings, which was even in the regulation black the military seemed to like.

"Hmph." Raja couldn't quite bring himself to speak, for fear of venting his displeasure at being whisked far from home. Well, not that far actually, given that his hometown was but twenty kilometers as the crow flies. But on an island no different from Alcatraz itself, what with all the fences and cameras abound, they could be thousands of kilometers away for all it mattered. The Ancient Wolfborn Romans sent their auxiliaries far from home to prevent desertion; the modern armies fenced and surrounded their own with a body of water. The lion was starting to see why island prisons were favored.

The wolf didn't look annoyed, merely tilting his ears and head curiously as canids did. "My name's Jian. What's yours?"

"Raja Jayakumar," managed Raja with a cough. "I would say I'm pleased to meet you, though that would be best suited for another time and place."

"You speak of enlistment like it's Hell itself," said Jian with a twitch of his nose.

"Oh, you have no idea."

"Everyone got their stuff?" yelled Sergeant Ming who had come to stand before the gathered recruits. "For those of you who have brought your own shit, I want everything turned out for inspection!"

No one moved for a moment. Then as if on cue, everyone turned their bags over, pouring the contents out before them. Many, like Raja, had brought generous amounts of snacks and consumables with them, knowing that a provision store on Pulau Saikang was too much to hope for. A sloth bear had brought plastic bottles of what looked like honey, but could easily be mead or other forms of moonshine. A komodo dragon, on the other paw, had brought shrink-wrapped steaks, and Raja briefly wondered if he was hoping for fridge space in the cookhouse, or intending to eat the meat half-rotten. Komodos had a reputation for bad breath, after all. From where he stood, Raja noted that the small-clawed otter in the second row of the platoon had brought along several cans of shellfish, including expensive Mexican Abalone. Sergeant Ming picked up one of the cans, scrutinizing it interestedly.

"You guys planning a party or something?" demanded Sergeant Ming. "You do know that recruits are not to bring food into camp, right?"

"No, Sir," clarified a Labrador recruit. "The list only mentioned camera cellphones—"

"'SIR'? WHAT THE FUCK 'SIR'?" yelled Sergeant Ming, causing everyone to jump. The splat of steak on brick could be heard. "DO I LOOK LIKE AN OFFICER TO YOU? YOU WILL ADDRESS ME AS 'SERGEANT', IS THAT CLEAR?"

"Yes, Sergeant!" said the Labrador timidly. His fur had stood up in his shock, giving him semblance to a sandy pincushion. Before him were several packs of the dry pellets dogs seemed to enjoy. Cats had their own variety of them.

"And flatten your fur!" commanded Sergeant Reski sharply.

"And what the hell is this?" demanded Sergeant Ming, pulling out what looked like a sleeping cap out of the Labrador's pile of junk. "Did you think that you are allowed to wear your own pajamas and shit? No one is to wear any non-issued equipment as long as you're here! You better not let me catch you with this again!" Sergeant Ming's hackles were bared to the full, increasing his size twofold. It would have been a comical sight, to see the smaller cat terrify a far larger dog, but Raja did not dare laugh. He was sure that in the real world—that is, the world outside the Army—the Labrador would have thumped the cat six feet into the ground, civil laws be damned. But this was the Military, where the number of stripes, bars, crests and stars counted first. One's species didn't factor into it, unless you were both carnivore and superior.

Sergeant Ming muttered a murderous "I'll be watching you" to the recruit before making his way to a sun bear who looked about to piss himself.

He never got his bottles of stuff back. After the 2-Sergeant customs inspection, Raja and the rest of the recruits made their way up to their bunkrooms, relieved of every possession that had the slightest chance of allowing one to enjoy their time in BMT. Raja had fared the worst, losing his PS4, IPad, IPhone and gaming laptop to the Sergeants, including four kilograms of beef jerky and coffee powder. That stuff wasn't cheap. Raja had believed he could have had self-control, but the way Sergeant Ming had also mocked his maneless form was totally unforgivable. It was known among lions that one's mane was to be respected, and yet the cat dared to call him a lioness before everyone else! He was bristling with rage by the time he reached the 3rd floor of the Company line, which had a lift they weren't allowed to use, by the way, and had to clamp his claws hard against the steel post of his double-decker bed to stop himself from throwing a nearby chair out of the window. The otter, who had been posted to the same bunkroom of 8 double-decker beds looked nervously at the lion before placing his near-empty personal bag into his locker. Raja glared at the drab cupboard before him, and without warning, gave it a swift swipe with unsheathed claws.

The screech reverberated around the spacious bunkroom, startling everyone. Raja roared, attacking his locker viciously, footclaws out as he kicked. Recruits yelled, and two of them caught hold of him. Raja snarled, flinging them aside. As he made to confront a nervous mousedeer, who should come towards him but a snarling tiger. Tackling Raja around the waist, the tiger slammed him against the badly scratched and impacted steel cupboard. Before the lion could so much as blink, the tiger flipped him around, pinning the side of his head against the cool metal surface. Raja wriggled and tried kicking backwards, but another slam of his head stunned him.

"The fuck you're playing at?" demanded the tiger. "You dare do your gang routine on your first day? Well, not when I've got something to say about that. Just what the fuck's your problem?"

"Are you both blind *and* deaf?" snarled Raja, trying to break free of the paws holding him down. He was a lion, and yet he couldn't even break free from this striped thug. "We've just had everything we've worked hard for taken away from us! And the Sarge insulted my honor! He called me a lioness! Don't you all feel the injustice?"

"Well, I feel you're a pussy," snorted the tiger, and Raja stiffened. "A lionessy pussy. This is the Army, not a holiday camp for cub scouts. If you can't accept that, tough." His own claws flexed against Raja's pelt. "But as long as you're here, you will keep your bloody temper under control. I swear, if I catch you jeopardizing the section again, I'll drown you with a bucketful of water."

"I'll like to see you try, asshole!" swore Raja, trying to pull loose. In that moment, he knew this was someone he could never be friends with. Lions had a saying; "No two kings may walk the same street", with many examples proven in history. It was believed that was how the first street fights started. There would be disagreements and fights, threats and promises broken, but no lion would bow to anyone.

A rumble grew in the tiger's throat. "You've been warned. Guys, get on with your business. We have a schedule to meet." He shoved Raja once more against dented metal, disengaging as he did. The rest of the bunkmates scattered and resumed their previous activities. No one dared to speak to the lion, now. He had just singled himself out from the rest of them, the greatest mistake a recruit could ever make. The weasel he had smacked inside the truck earlier gave him a knowing smile, before sticking his nose back in his cupboard. Raja eased his claws back and changed slowly into the green shirt and black shorts he had been issued with. Sitting down heavily on the uncovered mattress, the lion stared wordlessly at the sky outside the window. Already he could hear Sergeant Ming grilling another batch of recruits downstairs. It took all his control not to chuck the now-useless cupboard three floors down to the parade square.

Raja felt nothing but hopelessness. In the months leading up to his enlistment, he had always envisaged being brave enough to face the truth every male citizen had ever since Pura's independence. But he had only gone through the first—no, half a day—of his military service before breaking down into a violent mess, angry at the world for putting him into this. Was he really Raja Jayakumar, the lion who had achieved a gold award for his military fitness test? Did he really deserve being posted into the leadership training course in BMT based on that? Or was he the very reason for his undoing? There were countless enlistees who cheated the system, failing their medical physicals in the hope of getting downgraded. Somehow Raja had never considered going that route, believing he had the courage to face anything that would be thrown at him. He had to admit that he was ill-prepared psychologically, for his own relatives had never seen fit to share their own experiences. Cultural Honor, as his father had called it, for true courage comes only from adversity without expectance. A load of preyshit.

And to make matters worse, he had no one he could talk to on this godforsaken island of despair. He had tried speaking to his girlfriend Salrina about his fears a week before his enlistment, hoping for her support. This was the first of several unanswered calls. He couldn't quite say he blamed her, for how many would want to wait two whole years for their future mates? Not Salrina certainly, for she was always all about greener pastures and all that. His mother wouldn't be of much help with all her fussing, and he couldn't take back what he had told her about him being a man after reaching his 20th birthday just a week ago. Admitting that he needed her help went against everything he knew about personal pride, and it wouldn't do for his father to hear he was nothing more than a cub of a lion. *Raja*, he would drawl. *You disappoint Puja himself!*

"Raja?" said someone behind him. The lion snort-growled. Great, he'll now have to put up with crap from others. He kept his eyes and ears trained forward, refusing to meet his challenger's gaze. If anyone wanted to mock him, they'd better do it in front of him.

A pressure could be felt on the mattress as his challenger sat beside him. Raja turned to glare at the newcomer, what little fur he had left rising. It was Jian.

Jian was examining him with a tilt of his head, his coal-black nose twitching at Raja's scent. The only acknowledgement he made of Raja's expression was the skewing of his ears. Behind him, Raja saw that most of the bunkmates had already left to assemble downstairs. Only Jian and the small-clawed otter were still around, with the latter seeming to have difficulty with his short's drawstring. Many sizes smaller than any of the other recruits, Raja couldn't say he was surprised.

"You look like there's something bothering you, Brother Lion," observed Jian. "Problem getting over it all?"

"Yes!" spat the lion, making no effort to keep his voice down. The otter scuttered out of the bunkroom, stumbling as he did. Jian merely nodded.

"You want to talk about it?" asked the wolf quietly. "Surely there's more to it than the shit from earlier—?"

"Damn right there is!" burst Raja. Unable to hold back, he, a grown lion, placed his face into his paws. He felt the dampness seeping out through his paw pads, with his ears flushing. He felt angry against everything. Being conscripted against his will because of a constitutional quirk. How as a male of his family, he was expected to uphold the family tradition. The loss of his future mate. Being treated like shit, and surrounded by strangers who may make good on their vendettas. How many generations of conscripts had lost their love because of something they had no control over? How many had gone into the army with carefully guarded smiles, only to have them dashed when they realized the many personal sacrifices they had to make for the service of the nation, only to have it go unnoticed by all? To be scorned for a service they had no choice in serving. There were cases of job-seekers not being able to turn up for job interviews, all because the Military couldn't spare them for the afternoon. It wasn't their fault they had to serve, and it sure as hell wasn't because they took patriotism over their loved ones.

Jian was silent throughout the whole of Raja's tirade, pausing only to nod when he understood what ailed the large lion. Despite having the look of a goody-two-shoes, who wouldn't still be here, Jian was an attentive listener, stopping to clarify the parts he didn't understand through the cultural barrier. Raja knew the wolf was taking a big risk not going down to the parade square to assemble with the others, but somehow he couldn't bring himself to tell the wolf to do what the Sergeant had commanded.

"So, tell me, Jian, what is there to look forward to?" whispered Raja. He had given up dabbing his tears, and instead took to staring into blank space. "I might as well jump these three floors down. Who knows? I might even land on the Sarge. The others would be more than pleased."

"The weekend break. The loving family you will return home to. Like-minded comrades," replied Jian.

Raja glared at him. "Are you serious?"

"You might not see that about your father, but we both know your Ma cares," Jian pointed out. "I saw her with you."

"You don't know her!" said Raja, throwing his paws up. "She's always fussing and telling me what to do! Doesn't she know I'm already old enough to make my own way to this death camp? She even cleaned my whiskers right after I was done with lunch! All in front of the other recruits!"

"But she took the time out of her busy schedule to come all the way to see her son off," said Jian softly. "Did you know what mine told me? 'Jian, you're a big boy now, so you'll make your own way to camp. Don't call me at night, as I might be meeting someone. I can't take any calls on weekdays. I love you.'"

Raja stole a glance at Jian, who had a sad smile on his lips. It took a full minute for those words to sink in, and everything he knew came rushing back.

He had been as fortunate as anyone could ever be, despite what he had endured. Salrina was the only lioness he had met, but did that really mean she was for him? After all, if one truly loved another, wouldn't care and understanding bind them both, even in the span of two years of on-off visits? Sure, his mother could be insistent in the manner in which she behaved with regard to him, but despite the embarrassment she might have caused, hadn't it all been for his own good? All that fussing and checking on him; it was to make sure he looked and felt his best.

Raja didn't like to admit it, but it took a complete stranger and tumultuous events to show him what he truly had. His girlfriend was merely a passerby in his life, having left him when she was needed the most. The sound of her name was enough to make him realize how foolish he had been all these months, a moth chasing a dying flame. Even after the flame had burned away, wouldn't the moth need to find another? He would probably be burned again, but hey, no one said the circle of life was without its own share of preyshit. But first, he would need to find himself. He was now in the greatest challenge of his life, but he had the support of those he cared about, with a new friend to face it with.

The caterwaul of the Sergeant down below could be heard, followed by the chorus of Raja's name. The recruits would now be in push-up positions until they arrived. Jian cocked an ear at Raja, a sense of calm emanating from him.

"You know, they will punish you for being late in assembling downstairs," said Raja carefully. "You shouldn't have waited for me."

"To me, it isn't every wolf for himself," said Jian calmly. "It looked like you needed me more than Sergeant Asshole did." For the first time that day, Raja smiled. The wolf and lion ran down the stairs in quick succession, their ears flat on their heads as the yelling downstairs got louder. There would soon be hell to pay. The greatest of problems could never be solved in a day, but Raja knew that no one was ever alone in the sharing of this journey, which had been braved and surmounted by many generations of those who came before.

* * *

One generation later...

Raja shuffled his feet from boat to concrete pier, stepping under the shade of the sheltered jetty. Past him, old and young alike moved, all walking the neverending stretch of the all-too-familiar jetty. It had changed little since the last he'd been here. The electronic signboard was now smashed, supplanted by a full-color banner extolling the virtues of having a positive mindset. On it, the photos of a lion, panda, tiger and small-clawed otter stood in the respective service uniforms of the Army, Air Force, Police and Navy. Mouths set in a confident line, they stared off into the distance towards the right of the viewer, framed by the caption: Together We Defend.

Raja had to admit it was rather comical. The panda couldn't possibly fit into the cockpit of all those sleek, new aircraft, and the otter didn't look like he could withstand the average wave without being bowed over. But hey, inclusivity was part of what the Armed Forces was all about, right?

"So you got all that?" said an older wolf to a younger tiger. "Always be helpful, don't talk bad about your superiors, and remember to wash your underwear..."

"I *know*, Pa," growled Tyrin. His striped brow creased in a frown. "Stop embarrassing me."

"It's all for your own good," Jian snorted. He grimaced towards Raja, one of his ears skewing as he did. The lion had to admit, even after all these years, he had always found that cute, and a smile showed on his muzzle.

Conscription brought people from all walks of life together, for better or for worse. Having to deal with prejudiced bunkmates, and an overbearing control freak of a tiger was a major downer during his training all those years back. But Raja had to admit he would gladly brave ten times worse if it meant that he met Jian.

He and the wolf got through thick and thin together, supporting each other during the highs and lows of their training. But graduate they did from training, making right all those moments of despair. They were then posted to their new units, where they would remain till the end of their two-year cycle. Raja, to his father's dismay, ended up as Technical Specialist instead of OCS. On the plus side, he did get to test out the cool new equipment before everyone else in the service. With that experience under his pelt, along with his polytechnic diploma, the lion found a job with a military supplies contractor when he completed his term. He still had to deal with the military, but at least he didn't answer to them.

After Jian was posted to OCS, along with the top 5% of the recruits following completion of BMT, Raja hesitated to stay in touch with him. Rumors abounded of those hailing from OCS being as hoity-toity as befitted those who could now lord over others, and he didn't hear from him for months.

But Jian was full of surprises. Right after completing his 9-month stint, he celebrated by inviting Raja to a celebratory dinner in his apartment. The wolf hadn't contacted the lion earlier, as he didn't want any distractions to interfere with training. Only recently, he had moved out of home after signing on as a career officer, not that his mother cared. For all his support for serving the nation and doing the best one could, deep down, Raja realized the wolf was someone he was comfortable with. He helped others simply because he wanted to, not merely because of duty to country, or anything like that. They laughed, they joked, and talked about trials and tribulations faced.

One thing led to another, as life had a way of doing. Get-togethers became meet-ups, and meet-ups became dates. And soon, Raja realized that for all that had happened, things eventually worked out for him after all. His ex-girlfriend was just a bad memory, and his time with Jian was the present.

Raja was initially nervous when Jian suggested they adopt a cub. They were only 26 then, with Raja having left the service only four years prior. Such a disruption might affect their own careers. But the lion could never say no to the wolf, especially when he showed those puppy eyes, so they checked into the adoption center together. It wasn't easy for two young fathers, but with love and determination, anything became possible.

And here they were, sitting before their son at the cookhouse, where Tyrin ate his last meal. The young tiger scowled as he chewed, and Raja couldn't help but wonder if it matched his own expression 27 years back. The smell of the chicken rice was even similar, and Raja briefly pondered if the recipes were passed down from one generation of cookstaff to another.

"All recruits, please say goodbye to your parents and report to the parade square," growled an officer over the PA system. A bear, by the sound of it. A piece of chicken hung from one's of Tyrin's fangs before it fell. Averting his face from his parents, the tiger got up from his chair, turning towards the parade square. His black messenger bag slapped against his side, not much larger than his hips.

"Raja, don't you have something to tell Tyrin?" asked Jian, nudging Raja's arm. Tyrin cocked an ear back, angling his head back slightly.

Raja cleared his throat. "Of course. Tyrin, please hang on a moment. This won't take long."

Tyrin turned towards him, letting out a sigh. Despite his frown, Raja could see a hint of moisture in his eyes. "What is it, Raj Pa?" he breathed.

Raja clasped his son's fingers in his paw, taking a breath before he spoke. "I want you to know that your father and I are proud that you made it into training with a gold fitness award. In life, you will meet many kinds of people. Some are passing whispers to be forgotten. But others are there for you to learn about yourself. But remember that whatever happens, we will always love you. Go now. Enjoy your time here. Nothing will go wrong."

Tyrin stared at Raja for a long moment, and without warning, reached over the table and hugged him and Jian both. And then he was off. Off to join the many others who had come from separate paths, coming together to partake in the same journey. A journey that had been traversed by so many before them.

For Tyrin, this included both his parents. Jian leaned against Raja and smiled.

"You didn't tell him what problems he might face, such as that control freak in our section," giggled Jian. "I'm shocked."

"I might not have met you then." Raja nuzzled his mate in response.

And now for something completely different!
A great story, Mike!
Mike? Are you still there?
Mike…?

Hoodies and Horses

by Michael D. Winkle

FABULA: THE FORUM OF LEGEND AND FOLKLORE
—Superstitions
—So-Called Arthur King: Medieval Legends and Lore
—Who Has Got My Tailypo? Classic Folk Tales
—Greasy, Grimy, Gopher Guts: Children's Songs and Stories
—Hanging from the Door Was a Bloody Hook: Urban Legends
    Bloody Mary
    The Ghostly Hitch-hiker
    Slenderman
—Hoodies and Horses

AnteriorBioBlade
Here's the article I published in the school paper my last semester as a senior. No one laughed at it too much, so I thought I'd share it on the board.

* * *

FOLKLORE OF THE OKLAHOMA/ARKANSAS BORDER

I grew up along the Oklahoma/Arkansas border, in the area between Fort Smith in the north and the Ouachita National Forest in the south. Over the years I heard (and told) many campfire stories and urban legends, some of which carried a unique local flavor. I finally wrote a few down.

1. Equus, the Horse-Man of Western Arkansas
Years ago, during World War II, there was an "agricultural lab" near the Oklahoma/Arkansas border. People thought they just grew crops, but much weirder experiments took place there. The military tried to

breed half-human and half-animal monsters to serve as "super-soldiers" in Europe and Japan.

Well, the A-bomb put an end to their funding, and the government tried to hide all traces of the experiments—by killing their semi-human creations. But they had succeeded in their super-soldier project a little too well: the beast-men fought back. The military had to blow the station off the map; the newspapers of the time just said that a "big fire" ruined the agri-station beyond repair. But one super-soldier survived: Equus.

Equus, which is Latin for "horse", has a horselike head and mane on a manlike body. His hide is covered with short fur, and he has a long horse tail. He has humanlike hands, but he leaves round hoofprints wherever he walks.

The horse-man roams for miles along the OK/AR border, but he always returns to the ruins of the agri-station. He likes his privacy. Teenagers who park on the country roads nearby say Equus will attack you if you linger too long, banging on the windows and hood. Some people say he even carries an ax to chop on cars—and their occupants, if he breaks in!

2. Equus and the Farmer

A farmer who lived near Sallisaw woke up one night to hear a commotion coming from his barn. His horses neighed and whinnied wildly, and a voice called out, "You are free, my brothers! You are free!" The farmer stepped out with a shotgun but couldn't see anything in the dark, though he heard his horses snorting and stamping.

The next morning the farmer found his animals grazing here and there in his pastures. He and his family rounded them up, and that evening he put them in their stalls and locked up the barn.

That night, though, he heard the horses neighing and snorting again, and again a voice cried, "You are free, my brothers!" The farmer shot in the direction of the shouting, and he heard a shrill yell like he'd hit a big stallion.

In the morning the horses just stood around grazing again. None of them had been injured.

On the third night the farmer and his sons waited up with rifles and shotguns, but Equus never returned. The horse-man had finally realized that his "brothers" were not that keen on gaining their freedom.

3. Impersonating Equus

My best friend's cousin decided to make an Equus costume. It was mostly a green World War II soldier's uniform topped with a horse mask.

The mask had a long, black mane, and he stained the face and muzzle with camouflage make-up. He even made a helmet that fit over the back of the horse's head, with ears glued to the outside.

The cousin had the great idea of hanging out at lover's lanes, going up to cars, and banging on the windows as the horse-man. Well, he did it successfully a few times, with my friend waiting in a car so he could get away quick. One night, though, my friend couldn't go, so Terry (the cousin) went by himself. He never came back, and no one ever saw him again.

The theories are that someone saw him as Equus and shot him—then buried him in secret when they realized their mistake. Or that the real Equus took him down.

A third theory, more recent, is that the gnomes (see stories 5 and 6) grabbed Terry as they have supposedly taken livestock, thinking him some sort of weird animal. This became the favorite theory after story number 7 started making the rounds ("Equus vs. Gnomes").

4. Equus and the Axe-Man

The kids around Poteau always talked about the half-horse half-man Equus as a monster, until one night at Camp Kiamichi many years ago. The Boy Scouts sat around the fire and told stories about how Equus was created to be a super-soldier in World War Two, but he turned on his masters and destroyed their lab. They told about how he attacks teenagers parking on back roads, and kills farmers, and eats hunting dogs. Then, around midnight, everyone crawled into their tents to go to sleep.

A couple of boys woke an hour later. There were safety lights on phone poles in the camp, and one shone on the side of their tent like on a movie screen. As the boys watched, a shadow slid up on the canvas wall—a shadow shaped like a man, holding a huge axe! The shape crept closer and closer to the tent—then a second shadow slid up beside the first. The second shadow had an outline like a man's—except for a long muzzle like a horse's! The second shadow jumped on the first, and a chorus of yells and whinnies and crashes woke the whole camp.

When the camp counselors finally assembled, they found a man unconscious on the ground and an axe embedded in a light pole. The man turned out to be an escaped lunatic from the Vinita mental hospital. He had killed three people on his way across the state and would have killed no telling how many Scouts at Kiamichi if Equus hadn't stopped him.

That's when kids around Poteau changed their tunes. Now they say Equus is the guardian of the woods, ready to help those in trouble and punish those up to no good. But it's still hard to find anyone who will stay overnight at the old camp grounds.

5. Gnomes of Gnomedal

Down near Heavener, about two hundred years ago, the first settlers found a huge slab of stone, about twelve feet by twelve feet, with Viking runes carved into it. The runes, translated into the Roman alphabet, spell GNOMEDAL. Some scholars believe the runes stand for the name of a Viking leader and the date of his arrival; others say it's all fake. Still others think GNOMEDAL means just what says: a "dal" (valley) of Gnomes.

People claim to have seen gnomes (earth spirits or dwarves), swaddled in cloaks and hoods, wandering across roads and fields at night. My aunt found one on the back porch of her farmhouse once, trying to steal a bucket of new potatoes she had dug up that day. It hissed like a 'possum and ran away awkwardly in its long robes. Other people claim the gnomes have taken chickens and even cows.

[Similar beings reported in other parts of the country have been dubbed "Hoodies" due to their monkish attire, but around here they're still gnomes.]

6. The Girl on the Road

About five years ago a girl from our high school took a short cut from Poteau to Fort Smith along some country roads. The forest trees cut off the sunlight, and the farmhouses were few and far between, but she didn't worry because it was daytime.

After driving for half an hour, she saw something on the narrow road ahead. It was a young woman about her own age in a dirty, torn blouse and skirt. She lay sprawled in the middle of the road, barely able to crawl, her hair disheveled and her face bruised.

The girl from Poteau thought this unfortunate person had been beaten, raped, and dumped on this deserted country lane. She stopped the car and started to get out, when suddenly she spotted movement among the trees to either side. Several people she called "Satanists", but really short, crept through the brush toward her car. It seemed like the beaten woman was bait to get someone out of their vehicle.

The girl from Poteau knew she could not get the beaten woman into her car before the "Satanists" reached them. All she could do was jump back in and drive on to Fort Smith. She drove straight to the Sheriff's office, but the deputies found nothing on the country road, though patrol cars followed it all the way back to Poteau.

To this day, the girl driver says she can hear the woman in her dreams screaming "Help me!"

The Sheriff's office said there was no evidence of Satanic activity in the OK-AR border area, and they may be right. Since the high school girl insisted the "Satanists" were short, like Munchkins, they may have been gnomes instead.

Needless to say, the Poteau girl never drives down country roads any more.

7. Equus vs. Gnomes

One fall afternoon a few years back a hunter heard a commotion in a thicket near his deer stand. Voices yelled in a language he did not understand, and an animal brayed and whinnied like a horse—yet not *entirely* like a horse. As the hunter watched from his vantage point, a tangle of bodies spilled into the clearing below. Four of the characters were short, covered with brown robes and wrappings from head to toe "like them desert terrorists." The fifth combatant nearly made him fall out of his tree: It stood like a man, but it had a horse's head. It wore green combat fatigues and even a belt with a knife sheath and canteen.

There was no knife in the sheath—unfortunately, because Equus sure could have used it. The gnomes each held a noose or lasso, and each looped his or hers over the creature's head as fast as he could yank them off. One gnome edged too close, and Equus kicked him into the brush as if making a field goal. That one did not come back.

Equus panted and slathered by now, though, and the remaining gnomes secured their ropes on him. It's not clear how the dwarfish beings intended to subdue him, but the struggle never reached that point: the hunter fired his rifle into the air. The gnomes scattered immediately. Equus staggered into the trees a minute later—but he saluted the hunter in the deer stand.

When asked why he didn't shoot the horse-creature to prove he existed, the hunter replied, "I'm from a family of veterans."

* * *

HeWasAdopted

Great article, Anterior. I remember stories about Equus when I was a kid. Why do they tell you things like that when you're out camping, and it's night?

AManAPlan

The gnomes sound like Jawas, with their hoods and short stature.

ThatsWeaZEL

I was thinking more like those little hooded dwarves in *Phantasm*. Cheapest-looking movie I ever saw, but I couldn't sleep after the first time I saw it.

WoodbineTwineth

As the resident old fogey on the Fabula Message Board, I'll mention that the Equus stories go back at least to the 'fifties. He's a long-lived critter, for sure.

TheGreatShamaz

Didn't Jan Harold Brunvand say that "lover's lane" horror stories started in the 'fifties? If the Equus stories really go back to the Second World War, they may be the tales that all the later legends came from! The Hook, The Grunch, The Boyfriend's Death, The Killer in the Back Seat, Humans Can Lick, Too…

WoodbineTwineth

You'd have to find some fogies older than me to learn that. Or better yet find some mention of Equus in a contemporary publication, like the FWP archives.

AManAPlan

I thought the Federal Writers' Project ended before WWII.

WoodbineTwineth

Some states continued it independently until 1943.

AnteriorBioBlade

Uh—guys, there's something I didn't mention in "Folklore", because I didn't want to get a weird rep my last few months at Poteau High, but—I saw Equus myself when I was a kid.

My friend Billy Ray and I played around this old strip-mining pit that was in an unused area of Billy's family's land. In retrospect that was pretty dangerous, because the walls of the pit were completely vertical, and if you fell into the murky water at the bottom, you'd probably never climb out again.

One day we were chucking stones into the pit (we had the improbable idea of filling the whole thing in) when we spotted movement in the brush by the trees. We paused and watched and in a few moments a tall figure lurched out of the thistles. (We had been uncharacteristically quiet in our determination to fill the pit; I think the clatter of stones plus the lack of our usual jabber puzzled him.)

Anyway, there was a tall figure several yards away, attired in rumpled green clothing, a belt with a knife in a sheath, and a wide-brimmed green hat (not a helmet, at least not that day). Wide as the last was, it could not conceal the big rounded muzzle or the tangled mane of black hair.

Billy Ray and I froze like statues, so it took a few seconds for Equus to spot us. He did a double-take and let out a very horsey snort. His eyes were big and weird and *knowing*, if you understand what I mean, under his hat. He smiled, or I think he did, but a horse's muzzle just isn't built for that.

More than that I can't tell you, because Billy Ray and I ran away screaming. We never went back to the strip-mining pit, and, after a day or two of ridicule from family and friends, we never mentioned the incident again.

All right. Gentlemen, start your mocking.

HeWasAdopted
No mockery here, A.B.B. I heard plenty about Equus growing up.

TheGreatShamaz
I'm not completely mocking, Anterior, but every rural community has a "Goatman" or a "Lizard Man" or a "Mothman" haunting the nearby woods. Heck, Maryland even has a Bunnyman!

WoodbineTwineth

They say every legend has a grain of truth.

AManAPlan

I think there may be animal-like beings out there that are just as smart as people. Remember Gef the Talking Mongoose?

ThatsWeaZEL

That brings up a question which has plagued mankind since time immemorial:

Who would win in a fight? Rikki-Tikki-Tavi, Gef the Talking Mongoose, or Sredni Vashtar?

TheGreatShamaz

Well. Rikki certainly has the warrior spirit, and Gef had poltergeist-y powers (throwing things around while hiding behind the walls). But Sredni Vashtar was some sort of demigod—a spirit of violent and bloody vengeance, at that. So I'd have to go with Sredni.

HeWasAdopted

Can I suggest a write-in candidate? Emmett Otterton, if he's been eating Night Howlers.

MonsterEnergyDrinkModerator

Back on topic, please.

WoodbineTwineth

A.B.B., don't you live near the country lanes of "The Girl on the Road?"

AnteriorBioBlade

Yep. The shortcut to Fort Smith starts only a few miles down from me.

HeWasAdopted

AManAPlan and I don't live too far from Anterior, for that matter.

WoodbineTwineth

Mrs. Twineth and I are half-inclined to go camping this weekend. Maybe we'll drive the backroads of Equus and gnome infamy instead. Who knows? Maybe we'll see something.

AnteriorBioBlade

I'll email you the directions, Woodbine, but be careful. Reading about Equus is one thing. Seeing him is another. Don't even get me started on the gnomes.

AManAPlan

I'm with Anterior. Have you ever read the Missing 411 books? There's a cluster of mysterious disappearances of people right on the Oklahoma-Arkansas border—right in the "Equus Area."

WoodbineTwineth

Don't worry, folks. We're fond of seeing the countryside— from the inside of a locked SUV.

TheGreatShamaz

My brother claimed he saw something like Equus in Wisconsin once, only it had the head of a German shepherd. I always thought he was F@* * *&ing with me, but…

ThatsWeaZEL

Sounds like the Bray Road Beast. There's a thread about it somewhere on the site.

HeWasAdopted

Anyone hear from the Twineths? Or have they become another statistic?

AnteriorBioBlade

Don't let them fool you; they're used to camping, and they don't spend all their time on their phones. Give them a day or two.

Woodbine Twineth

OMG OMG OMG You won't believe us, but it's real!! Equus and the gnomes, but the gnomes aren't gnomes!!

We were driving along that shortcut and along any side roads that looked interesting. We were based at a Motel 6, and we spent all Saturday on those country goat trails. We decided to spend most of Sunday doing the same before giving up. Down some godforsaken little road we came to a high fence with a locked gate. Chain link, ancient and sagging, and buried in vines. I think it might be the "agricultural station" where they created Equus.

We were interested enough to get out. Judging by the rusty posts visible from the gate, there had once been an inner fence. There was even a guard kiosk, gray and weathered. We stepped up to the double gate; a chain and lock held it shut. Both looked relatively new. The forest grew right up to the fences.

We could see a few buildings and Quonset huts across an expanse of cracked asphalt. After a couple of minutes, I heard movement in the brush, then guttural voices. I couldn't make out any words. I suggested to Mrs. Twineth that we leave.

Too late; there was a loud bark, and four or five small beings crashed out of the bushes. They wore monk hoods, and the tallest only came up to my solar plexus. My wife got in the driver's side, but the "gnomes" seemed to focus on me. Before I could open the passenger's door a small but heavy body jumped right on my shoulders. We both crashed against the Outback and slid down. I hooked my arm over the side mirror to keep from hitting the ground.

The first creature scrambled back up, and a second scampered at me. Mary (my wife) tells me the others were trying to get in the driver's side. I had my hands full with just two. The little horrors had thick branches with which they smacked me on the face and chest. Even the arms sticking out of the ends of their sleeves were wrapped in gauze.

Anyway, Mary screamed and beat the horn, and I just fended off the sticks. Then—

A big brown hand with chisel-thick nails clamped down on one of the gnomes. It gripped the cowled thing's shoulder and yanked it up like you'd pluck a dandelion. And the little goober kept on going, tossed away like an empty beer can.

A backhand slap took care of the second hooded gnome, and there I was face to muzzle with him. Equus. Combat fatigues, helmet with ear-holes, and all.

He held out his hairy hand—definitely a hand, though with hooflike black nails—and I accepted it. It was hard as iron and bristly as a whiskbroom. He pulled me up, and I only came up to *his* solar plexus. For a second I was way too close to his flaring nostrils, his big, knowing eyes—a sort of russet brown—and his blocky yellow teeth.

Then, with bobcat-like snarls, two more gnomes sprang up on the vehicle behind me and dropped on my horsey savior. I thought of old-time Christmas paintings—Tiny Tim on Bob Cratchet's shoulder. That's how the cowled ones were clinging to Equus.

I'd like to say I came to his aid, but all I did was scramble for the door and climb in. I slammed the door and locked it, and from the relative safety of the cab I watched Equus fling off his diminutive attackers.

I don't know if more came, or if the beaten ones just kept returning, but the hooved super-soldier would smack one down only to have another jump up at him.

The unexpected attack wasn't what made me wet my boxers, though. That wasn't what made me scream at the missis to get us the F@(k out of there.

During the melee, Equus caught a couple of "gnomes" by their cowls and yanked the monkish hoods right off. And I saw that the "gnomes" weren't gnomes. One had a head of tannish-gray fur, big, round, pink ears, beady black eyes, and a long, pointed snout. It was a 'possum's head. The other had the gray-brown fur and black mask of a raccoon. *The "gnomes" of A.B.B.'s article are more human/animal hybrids, they've just been hiding the fact under those cowls!*

We made it back home, somehow, but as long as the Subaru is half-packed anyway, we're leaving again. Mary wants to visit her folks in South Dakota—that's what we're going to say, anyhow.

You may not hear from us for a while. This crap's too crazy for us. Anterior, you and the others be careful.

ThatsWeaZEL

LOL—Nice story, Woodbine, but enough's enough. I might have fallen for a glimpse of Equus in the distance, like a blurry Bigfoot film, but raccoons and 'possums dressed as monks? Come on!

TheGreatShamaz

The WoodbineTwineths want you to update your article, Anterior, featuring them as the hapless heroes.

MonsterEnergyDrinkModerator

Okay, okay—Let's give the WoodbineTwineths the benefit of the doubt. I happen to know they are both professors at NSU, not thirteen-year-olds.

TheGreatShamaz

Well, it is a bit much, Monster. I've been on a dozen ghost hunts, and I've never seen so much as an orb. And the Twineths hit the jackpot on their first try?

ThatsWeaZEL

It sounds like Anterior's not that far from the "agricultural station." Maybe he could brave the woods and bring back proof—if he's got the gonads.

AnteriorBioBlade

I do know the shortcut, Shamaz, like I said. I've even taken it to Fort Smith a time or two. It's about twenty-five miles of country lanes, though, with all manner of side roads. I'll try contacting the Twineths and see if they'll give me directions to

I AM THE ONE YOU CALL EQUUS. YOU HAVE SEEN ONLY THE TIP OF AN ICEBERG. DIDN'T END WITH THE WAR. ANIMAL/HUMAN MANUFACTURE STILL GOING ON.

I MEAN NO HARM BUT OTHERS DO. OTHER MEN. OTHER ANIMAL PEOPLE.

NOT SUPERSOLDIERS. NOT LABORERS. REPLACEMENTS.

REPLACEMENTS FOR HUMANITY.

THE REAL BATTLE HAS YET TO BEGIN.

WATCH YOUR BACKS

SEMPER FI

ThatsWeaZEL

Oh, boy—Anterior, you in on this too? I think we're being had, guys!

AnteriorBioBlade

It happened!!!! I was writing that post when I heard a crash in the kitchen. I got halfway down the hall when I saw him.

Jeez Louise, it really was Equus, in a drab, olive green uniform and helmet! No army boots—he had hooves for feet! His head—well, it was a horse's head, but not quite. A bit wider behind the muzzle. And—you know how horses' eyes are sort of on the sides of their heads? Equus' wrapped around the front a little. You could see their whites.

I admit it—I gave a Wilhelm scream and ran for the back door. Had on only my pants and socks, and I was lucky I had *that*. Equus let out a "Whuff!", then he yelled "Wait!" Yes, he talked. "Wait! You are in danger!"

Maybe of a heart attack. Or a car crash, 'cause I jumped in the Silverado and rooster-tailed outta there!

When I came back (with HeWasAdopted and AManAPlan), he was gone, back to the woods behind the addition. AManAPlan took pictures of his hoofprints, but they just look like any horse's hoofprints.

Then we came in. A few muddy prints in the hall led to my room. And my PC. And we saw what he posted, using my account.

TheGreatShamaz
Okay, I'm throwing down the bull@* * *$% card. Hell, the whole bull@* * *$% deck! It's not gnomes we got down in Arkansas, it's trolls!

MonsterEnergyDrinkModerator
Okay—Okay—Hold it down, fellows. Hoax or not, we can still discuss things civilly.

TheGreatShamaz
Well, how about it, Anterior—you still with us?

ThatsWeaZEL
Guess Equus got him.

TheGreatShamaz
He'll show up sometime and yell "April Fool!"

ThatsWeaZEL
It's June.

AnteriorBioBlade

This is HeWasAdopted—Chuck Olafsson—using Anterior's account. I'm here with him now. It certainly looks like someone was here. Someone who left hoofprints.

AManAPlan here, too. I've uploaded the hoofprint pix to Photobucket, but, like A.B.B. said, they just look like hoofprints!

TheGreatShamaz

Wait a minute. How would Equus know what the Internet is? How could he know about you, and where you live?

AnteriorBioBlade

Dude, Equus has 75 or 80 years experience behind him! He probably learned about computers and the Web as soon as they came out. All he has to do is Google his own name by now. And he probably goes on reconnaissance missions every night. What else does he have to do? He probably has a dossier on everyone in every neighborhood up and down the state line!

ThatsWeaZEL

If you're not all S* * *!tting us, what's it all about? I've read Illuminati-UFO-Area 51 crap about "them" trying to create a slave race out of genetic material from cattle mutilations and such. And Equus was always called a super-soldier. But what's with these "replacements"?

AnteriorBioBlade

For us, I guess. I mean, Homo sapiens. Maybe someone somewhere has decided that Mankind has fu@%ed up the earth long enough. Maybe they think half-animal species will be friendlier to the environment.

ThatsWeaZEL

Uh, people, I'm more interested in how Equus said our lives were in danger. Especially because a big brown UPS van has just pulled up in my driveway, and I haven't ordered anything recently.

AnteriorBioBlade

AManAPlan has just come in from the living room. A big brown van's pulling up in front of my place, too!

AnteriorBioBlade

HeWasAdopted says someone's getting out. No, several people. Just a minute.

AnteriorBioBlade

I thought they were in UPS uniforms, but those are brown, not gray. They look more like SWAT

Post Deleted

This post has been deleted by an administrator.

Post Deleted

This post has been deleted by an administrator.

Thread status: Not open for further replies.

* * *

Page Not Found

That page cannot be found. Either the address is incorrect or the page is no longer available.

Michael D. Winkle

About the Authors

Rob Baird

Born in 1985, Rob Baird wanted to be a lawyer until his dad insisted he learn something practical. And so, anthropology degree in hand, he promptly set about… writing furry stories for the Internet to gnaw on. "Anthropomorphism" is right next to "anthropology" in the dictionary, and everything goes better with talking animals.

Ten years and a couple million words later, he has a comfortable, coffee-soaked niche at the intersection of science fiction, folk music and your local bar on trivia night. He hopes it makes his folks happy, 'cause it's a lot of fun; you can read the results on SoFurry and in FurPlanet's *Taboo*. Deep space is his dwelling place, but the commute's a pain so he also maintains a residence in Berlin, Germany.

Stephen Coghlan

Writing from Canada's national capital (you know, the oft-frozen land between Alaska and the rest of the U.S. of A.), Stephen Coghlan is a professional construction worker by day, a father and husband by night, and a builder of fantastic worlds (aka a writer) in what few moments he manages to scrounge up between. One can follow the progress of his works on his website at scoghlan.com or check out his upcoming novel, *GENMOS: The Genetically Modified Species*, from Thurston Howl Publications.

A fan of anthro stories and characters since early childhood (I'm looking at you, 80's Canadian TV), he was always fascinated by the furry community, but he has no fursona of his own. Instead, he lives vicariously through the characters that he creates.

Searska GreyRaven

Searska GreyRaven has been writing ever since someone gave her a crayon and hasn't stopped since. She makes her home in sunny South Florida with her partner-in-crime, keeps stinging insects for kicks (and honey), and is fond of sporks.

You can find her on twitter @SearskaGreyRvn, SoFurry (Searska_ GreyRaven), and the Furry Writers' Guild forums.

Gullwulf

Gullwulf is a seagull werewolf born in February 1993, a newcomer onto the furry scene but not a new writer by any means, with a terrible addiction to french fries and junk food. She dabbles in fantasy, historical, and horror fiction, and when she's not writing, she's usually thinking about writing or is attending theater shows and watching for a full moon. Or possibly hanging out with friends, who then have to listen to her historical rants.

Sometimes she makes for good company! She can be contacted at twitter @gullwulf, on her FA profile of Gullwulf, and on FurryNetwork as Gullwulf.

Devin Hallsworth

Devin/Debra Hallsworth is a farm guy/girl/whatever from rural Canada, hailing specifically from the province of Alberta/Texas Lite. Being born on a farm made liking animals ridiculously easy, but writing furry fiction came about only after getting onto the internet and stumbling across some stories. He/she/shi has been an avid reader of fantasy and science fiction since childhood, but the idea that writing was something anyone could do didn't take hold until after having been exposed to writing communities such as the Transformation Story Archive mailing list and the great folks who reside there.

This is the first sale in any publication by this author, but if you are interested in schlock/kitsch/previous works there is a small collection of short stories posted on Shifti.org, a site which itself is definitely worth a perusal by any fan of furry or transformation fiction.

Check out:

http://shifti.org/wiki/Main_Page and

http://shifti.org/wiki/Category:Devin_Hallsworth

Taylor Harbin

Taylor Harbin is a professional historian from southeast Missouri. Easily distracted by the internet, he composes all of his work on a manual typewriter. His fiction has appeared in *The Bards and Sages Quarterly* magazine.

He can be reached through his blog at www.gutsofimagination. blogspot.com

Madison Keller

When she was young, Madison Keller wanted to be one of the X-Men. While that dream never came true, her dream of writing did. Now she is the author of several epic fantasy novels and a plethora of short stories spanning multiple genres.

When not writing she can often be found bicycling around the woods of the Pacific Northwest or at the dog park with the original Kerka, her adorable Chihuahua mix.

John Kulp

John Kulp (1994—present) is a small-clawed otter born in Waukesha, Wisconsin. He has steadily moved Southeast his entire life. After attending the University of Pittsburgh for a double degree in Computer Science and Japanese, he relocated to Baltimore to work at a start-up as a full stack web developer.

John currently resides in the Baltimore Inner Harbor, where he's evaded several attempts by the Coast Guard to remove him. He enjoys playing the board game Go, running along the shore, and imbibing impossible quantities of tea. His weekends are spent in a flurry of board gaming and tabletop role-playing. You can follow his antics put shamefully on display for all to see on Twitter at @RunningOtter.

Alan Loewen

Born in late 1954 in Easthampton, New York, Alan Loewen is the product of a long line of German Mennonite farmers on his father's side and a long line of Episcopalian whalers and fishermen on his mother's side. His stories come from a plethora of experience he has gathered over the years in working as a factory worker, inner-city security guard, park ranger, youth worker, radio personality, stage actor, stage and parlor magician, an ordained member of the clergy, computer salesman, counselor for mood disorders, life coach, and a host of other vocations.

A lover of anthropomorphic art, cinema, cats, Neolithic survivals, oriental cuisine, gardening, used bookstores, old houses, and sacred architecture, Loewen presently lives in Gettysburg, Pennsylvania. Married and with three sons, he shares his home with a Sheltie, a sun conure lovingly dubbed "The Death Chicken," and way too many cats. You can read more about Alan on his Amazon author's page.

Mary E. Lowd

Mary E. Lowd writes stories and collects creatures. She's had three novels and more than seventy short stories published so far. Her fiction has won an Ursa Major Award and two Cóyotl Awards. Meanwhile, she's collected a husband, daughter, son, bevy of cats and dogs, and the occasional fish. The stories, creatures, and Mary all live together in a crashed spaceship disguised as a house and hidden in a rose garden in Oregon.

Learn more at www.marylowd.com, or read a great deal of her short fiction online at www.deepskyanchor.com.

Bill McCormick

Bill McCormick (1961—present) began writing professionally in 1986 when he worked for *Chicago Rocker* magazine in conjunction with his radio show on Z-95 (ABC-FM). He went on to write for several other magazines and later transitioned to blogs. He currently writes a sports blog at JayTheJoke.com, as well as a twisted news blog at WorldNewsCenter. org. The latter provides source material for his weekly radio show on WBIG 1280 AM, FOX! Sports. Yes, you read that correctly, he does a show about anything other than sports on a sports radio station.

In 2011, Bill started submitting some fiction short stories to various publishers. Much to his surprise, and the consternation of linguists everywhere, they began publishing his efforts. Bill has expanded his repertoire to include comic books and graphic novels as well as his own stories. He has currently penned everything from dystopian nightmares to cuddly children's stories.

Bill is a big fan of nicotine, vodka, music, and this bottle blonde who keeps waking up in his bed.

Elizabeth McCoy

Elizabeth McCoy has written for Steve Jackson Games (her newest being GURPS Aliens: Sparrials, expanding on the furry race of filches and con artists), small-presses (*Furry! The World's Best Anthropomorphic Fiction!* and *What Happens Next*, both edited by Fred Patten) and herself, self-publishing her furry "Kintaraverse" short stories (most originally in *PawPrints Fanzine*), the AI-focused *Queen of Roses*, and her human-populated fantasy-romance *Lord Alchemist* series. Check www.elizabeth-mccoy.com for links to her eBooks!

She still lives in the Frozen Wastelands of New Hampshire, still has the same spouse and child as before, but many of the cats are new. She is still awkward talking about herself in the third person.

Ken MacGregor

Ken MacGregor's written work has appeared in dozens of anthologies and magazines. His story collection, *An Aberrant Mind* (Sirens Call Publications, May 2014), is available online and in select bookstores. He edits an annual anthology, *Amanda's Recurring Nightmares* (since 2014), for the Great Lakes Association of Horror Writers. Ken is an Affiliate member of HWA. He has also written TV commercials, sketch comedy, a music video, and even a zombie movie.

Recently, he co-wrote a novel and is working on the sequel. Ken lives in Michigan with his family and two cats, one of whom is dead but still haunts the place. He was born at the end of 1966, in Detroit, just a couple months before the city went berserk. It has mostly recovered. It was not Ken's fault.

MikasiWolf

A Design Engineer during office hours, and a writer outside them, MikasiWolf (1990—current) started his journey through the labyrinth of prose and wordcraft since 2007, months before discovering furry fandom. He has never been without inspiration since. Though he occasionally dabbles in the wetwork and complexity of art, he considers himself more of an artist of words. His stories have appeared in *The Furry Future*, edited by Fred Patten (FurPlanet Productions, January 2015), VancouFur 2015 conbook, What The Fur 2015 conbook, Anthrocon 2015 conbook, *Claw the Way to Victory*, edited by AnthroAquatic (Jaffa Books, January 2016), and *Gods with Fur*, edited by Fred Patten (FurPlanet Productions, June 2016), as well as in this here anthology. ;)

Despite the sweltering heat, he currently resides in the midst of an urban jungle. He spends his time picking up the pieces after his dog codenamed Taro, writing, and enjoying video games with a good premise. He can be found on: https://twitter.com/MikasiWolf, and http://www.furaffinity.net/user/mikasiwolf. Feel free to DM him with any comments you may have! Or if you just wanna talk. He doesn't bite...yet.

Field T. Mouse

Field T. Mouse, born in 1984, is a lifetime resident of rural Indiana, where he lives alone with his thoughts. Though he went to school for fine arts photography and other creative pursuits, he's been interested in and practicing writing from a fairly young age. Having a quiet, introverted nature, he's always found the written word to be far more comfortable than the spoken.

His stories tend to feature prey protagonists. Identifying as a mouse, he feels better able to channel what he perceives to be their particular point of view. Field also has a story published in FurPlanet's anthology *Gods with Fur* (2016).

Tom Mullins

Tom Mullins, known to some of his friends as Killick, was born in England in 1988 and brought up in Australia, and has the inconsistent accent to prove it. He is a librarian at a Queensland university where he assists medical students and doctors with referencing software and improving research skills, yet he still struggles with PowerPoint. Tom lives with his amazing partner in Brisbane, a city with summers so humid you could swim through them. At home he enjoys playing board and video games, and has fallen in love with classic and cult movies that he's never seen before.

"Shells on the Beach" was partially inspired by events detailed in comedy legend Spike Milligan's war memoirs, including his military training with an obsolete howitzer where his regiment were forced to yell "bang" as they had no ammunition to practice with.

Tom's arch-nemesis is cheesecake.

BanWynn Oakshadow

BanWynn Oakshadow (1962—present) is a writer, photographer and artist who grew up in rural Ohio, and now resides in Sweden. His photography and flash fiction attempt to capture eternal moments of either growing up as a farm boy in the rural Midwest or American Indian history and lore. He 'walked' for three years with a Dakota medicine man, and was an ethologist after college. He loves to use animal species with their unique adaptations and personalities as metaphors and characters in his speculative fiction and poetry.

He frequently writes about Child abuse, Mental Illness and Spirituality. He contributes to, and is collecting works for, anthologies on these subjects. He currently has three novels submitted. His current project is editor of "Zen Torn Inside Out", a poetry anthology for, from and about Adult survivors of Child Abuse, Rape and Mental Illness.

Angela Oliver

Angela "LemurKat" Oliver is an author and illustrator. She has a degree in Zoology, and isn't afraid to use it—at least in her writing. Her debut novel, *Aroha's Grand Adventure* (CreateSpace, March 2012), is a middle-grade novel about a flightless bird's perilous journey across rivers and through mountains, in a quest to find home. In 2007, Angela visited Madagascar and fell in love with the country, its animals, and its people. This inspired her "epic lemur saga". Set in the same alternate-world Madagascar as *Hunter's Fall*, book one, *Fellowship of the Ringtails* (CreateSpace, June 2013), is currently available on Amazon in eBook and paperback. The second in the series, *Tail of Two Scions*, will hopefully be released in late 2017—as long as the characters co-operate!

Angela also creates miniature works of art and spent two-and-a-half years illustrating almost every animal in the world (from Aardvark to Zosterops). These images were used to create the ecological trading card game, *ZooTrophy*, as well as appearing on postcards and online. Angela Oliver currently lives in Christchurch, New Zealand, with her husband, and overactive imagination. You can find out about her projects via her website: http://lemurkat.co.nz

Frances Pauli

Frances Pauli (1971—still kicking) writes multiple books and series across the Speculative genres. Though she has difficulty sticking to a particular box, her fiction usually touches on themes of magic and spirit, often includes romance, and occasionally wanders into dark or humorous corners at random.

Frances posts furry serials and short fiction on various social sites as Mamma Bear, and maintains a blog and listing of her works in print at francespauli.com When not writing, she crochets, shows hairless dogs and keeps far too many tarantulas for her family's comfort.

Jefferson P. Swycaffer

Jefferson P. Swycaffer (1956—present) has been a furry fan since just about the beginning. He came within a fine camel's hair of naming the genre, referring to it as "fuzzy fandom" in an article around 1984. He has published nine science fiction novels, and several more on Amazon as Kindle eBooks; several of these books have been "furry" to one degree or another. In science fiction, his "Marterly Trilogy"— *The Empire's Legacy* (New Infinities, August 1988), *Voyage of the Planetslayer* (New Infinities, October 1988), and *Revolt and Rebirth* (New Infinities, December 1988)—examined the question of genetically engineered "slave races" and the morality of altering nature to serve mankind.

In somewhat less serious work, he wrote an X-rated crossover with Steve Crompton's "Demi the Demoness" comic book. Jefferson is emphatic in considering himself a fan first, including service as the Secretary for ConDor, San Diego's longest-running annual science fiction convention, and a professional merely as a matter of fortuitous contingency.

Lisa Timpf

Lisa Timpf is a freelance writer who lives in Simcoe, Ontario, Canada. Her previously-published stories include two tales in *New Myths*, "Roxy" (#32, September 2015) and "Into the Ring" (#34, March 2016), which feature AI-enhanced police dogs. Her work has also appeared in venues such as the quarterlies *Third Flatiron* and *Scifaikuest*, the annual *The Martian Wave* (2015 and 2016 eds.), and *Chicken Soup for the Soul: My Very Good, Very Bad Dog*, ed. by Amy Newmark (Chicken Soup for the Soul Publishing, February 2016).

A current dog owner and former cat owner, Lisa particularly enjoys writing stories that involve nature and animals. Other themes her stories touch on include memory loss, aging, sports, and the vagaries of relationships. When not at her laptop, Lisa likes gardening, bird watching, and tossing fetch toys for her seemingly-tireless Border Collie, Emma. Lisa was born in 1959, and has a Physical Education degree from McMaster University.

Michael D. Winkle

Michael D. Winkle was born in Oklahoma in 1959 and has lived in the same general area ever since. He has worked as library assistant, bookkeeper, and in the usual array of "writer experience" jobs, from car washer to postal worker. He graduated with a B.A. in English from Oklahoma State University. He is the author of thirty or so professionally published stories and articles, including "Wolfhead" (*Tales of the Witch World 3*, edited by Andre Norton; Tor Books, July 1990); "The Autumn Beast" (*Here & Now Magazine #5/6*, Spring 2005); "Curious Adventure of the Jersey Devil" (*Panverse 2*, edited by Dario Ciriello; Panverse Publishing, September 2010); and "Origins" (*Gods with Fur*, edited by Fred Patten; FurPlanet Productions, January 2016). He also had "something", whether article, story, or serial chapter, in all twenty-five issues of the lycanthropic fanzine *Fang, Claw, and Steel*.

He hopes that his trickle of published short stories will eventually gather into a torrent of published novels.

J. N. Wolfe

J.N. Wolfe currently prowls the west coast of Canada, where the hunting is fine with milder, more enjoyable winters. When the day's hunt is complete, he tends to be holed up in his den chasing various pursuits, writing being one of them. The younger wolf has written in spurts throughout the years, never really figuring out how to properly tell a story until his older self completed a writing class with Gotham Writers.

Since then, he has renewed his love for the Word, and hopes that his characters will have the chance to live not only within him, but to lead new lives within other readers and writers.

J.N. Wolfe was born in 1978 and considers himself a greymuzzle.

About the Artist

Teagan Gavet

Teagan Gavet is a professional illustrator, graphic novelist, and freelance rambler. Find more at: http://www.teagangavet.com
http://www.furaffinity.net/user/blackteagan

About the Editor

Fred Patten

Fred Patten (1940—current) joined the Los Angeles Science Fantasy Society in 1960 while in college, and has been an active s-f & fantasy fan ever since. He began writing for and publishing fanzines in 1961 (see http://www.zinewiki.com/Salamander), and has written over a thousand reviews of anthropomorphic literature since 1962, irregularly for s-f fanzines in the 1960s, 1970s, and 1980s; for *Yarf!* from 1990 to 2003, for *Claw & Quill* in 2004-2005, for *Anthro* from 2005 to 2008, for *Renard's Menagerie* in 2008, for *Flayrah* from 2011 to 2014, and for *Dogpatch Press* since 2014. He has written two non-fiction books and edited ten anthologies of furry fiction. He founded the Ursa Major Awards and has been on its administrative Anthropomorphic Literature and Arts Association since 2001. He is a member of the Furry Writers' Guild and the Furry Hall of Fame. He co-founded Japanese anime fandom in 1977, and was awarded the Comic-Con's Inkpot Award in 1980 for helping to introduce anime to America. He writes a weekly column on animation, *Funny Animals and More*, for Jerry Beck's Cartoon Research.

A stroke in 2005 has left him hospitalized, from which he carries on his fan activities via a MacBook Pro laptop.

About the Authors